KHAKI ON BROKEN WINGS

KHAKI ON BROKEN WINGS

Cases That Shocked India

Police Diaries Book 2

Amod K. Kanth

BLOOMSBURY
NEW DELHI • LONDON • OXFORD • NEW YORK • SYDNEY

BLOOMSBURY INDIA
Bloomsbury Publishing India Pvt. Ltd
Second Floor, LSC Building No. 4, DDA Complex, Pocket C – 6 & 7,
Vasant Kunj, New Delhi, 110070

BLOOMSBURY, BLOOMSBURY INDIA and the Diana logo
are trademarks of Bloomsbury Publishing Plc

First published in India 2023
This edition published 2023

ISBN: HB: 978-93-88912-10-5; eBook: 978-93-88912-12-9
2 4 6 8 10 9 7 5 3 1

Typeset in Manipal Technologies Limited
Printed and bound in India by Replika Press Pvt. Ltd.

CONTENTS

Author's Note

This book is based on my recollections of police investigations and court proceedings, formal and informal sources, wholly or substantially corroborated by documents in the public domain, including authentic media reports. Being associated with these inquiries, cases and proceedings, I am aware of the findings and true facts of these cases and the relevant legal provisions on which I have expressed my honest opinions in good faith, serving the larger public good and the national interest within the provisions of our Constitution and the laws. The facts and opinions articulated are true to my belief, written without any improper and indirect motives or to cause any harm to anyone. This book is entirely intended to inform and educate the readers on some vital issues of public interest in consonance with public policies and in furtherance of the free flow of information and the right to know, which is well recognised within our Fundamental Rights, having due consideration to the obligations placed on me as a former IPS officer.

Preface

Ever since I donned the khaki uniform of a police officer, to support me in my official work and to maintain a completely authentic account of whatever I did and whatever happened around me, I recorded all the relevant facts and figures briefly in my personal police diaries. As an investigator and as a part of India's criminal justice and juvenile justice systems, I have always believed that discovering the truth was my solemn duty, since the truth held the key to solving the problems in any situation, whether it was to investigate a crime or maintain law and order. Any crime or incident warranting an inquiry or investigation requires an authentic and truthful reconstruction of the events. It helps immensely if, as an observer or as a participant, we record the facts contemporaneously, closest to the time and place of occurrence.

Through my active participation in law enforcement for 34 years and an equal number of years in the voluntary sector, I have been able to understand somewhat how truth can be distorted, mutilated and at times even falsified completely in the criminal justice system (CJS) in which we operate—with the police as investigators and inexorably intertwined with the broken wings of the CJS, the lawyers as the prosecutors and defenders of the accused and the victims, the judges as the final dispensers of justice and the prisons or correctional services as the repositories of the proceeds of the entire process. Time and again, the question asked by those who perpetually remain at the receiving end is whether truth has prevailed and justice given to the victims, who are mostly the needy and helpless, the poor and deprived. Most of the stakeholders—with the exception of the rich and powerful—the victims of crimes and injustice and even the witnesses, accused and perpetrators, remain equally ignorant about the laws of the country and the labyrinth of systems in which they get pushed around—eyeless in Gaza.

My experience with India's criminal justice system is that it is alien, colonial and archaic. But I can't resist admiring the legal provision in the Criminal Procedure Code that makes it obligatory for a police officer to record the 'case diaries' in the present tense, and simultaneously, as and when the investigation or inquiry proceeds. If we don't enter the philosophical domain of 'absolute or relative truth' and it is to be explored with reference to an event and the attendant circumstances in question as it unfolds, the truth remains immutable. But when the facts thus collected have to be presented as evidence—even though they are mostly inadmissible under the law—for judicial scrutiny, the distortions of the truth begin.

In this book I have attempted to describe how the rich and influential people, in connivance with the those who operate the CJS, exploited the loopholes in the system in some of the most sensational and heinous crimes that dominated national headlines and still continue to remain fresh in the public's mind. In the Jessica Lal murder case, despite compelling evidence, the court came close to acquitting the accused, prompting newspaper headlines such as 'no one killed Jessica'. In Sanjeev Nanda's BMW hit-and-run case, the money power and unprecedented intrigues between the lawyers along with a planted witness and a powerful family, almost dictated the judicial pronouncements. Through the international crook Charles Sobhraj's sensational Tihar jail break case, I lay bare the manipulations in the country's highest security prison. And through the investigations in Romesh Sharma's cases, I present how a politico-mafia lord influenced the system while terrorising his targets and extorting properties worth hundreds of crores.

The first-hand material about these landmark cases that I had the opportunity to handle remained confined for decades in my old, yellowed diaries, personal papers and the media reports I had collected and maintained along with my occasional reflections. They would have disintegrated and disappeared had it not been for Bloomsbury India, which encouraged me to write my first police memoirs—*Khaki in Dust Storm*—and now this book, *Khaki on Broken Wings*. I am thankful to my close associates Umang Lal, Dilip Sharan and Soni Sangwan, who remained a part of me in this exploratory journey. No words are enough to thank my wife, Rekha, and my son, Pratinav, for remaining extremely indulgent and supportive of my efforts.

I

Exploring Arunachal with a Tribal Patriarch

'You are a genius, Sir!'

Picturing him as a political acrobat, I would say this with amusement to one of India's longest-serving chief ministers, the chief minister (CM) of Arunachal Pradesh, Gegong Apang. He could, as I had observed, accomplish several gymnastic feats in politics and life simultaneously, juggling with 5–6 balls at a time, always keeping two in his hands while the others were in the air.

He would laughingly ask, 'Why do you say so, DGP (Director General of Police) saheb?'

I would reply, 'I am always amazed to see you quite happily dealing with all your personal or official problems with complete ease, without any grudge or anxiety. You look so comfortable, Sir!'

He would smile and then give me a long discourse about the history, geography, tribal intrigues, traditions, culture and social structure of Arunachal Pradesh. These wonderful chats during the several hours of road journeys with him were a great source of learning for me.

Since taking over as DGP, Arunachal Pradesh, in January 2005, sometimes, as a part of my duty, I travelled long distances by road to different parts of the state with the chief minister.

I did not know why he took me along. Actually, his convoy always included some policemen, but probably he thought that if the DGP was a part of his convoy, it would add some extra stature to it.

Most of the times I agreed to go with him. Not only was I directly responsible for his security, I believed it would give me first-hand information about the situation in the state.

All these trips were a unique experience for me in many ways. I listened attentively to his lengthy talks, which were interrupted by frequent bouts of sleep, with his whole stout body appearing to hang towards one side by the seat belt. Considering it my duty to accompany him, I never complained or expressed my unwillingness to do so, but actually I was very uncomfortable physically. I also became unwell at times as I was not used to such trips. But, in retrospect, I realise that I gained immensely from his company. My understanding of that fascinating part of India inhabited by amazing people, who I served as a policeman, increased tremendously. I learnt a lot, and all my learning came to me in a very natural and practical manner.

Gegong Apang often talked about his matrimonial alliances during these road journeys. He would point out and say, 'You know Amod ji, this village, which we are passing through in this hilly tract, is owned by me and my family. And in a village a little further from here, my wife lives with my children.'

I would be surprised to hear that. I would eagerly ask, 'How is that possible, Sir? I know you already have a family somewhere else.'

He would then explain. 'In your system, you follow monogamy. But here, in our social life of tribals, the ways and traditions are very different. We all have to follow and respect them. This ensures our good living. Our tradition allows us polygamy. Often polygamy is highly functional and useful for maintaining amicable coexistence among the people who live here, who cling to their traditions. They willingly accept me as their leader when I follow the traditional practices.'

As I showed interest, he would explain further, 'In ancient and medieval India, polygamy was common among the rulers for developing political cohesion in the society. My marriages help me tremendously in resolving some age-old quarrels and disputes among the tribes of these hills. This also aids in stopping the possibilities of skirmishes and battles among them.'

When our convoy of about a dozen vehicles crossed villages in the hills, children and often groups of people would run after our cavalcade, shouting 'Jai Hind, Jai Hind!' Many of them would also hold the national flag, our tricolour, in their hands.

No other part of our country appeared to me as patriotic as these places. To my big surprise and also my heartfelt joy, I discovered that the common language of the people was Hindi, albeit influenced by local dialects. I would have never believed this extraordinary aspect of this remote part of India, which was often under threat from China, if I had not witnessed it myself.

Mr Apang usually sat in the front seat of the car, next to the driver and I would sit in the back seat along with a trusted assistant of his. Seeing an overwhelming demonstration of affection and unflinching support by the local people, once, just out of curiosity, I asked the assistant, within the CM's hearing, 'What makes these tribal people appear to be so friendly and loving towards the CM? What do you give them when you go out of the car to embrace them? How have you won this kind of loyalty of the people? They seem to welcome you everywhere with open hearts.'

The assistant replied, 'I give each of them, especially the Gaon Buddhas (village elders), some cash on behalf of CM saheb. I always carry cash in my bag when I am with him. These people lack hard cash and feel very happy when they get some. In fact, some of them still live in the barter age. Our CM saheb gives them a little token to keep them happy and loyal. It is like extending his blessings to them.'

I completely failed to appreciate all these narratives and explanations. My automatic reaction was to immediately ask what the need was to do all this and how it was managed financially. I felt that this was fundamentally wrong according to the rule book and being the DGP of the state, how could I witness such happenings and let them continue?

The CM would then try to assuage my feelings through a long explanation, 'See Amod ji, I do this from my individual funds. It is important to keep the village elders and the hard-working persons happy. This little gesture acts as an elixir against all the petty grievances which they often harbour in their hearts.' He would say this to convince me, but at the same time, he was intelligent enough to ensure that whatever he did, it did not appear to fall short of following the rule book.

Mr Apang was a Congress veteran—a patriarch who had earlier remained the chief minister of Arunachal for nineteen years, from 1980 to 1999. He maintained a close association with all segments of the society, including other political parties. That's how, after having lost his position, within just three years he was again back in power, from 2003 to 2007, when I was serving there.

I was transferred out of Arunachal Pradesh, having earned Mr Apang's wrath when I took some legal actions to implement the Supreme Court directives on police reforms (often called the 'Prakash Singh Case') with the help of the highly supportive and forthright chief secretary of the state, Tabom Bam.

Mr Apang was eventually embroiled in a corruption case involving allegedly irregular bank and cash transactions running into crores of rupees.* This was what was called the 'head-loading' in the Public Distribution System (PDS) goods in the

* 'PDS Scam: Apang Held, Remanded to 7-day Police Custody', *Times of India*, 24 August 2010, available at https://timesofindia.indiatimes.com/india/pds-scam-apang-held-remanded-to-7-day-police-custody/articleshow/6425976.cms; and 'Ex-Arunachal CM Apang Arrested for PDS Scam', *Times of India*, 25 August 2010, available at https://timesofindia.indiatimes.com/india/ex-arunachal-cm-apang-arrested-for-pds-scam/articleshow/6429045.cm

name of several remote and inaccessible places in the hills. The charges have been under investaigation by the Central Bureau of Investigation (CBI).

I found Mr Apang to be an interesting character. He was a self-made man and a leader who had risen from humble beginnings to the level of national politics, with the reputation of enjoying a complete command over his people. Though I did not agree with his ideas or the way he practised his politics, I was certainly impacted by my interactions with him.

2

Retrospections in Shangri-La

My professional and personal life has been full of ups and downs. In my stormy and challenging police career, my posting as DGP Arunachal Pradesh from 2005 to 2007, though less eventful, actually turned out to be very meaningful for me. This was not my first tenure in the North-East, the earlier being as Deputy Inspector General (DIG) of a police range during 1996–1997 in another fascinating state, Mizoram.

Having been involved during my postings in Delhi in several important and hugely hyped cases of policing which created turbulence all over the sociopolitical landscape of the country, many disturbing thoughts would often haunt me with scores of unanswered questions.

Troubled by the memories of the sensational crimes I had handled as the senior supervisory officer of the investigating teams, I became restless. My mind was overwhelmed by the innumerable questions about the criminal justice system, my experience as a law enforcement officer and the state of policing of India.

The Arunachal Pradesh posting was, professionally, very important and significant for me. It offered me the opportunity for appropriating, spacing out and settling several intensely conflicting and severely disturbing beliefs, thoughts, ideas, desires, ponderings and memories.

The multiple dimensions as a human being which surfaced at that time had actually been developing within me for several years, having their roots in my highly challenging experiences, especially while in Delhi Police and the CBI. These extraordinary experiences produced some novel yet realistic ideas and strategies for effectively handling the unique situations I faced. Remarkably, many of the actions taken then resulted in popular demands for changes in the criminal laws directly connected with the functioning of the police.

At Itanagar, the capital of Arunachal Pradesh, I lived in a bungalow called the 'Police House', which was built on a hilltop. The day I landed there, it reminded me of how the great novelist James Hilton portrayed the fictional place in his novel *Lost Horizon* (based on which Frank Capra, the celebrated film director of 1930s, made a popular movie). He described the entire piece of land bordering India and Tibet as 'Shangri-La', meaning a real Garden of Eden, carved out on earth.

Initially, I was somewhat of an 'outsider'. In fact, the police administration itself was layered and structured, with divisions between the 'local' police officers and the 'outsider' police officers quite clearly marked.

As I settled down, the heavenly atmosphere of the place started having its impact on me. Quite naturally and at times spontaneously, my regular wanderings in the state resulted in the surfacing of numerous thoughts lying buried inside me, which also brought up unanswered queries so far embedded deep within my heart. The heavenly views and the sights would fetch answers to my numerous convoluted thoughts and questions.

In just two years of my stay in the state, I travelled to almost all the regions and soon began to recognise every nook and corner of the place, even the size of a particular fern, the smallest rivulet and all the culverts on the way.

My regular field visits as the head of the state police were highly inspiring, enriching and professionally productive experiences for me. All the places I visited were a treat to the eyes and a divine enlightenment of the soul. I could heal my psychological wounds of police life which I had been carrying within me all this while as a huge baggage.

The entire two years of my posting were, by and large, peaceful, except for a few minor skirmishes amongst some twenty odd major tribes in the state. By the definition of 'crime' as I had understood it in my career of police service, Arunachal Pradesh had a minimal crime rate.

There were some sporadic incidents of insurgency, mostly originating from the neighbouring states of Nagaland and Assam. They were mainly in the two Nagaland-adjacent pockets of Tirap and Changlang districts, which I visited a couple of times. They were heavily influenced by the National Socialist Council of Nagaland (NSCN–Khaplang/Muivah), like the adjacent areas of Nagaland demanding Greater Nagaland. I had to tackle the problem of extortions there, including some cases affecting government servants.

The home-grown ultras and militant groups caused the state police some worry. My actions to address the specific problem with limited counter-insurgency operations had some positive effects. In retrospect, I feet the problems were no big deal as compared to the prevailing scenario in the other strife-torn parts of the North-East. One reason for a better situation in Arunachal was that the local people were inherently innocent, simple, friendly and peace-loving.

I found it to be a natural but extraordinary achievement that in spite of my apex and rather inaccessible position as the head of the police department, very soon I had several local friends who appeared to have happily accepted me as one of their own. It was a wonderful thing to happen and it also turned out to be helpful in many ways. In these people I saw traits of pure humanity, something rarely seen in metropolises like Delhi.

In the midst all these pleasant happenings, a rather different experience was the emerging insurgency led by Gangte Tugung, a self-styled gang leader of a terrorist outfit, holding the rank of the chairman of the so-called United Socialist Council of Arunachal (USCA). He had escaped from jail and the state police were on the lookout to catch him. With the efforts of my efficient team, we searched the police records and found some important facts about Gangte Tugung and his gang. This process and the actions taken later became the guidelines for police actions towards curbing insurgency in the state.

I recall the eventful day of 21 February 2006. It was a day when several events took place, which was a lot considering our usual laid-back times in Arunachal Pradesh. It was drizzling since morning, and the weather was giving indication of turning rough at any moment. The Arunachal Police Mess had been renovated, and its opening ceremony was scheduled in the evening. Considering the personal interest I had taken in the renovation and the general excitement around, I expected a good gathering of the family members of the local police officers and a mixed group of locals and officials. A performance of a team of musicians consisting of policemen, their families and some local artists was scheduled.

There was an apprehension based on the experience in the previous years that the family members, particularly the young boys and girls, would not participate. But we were pleasantly surprised to see that, ignoring the inclement weather, almost everyone who was invited came to the event.

The evening turned out to be beautiful. Our own police band, revived a little earlier, performed admirably and there were some great singers among the policemen. A variety of games, especially tambola, were played. The animated chatter of ladies and the laughter and shouts of youngsters filled the place. Everyone had a gala time.

It was a very satisfying experience for me. I had, in my own way, worked hard to break down the social barriers and encouraged bonhomie and camaraderie amongst the policemen, their families and the general public. The event created a sense of belonging among everyone. They could feel they were all a part of a self-developed, homogeneous group—including those who had personal reservations about one another previously.

I was happy. The merrymaking filled me with a pleasant glow. All the diverse currents in my inner self seemed to be settling down inside, finding cosy corners where they could easily fit themselves. I developed an intense desire to take a deep dive into my emotions and have a frank dialogue with myself. I remained quiet and calm, watching everyone indulging in one activity or the other, but my mind took a flight to a world where I could boldly debate on all the pressing questions filling my mind.

In the midst of all the mirth and gaiety, I started thinking about the highly complex functions of the criminal justice system of India, the differences between police set-ups of Delhi and Arunachal and the systems under which they operated, trying to resolve the dilemma between tradition and the need for change.

Busy with my thoughts, I didn't realise that I had left the party and returned to the Police House. I found myself standing at the window across my work table overlooking the hills, which were full of greenery, and which I knew were a treasure trove of a large variety of flora and fauna.

This was where I would often stand, looking out of the window, holding a mug of my post-supper coffee, lost in my thoughts. Sometimes I would almost freeze in the cold, standing for hours, lost in my thoughts, until someone called me. It was my favourite place in the house.

3

Plugging Holes in Hawa Mahal

Every stage of an individual's life has a certain amount of uniqueness. My posting in a remote border state of the country as the police chief was also unique in that sense. It gave me an opportunity to find answers to many of the questions which had filled my mind for years, making me somewhat vexed and restless. The answers came from within myself. But the serendipity happened only at Itanagar, in Arunachal Pradesh.

I would often look out from the large window of my camp office and walk in the sizeable open spaces of the Police House. The grounds had a hall called 'Hawa Mahal'. It was an open-air built-up space without walls, with only a canopy overhead. It overlooked a deep valley with a rivulet, and there were hills beyond. I enjoyed talking to myself there, right in the lap of nature. I often saw my mirror image—my alter ego—quite separate from me, over the placid hills and valleys spread in front of me.

In the camp office, the new white curtains adorning the window, brought from Delhi by my wife Rekha on one of her occasional visits, would often cling to me while blowing in the pleasant breeze and remind me of her. This would encourage me to begin a dialogue with myself again.

The questions in my mind arose from a complex mix of multiple planes of memory connected with a wide spectrum of pressing issues about the day-to-day and mundane affairs of places ranging from Arunachal to Delhi. There were also many intricate questions about the grave aspects of the events either in the National Capital Territory (NCT) or the remote territory of Arunachal Pradesh, many of them concerning the criminal justice system of our country.

While working in Arunachal Pradesh, and then later in other positions, my mind would be continuously thinking in the background. My mirror image or the alter ego I had created of myself often talked to me and asked me to define my overall being and my character, as I understood it. I passionately described my life and my personality, 'My early life contained a lot of uncertainty. I had a chaotic academic career, especially in the 1960s, followed by a couple of years of courageous and, at times, penniless life-experiments until the early 1970s.

'As the mediocre fifth child amongst nine brilliant siblings, the penury of the early years might have been the basis for what happened in the 1970s. I had an adventurous start as a lecturer in Jamshedpur when we created a college amongst the tribals of Jharkhand. I qualified for the Civil Services and got into the Indian Police Service (IPS) in 1974. Due to my unusual background, I was quite different from my batchmates at the training institutes at Mussoorie, Mount Abu and Hyderabad.

'With the start of a new career began a new life. During most of my service of nearly thirty-four years, I had numerous active and eventful field assignments. The journey as a policeman was full of several mammoth events and extraordinary experiences which became landmarks in the history of the criminal justice system of India.

'I believe that I was fortunate to have so many opportunities to work as an investigator in several tumultuous high-profile criminal cases. Each time when these events occurred or the cases came up, I happened to be in critical positions as one of the officers directly involved in crime control or investigations, either in the district police or the crime branch or as one of range police chiefs or in the CBI—the premier national investigation agency. Each time, I was officially assigned to investigate these cases.'

Continuing the discussion, my alter ego said, 'You appreciate and at the same time have reservations about the system in which you operate. As one of the agents of this system, holding the key position in law enforcement and often one of the prime movers of the system, you have openly talked about the need for a change. Many others have also done so. You ostensibly agree with a few and disagree with many of them and you have often expressed this in meetings, presentations, writings and television talks. You appear to have some firm beliefs about the mandated rule of law as it exists in a democracy like India's. Definitely, the rule of law should be the hallmark of the Indian political, administrative and legal systems. You believe that the rule of law draws its entire meaning as well as strength, legitimacy, efficacy and authority from the Constitution of India.'

My alter ego continued, 'But, as you have expressed many times, you have reservations about the way the rule of law is implemented in India. You do not seem to have any reservations about the essence, efficacy, core philosophy or the main objectives of the rule of law. Your complaint is against the misuse which takes place by manipulating the existing system. You feel that the system itself offers scope for misuse. It is designed on the belief that its implementors will be righteous, honest, forthright and virtuous. It is meant to be a tool in the hands of the virtuous to kill the evil. But as you point out, often this tool goes into the hands of the evil-doers themselves and then the system becomes the means to shield the wrong doers. The rule of law dwells in the realm of rationality but if evil manages to walk on that path, it creates a helpless situation. You believe that the set of laws that govern the criminal justice system and the so-called trinity of laws, that is, Code of Criminal Procedure or Criminal Procedure Code (CrPC), Indian Penal Code (IPC) and Indian

Evidence Act, coupled with the Indian Police Act of 1861, are all archaic in character.'

I answered, 'The CrPC, IPC and Indian Evidence Act along with the Indian Police Act of 1861, through which we have been primarily operating, are all anachronistic in many ways, continuing in India since the 1860s. Mainly formulated by the brilliant lawmaker Lord Thomas Babington Macaulay, this sheet anchor of India's legal system was implemented by the British to achieve their imperial goals. The British did not leave any stone unturned to subjugate India after the revolt of 1857 or the First War of Independence.

'The police and the judiciary, along with the English education system, were based on Western models with the prime objective to crush India and keep it subjugated. The core objectives of the system had no place or provision for providing justice to the common people of India. After Independence, for whatever reasons, we retained the criminal justice system established by the foreign rulers and this continues even today. The system is not designed to suit our country's requirements. To make it workable, we often apply patches and do some mending through reforms, but the problems continue.

'Earlier, the British were experts in using the system for supporting their wrongful rule; now certain shrewd and skilled minds use the holes deliberately left by the British in the system to support and protect the wrongdoers in India. The so-called learned and famous lawyers of the country often use their intelligence and skills for saving criminals. They are able to do so because they are experts in the misuse of the system. This cannot be stopped until we dispense with our outmoded system.'

My alter ego pointed out the series of suggested and cosmetic police reforms, progressive amendments to the Constitution and the numerous laws that were modern and comparable to any good police and justice system working anywhere in the world. It asked, 'How do you see the reforms done in the post-Independence era?'

I replied, 'I always favour reforms and changes. These are steps to improve our system. They definitely serve the needy while making our lives better and the functioning of the police more efficient. I completely support the public oversight and the complaints redressal authorities, separation of divisions handling crimes and law-and-order, protection of officials in crucial positions who function lawfully, more budget and manpower, better infrastructure, more use of technology, smarter actions by the police, newer roles for the police, prosecution and judges, speedier delivery of judgements in fast-track mode, newer agencies for intelligence work, constructive use of media and so on.

'At the same time, there is an urgent need for plugging the loopholes that make the system porous and permits persons with resources to take undue advantage. Today, the rich and the powerful can easily hide the crimes they commit with the help of high profile and learned lawyers. These lawyers take fat fees for their expertise. This is all technically possible and hugely prevalent within the law. It becomes possible because the system itself offers scope for such aberrations on the path of justice. In this way, falsehood prevails and truth meets an unceremonious death.'

My alter ego then asked, 'All these past cases are now closed and the guilty have been punished or let off. Why do you keep discussing these cases?'

I answered the question with some passion, 'Some of the high-profile cases and events that rocked the whole nation when they took place still ignite curiosity and excitement in the minds of the media and public and show the unquenched thirst for suitable information and analysis. They need to be revisited for our better understanding and possibly better learnings, which can then be used for changes in the crucial aspects of our criminal justice system. Some of these cases can be used to analyse the deeper layers of the system and discover the loopholes which often get misused, defeating the entire purpose of the justice system.

'To me, it appears worthwhile if some of these cases are reviewed and examined in the light of the new aspects that surfaced later. For example, several details of some of the classic cases I handled have remained in my personal files and diaries. They came into the public domain through the media, but can be studied more coherently with the help of my personal papers which I prepared and used during that time. These papers need to be added to the main stories of the cases, as this may help us to study our justice system, which is the main purpose of this book. It would be interesting to go back in time and re-examine these cases which became the subject matter of public debates on the basic issues involved. Those issues are very much alive and highly relevant even today.'

My alter ego asked, 'Much has been written on the criminal justice system of India. Even movies and TV serials have been made on many of the famous cases. What is your primary objective behind writing again about some of these well-known cases?'

I answered, 'My objective is to kindle ideas and thoughts regarding the real situation of the police as the "prime mover" in such situations and also discuss the roles of the other stakeholders, namely, the judges and magistrates sitting at the top, with the prosecution and defence lawyers assisting them in matters of law and evidence. Equally important in this effort will be to add the aspects of our post-judgement processes, especially when they demand custodial measures, and the role of the prison system prevailing in our country. Without inclusion of the role of jails and the correctional services, the analysis of the criminal justice system will remain incomplete.'

My alter ego questioned me again, 'What makes your stand unique and novel? Why do you think that these episodes are important even in today's scenario?'

I replied, 'While in service as an IPS officer or even afterwards, I had a deep involvement with civil society organisations dealing with hardcore problems involving the enforcement of criminal laws, especially those related to social legislations meant for the most-needy, deprived, poor and vulnerable segments of the society.

'I had several opportunities to get directly engaged in the implementation of laws as an enforcement officer. I was fortunate to play an active, and at times pivotal, role in the introduction and launch of some new laws. I helped to put in place systems and processes which would legally bring together the criminal justice and the fast-emerging juvenile justice systems in India.

'A realisation-based and experience-driven feeling emerged and started growing within me that the police system should not actually be of the kind it has been in the past. It must function with much deeper roots in the changing socioeconomic and politico-governance set-up.

'Though I was convinced about my opinion questioning the effectiveness of the Indian police set-up, I always preferred to enforce the law and abide by the rules as they existed. It was perhaps due to these questions, which were like thorns in my heart, that I looked to extend my role as a humanitarian policeman and I had the good fortune to set up Prayas Juvenile Aid Centre (JAC) Society.

'During the next twenty years of my service as a policeman, my role with Prayas evolved. While continuing hardcore policing, I believed that life and profession could not be completely compartmentalised, and this belief paved the way for my deeper involvement in police work and maintaining a harmonious balance with my social work.

'In 1988, the celebrated first lady IPS officer, Kiran Bedi, my senior in the cadre, had set up the Navjyoti India Foundation for drug de-addiction, and I started Prayas for the neglected and delinquent children in Delhi. Both these non-governmental organisations (NGOs), formed as separate legal entities (as societies), were headed (as their President) by Police Commissioner (later Director CBI) Vijay Karan, an outstanding innovator and humanist to the core.'

My alter ego then asked, 'What do you mean by giving the information about your social service enterprise within the police set-up? Do you mean to say that the police should be different from what it is today, and become socially relevant in the Indian system of public administration?'

I answered, 'The real objective of a policeman, the purpose and justification of policing with its wide-ranging powers, has to be to serve those who need them most—the common people, targeted beneficiaries, needy, poor, helpless, vulnerable, elderly, children, women and similar groups and individuals.

'By the time Prayas was born, purely out of necessity, to take care of children and youth in crisis, my ideas regarding the thin dividing line between governance and social work by the police had become clear. Along with my hardcore police work, I was equally involved in providing services to the children requiring protection, governed under the Juvenile Justice (Care and Protection of Children) Act 1986/2000, which included provisions for the juveniles or Children in Conflict with Law (CCL) and the Neglected or Children in Need of Care and Protection (CNCP). I had the opportunity to closely participate in the formulation and implementation of this basic law for children in India creating a parallel juvenile justice system with an expanding and altered role for the police.

'While working with the government and non-government agencies at different locations across the country, we discovered that the children who worked in menial jobs as well as those who were beggars, vagrants, missing-and-found and so on—all covered within the legal definition of CCL and CNCP—were about 35 million in number. That was a huge figure. All of them deserved a better life. My challenge was to bring the police and the social service sector together, on one platform.

'In due course, we defined and codified the desired roles for the police in the social service sector and developed integrated partnerships between the government and communities, operated through the Civil Society Organisations (CSOs). The major task in this process was to combine the two different systems, that is, the criminal and juvenile justice systems, in order to serve the real "clients" or "customers" of the community-based policing. The opportunity to highlight this came during one of the annual IGP/DGP conferences which are invariably attended by the highest in the government including the prime minister and the home minister; through a well-researched document, I presented and also defended my views on "Community Policing in India".'

All this discussion brings up the important question—what are the core issues of the system of the police and policing in India? There are several statistics of increasing or decreasing crime rates in different parts of the country. There are numerous examples of changes brought about in the intensity and volume of crimes due to extraordinary measures and concerted efforts put in by police leadership.

Many meaningful changes are often brought through community participation or changes in the policies or policing methods or the leadership or certain positive support provided by the political, administrative or judicial bodies of the country.

I had ample opportunities to witness and participate in instances of dramatic or heroic acts of policing and the sacrifices made by policemen, reflected in a huge number of them being martyred. Every year, 21 October is the Police Commemoration Day, when we remember and pay tributes to our martyrs, including the forgotten or overlooked ones, and adorn them with awards and recognitions.

Some of the haunting questions regarding the peculiarity of the role, status and position of Indian police in the criminal justice system are:

- What are the points of pulls and pressures between the Indian bureaucracy, the judicial processes and the democratic system in practice?
- What is the extent of the out-of-law interference in the law enforcement functions by politicians who acquire control over them and are supposed to exercise some kind of supervision?
- What happens to the basic functions of the police in finding truth and enforcing laws, thus becoming the main body to render justice, if the police gets influenced and becomes subservient—or even corrupt and partisan?
- What is the importance and legal relevance of the evidence collected by the police as investigators in the criminal justice system?
- How could it be understood that the investigations done by the police should be based on concrete proof that stand the scrutiny of trial in the court and be proven conclusively before a judge and also serve the ends of justice?
- What is the efficacy of the judicial system when, sometimes, the evidence painstakingly collected by the police gets manipulated in the course of the court proceedings by the learned lawyers and their support systems, and the police investigator involved has to just remain a helpless and silent spectator in the court?
- How does justice get done when, along with truthful and sincere policemen—with or without honest prosecutors—the judge also seems to be helpless in not being able to do anything except follow the ways in which the evidence gets placed and disposed of in the court?

- How does it impact a police investigator who does hard work to collect facts, chases and catches the accused persons, undertakes their prolonged interrogation, relentlessly follows up with timely action (time being an essential factor for each investigation), tries to re-create the sequences of events, and enables the case to stand on its feet as per the law, but during judicial scrutiny finds that the evidence is inadmissible?
- How much does it demoralise the policeman who has done all the hard work of investigation, when the witnesses become hostile in court and the judge berates him or her for doing a shoddy investigation?
- What is the actual role of the police in investigation? Is it the main investigating apparatus to unravel truth and get the judicial and administrative processes started?
- How can the police itself strengthen or weaken a case and other legal processes by its fair or unfair, committed or careless, actions during collection and presentation of evidence, for a proper or improper outcome?
- What is the efficacy of the role of the police in evidence collection and how do the judiciary and other authorities treat evidence and findings provided by the police?
- How does the strategy deployed by the culprits or other stakeholders often counters the sincere efforts of the police department and cause them to fail?
- How do dishonest police officers shatter or blur the truth by disrupting and manipulating the entire police and legal processes, especially in big cases or critical law-and-order situations?
- How do the biased and predisposed investigations or enquiries, partiality and red-tape in the police department contribute to falsifying true justice?
- How does the ill-equipped, overburdened and understaffed police, prosecution and judiciary weaken the processes of the criminal justice system?

- How do our ill-provided, understaffed, outdated and terribly overburdened prisons, in spite of myriad reports of committees and plans to bring about reforms, remain bedevilled with serious loopholes? How do hardened criminals and powerful inmates take advantage of the situation?
- How does the archaic character of the Indian police system make it inherently weak and completely unsuitable for an aspiring and transforming country?
- Why does this outdated structure of the Indian police within our criminal justice system, firmly embedded in its colonial foundations continue to exist—as against the Indian Constitution, which is far ahead of its times in its true spirit, provisions and ethos?
- Why does a policeman in India often indulge in unlawful and corrupt practices? How does the system itself create compulsions and provide opportunities to a policeman to get lured by the extralegal and corrupt ways of working?
- Why is the practice of filing a First Information Report (FIR) and the basic system of criminal investigation, which completely distrusts the police, so challenging, intimidating, inaccessible and abnormal to a common person?
- What is the true nature and state of governance in India—based on honest and truthful reporting of crimes or events and pursuit of investigations and enquiries in the Indian criminal justice system?

4

Negotiating the Unruly Rule of Law

The process of a criminal case—what is called a 'cognisable' crime, that is, a crime where the police is empowered to investigate, arrest, conduct searches and so on—begins with the lodging of a first information report (FIR) at a police station. In a non-cognisable crime, the judicial or metropolitan magistrate is empowered to conduct an inquiry or authorise the local police to inquire or investigate.

Whenever a crime takes place, the victim or anyone else, including a police officer having direct knowledge of the crime, either reports it to a police officer having the jurisdiction or lodges a complaint at the nearest police station.

On receiving the complaint, the attending police officer at the police station either accepts or refuses to register an FIR, depending on the nature and facts of the complaint or the information received by the station house officer (SHO) or the designated duty officer at the police station. For a non-cognisable crime, an FIR is not registered. Instead, a complaint is lodged in the Daily Diary (DD) or the General Diary of the police station with the advice to the complainant to go to the concerned magistrate.

Once an FIR is registered, the police officers led by the SHO at the police station are legally bound to commence the investigation. The duty of investigation is assigned to a police officer or a team of policemen headed by a senior police officer empowered to investigate.

As a matter of legal duty, as primarily laid down in Sections 154 to 173 of the CrPC, from the registration of the FIR to the conclusion or preparation of the final report, the investigation has to be carried out by the investigating officer (IO), independent of any external influence, including the courts. The IO has to legally operate under the supervision of the police officers superior to him or her in the police hierarchy.

The elaborate legal provisions and the police rules and manuals that help the system to operate, are in the nature of standard operating procedure (SOP). As per the existing and relevant laws, as soon as the investigation is complete, a final report is prepared under Section 173 CrPC, which has to be submitted to the empowered magistrate or judge. The final report is called a 'charge sheet' when the IO finds sufficient evidence to prosecute the accused person(s) through the SHO or the superior officers, as required.

The IO has to also submit a report to the Magistrate or the competent court, through the SHO or his or her designated superior, about the complaint being false or a mistake of fact, or the case being 'untraced' or the evidence being insufficient, or the evidence, while being adequate for trial, may not be conclusive.

The FIR and the charge sheet are two crucial steps in the investigation of cognisable offences in a criminal case. The charge sheet is processed and presented by a prosecutor, who is supposed to be independent of the police and the IO, and the trial, which is the main judicial process as the case begins in the empowered court.

The judicial process, both in the cognisable and non-cognisable criminal investigations or inquiries, actually commences with the registration of a case with the police or the magistrate. It continues at every step, from lodging the FIR or complaint to the final report and includes searches, arrests, bail matters and so on, since the magistrate or the empowered judicial officer having the jurisdiction has to be kept duly informed at every stage.

In a criminal court, there are only three legally empowered functionaries—the magistrate or judge presiding over the judicial process, the prosecutor who presents the case in the criminal court as an independent officer who operates under the home department of the government while representing the police or the investigating agency and the defence counsel who fully represents the accused.

The prosecutor, including special counsels appointed to substitute or work alongside the regular prosecutor, is the government lawyer who mainly assists the court, while representing the State, including the police, in the court. Similarly, the defence lawyer, who receives a *vakalatnama* signed by the accused, represents the accused. This *vakalatnama* is an authority through which the defence lawyer embodies the accused, with his or her permission, and remains fully responsible to safeguard the accused and argue on his or her behalf in the court. Under the jurisprudence, both the prosecutor and the defence lawyer are supposed to assist the court to find the truth and render justice.

Along with these three key persons in the judicial proceedings, there is a fourth most-visible, omnipresent and key—albeit extrajudicial—person. This is the representative of the police, who may be required to be there with the final report or the charge sheet and the corroborative evidence.

For some reason or the other, most of the time, this police representative is not empowered or legally required to be there in the courts, but remains as the person in khaki (or plain clothes) as the IO's representative, to appear as a witness or to produce the witnesses or the case material. This representative may be the innocuous functionaries like the 'naib court' (court clerk from the police) and the 'pairvi officer' (police lobbyist from the department).

These functionaries without whom India's criminal courts might come to a grinding halt are totally subservient to the court and to the court officials including the prosecutor, and mostly operate through the well-established but legally unwritten processes.

Thus, the four well-defined wings of the criminal justice system are the police and investigating agencies, prosecution and defence teams, courts and judicial bodies, and the jails or prisons—the so-called correctional services. The last one is the depository, if not the dumping ground, of the overall system.

When the accused persons or the offenders are taken into custody on being arrested, the police have the power to keep them in a police lock-up for twenty-four hours (excluding the journey time). Or they may produce them before a magistrate for being sent to judicial custody or jail.

In India, 75–80 per cent, or even more, of the population in the overcrowded prisons happens to be the 'under-trials', despite the golden principle of the borrowed Indian jurisprudence that an offender is presumed to be innocent until proven guilty. The convicted inmates of the inhumanly teeming Indian jails constitute less than 25 per cent of the 4.5 lakh prisoners who are sent there through the judgements and orders delivered by the judiciary.

Logically and legally speaking, the prisons and correctional centres, besides the 'judicial lock-ups' which are essentially required to be there alongside the courts where the prisoners are kept and produced during the proceedings, should not be under police control or custody. But in practice most of the jails and lock-ups are entirely protected or controlled by the police, and at times they do not even have a token presence of prison officials.

Surprisingly, even the juvenile homes are mostly protected by the police and they hold custody of the juvenile offenders when they are being transported from the homes to and from the Juvenile Justice Board. All this is against the juvenile law applicable throughout the country.

So, in the courts and the other judicial and semi-judicial bodies, the most active and the visible set of functionaries are the police. The police is present everywhere in the criminal justice system, from the first to the last steps of its structure.

Being involved for a long-time in the functioning of the criminal justice system, I had the opportunity to work in its various spheres. While posted in the ever-boiling-pot of Delhi Police or the CBI and also posted in places as diverse as Pondicherry, Tamil Nadu, Goa, Mizoram and Arunachal Pradesh, I gained a reasonably good experience of the functioning of the Indian police in our federal structure.

During my tenure in the CBI, I made official visits to USA for some investigations through the Interpol and the Federal Bureau of Investigation (FBI). I found the American police system to be quite complex. But when I look at the Indian police in all its formations and dimensions, it is not less mind-boggling.

The most prominent features relate to the constitutional provisions under which police, crime control and law-and-order, barring a few exceptions, are included in the State list, as against the Union or Concurrent lists. The union government is directly responsible for the 'sovereignty' and 'territorial integrity' of India and thus is also the creator and controller of the multiple central police organisations and forces. It is also responsible for the Union Territories including the NCT of Delhi, which are almost of the same size as the combined strength of all the police forces of the states.

In practice, however, in most situations of crime and law-and-order, including many having direct bearing on security or on inter-state issues, the union government, unfailingly, gives up its responsibility. This creates uncertainties about the national character of the Indian police within its federal structure, which, unlike the USA, is primarily governed by nationally applicable basic criminal laws, that is, IPC, CrPC and Evidence Act and the Indian Police Act.

My postings provided me with a variety of experiences that gave me the advantage of having a macro view of the system and, at the same time, have a hands-on experience within the field at practical level. I had some unique experiences of the apex level functioning of the system when I was working in the ministry of home affairs with the minister and in the CBI, conducting investigations and travelling extensively across India and abroad.

I could see that within the Indian system, which appeared to be cast in iron from outside, there were built-in flexibilities and endless possibilities of manipulation everywhere. Manipulation takes place right from the stage of the FIR or complaint, at the lowest level, when the criminal case gets initiated by the police and continues right through the court case—in trials, appeals up to the highest levels, and when the courts give the final verdict. But even beyond this final verdict, as provided in the Constitution and the basic criminal laws, one appeal doesn't conclude the criminal proceedings in the Supreme Court due to the practice of having several benches and reviews. Even after the final verdict, some manipulations take place. There are several examples in the past of high-level manipulations even in prisons, which clearly shows the loopholes in the criminal justice system of India.

This volume of my police experiences has some thought-provoking narratives of some of the classic cases I had handled. They include the Jessica Lal's murder and the Sanjeev Nanda BMW hit-and-run cases of 1999, Romesh Sharma's land mafia cases deeply connected to a leading corporate and political nexus and the sensational escape of

Charles Sobhraj from the high-security Tihar Jail in Delhi. Some other cases that I was connected with, which I will discuss separately, which presented multiple dimensions were the assassinations of Rajiv Gandhi, Lalit Maken, Arjun Dass and General A.S. Vaidya, and the landmark economic offences, share market and corruption cases of Harshad Mehta, V. Krishnamurthy and the Jain hawala case.

Despite meticulous and legally perfect management of the cases, and the hard work and sincere efforts of the IOs, the police became embroiled in the murky affairs of each of these cases, at times due to the manoeuvrings by some dishonest police and criminal justice officials, clandestinely involved with the accused and their resourceful lawyers who were manipulating the system. The IOs and prosecutors found it extremely difficult to present the evidence, so painstakingly collected, while adhering to the core objective—victory of truth and justice.

Through my narration of these well-known cases and some details which somehow remained only in the media and public domain, I shall attempt to highlight the systemic failure of the Indian police within the criminal justice system. At the same time, I will describe the good, sincere, honest and dedicated efforts put in by several policemen.

Though the peculiar role of the police within India's legal and administrative system is the underlying theme of this book, my purpose is not to pass judgements on the police, the judiciary or the other stakeholders of the justice system since it were they who gave me the opportunities to learn and serve, in the first place. My sole objective is to highlight the dangerous infrastructural, procedural and attitudinal maladies in the police system alongside the criminal justice system, and more importantly, how it is prone to collapse when deliberately manipulated by some people.

5

Idyllic Itanagar to Tragic Jessica

'May I come in, Sir?' It was the much familiar voice of a lady.

'Come in,' I replied, without moving my position next to the window, or my gaze from the mesmerising morning scene outside. I was in my camp office at Itanagar where, as usual, I was looking out of the window, without knowing for how long.

The lady was Bharti, who had brought my day's itinerary, newspapers, letters, emails, files and, of course, the coffee mug, which my home-staff, Dass, had filled with my favourite tea, especially brought lovingly for me from the tea gardens of Wakro in Lohit district.

I had come to Arunachal Pradesh as the DGP a little while earlier. The view from this window offered me so much solace that standing there, remaining oblivious of the passage of time, became a part of my daily routine. I owe that window and the view a lot for helping me resolve many of the riddles that routinely cropped up in my mind and often pierced my heart like thorns.

The combined effect of water flowing down the hill, the mountain breeze blowing inside the room through the open window, making the panes vibrate rhythmically with a sweet musical sound and the vibrant foliage outside, was magical. This was in stark contrast to congested Delhi, from where I had come. Delhi may be the hub of all action and the seat of power—and truth be told, I did miss it—but here in peaceful Arunachal

Pradesh, the distance between me and the circumstances of my transfer from Delhi gave me an opportunity to put my life in perspective. My posting here was like a breath of fresh air, away from the web of political intrigues and power struggles of the national capital.

Bharti Hazarika, my senior personal assistant, was a seasoned police professional. Morning was when she helped me to document my thoughts about the criminal justice system of India and my reminiscences about the important cases in which I was an investigator or a supervisory officer. In fact, it was partly her encouragement and ultra-fast typing skills that had made me start writing.

As Bharti settled down, I asked my standard question, 'So where were we?'

'Sir, we had to start the chapter on the investigations in the Jessica Lal case. Something about the case seemed to be troubling you when we started talking about it yesterday,' she reminded me.

'Ah, yes. The Jessica Lal case. The Trial Court judgement is around the corner. But I have a feeling that justice for her soul will be much delayed,' I said. This premonition came true sooner than I had expected.

Talking to Bharti about Jessica Lal took me back to the corridors of power in Delhi. Whose son are you? Whom are you close to? Which clique or faction do you belong to? These are the routine questions there.

I vividly remember, just a few days after this conversation, while reading the papers typed by Bharti, I received a call from Delhi which roused all the bruised and sore thoughts of the Jessica Lal case.

'Hello,' I had answered the phone by habit on the third ring.

'Hi Sir,' said the girl at the other end. The voice was familiar as was the number she was calling from. I took a moment to realise it was Barkha Dutt, the spirited journalist from NDTV.

'Have you heard?' she asked.

'Heard what?'

'He has acquitted all of them,' she replied.

For a moment I couldn't believe my ears. The 'he' was Additional Sessions Judge (ASJ) Sunder Lal Bhayana and 'them' were the nine accused in the sensational killing of thirty-four-year-old model Jessica Lal at the trendy restaurant of the rich and famous in Delhi, Tamarind Court (whose actual name was 'Once Upon a Time'), at Qutub Colonnade.

The killing made headlines not just because of the victim and the presence of almost all of Delhi's Page Three crowd but also because of who the prime suspect was—Sidharth Vashisht alias Manu Sharma, the son of Haryana minister Venod Sharma and related to the former president of India, Dr Shankar Dayal Sharma.

The five-word initial pronouncement by Judge Bhayana that 'All accused persons are acquitted' unleashed a tornado of emotions that engulfed my peaceful assignment in the serene state of Arunachal Pradesh and turned it upside down.

Ever since the murder in April 1999, with something going wrong in the trial at every stage, on its anniversary every year I would invariably be at the centre of a media storm. Journalists tracking the case would do articles on it and speak to me as I was the senior officer who had closely supervised the investigation since the beginning.

When Barkha told me about the shocking verdict that day—21 February 2006—she was already planning a campaign called 'Justice for Jessica', and some people in Delhi had decided to make me the scapegoat they needed to save their face.

I was, of course, unaware of how the coming days would unfold, but even in my remote location, I was certain of one thing—our investigation and the evidence our team had painstakingly gathered was sufficient for a conviction and now, post the judgement, the need to immediately appeal against it in the High Court was very urgent.

After dropping the bombshell, the judge had risen for the day, while the reporters jostled with one another, trying to get more information from him. He obliged them briefly, giving the grounds for the acquittals, as he left the court premises. The judge had concluded that Manu Sharma had been framed by the prosecution. Agreeing with the defence counsel, the Court appeared to accept the story that Manu Sharma was being victimised by the IOs due to extraneous and political influence, under pressure from senior officers. Accordingly, the evidence was fabricated.

The judge went entirely with the defence theory that the Tata Safari car, in which the main accused had come to the scene of crime and which belonged to Piccadily Agro Industries (owned by Manu Sharma's family and which was used to establish Manu Sharma's identity and his involvement in the case), had been actually picked up by the police from Karnal and planted at Noida, just to frame and entrap him.

According to Judge Bhayana, there was no evidence from the spot to support the story of the much-publicised Home Guard-turned-constable Shrawan Kumar hitting and breaking the windowpane of the Tata Safari when, subsequent to the crime the same night, the vehicle was being taken away from the scene of the incident by Manu's co-accused, Vikas Yadav and Tony Gill. He believed that the story of the broken glass pane was introduced by the IO to create false evidence against the accused persons.

The non-recovery of the murder weapon and the failure to establish a complete chain of circumstantial evidence of the incident, all indicated that the police had decided to fix the innocent accused in the case although there was no evidence on record about his involvement. 'The prosecution had miserably failed to prove its case beyond reasonable doubt against any of the accused persons,' Judge Bhayana concluded.

The dark clouds and the constant drizzle in Itanagar that evening when I had heard the acquittal news seemed to be in keeping with my sombre mood. I was unable to shake off the sense of foreboding I had in the evening, all through the festivities during the opening of the newly renovated police mess. My troubled thoughts in the midst of the laughter of children, chatter of guests and the anchor calling out the numbers at the tambola game, had persisted.

The media had accepted the Jessica case verdict as gospel truth and projected that the might of the judiciary prevailed in all its authority—leaving the police officers and prosecutors red-faced.

What no one thought to question that day was a point raised later, during the High Court appeal, by the Additional Solicitor General (ASG) Gopal Subramanium. He said, 'The learned Trial Court even on 21.02.2006 heard arguments and sought clarifications from both the parties and was able to pronounce the judgement running into 179 pages the same day.'

The judge, who was elevated to the High Court Bench within a week of this controversial acquittal, was apparently in a great hurry after delivering the judgement to go to the High Court for a meeting when he was accosted by the media for comments.

Initially, in the cacophony of the police-bashing in the media, only one legal expert, Senior Advocate Ashok Arora, had the courage to tell the media, 'It is not that there is *something* wrong in the judgement. In fact, *everything* is wrong.' He even filed a petition with the Supreme Court bench headed by Chief Justice Y.K. Sabharwal seeking that Justice Bhayana's elevation to the High Court and swearing-in be postponed. This was turned down, as was a similar request he made to President A.P.J. Abdul Kalam.

While I was in the company of my officers and their families at the police mess function the previous evening at Itanagar, the national media was abuzz with this case, with no one—the concerned or the unconcerned, the serving or the retired officers—prepared to analyse the case dispassionately.

Initially dumbstruck, the top leadership of Delhi Police was silent till they coined or borrowed expressions like 'colluding officers' who 'botched up the case'. These terms got stuck in my throat like a fishbone. Since my name as joint commissioner of police (south range) had figured in the case right from the beginning, naturally, the media was keen to take my statements and responses. News channel NDTV, where their presenter Barkha Dutt was very active, preparing to launch the 'Justice for Jessica' campaign, was again on the phone that evening for my quick reaction.

Obviously, so far away, there were no details available to me except for the broad contours of the case and a few grounds—such as the non-recovery of the murder weapon, a .22 pistol that was used for the crime; three main eyewitnesses Shayan Munshi, Shiv Das and Karan Rajput turning hostile; and the theory of two weapons being used, indicated by different firing marks on the two empties of bullets as per the Central Forensic Science Laboratory (CFSL) report—on which the judge had given his order.

By evening, there were already attacks in the media on the Delhi Police team that investigated the case. So, the next day I found myself defending the team and stating that despite the witnesses turning hostile, we had a strong case for appeal with ample direct as well as circumstantial evidence which could result in conviction.

The media uproar started building up, picking bits and pieces of information from the judgement and combining them with the previous adverse reports about the case, putting the police and prosecution in the dock.

The acquittal judgement delivered by Justice Bhayana commenced with the prime accused Manu Sharma. He had allegedly shot Jessica dead because she had refused to serve him a drink as the party was over and the bar was closed. There were eight others who were acquitted. Among them was Vikas Yadav, the son of a *mahabali* (don) politician and a member of Parliament, D.P. Yadav. Vikas Yadav's other claim to fame has been that later in 2002 he was accused, and later convicted, of killing Nitish Katara as he could not accept his relationship with his sister. Nitish Katara's mother, the irrepressible Neelam Katara, fought for years to get justice for her son.

Among others who were acquitted were Manu's close friends and co-accused, Alok Khanna and Amardeep Singh Gill alias Tony, both senior officials with the Coca-Cola company; Shyam Sunder Sharma, Manu's uncle and son-in-law of former resident of India, Shankar Dayal Sharma; Yograj Singh, a former Ranji cricketer and father of test cricketer Yuvraj Singh; Harvinder Chopra, a chartered accountant and the manager of Venod Sharma's Piccadily group of industries; and two others, Vikas Gill alias Ruby Gill from Chandigarh and Raja Chopra, both businessmen, family friends and associates of the Sharmas.

Amit Jhingan, another accused in the case, a young businessman friend of Manu Sharma, who had been arrested earlier, had already been discharged due to inadequate evidence at the stage of the charges being framed against the accused.

Two other crucial but absconding accused persons who had been declared 'proclaimed offenders' by the court were Ravinder Sudan alias Teetu from the US, who had supposedly disposed of the murder weapon and Dhanraj, D.P. Yadav's driver, who had abandoned Manu Sharma's Tata Safari that was found in Noida. Their trial had yet to commence.

The part played by some of these accused persons was not less important considering the manipulative way they acted, but they were not in the spotlight and their roles were defocussed as the complete media glare was monopolised mainly by Manu Sharma, and partly by Vikas Yadav.

6

Media Assaults with No Rebuttals

There were opportunities to play up each and every incident, item and character related to the Jessica Lal case from the time the crime took place on 30 April 1999 until the day of the judgement, 21 February 2006. The prominent incidents included the initial circumstances of Manu's identification, his dramatic escape and innocuous surrender, D.P. Yadav's intricate hide-and-seek games and the highly 'filmy' surrender of Vikas Yadav in my office at the Delhi Police Headquarters with the entire media in tow.

The mockery of the judicial process through a fake anticipatory bail obtained from a Manipur judge by Vikas Yadav came to light later, but by that time the media had got used to any unusual event happening in this case. In the midst of some media glare, involvement of the home ministry, which had already asked for a report from us, alongside the High Court taking suo moto cognisance, another event took place. This was the controversial transfer of my batchmate and friend, Yudhvir Singh Dadwal, the joint commissioner of police, New Delhi range to Arunachal Pradesh, since he was present at the party where the crime had taken place. Each aspect of this case and each person involved at every stage, all proved that facts, like truth, are stranger than fiction. ,

Between the day of the murder and the filing of the charge sheet on 3 August 1999, there were endless media stories that detailed the arrests as they took place. The first to be arrested were Amardeep Singh Gill and Alok Khanna on 5 May. They were picked up following the raids by Delhi Police at Manu Sharma's house. Manu, the main accused, whose every step was followed by the media, was arrested on 6 May There was an incessant media interest in the case between the morning of 30 April when the crime came to light and 6 May when Manu was arrested in Chandigarh, and beyond, with regular doses of spicy and intriguing stories.

Two days later, on 8 May, the glamorous socialite Bina Ramani, her husband Georges Mailhot and daughter Malini were arrested under the Excise Act for running an unlicensed bar, Tamarind Court, at Qutub Colonnade where the murder had taken place. The involvement of former President Shankar Dayal Sharma's son-in-law, Shyam Sunder Sharma, in the case and numerous gossip-stories about the Ramanis and other celebrities who had attended the party, used up a lot of newsprint and airtime.

After Barkha's phone call, my mind travelled back over the years, recollecting the different stages of the investigation—arrests, the framing of charges and the subsequent trial. The wheels of the media factory had started rolling from the moment the girl was shot and continued all through the case.

In Delhi in those days, the concept of celebrity bartenders was very new. Mother–daughter duo Bina and Malini Ramani were socialites, famous for their ability to create hotspots that worked as celebrity magnets. To her credit, Bina Ramani had incredible business acumen and she was among the early persons to spot the potential of the real estate in Hauz Khas Village. But when her restaurant there ran into some excise issues, she moved to the area around the Qutub Minar to create a new kind of party place for the nouveau riche of Delhi, who always have more money than opportunities of spending it.

Tamarind Court, named after the tamarind trees in the courtyard of the well-known Qutub Colonnade, had been going through its soft launch phase. The excise licences had not yet come in. But small things like laws had never deterred Bina Ramani and she had gone ahead with her launch by bending the rules. Since she was not allowed to sell alcohol without an excise licence, she had come up with the unique idea of hosting 'Thursday parties' to popularise the destination. These were supposedly by-invitation private parties. And the attraction of these private parties were the celebrity bartenders, generally models or designers who were friends of Malini.

Within just a few weeks, for the rich and the famous, the Thursday parties at Tamarind Court had become the place to be seen. On 29 April 1999, Bina had another one of her Thursday parties, this time ostensibly as a farewell for her husband Georges Mailhot, who was going abroad for six months. There were several celebrities present that evening. An international event was being held in Delhi that week and some of the names and faces generally found in the business papers had also congregated at Tamarind Court that fateful Thursday night. At the bar were models Jessica Lal and Shayan Munshi, among others.

You can imagine the media interest in such a party even without a sensational murder taking place. As soon as the news of the shooting started coming in, the media spotlight turned on us. For the media, the first report was of a shoot-out at a fashionable and trendy restaurant. When they spotted Malini Ramani and other Page Three faces at the cremation ground in Punjabi Bagh, the headlines started grabbing more attention.

It was but natural that the entire progress in the Jessica Lal murder case was published and telecast in full tabloid-style of juicy reporting—from the incident reports, the arrests, the filing of charge sheet to the framing of charges in the court on 24 November 2000.

We were routinely accused of having conducted a shoddy investigation, of having failed to present a water-tight case. The media reports also carried details of how the case crumbled when the key witnesses Shayan Munshi, Shiv Das and Karan Rajput turned hostile in May 2001 and the vague and unsure manner in which the Ramanis identified Manu Sharma in the court. All these events dealt persistent and unrelenting blows to the case. When on 12 April 2005 Manu Sharma was granted regular bail, Jessica's reluctant sister Sabrina seemed to finally give up on the case; it was a big setback to the prosecution.

Seven years after the crime was committed, on 21 February 2006 came the verdict, delivered by the Trial Court of the Fifth Judge in Delhi, S.L. Bhayana. It turned out to be one of the most debated judgements given by any court in Delhi. For the majority of people taking active interest in the case, it was seen as the predictable end of a hazardous journey on a bumpy road through the trial, prosecution and defence battles, winding up on a disappointing note for us.

For me, sitting in Arunachal Pradesh, the information, mostly coming through the print media-reaching late in remote hills, was all second-hand. All I had was the judgement and the one-sided versions in the media since the Delhi Police did not come out with any formal statement. And when they came, the biased and apparently intriguing statements—made by Dr K.K. Paul, then commissioner of Delhi Police and other senior officers—like, 'Police Chief Says Jessica Case Was Fixed' and 'Can Guilty Officers Be Punished?' caused a great mental turmoil to me, my family and my team.

There was no one to explain the Investigating Officer's so-called controversial decision to send the empty bullet shells along with a questionnaire, as well as the bullets and metal pieces found on the scene of crime, along with the live cartridge found in the Tata Safari and the metal pieces recovered from the skull of the victim, for forensic examination.

There was no one to explain how or why it was not a mere coincidence that prime witness Shayan Munshi introduced the two-gun theory during his well-orchestrated dramatic appearance in the court at a time when the forensic expert came out with a report supporting the accused persons. This was brought into the proceedings of the court of the committal magistrate against the prosecution's persistent and justifiable arguments, with the defence claiming its legal privilege to examine or not to examine a witness, and to produce or not to produce a document as evidence.

There were several aspects of the case, deliberately made controversial, as it unfolded over the years in the court, where direct as well as circumstantial evidence was overlooked and side-tracks were used to obfuscate the case. The independent corroboration, deposition and on-the-spot conduct of the alert Home Guard Shrawan Kumar, which led to the recovery of the Tata Safari vehicle, was unceremoniously dropped by the judge. Shrawan Kumar had tried to stop the fleeing Tata Safari and damaged the driver-side rear glass in the process, leaving excellent evidence which was brought before the court. This was not given credence while issues like the two-gun theory were introduced.

There was no one in Delhi Police to explain the finer points like how, in the absence of a regular medico-legal unit of a police post at Aashlok and Apollo hospitals, Jessica's clothes could have been thrown away by unmindful staff while doctors worked on trying to save her life and that these clothes had no evidentiary value. These clothes were given greater weight than the direct corroborative evidence that established Manu Sharma's presence at the scene of crime.

7

Back to Delhi: From Media to Method

No one attempted to read through the Trial Court judgement to point out the endless contradictions and errors—even on the well-known points of evidence which were repeatedly published in the media. All these news items and the numerous uninformed opinions being expressed constituted the perfect ammunition for the media against the completely undefended team of investigators and senior police officers, who were deeply concerned with the state of affairs.

I was filled with rage and frustration in the distant, isolated hill-top Police House of Itanagar, longing to point out all the flaws in the judgement. My wife Rekha was in Delhi and her anguish while going through the newspapers matched mine as we talked on the phone about what needed to be done.

The media and I had developed an interesting relationship over the years. I had faced the media in all conceivable situations, relating to my police work and also my work in voluntary and civil society organisations. Never in the past had I felt any need to consult anyone about the if, how and why of speaking to the media when they approached me. I always gave them spontaneous answers and expressed frank opinions on their questions, whether they related to the police, social issues or the welfare of children.

Over the decades, in my sensitive and somewhat eventful police career, I had learned the lingua to communicate with the media, the pitfalls I could land up in and also the advantages that could be derived, within and also outside my police work. My friends and foes—in both the police and media—were almost equal in number. But being so far away from the real action, I was at a loss to decide my future course of action. I was literally on the horns of a dilemma—to speak or not to speak.

As there was mud-slinging on me too and because the clear open-and-shut case was deliberately made complex to hide the crime, I was looking for some kind of opportunity to bring the facts in focus. But I could not trust anyone for the task except my team and a few friends in the media on whom I had unflinching faith.

The information about the events taking place was reaching me through Rekha and also from a friend holding a high position in the government media. Close friends from the media and police were also constantly updating me through mobile and telephone. I was getting the news, both from electronic and print media, in real-time from them since newspapers from Delhi reached Arunachal after a gap of nearly two days.

'What is happening over there?' I would ask Rekha in anguish, to get her viewpoint, when she called from Delhi.

'Amod, someone has to speak out the truth to the courts again. There must be a loud voice raised to curb the sheer injustice taking place,' Rekha would counsel me. 'The headlines are so one-sided, the news reports are contradictory. Even the judgement is clearly wrong—but no one dares question the factual errors of the judgement,' she would say, expressing her distress at seeing me and my team being criticised and our work being ignored and literally thrown away.

As usual, I was much less distressed over the happenings than my close relatives and friends. They were almost equally divided on what my expected reaction should be. Some wanted me to come out and clarify the points, which was not so easy to do. Others wanted me to lie low, which was much more difficult and against my grain.

My long-time, much-respected senior in the police department, Ved Marwah, guided me at that juncture. I had a long and detailed telephonic discussion with him. Very wisely, he advised me to keep away from making any decisive comments in the media or any interaction with the media persons on the issues which were sub-judice.

Some other seasoned media veterans also told me to keep away from the muck floating around and concentrate on the appeal that had to be filed through my team in the existing hostile situation within the Department. If I spoke up, the risk was that I would become the face of the perceived police debacle and an easy target. All the blame would be pinned on me. My image had already been badly hit by the court verdict. It could get worse and I could become the focus of media and public criticism, making our legal task in hand more difficult.

My conscience, however, would not let me rest. I could not leave my team to the wolves and go into hiding. In hindsight, I realise I was not sure at all about the repercussions of opening my mouth.

Though I was away from the hounds of Delhi, the period from 21 February 2006 to the first week of March was one of the most anxious times of my life. The local media in Itanagar, perhaps because of the detachment gained from distance, did not give much space to the happenings in Delhi, though they were aware of my role in the case. It was my own indignation at what was happening which was the cause of my discomfort.

I would often switch on the television and surf channels. I would watch the endless discussions going on amongst the celebrities, intellectuals, activists, media experts and retired police officers. The general trend of the discussions was based on vague assumptions and muddled deductions, presenting a distorted view of the actual case.

The electronic and print media did contact me during this period, but my response was circumspect and restrained—the matter was sub-judice. I made some general statements about the strength of the case while trying to explain how the investigators had made great efforts and done their job honestly. By then I had some idea about the judgement but had not read it completely. I was still able to point out, rebut and give limited counter-views to some baseless and highly misleading points being made about the case, mostly taking leads from the judgement itself. But I was cautious—that was not the right moment to put across the points of our defence.

My alter ego pestered me continuously all the time. It said, 'You have to go to Delhi and speak the truth. See, no one has attempted to even read the judgement and point out the numerous contradictions and errors, even on the points of evidence which are known so well to everyone and have been repeatedly published in the media earlier, with all the details. The truth is getting openly strangulated. Just rush to Delhi to save the case.'

After a lot of deliberation, I decided to take charge of the case, either on leave or while posted at Arunachal Pradesh. I would visit Delhi whenever required to fight the case in the High Court through lawyers who were engaged and also defend our team while preparing our case within the police department.

8

Police Diary, Recall and the Team

Before reaching Delhi and soon thereafter, I had a detailed telephonic discussion with the investigating team and also with Special Public Prosecutor (SPP), Suresh K. Saxena. All of them were completely bewildered by the turn of events. Based on our discussion about the judgement and the strong evidence we had, we decided to fight it out to save the case. I was prepared for the battle and so was the team which had worked diligently to prepare the best possible case that should not have failed.

As the aircraft was circling over Delhi airport waiting for the air traffic controller (ATC) to give it landing clearance, my alter ego constantly talked to me, encouraging me to go and stand tall, as the truth was with me.

So when I landed in Delhi, I was mentally prepared for the battle to restore truth and justice, which were practically erased by the nefarious deeds of the perpetrators and their collaborators. Though I still had to figure out the details of the judgement, I was certain about one thing—I was not going to let my team down or my professional reputation suffer.

My alter ego quickly reminded me of all the key events and the facts of the case and constantly gave me a boost with its in-depth analysis. It suggested, 'See Amod, you should always be clear about all the facts of the case, if you really want to win. The best way to do that is to see the episode from all the different angles and analyse the facts in the light of each angle, separately.'

One clear, truthful angle was that the murder took place with witnesses all around, for a trivial reason. It was not a pre-planned and conspired murder; hence the evidence collected through an unusually fast and meticulous investigation had all fallen into place. The case turned out to be a mammoth and murky one because the accused persons belonged to a highly influential class of the society.

Another angle was that the case became an example of the misuse of the judicial process. It clearly demonstrated the scope of manipulation in the criminal justice system, thereby questioning the efficacy of a fair investigation turning into a highly unfair trial within the Indian jurisprudence.

The third angle was that the case reflected how the media had immense power to cause twists in a case and turn around even judgements of the courts of our country.

The fourth angle was the exposure of the late-night parties of the Page Three crowd, the wealthy and the high-and-mighty. The crowd at these parties included not only politicians, police officers, film and sports stars but also artists, fashion designers, media persons, business persons and leading professionals like doctors. All these persons were present in the party in which Jessica Lal was murdered.

While in service, I had the habit of maintaining a daily account of my work in my personal 'Delhi Police Diary'. These diaries were much in demand—they had our name printed on it and given every year to us as well as the media persons as a new year gift. Through my aide-memoire, personal scribblings and daily reports in my diaries which I had scrupulously maintained for over two decades, I tried to recollect the incidents from 30 April 1999 onwards. I believed that ours was a perfectly built case, handled by a team of qualified and thorough professionals.

Within five days of the crime, I submitted a very detailed 'Supervisory Note' to the commissioner of police, Delhi, Mr Virendra Narain Singh. Copies of this note were addressed to my subordinate officers—Sudhir Yadav, the newly posted deputy commissioner of police (DCP); Vivek Gogia and R.S. Ghumman, the two Additional DCPs of South District; O.P. Mishra, assistant commissioner of police (ACP); and Surender Sharma, the station house officer-cum-investigating officer.

Now, when I picked up my supervisory note again, I found that it summed up the entire case in terms of the future investigation in a very practical manner. Soon, I could put together all the material which I had with me and I was ready to take charge of the battle to establish the case and present the truth, with or without the top cops in Delhi Police cooperating with us.

The case had started with three phone calls early in the morning on 30 April 1999. The first was from Vivek Gogia. He was the Additional DCP, South Delhi District. Essentially the number-two officer in the district, at that time he was officiating as the DCP South District because the top slot was vacant.

Gogia was a keen officer who had worked with me earlier on several occasions. We and our families had also spent a lot of time together in Mizoram when we were posted there. He was still like a probationer, getting into minute details to learn about any investigation. Little did he know at that time that he was handling an explosive substance, which would test his mettle in the not too distant future.

'Sir, there was a murder in the jurisdiction of Police Station Mehrauli,' he informed me.

'Victim?' I asked.

'Female, thirty-four,' he replied.

He quickly filled me in on the details that were available at that time. We knew the identity of the victim, the physical description of the suspect, we also had the licence plate number of a Tata Safari, the vehicle in which the suspect and his friends had come in and which his friends had come back later to try and retrieve from the parking lot. Gogia also told me that the place was the popular nightspot, Tamarind Court, at the Qutub Colonnade in Mehrauli.

I had barely replaced the receiver on the cradle when the phone rang again.

'Mr Kanth?' asked a deep, husky voice.

'Yes,' I replied, trying to place the owner of the distinctive voice.

'I was there,' the voice said cryptically.

By now I had recognised the famous voice. It belonged to the Hollywood action star Steven Seagal. He was in Delhi and had spent a day with us at the Tughlakabad Children's Centre of Prayas. Few people knew this, but Seagal, a practising Buddhist, was a philanthropist and deeply engaged with disadvantaged children. As he spoke on the phone, I remembered how much he had enjoyed his time at Prayas and how he had mingled so wonderfully with the children. Within moments, he had gained their affection and they were literally clambering all over him. In fact, newspapers had also carried photos of his playful conduct with the Prayas children.

'Where were you Mr Seagal?' I asked, still wondering what this big man was so worried about.

'I was there at the party last night where later the girl was shot,' he replied.

By now, I realised where his anxiety stemmed from. Steven Seagal was one of the celebrities who had attended Bina Ramani's 'by-invite only' party. He didn't want any negative publicity.

'What made you go to that place?' I asked, trying to reconcile the gentle image of Steven Seagal playing with children at

Prayas with the image of the Hollywood star quaffing alcohol at a happening party place of the Capital.

He appeared a bit embarrassed by my question, and I let him wriggle out of it gracefully.

'Did you see the girl being shot?' I asked, trying to determine if he was a witness.

'No, I had left before that,' he replied.

Since he was not a witness or connected to the crime, I told him to relax and that I would get back to him if the police needed him for anything.

The moment I put the phone down, it rang again. This time too, I was greeted by a husky, 'Hello.'

My early morning brain thought Steven Seagal had called back with some more queries or information and I said 'Yes' without much preamble.

'Babua, it is me,' was the response from the other side.

'Daddu!' I exclaimed, quickly recognising the voice.

This was Yudhvir Singh Dadwal, the joint commissioner of police of the New Delhi Range and my batchmate. He later went on to become the head of Delhi Police as the police commissioner. We were friends and he was well-known for his Texas-style drawl and anglicised Punjabi style of speaking. For him, I was 'Babua', an affectionate distortion of 'Babu' a term common in Bihar, our home state. I and his close friends called him 'Daddu', a shortened form of his surname 'Dadwal'.

'I was there last night,' he said.

By this time, I did not need any explanation of what 'there' was.

'Did you see the shoot-out?' I asked directly.

'No dear, I was there for only a short time and had left even before midnight. Since I had office next day, I did not want to stay too long,' he replied.

'Everyone was there, you know,' he continued, rolling off the names of several of Delhi's Page Three regulars. Dadwal was a good cop who worked hard—and partied hard, too. That day, his lifestyle took him to what should have been just another party, but turned into a crime spot. Though the fact that he was present at the party did not have any bearing on the murder and the subsequent events, he did have to pay the price for being at an unlicensed bar and ended up getting posted out of Delhi shortly after the incident.

I can still recollect the somewhat similar sounding, husky and anxious voices of Dadwal and Seagal on the telephone, both trying to find out the implications of their presence at Qutub Colonnade. The initial reports estimated that nearly 300 to 400 persons had attended the party that night. They had all come and gone at different times. Many of them were among the popular celebrities of Delhi. Each could now get investigated as a witness or someone connected with the case. So all of them were disturbed and worried, considering the media glare, popular interest and the growing controversies around the case.

By habit and training, my first act in any important crime investigation was to visit the scene of crime and attempt to go directly or indirectly into all the facts and details of the incident. If it was a case that needed my supervisory inputs or guidance, then I would take charge to summarise, scrutinise and classify the crime details and related facts in order to give a definite direction to the investigation.

I had done the same in the Jessica Lal case (as evident in the FIR No. 287/99 u/s 307/302 IPC/PS Mehrauli, South Delhi District). Usually, the investigation reports of a crime of this nature were prepared in the name of the DCP or ACP, and in that case also, it was done by the Add. DCP Vivek Gogia, an IPS officer, directly reporting to me on that day. Gogia had remained away from Delhi for a long period and was still learning to go deeper into the details of such an investigation. So when I visited the site the next day, I looked into all the obvious and the not-so-obvious evidence thoroughly, giving the investigating team detailed guidelines as 'pointers for investigation'.

A quirk of fate brought me back in contact with Suresh K. Saxena, the SPP in the Jessica Lal case. My association with him went back to 1991 when I was investigating the Rajiv Gandhi assassination case. I was a part of the Special Investigating Team (SIT) of the CBI and he was its additional legal advisor and public prosecutor. Having earlier been the chief prosecutor handling several sensational and landmark cases, his experience was invaluable.

While investigating the Rajiv Gandhi assassination case, as we lived together for months under heavy security cover at the Chepauk State Guest House in Chennai (then Madras), he gave us insights into the actual application of law in any event or human affair, irrespective of whether it constituted a crime or not. Saxena had unmatched experience of court craft that he could deploy deftly in the Jessica Lal case.

I had developed and practised a method of investigation in the Rajiv Gandhi assassination case, which I could apply to the investigation of the Jessica Lal case too. When I requested all the investigators in the Jessica Lal case, including the senior officers, to submit their special case diaries to Inspector Surender Sharma, the chief investigating officer, I was actually following the same method we had used earlier.

9

Revisiting the Investigation

Back in action in Delhi now, I found that, in my preliminary supervisory note which I had recorded soon after visiting the scene of crime the day following the event, I had pointed out some details—for example, the first information was given to the Police Control Room (PCR) as well as the respective police station at about 2:11 AM. Later, during the course of further investigations and trial, the IO had been directed to clarify this with reference to the police station and PCR records, about the time and persons in the picture when the PCR and police station staff arrived at the scene of crime and how they responded.

In the developments of the case, a number of such facts were added to the main report within a day of the crime. The recording of the minute details of the first round of the investigation of the case was very important because these details would play an important role later, as saviours of truth when the case was being systematically sabotaged.

I give details of the investigation and the case we built, based on the statements of witnesses, accused and others, in the pages that follow. It was for the courts, of course, to decide on guilt and innocence.

The first PCR call about the crime received at the police station was marked to SI Sharad Bishnoi (called Sharad Kumar, too). Since he was already on another call, SI Sunil Kumar along with Constable Subhash was sent to the spot. SI Sharad Kumar also reached the place along with Constable Meenu Mathews.

All of them reached the crime scene almost simultaneously. By then, Jessica had already been taken to Aashlok Hospital. So SI Sunil Kumar immediately proceeded to the hospital to follow up the investigation without loss of time.

Aashlok Hospital, located in Safdarjung Enclave in South Delhi—a stone's throw away from my present home—was a small hospital named after two doctor brothers, Ashwini and Alok (hence Aash–Lok) Chopra who were the co-owners and ran the hospital. Why the hosts of the event took Jessica, who was in a very serious condition, to this hospital was a fact to be explained and understood later.

At the hospital, SI Sunil Kumar found Jessica to be unfit for making a statement and the FIR was recorded on the complaint of her co-bartender and eyewitness on the spot, Shayan Munshi. Shayan was a model friend of Malini Ramani and was doing a course at the Institute of Planning and Management in South Extension, New Delhi. Also known to be a close family associate of Bina Ramani who lived in Saket, Shayan Munshi, was the key and the most natural witness, as he was standing with Jessica Lal near the serving counter of the bar, when she was shot.

Shayan Munshi had accompanied Bina Ramani and the injured Jessica to Aashlok Hospital in another car after the shoot-out. In his statement recorded by the police, he said he had come to attend the party at Qutub Colonnade on 29 April 1999 as he knew Bina Ramani. He said that the party was over when Manu Sharma and his friends entered the bar almost forcibly. There were just 5–6 people in the bar at the time. Among them was a waiter, perhaps to wind up the things.

Munshi described the main accused as about 30–32 years old, fair complexioned, heavily built, with a round face and wearing a white shirt. He came into the bar, got behind the bar counter and asked the waiter for two drinks. The waiter refused to serve him as the party was over. Jessica Lal and Malini Ramani, who were also present there, tried to convince him that the party was over and no drinks were available.

The man then said, 'I will do it my own way.' When Jessica Lal tried to calm him down saying that there was no need to be angry, the man took out a pistol from his pocket and fired a shot towards the roof and then, aiming at Jessica Lal, fired another shot at her. The bullet hit her over her eyebrow and she fell down. Meanwhile, Bina Ramani, who had also arrived on the spot, was stunned, but she immediately ran out to call an ambulance and the police. She decided to take Jessica Lal to Aashlok Hospital in Safdarjung Enclave in her car.

Shayan Munshi further said that he got into another car and followed Bina Ramani to the hospital. He said that the person had shot Jessica Lal with the intention of killing her and that he could identify him if he came face-to-face with him. On the basis of Shayan Munshi's complaint recorded at Aashlok Hospital, which was read over to him in full public view and hearing, SI Sunil Kumar sent the *rukka* (the first report of a crime) to Police Station Mehrauli, which falls in the jurisdiction of the South District. Since Jessica Lal had not been declared dead by that time, a case under Section 307 IPC (attempt to murder) was registered and the investigation started.

SI Sunil Kumar, as required, came back to the crime scene and joined SI Sharad Kumar who was present there, leaving behind some police officers at Aashlok Hospital who had also reached there by then. At the crime scene, he began the routine activities mandated for such investigations, like the scene of crime inspection, preservation of the site, preparation of a site plan, collection of evidence, initial examination of the available witnesses and so on. All this was recorded in two places—the case diaries which fulfilled the requirement of the statutory documentation of the progress of the case and the police supervisory notes.

The language of the FIR being Hindi, became a source of controversy during the course of the trial. But here it needs to be underlined that investigations in India are routinely conducted in Hindi or the local languages, sometimes even Urdu. SI Sunil Kumar stated that he recorded the FIR in Hindi as he was comfortable in that language. This is the usual norm in Indian police investigations as the local language is also the most suitable medium of communication for the majority of witnesses and for facts and evidence to be brought on record. Even as IPS officers, while under training in our respective states and cadres, we are made to learn the local language and dialects in which we are supposed to conduct our routine official work.

Since Shayan Munshi, like what many of us do, was talking in a mixture of Hindi and English, SI Sunil Kumar never suspected that when the time came for him to take the witness stand in court, he would take a plea that he did not know Hindi, a crucial point on which the defence attorney placed his arguments, enabling Shayan to escape from being the prime witness in the case. Whatever the nature of the developments, Shayan's statement had been consciously 'Read Over and Accepted as Correct' (RO&AC) before being properly signed by him, and converted into an FIR that became the basic document for the investigation of the case.

In my resurrected note to the subordinate officers which had been duly endorsed and even appreciated by the Commissioner of Police V.N. Singh, I had given clear directions to the concerned officers to find out who all were present on the spot at the time of the shooting. I also mentioned about some persons returning to the parking area of the crime scene to retrieve the Tata Safari left by them there.

My report mentions as to how and why a Home Guard named Shrawan Kumar came to the spot and, apparently with directions from his seniors, maintained a watch on (Manu Sharma's) vehicle Tata Safari CH01W-6535 and what exactly he did.

SHO Surender Sharma told me the next day that it was the same person to whom he had given directions not to allow anyone to take away the vehicle without verification. The Home Guard had noted down the registration number of the Tata Safari, first on his palm and later on a piece of paper to inform his seniors.

As confirmed to us subsequently, Shrawan was indeed deployed on duty outside Qutub Colonnade during the initial investigation of the crime. Around 4 AM, he saw someone trying to drive away the Tata Safari and attempted to stop the vehicle. He struck the window of the fleeing vehicle with his danda (stick). We had not found his presence on the spot so credible initially. Later, most appropriately, he was recruited as a Constable when it was mentioned to us that Shrawan Kumar had done a commendable job and deserved to be rewarded. At that time, in order to ascertain the truth and the actual sequence of events, I wanted the DCP to look into the respective roles of the other officers, including that of SHO Surender Sharma who was about to take over the case as the Chief Investigating Officer of the case.

It would be interesting to recollect, based on the facts recorded in my diary, how I understood the case in the first instance. During the forenoon of 30 April 1999, when I first visited the scene of crime, I had already been told that the restaurant where the crime took place was listed in the Delhi Police Licensing Branch records as an 'eating house' in the name of 'Once Upon a Time'. But the actual situation we found was altogether different. The restaurant had a signboard saying 'Tamarind Cafe'. The place had been sealed after the initial investigations to preserve the scene of crime and it was reopened in my presence.

I went inside the building along with other officers to find the scene of crime in a typical post-late-night-party condition with bottles, mostly soft drinks and some empty liquor bottles, strewn all over. I made some specific observations expressing my dissatisfaction over the somewhat careless management of the crime scene. I raised questions about the apparent cleaning of blood from the spot although it was later alleged to be a deliberate attempt of destruction of evidence and also some negligence in handling the crime-scene. It was mentioned that immediately after the crime and when Jessica was being taken to the hospital, someone, maybe the owners of the restaurant or the Ramanis could have ordered cleaning of the blood lying there.

The SHO, Inspector Surender Sharma, told me that he had come to the scene of crime immediately after the incident along with the other policemen, after the PCR officials had arrived. It was obviously required to investigate and explain how the owners of the bar could clean up, in a very short time, the entire area and remove important things like empty and used liquor bottles, glasses and so on. I gave directions on the spot that all this should be carefully examined and explained, whether it was done unmindfully or deliberately.

The SHO was particularly directed to collect all the relevant evidence and material, including the coupons which had been freely sold in the bar to serve liquor to an estimated 200 people who could have been present in the party. The number of people who attended the party with the exact identity of each one and their examination became a long exercise for our team.

The number of people to whom coupons were sold was reported as 200 by those who had been issued coupons for the liquor. Decidedly, a thorough examination of the entire accounts and transactions at the bar had to be done for the murder case as well as the Excise Act case. The number of people who were present at the scene of crime or visited the place or attended the so-called 'Thursday Party' by invitation or otherwise remained a subject matter of investigation—the initial information was 300–400 persons, but the liquor coupons were claimed to be sold to only around 200 persons.

This second case, under the Excise Act, was immediately registered against the Ramanis for illegal sale of liquor in fairly large quantities to the guests, invitees and others at what was called the 'Thursday Party'. I gave detailed 'Pointers to Investigation' to the South District officers, including the area SHO, to be followed up by the special team that was constituted under the Additional DCP Vivek Gogia.

Meanwhile, the information about the evidence of the Tata Safari vehicle was being broadcast through the wireless network of Delhi PCR. Fortuitously, I had spoken to Kiran Bedi, then serving her forty-day Chandigarh Inspector General of Police tenure, about the vehicle registered in the Transport Authority of her Union Territory.

The Chandigarh Police acted very quickly and collected the information about the ownership of the Tata Safari. It was in the name of a company called Piccadily Agro Industries Limited, Bhadson, Indri, Distt. Karnal, owned by the well-known politician Venod Sharma. His son Sidharth Vashisht alias Manu Sharma was a director in the firm. We also found out that the particular vehicle, Tata Safari, was generally used by Manu Sharma.

In less than ten hours since the investigation started, the needle of suspicion was almost fixed on the real accused, identified as Manu Sharma, through the vehicle's ownership and identity of its user, as well as the description given by Shayan Munshi. The senior officers who received the information regarding the ownership of the Tata Safari transmitted it to the SHO/IO Surender Sharma, and he acted on it to proceed further with the case.

This was a natural flow of events linked to one another and the typical unfolding of a case, as it should normally happen. As the Chief Investigation Officer, Inspector Sharma later made a truthful statement in the Trial Court about the identity of the accused being established on the basis of information given by the 'senior officers'. But this statement was interpreted by the Trial Judge Sunder Lal Bhayana as that Manu Sharma had been 'framed in the case under the instruction of the Senior Officers'.

On 30 April itself, it was duly recorded in the case file that a special police party had been sent to Chandigarh and Haryana to secure and apprehend the main accused, Manu Sharma, who was absconding by then.

As a first round of follow-up action, the police raided Manu's sugar factory and all other establishments during the next few days. Manu's father, Venod Sharma, was contacted at his house. But he managed to avoid interrogation at that stage by making use of the typical health and medical excuse. He was hospitalised at Chandigarh for the treatment of some illness or ailment. This is the modus operandi often adopted by highly placed offenders and connected persons to evade investigation. The illness excuse is often accepted in routine and is an indicator of a weakness in our criminal justice system due to which effective investigations often get blocked.

While vigorous efforts were being made to locate and arrest Manu Sharma, information came in that he was in the close company of two of his friends, Amardeep Singh Gill alias Tony and Alok Khanna. These two friends were General Managers in the Coca-Cola company and had their office in Gurgaon. Since they were directly involved in the crime and also present with Manu Sharma on the scene of crime, the duo were arrested on 5 May 1999.

After that the investigation began taking shape and the sequence of events on the fateful night started becoming clearer. We found that Amardeep Gill alias Tony was at his Friends Colony home that evening when Manu Sharma called him to say that he and his friend Vikas Yadav would come to his place for an outing to Qutub Colonnade at Mehrauli. Manu Sharma and Vikas Yadav arrived at Amardeep's house at about 10 PM, to be joined by Alok Khanna who came at about 10:15 PM. The four of them had a few drinks together at Amardeep's house, and at about 11 PM, they proceeded to Qutub Colonnade in Manu's Tata Safari vehicle.

Working on the details gathered from the statements of Amardeep and Alok, and also on the basis of the corroborating statements of other witnesses, we pieced together the entire story by 5 May and were ready with the case-related sequence of events on our records. Most of these details were later presented in the charge sheet. The report was further corroborated and firmed-up through many other pieces of evidence, including documents which the investigation team gathered.

The investigation was carried out smoothly and the evidence was gathered painstakingly, with the examination of more than a hundred witnesses during the early part of our probe. Interestingly, many witnesses were duly examined in the court as well and they deposed appropriately. In spite of all these efforts and developments, our criminal justice system, as it operates, gave scope for getting the entire case sabotaged and opportunity for a conspiracy to falsify the most expeditious, hard and honest work done by the police during the investigation.

Whatever the result in court that came out later through distortions and manipulations, the investigating team of the police was happy at that time to have successfully solved the case and collected the crucial evidence within a week of the incident. By the time the charge sheet was filed, we, as a team, were satisfied that we had put up a water-tight case in spite of all the obstructions we had faced.

Actually, for us, in the technical terms of a police investigation, this case had nothing extraordinary about it. It was not a tough investigation or a blind case where we had to encounter a dead end. A detailed supervisory report by me, updating the commissioner of police was on record, which had also been submitted to the ministry of home affairs, government of India, due to the interest generated in the case through the national media.

For us it was a simple, though elaborate, case in which a girl had been shot dead in full view of many persons in an illegal bar. In our police department we handle such cases routinely. This case was clearly and correctly worked out, with the identification of the main accused within hours, arrest of the accomplices within four days and the murderer himself on the sixth day of the crime. The hazardous aspects of the case were the unusual number of Page Three socialites and celebrities with their hangers-on and the different characters involved who proved to be men of straw during the trial. What made the incident newsprint fodder was that the bartender girl was a model, the bar was run by socialites, the witnesses were celebrities from the world of glamour and the accused was the son of a highly connected politician from the ruling party.

My initial opinion that this was an 'open-and-shut case' was later portrayed in the media, judiciary and my own department as my shortcoming and limitation in understanding the enormity of the case. As it was widely covered in the media, the entire country knew that Manu Sharma was the prime suspect in Jessica's murder and what we filed in our reports was hard-core evidence. But we were mocked and accused that we took it all too lightly.

10

We Unfold and They Cover Up the Trails

How the events took place leading to the occurrence of the crime was crystal clear to us, and it was recorded in our case file and reports. Manu Sharma, Vikas Yadav, Amardeep alias Tony and Alok had met at Tony's Friends Colony house in the late evening, a few hours before the crime took place, just for a get-together, without any inkling that they were going to commit such a sensational murder. After meeting there, following a couple of drinks, they went together to Qutub Colonnade, the happening place in the city.

They arrived there when the party was almost over. The bar was closed but they demanded drinks. When they were refused, Manu Sharma took out a pistol and shot Jessica Lal. They immediately fled from there. While fleeing, Manu Sharma also bumped into Bina Ramani who was at the scene of crime, and her attention was drawn on hearing the sound of gunshots. Bina Ramani actually questioned Manu about the weapon and followed him but he hurriedly left the scene of crime and disappeared.

According to the statements of Tony and Alok, the Tata Safari car in which all of them had come together to Qutub Colonnade was later driven away from the scene of the crime by Vikas Yadav, who had come back to the spot along with Amardeep. When Vikas was driving away the Tata Safari, the

Home Guard Shrawan Kumar tried to stop him and hit the rear windowpane of the car with his stick. Vikas took the Tata Safari to Tony's house in Friends Colony, then to his house at 15 B.R. Mehta Lane where it was handed over to his driver Dhanraj. The Noida Police found the abandoned vehicle which was taken over by the SHO Mehrauli Inspector Surender Sharma when he was told about it. We were also able to establish the ownership of the vehicle based on the registration number with the swift assistance of the Chandigarh Police.

Among important recoveries from the crime scene were two empty cartridges with 'C' markings on them. They were found behind the bar counter. An inspection of the scene of crime had revealed no blood there. Investigations disclosed that Surender Garhwali, aka Chander, a cleaner employed at the restaurant, had been asked to clean up the place and remove the blood. Later, during the Public Interest Litigation (PIL) hearing in the High Court, he said that though he did not know who asked him to clean the blood, he did recall that it was a male voice.

All these facts were put together after extremely fast and efficient investigations. If you look at the investigation reports of the time—the notes made by the subordinates, top-up supervisory notes made by me over them and also the progress reports submitted to me by my juniors—as early as 6 May 1999, the investigation process had made substantial progress and appeared to be on excellent grounds.

Manu Sharma, the main accused, along with Tony and Alok as co-accused, had all been traced and arrested by 6 May 1999. The role of Vikas Yadav, son of former Member of Parliament D.P. Yadav, had also come out clearly. Vikas, who lived with his father in the official bungalow allotted to his father in the VIP area near Connaught Place at 15 B.R. Mehta Lane, was the one who returned to the scene of the crime, having escaped after the murder, and drove away Manu's Tata Safari from Qutub Colonnade.

With the arrest of Tony and Alok, and later of Manu, the details of the crime and its cover-up—the evidence, the movements of the accused after the incident, the connected circumstances, witnesses—started getting revealed, one after the other. The extraordinary speed at which the investigation was moving, the way the case was becoming clear, and also the strong evidentiary material we had gathered, were reasons enough for me to confidently make the statement that this was an 'open-and-shut case'.

Manu Sharma was finally arrested on 6 May 1999 at Chandigarh. At the same time, his arms licence was handed over to Inspector Lamba. He was first taken to his house at Chandigarh for the recovery of the diary which contained the address of Ravinder Sudan alias Teetu, who had been given the gun used in the crime by Manu. Manu was then immediately brought to Delhi to obtain his police remand from a magistrate for his custodial interrogation and a detailed confession. Though such a confession is inadmissible as evidence under the law, it is very useful for investigation.

Manu Sharma's confession was recorded in Hindi and transcribed in all the modes—video, audio and text. The confessional statement was properly translated into English, too, and both the Hindi and English versions were kept as supporting evidence. The narrative emerging from the confession was almost the same in sequence and detail as we had weaved together from the information that the investigating team had gathered during the first few days after the crime. His confession gave us more clarity about the sequence of events which led to the crime and also the events which followed later.

What we learnt from the confession were the precise details and the manner in which Manu was protected by those harbouring him following his escape after the crime while he stayed overnight in Delhi and subsequently when he left Delhi under cover. This was all supported by the actual witnesses and others who, privy to the crime, had helped in his movements and attempted to protect him from the legal process. We also got concrete information about how they attempted to dispose off the crime weapon—the pistol—after it was retrieved by Manu from the place not far away from the scene of the crime where he had first hidden it.

We also got clarity about how Manu and his friends used different cars, taxis and even an auto-rickshaw on the night of the crime for different purposes in order to save themselves from being caught by the police. Delhi Police had begun its search for Manu's Tata Safari, which was removed from the site of the crime by his co-accused, right at the start of the investigation itself. All sorts of evidence was continuously analysed by Delhi Police, and the line of investigation was being updated and revised based upon the videographed confessions of Manu Sharma, which was later produced in the court as a piece of evidence.

The statement of the crucial witness, namely, Dinesh Kumar Sharma, a guard of Amardeep's building, was taken and probed deeply because he could give details with descriptions about the continuous coming-and-goings of vehicles along with the accused persons during the night of the crime. This was all clearly corroborated with the statements of the accused Amardeep—the owner of the apartment—and the other accused.

The police was on alert and was cautiously yet relentlessly taking the investigation forward in Delhi, Chandigarh and beyond while, simultaneously, it appeared to us, continuous efforts were being made by the accused and suspects to cover up and manipulate the evidence.

The invesigations indicated that Shyam Sunder Sharma, known as Shyamjee, who was Manu Sharma's uncle, helped in the disposal of the murder weapon and facilitated the movements of his nephew.* Assisting, allegedly, was Harvinder Chopra, the

* 'On the Trial Court Judgment', *Outlook*, available at https://www.outlookindia.com/website/story/on-the-trial-court-judgment/233421

chartered accountant of Piccadily Agro Industries, besides his childhood friend Ashok Dutt. Ashok Dutt, however, later said in his confession to the police that Shyamjee had never told him that Manu had committed a big crime and had shot dead Jessica.

Manu and his non-resident Indian (NRI) co-accused Ravinder Sudan alias Teetu escaped from Delhi, and in this bid, they allegedly took the help of Harvinder Chopra who was a family friend of Shyamjee as well as Vikas Yadav. He helped them by hiding Manu temporarily in the house of his father in-law Chander Prakash Chhabra at Saket. Chhabra initially helped due to his son in-law's request and later told the police how he was misled to allow the main accused Manu Sharma in his house. He did so due to his relationship and in confusion.

Dr Ruby Gill alias Vikas Gill of Chandigarh, another family friend and a close associate of Shyamjee, according to our investigation, helped them to escape from Delhi. On the way from Delhi to Chandigarh in Vikas Gill's Ford car, they dropped their friend Ravinder Sudan alias Teetu, who was with them, at the Inter State Bus Terminal (ISBT), Kashmere Gate, with the crime weapon, that is, the pistol with which Jessica Lal had been shot. Ravinder Sudan was given the task of disposing off the weapon in some untraceable and unreachable remote area. Being an NRI scheduled to leave India for USA soon, he would not be available for investigation and legal action.

When Manu Sharma reached Chandigarh, he went to a house in Panchkula, under the protection of a family friend, Yograj Singh, a cricketer and the father of the famous Indian cricketer Yuvraj Singh. The police confirmed that Manu Sharma stayed with Yograj in hiding as Yuvraj Singh's grandmother-in-law, Ms Gurmeet Kaur, innocently identified Manu Sharma when the police showed her his photograph.

Yograj kept on changing the place of stay of Manu Sharma and in that bid, he also kept him with one of his friends, Kulvinder Singh Gill, living in a small town called Mahni Khera in Punjab.

Kulvinder was a small-time Punjabi stage and film actor, and taking advantage of his friendship, Yograj convinced him to keep Manu Sharma at his place as a guest by falsely introducing Manu as Harkirat Singh, a USA-based NRI filmmaker, who wanted to study rural Punjab for one of his film projects. Later, when the police interrogated Kulwinder, he was stunned and confessed that Manu Sharma had stayed at his place pretending to be Harkirat Singh.

While as per our investigation, Shyamjee was trying to hide his nephew Manu in Punjab and Chandigarh, he was also ensuring that Teetu, who had presumably disposed the crime weapon, was able to escape from India. He asked his friend Ashok Dutt to make the arrangements. They wanted Teetu to go to USA and become untraceable before the police smelled his involvement and initiated measures to arrest him. Teetu's escape on 4 May resulted in a major loss of evidence for the police.

The police, however, was able to track all the frantic efforts made by Ashok Dutt to set up Teetu's escape. Though he admitted in his confession to the police that he helped Teetu to leave India, he claimed to be innocent. He said Shyamjee, his friend, told him that Teetu wanted to go to USA because his mother was seriously ill there.

On 10 May 1999, SI Vijender Singh, in a smart move, took Ashok Dutt to a telephone booth, Shamim Khan Telephone Centre, run by Ayub Khan, near Okhla Phase-II Railway Yard, to speak to Teetu on phone. From this telephone booth, with proper documentation of the recorded telephone number, highly convincing calls were made to New York on the telephone number of Ravinder Sudan. Ashok Dutt spoke to Ravinder Sudan thrice—for 195 seconds, 44 seconds and finally for 178 seconds. The entire conversation between him and Ravinder Sudan in Punjabi was duly recorded by SI Vijender who paid ₹447 for the calls and took a printout of the bill. An audio cassette of the taped conversation was also prepared, properly sealed and taken into police custody. It was produced in the court as evidence.

What transpired between Ashok Dutt and Ravinder Sudan tentatively established the fact that Ravinder Sudan had taken the weapon from Manu Sharma, and he had acted under the direction of Shyam Sunder Sharma who was, as usual, referred to as 'Shyamjee'. Since Ashok Dutt and Ravinder Sudan knew each other, the conversation was by and large smooth, although due to his guilty conscience, Sudan did not express much.

Ashok Dutt enquired about Teetu's whereabouts and asked why he had not told him about 'something' in his possession. Ashok told him that his (Teetu's) sister and friends were being harassed by the police and wanted to know where he had kept the weapon. Teetu replied that it was known to Shyamjee. Ashok Dutt again informed that Teetu's sister and relatives would be apprehended and that people at high levels had been contacted. He wanted Teetu to come back otherwise Interpol (International Criminal Police Organisation) would catch him.

When asked repeatedly about the weapon, Teetu never denied his knowledge and always spoke about Shyamjee. At one stage, Teetu said he would talk in detail after about ten minutes. But, presumably after consulting someone, when Ashok contacted him again, Teetu did not speak further.

Finally, when Teetu had left for USA and the situation was found to be untenable, Manu Sharma, on the advice of his uncle, surrendered to the police. Inspector Raman Lamba arrested him and brought him to Delhi. After that we immediately started work on his confessional statement and the follow-up by way of corroborations and the investigation on the new facts emerging alongside the collection of evidence.

After Manu Sharma's escape following the crime, the resources, contacts and confidants of his father, Venod Sharma, were actively utilised. Once the chain of events was almost completely established—within fifteen days of the crime—it became clear that Harvinder Chopra, the chartered accountant of the Piccadily group of companies, who had harboured Manu at his father-in-law Chander Prakash Chhabra's house in Saket, Delhi, was orchestrating the moves.

Among others who were found actively helping Manu Sharma was the harbourer and conspirator Raja Chopra, who provided the vehicle for Manu; Vikas Gill, who actually accompanied Raja Chopra to Harvinder's father-in law's house at Saket; and Ravinder Sudan, who accompanied Manu and Vikas Gill during a part of the escape and carried away the weapon of offence, for disposal.

Earlier, on 30 April 1999, when the investigation had just commenced, the police questioned Harvinder Chopra based on leads gathered from the Tata Safari used by Manu Sharma and the co-accused, and he had confirmed about the Piccadily group's ownership of the vehicle. Harvinder later disclosed to the police that at about 11 AM, Manu Sharma had called him to say, initially, that his vehicle had met with an accident. But when Harvinder spoke to him a couple of times to ask for details of the accident, Manu Sharma admitted that he had shot a girl in a restaurant. Harvinder said that he had consoled Manu and assured him that he would handle the matter, and fixed up his shelter at his father-in-law Chander Prakash Chhabra's house.

Manu Sharma's friend and co-accused Vikas Gill had confirmed that when he visited the house of Manu Sharma's father Venod Sharma at Chandigarh, he was told that Venod Sharma had gone to a lawyer. Simultaneously, Raja Chopra, a family friend who was also helping Manu Sharma, also confirmed that he knew Manu Sharma had shot a girl in a restaurant. Similarly, Raja Chopra, who was in the know of things and had gone with Manu Sharma to Harvinder Chopra's father-in-law's house, also confirmed about a bald, middle-aged person accompanying them. Vikas Gill escorted Manu Sharma and Ravinder Sudan alias Teetu in a Ford car from Saket to Chandigarh. On the way, as Manu Sharma disclosed and Vikas Gill confirmed, Teetu was handed over the pistol by Manu Sharma and dropped off near ISBT (Inter-State Bus Terminal), Kashmere Gate.

On the way to Chandigarh, they stopped at a petrol pump near Sanjay Gandhi Transport Nagar and, by mistake, they filled diesel instead of petrol in the Ford car and the vehicle stopped functioning. To establish this point, Rakesh Kumar Atri, a helper in the petrol pump, was examined, and he stated that on 1 May 1999, at about 3:30 PM, two persons had come in a white Ford car in which diesel had been filled instead of petrol. Since the vehicle stopped running, he had got it parked behind the petrol pump where the cashier's scooter was also parked.

Rakesh Kumar Atri also told the police that he had taken both the persons on a two-wheeler scooter to the Sanjay Gandhi Transport Nagar bypass, where the duo got into a Tata Sumo vehicle, and he returned to the petrol pump. He identified these two persons as Manu Sharma and Vikas Gill. The Ford car was pushed into a corner at the petrol pump (Ameesh Enterprises). Manu and Vikas hired a Tata Sumo from that point to cricketer Yograj Singh's house in Panchkula.

An apparently guileless Chander Prakash Chhabra, who acted under the obvious pressure of his son-in-law Harvinder Chopra, was a crucial witness to connect all these conspirators to Manu Sharma's escape. And, about subsequent harbouring he had correctly identified Vikas Gill alias Ruby Gill as the person who accompanied Manu to his house in Saket on 30 April 1999 and then took Manu away in his Ford car. He also identified

Ravinder Sudan's picture among the several photographs shown to him as another person who had come to his house on the same evening.

Another team of officers including SI Vijender Singh had worked out the movements of Ravinder Sudan and his escape from India in a Gulf Air flight on 4 May 1999. The best possible circumstantial evidence had been brought on record to establish the role of Sudan, who was declared a proclaimed offender and a fugitive located in USA while being charge sheeted as such.

About the same time, several witnesses were examined. These included Sahana Mukherji, the lady who had dropped Jessica to Tamarind Court at the beginning of the party; Rouble Dungley, who was in close proximity when Jessica was shot and who sprinkled water on her face when she lay injured; Rohini Sharma, an employee of Qutub Colonnade; Kamal Taneja, who gave some more details of others like Rohit Bal, Sanjiv Batra and Tarun Tahiliani, who were all present at the party.

Sahana Mukherji, who had a business of fabrication, told the police that she had brought Jessica from her house at Safdarjung Enclave to the party. Jessica was wearing a white shirt and blue denim shorts. She had immediately taken over her job at the bar. Sahana said that she had left the party around half-past midnight, leaving Jessica at Tamarind Court.

With all this information, this appeared to be a creditably well-connected case with ample material evidence to establish the charges against the main accused Sidharth Vashisht alias Manu Sharma and his co-accused along with the harbourers, with adequate circumstantial witnesses to support it. Going by the rulebook, there was neither scope nor need to introduce any new witness or to create any evidence. In any investigation, we are not supposed to examine and produce any additional witness in order to establish and prove the existence and presence of direct witnesses to prove any part of the transaction. What happened to these well-established facts and structured evidence on record during the course of the case trial was their systematic destruction, displayed in all its moral debasement in the public domain through the media.

11

Media and Family Perceptions

The role of the media is often crucial in investigations of prominent crime cases. The media, with their omnipresence and resources, shared or not, works with extraordinary drive and pace because they have to sell their news while competing with one another, without bureaucratic rules to slow them down. I have no hesitation in saying that I have often found them to be investigating and collecting facts ahead of the police, especially in the initial days after a crime is committed. Hence I always gave weightage to the first few days of media news in all my investigation work.

On 21–22 May 1991, I recall, when I was in the CBI and was assigned to investigate the Rajiv Gandhi assassination case by Director Vijay Karan, I hurriedly left for Chennai with my team of investigators and forensic experts. Before we arrived at the scene of crime at Sriperumbudur, about two hours from Chennai, at the Delhi and Chennai airports, we bought and read all the newspapers available. The local officers, experts and media persons present on the spot were completely floored when we discussed with them the minute details of the case almost as if we had witnessed the crime. We never told them that it was the result of their own efforts communicated through the media that had produced the wealth of information for us.

The stories of the Jessica Lal case that hogged headlines for years appeared to be somewhat different right from the first day.

The curiosity about what had happened was intense. It was a sensational case because several celebrities were present at the scene of crime. To the public, it could provide, off-and-on, some spicy news. Surprisingly, public interest grew more and more instead of waning, as it often happens, and the media kept fanning it.

The climax came after nearly seven years, with the much-awaited judgement—the acquittal—in February 2006. As expected, the case was reported in the media from all conceivable angles after the stunning judgement.

The headlines screamed, 'No One Killed Jessica Lal, Not Guilty', 'All Jessica Lal Murder Accused Acquitted', 'Getting Away with Murder' and so on. The reports in the media in the initial days were based largely on the court judgement and were a factual narration of reasons given for the acquittal. They did not really make any charges against the police or the prosecution. However, soon stories like 'Jessica's Case, Probe that Faltered at Each Stage', 'With Prosecutors Like This, Who Needs a Defence?', 'Police Chief Once Said about Jessica's Case "The Officers Conspired with the Accused"'.

Several stories in the media that hurt me and my team a lot. Some of these like, 'How Top Cops Let Jessica's Killers Off', 'Police Chief Says Jessica Lal Case Was Fixed' and 'DGP Face Saver: Money Power' soon filled the broadsheets, tabloids and television scrolls. Possibly because Delhi Police, led by a police commissioner who was convinced in a wrong direction, was made to appear as a weakling, with almost no defence offered on behalf of the investigators, we soon saw the stage set for the 'Justice for Jessica' campaign.

The media kept changing tack. The resultant public frenzy and media perceptions were widely divergent and often a far cry from the facts and evidence on record. The judgement was full of erroneous and misleading findings. Justice Bhayana told reporters after making his verdict public that the Delhi

Police had failed to sustain the ground on which it had built the case.

Justice Bhayana went on to mention specific grounds such as the non-recovery of the murder weapon, the use of two weapons, the witnesses turning hostile and the police failing to establish a convincing chain of circumstantial evidence leading to the crime, as the basis for his judgement. This was lapped up by people who were looking for reasons to substantiate the stereotype of a bumbling police force which was open to influences and bribes.

But the police was ultimately proved right when the Delhi Hight Court reversed the order.

Jessica's younger sister, Sabrina Lal, at one stage, became the symbol of the public outcry, 'Justice for Jessica'. During the previous years, Sabrina had captured public imagination, at least on celluloid, as the representative of the people's movement to seek justice for Jessica. Our experience with her was, however, somewhat different. Sabrina, it appeared, had given up concern about the case long before it reached the stage of actual verdict. Interestingly, when a mammoth fight for justice for Jessica was started by the media way back in January 2002, when Manu Sharma was granted bail, she had stopped taking any interest in the case. Even after Manu Sharma initially got bail in 2002, he had to remain incarcerated until 2005 because of the grim legal battle the prosecution and the police fought, without her cooperation.

Throughout the trial, the appeals of the SPP Suresh K. Saxena and the IO Surender Sharma to Sabrina that she should attend the hearings fell on deaf ears. They believed that her presence would have struck a sympathetic chord with the Court, but she never complied or showed any interest. For reasons only she could explain, she completely disassociated herself from the proceedings of the case from 2002 to 2006.

Even after the judgement came out, her initial statements had nothing against the police or the prosecution. In fact, she said that she believed that the evidence included a lot of documents, seizures and other material as well as the circumstantial evidence that could be relied upon for a conviction. She also said something that was on everyone's minds—she said that the judge should have made efforts to find out why the witnesses had turned hostile. At the same time, she also admitted that she had no clue about the judgement as she had not been in contact with the case at all since January 2002.

After the judgement, when I was in Delhi at my residence at Satya Marg, we spoke to each other on the telephone, followed by which she visited me.

'I am going to be with the Police Commissioner, visiting him tomorrow,' she told me at a time when our team was on a backfoot having suffered adverse judgement and media attacks.

'You must,' I told her, 'prevail upon the Police Commissioner to file an appeal against the judgement at the earliest, and tell him that all of us in the team were keen to help.'

'But I need to find out how the judge could acquit everyone in such an irregular way,' she replied in a note of anguish.

'I agree. It is in no way a fair judgement. We have so much evidence on record. Even if we discount the hostile witnesses, we have a lot of documentary and circumstantial evidence that proves the chain of events and the guilt of the accused.'

I ended my conversation with her with an appeal to convince the Police Commissioner to associate the concerned officers in the efforts to gain justice. She did not give me any assurance about that. But, following her meeting with the Police Commissioner, as coming from the Police Headquarters, the media gave a negative report about my conversation with her.

Much later in the day, Sabrina and her father, Ajit Kumar Lal, made a startling disclosure. They said that in December 1999, Manu Sharma's parents had visited them. But differences between the father and daughter were evident when Sabrina downplayed her own father's interview to a newspaper, calling into question his mental faculties. That interview, however, carried some very logical and well-informed comments by Ajit Lal. He had expressed his unhappiness about the functioning of the judicial system and he hoped that justice might still be done.

While Sabrina had merely questioned the reason for witnesses turning hostile, her father was more direct. He expressed deep shock at the conduct of Shayan Munshi, especially given the background of his close association with Jessica. He expressed his suspicions that Shayan was probably influenced by money. He also had a lot to say about Shiv Das and Karan Rajput turning hostile. He talked of a tape-recorded conversation between Karan Rajput and an associate of the opposite party where inducements were offered.

According to News18, the Lals were apparently aware that the witnesses Shayan Munshi, Karan Rajput and Shiv Das had all been bought over.* The question was why Sabrina did nothing to bring this information to light and, instead, chose to dissociate herself from the case and watch from the sidelines as the prosecution's case was being destroyed.

The answer came out in a sting operation by Star TV. While working on an exposé of why the witnesses turned hostile, they revealed that Sabrina Lal had made a substatntial payment to the star eyewitness Karan Rajput.

Sabrina's alleged payment to this critical witness who turned hostile caused very serious damage to the prosecution case.

* 'Sabrina Lall Answers Your Questions', News18, 20 December 2006, available at https://www.news18.com/news/india/sabrina-lall-254029.html

Under the circumstances, it could only appear questionable. We thought then that, some day when the hype subsided, she could talk about the payment made to a hostile witness without the knowledge of the police officers including me, whom she knew so well. She could also clarify about her conduct in becoming completely unconnected with the case except through the IOs, with whom subsequently she was unwilling to meet or cooperate.

Later, riding the media wave when she was becoming a celebrity and an icon, she started finding faults and without giving any valid reason, started attacking the police investigation and the investigators. She was, however, charitable enough to add that the police had enough evidence to prove that Manu Sharma had used his licensed weapon and ammunition that he had bought from a Haryana shop. In totality, Sabrina Lal and her father Ajit Lal did not have much to say against the police who had provided them with all possible support and confidence while making a simple request to them to be supportive in the case.

12

Rescue the Case: The Legal Way

The Jessica Lal case became a watershed in the annals of the criminal justice system of the country, with serious demands being made to bring about changes in the criminal laws. It was the topic of discussion everywhere. At times, the debates in the electronic media were ill-informed and superficial, with all kinds of trivial viewpoints being made by the so-called 'experts'. Most of these 'experts' appeared to be largely ignorant of the actual judgement and the appropriate legal recourses open to the police and prosecution, which we adopted later.

Taking suo motu cognisance based on media reports, the Division Bench of the Delhi High Court comprising Justices Vijender Jain and Rekha Sharma directed the Commissioner of Delhi Police Dr K.K. Paul to submit a report giving details of the investigation and the reasons for the failure of the case in the court. Obviously, while responding to newspaper reports when they initiated this PIL, the judges were shocked about what happened and said, 'How could all witnesses turn hostile and all evidence go missing?' The Bench directed the High Court Registrar to club the newspaper clippings and orders were issued accordingly.

Since Delhi Police led by Dr K.K. Paul had not committed or made any official statement about the examination of the judgement for an appeal—which was the most obvious legal course—or otherwise, the common perception was that through the High Court's intervention, a process of reinvestigation or retrial could be initiated, primarily due to the public outcry, fanned by the media. Without even looking into the judgement, several activists and NGOs were also demanding retrial and action against the police officials responsible for the failure of the case and the so-called shoddy investigation.

Although no statement or clarification came on behalf of Delhi Police or the Government, the two legal functionaries, IO Surender Sharma and SPP Suresh Saxena, fully aware of the case and in the picture right from the beginning, were required to be associated for further legal action. Taking detailed comments and opinion on each point about the case and the judgement, we suggested that Delhi Police should file an appeal based entirely on the evidence that was already a part of court record.

With the permission of the Court, further investigation could also be carried out, on the lines of what was decided by the former Commissioner of Police Ajay Raj Sharma way back in 1999, with regard to suspected manipulation of the cartridges in the ballistic report which had introduced the theory of two weapons in the case. This was consistent with a previous enquiry conducted in 1999 about the circumstantially absurd and apparently false forensic report that had come from the CBI's CFSL.

Based on a report submitted by DCP (South) Sudhir Yadav, I had made a suggestion right in the beginning for an independent enquiry, preferably by the CBI, since the doubtful ballistic report had come from CFSL which was attached to this organisation. Unfortunately, in 1999 as well as in 2006 following the judgement, instead of taking it to its logical conclusion, this report was completely twisted by the then joint commissioner of police (crime) and later the commissioner of police, who himself created serious doubts about the case.

Even our friend, the conservative and cautious Special Public Prosecutor Saxena, was not spared by the media and castigated for doing sloppy work. The screeching headline 'With Prosecutors Like This, Who Needs a Defence?' mentioned earlier, related to him. Public perception had been created through statements of Delhi Police itself that it was a 'shoddy investigation' and to support this point of view, entirely based on the court judgement, several loopholes were pointed out in the prosecution case.

It began to be mistakenly believed at that point of time that the IO had fallen short of the standard level of performance. People began to feel that the initial police team had collected no cogent evidence and could not properly record the statements of any of the witnesses regarding the involvement of Manu Sharma in the crime. It was ironic and so frustrating that such assaults came from within the Department—that the investigators deliberately did not prove both the evidence, the empties of used bullets recovered from the scene of crime and the live bullet obtained from Manu's Tata Safari.

It was unthinkable even for an ordinary person to believe that ballistic opinion need not have been taken, as was being told as an afterthought by Delhi Police top-cops, considering the fact that the two bullet empties found near the counter where Jessica Lal was shot and one bullet found in Manu's abandoned vehicle, were so closely connected to the pistol .22 calibre used by the accused. We were blamed for not providing substantial ground to Justice Bhayana through our reports and evidence to enable him to give a judgement against the accused. In our hearts we knew how mischievously the entire case was being twisted at every stage and, at times, we had to helplessly watch the drama in the court as silent spectators.

The day after Justice Bhayana's judgement itself, hastily concluding that the police did not investigate properly and recover the murder weapon and, consequently, the forensic report did not support the case, Senior Advocate Indira Jaising, during discussions in the media like others, analysed the case, practically supporting the judgement. She based her analysis on the non-recovery of the murder weapon, the ballistic report stating that the two fired cartridges were not fired from the same weapon, eyewitnesses turning hostile and the chain of events not being proved.

According to the media reports, Indira Jaising concluded that the Delhi Police must take the responsibility, both for the manipulation of the ballistic report and the conclusion drawn by CFSL about the use of two weapons on the spot. While arguing as to what ails the legal system, she agreed with Jessica's sister Sabrina that too much reliance was placed in the case on the eyewitnesses while the circumstantial evidence was overlooked.

It is rare that one particular case is subjected to so much diverse, detailed and multi-pronged scrutiny, resulting in all shades of views being expressed. While the case became the rallying point to protest against the collapse of the administration and criminal justice system in the country, the suggestion by the former Solicitor General of India Harish Salve, of a 'retrial or reinvestigation', appeared to be somewhat odd since the appropriate legal course was an appeal considering the evidence on record.

While all this was happening in the public space, slowly and steadily, the case was heading towards filing an appeal. By the first week of March, there was a perceptible shift in public opinion. Legal luminaries like Indira Jaising, who had earlier been so outspoken and critical of the supposedly shoddy investigation of the case, began to see the flaws in the judgement and the merits in the evidence. By this time, the legal experts had the opportunity to carefully read through the judgement and they could gauge the realities lying in its deeper layers. They now understood and appreciated the value of the evidence that had been collected and saw that the acquittal by the trial judge was seriously flawed on several counts.

In a media discussion, both Indira Jaising and another eminent lawyer, Mukul Rohtagi, who later rose to become the attorney general of India, felt that the State could go for an appeal in the case. They also pointed out that if the Trial Court had wished to interpret it, there was enough circumstantial evidence to convict the accused.

'A girl died, one person fled the spot, went into hiding, changed his car. It is ridiculous that the court could not give a verdict just because the witnesses were bought and they turned hostile due to certain reasons,' commented one eminent lawyer. The issue of the retrial of the Jessica Lal case also came up in the context of the unprecedented order given by the Supreme Court in the Best Bakery Case that became symbolic of injustice in the Hindu–Muslim Gujarat riots, where the investigating agency had been found to be conniving and allegedly not examined the witnesses at all. Another eminent senior advocate, P.N. Lekhi, however, felt that 'if there were a hundred retrials in the same circumstances, truth will not come out despite hundred-odd people being present in the party'.

Advocate Kamini Jaiswal made an obvious legal comment while stating that, based on the available evidence, there was no room for retrial since it would amount to 'double jeopardy'.

While eminent jurists like Indira Jaising were already changing their initial views, yet the suggestions of a reinvestigation or retrial lingered. Perhaps many in the legal fraternity had not really gone into the documents on record in depth.

A statement was made by the police commissioner (Dr K.K. Paul, as joint commissioner of police–crime), alleging that the 'Investigating Officer had manipulated the ballistic evidence', a point on which even the High Court had asked for a report.

Simultaneously, there were some interesting discussions in the media about the witnesses turning hostile. Senior Advocate K.T.S. Tulsi totally debunked this ground, along with the conflicting ballistic reports, for the acquittal. He pointed out that the Trial Court could have taken note of the post-crime conduct of the accused persons, which was important circumstantial evidence, to find out whether the chain was complete.

The ace criminal prosecution advocate Dayan Krishnan, who had dealt with the Parliament attack case, cited a Supreme Court ruling in the Anant Chintaman Lago case where the Apex Court had convicted the murder-accused based entirely on circumstantial evidence.

Former ASG Altaf Ahmad also felt that though the eyewitness accounts get primacy before the Trial Court, they are not absolute and even if they were relied upon by the Trial Court, the circumstantial evidence could become the ground for conviction.

Similar views were expressed by Senior Advocate Ashok Arora, who had earlier challenged Judge Bhayana's elevation to the High Court. He found the judgement to be completely wrong on all counts and also felt that ballistic reports were prone to tampering.

Meanwhile, Delhi Police was preparing itself, under the circumstances, to investigate their own IOs who had once done a commendable job for them. It was extremely frustrating for me at that point of time to have realised that our own people had taken a hostile stand against the investigating team and the supervisory officers, blaming us for no fault of ours, completely negating the effective and systematic manner in which the team had diligently completed the task.

Instead of scrutinising the judgement, as the topmost legal luminaries were already doing (our team was preparing an appeal against the judgement trying to introduce the same officially), most absurdly, the top cops of Delhi Police were agreeing with the distorted judgement. While the case was being deeply scrutinised in the High Court through the suo motu PIL, another Delhi Police team had begun the process of destroying our own case by not only finding non-existent faults but, to our utter humiliation, trying to somehow blame their own officers and prosecute them. Entirely based on the highly flawed judgement, a criminal case was registered, practically against the IOs, for committing 'criminal acts and illegalities'.

The case was already becoming the focal point for some kind of judicial reforms, including a Witnesses Protection Programme and changes in the law. Eminent lawyers like Dayan Krishnan and Ashok Arora strongly felt that it was high time that hostile witnesses were prosecuted for perjury (lying on oath). They believed that judges should punish them for making false statements as it was very important to uphold the sanctity and respect of the criminal justice system and protect it so that it did not reach the brink of collapse.

Gradually, my views expressed during the initial days—so far unheeded, pointing out that the police had no control over witnesses turning hostile, especially when there was a clandestine use of money and power—and my arguments on common platforms against the tampering of the ballistic report in the forensic laboratory began to gain credibility when similar opinions started coming from legal experts.

One of the most truthful of the witnesses was the NRI Deepak Bhojwani, a close friend of Jessica Lal. He had made some forthright statements in the beginning which were conveniently overlooked by the 'Justice for Jessica' campaigners. He said, 'I was the first prosecution witness to depose in the case. That period of my life was like a nightmare. I got all kinds of threats and was also offered money. My family was petrified and everyone around me just kept saying one thing—that I should stay away from the matter.'

A brave person who was disbelieved by the Trial Court, Bhojwani refused to be cowed down or bought over. He put up a strong resistance when there was an attempt to force him to retract from his initial statement. In the process, he decided to set up 'Mission Justice Society', an organisation to take up the issue of protection of witnesses. Based in Durban in South Africa, Bhojwani came out of the entire episode with his conscience clear, both during the trial and following the judgement, but neither the media nor the others concerned chose to treat him as a hero.

In the discussions that followed the acquittal, the highest in the land including President A.P.J. Abdul Kalam, Prime Minister Dr Manmohan Singh and Chief Justice of India Y.K. Sabharwal, expressed their concerns about the Jessica Lal case and the failure of the criminal justice machinery in the country.

Speaking at the conference 'National Summit of Legal Fraternity' organised by the Bar Council of India, the chief justice of India made an oblique reference to this case. He expressed his views about witnesses turning hostile after seven years and criticised the lawyers for the use of dilatory tactics while pleading for adjournments in the cases. He was quoted saying, 'We cannot live under an illusion, we exist because of the litigants who are consumers of justice; most people are gullible and believe everything their lawyers say and issues of moral turpitude have risen. Sadly, lawyers displayed casual approaches towards their clients.'

The 'Justice for Jessica' campaign launched by the media gathered over two lakh SMS-based appeals which were sent to the president of India. The President promised to act, as did many other leaders including Sonia Gandhi, the president of the ruling alliance, UPA. All of them wanted legal justice and a victory of truth.

Interestingly, Sonia Gandhi took up the case as it was a national cry and in her own way pulled up the government of the day. It was said that she intervened because of personal contacts with Jessica's family and partly out of her concern for such issues. Due to her intervention and the surging popular demand, Home Minister Shivraj Patil announced suitable changes in the law. A 'Criminal Law Amendment Bill' suddenly came into circulation and was actively considered by the Government.

The Jessica Lal case provided an opportunity to highlight the need for changes in the law. This had become the focal point of animated political discussions as former law minister Arun Jaitley mentioned having initiated similar changes during his tenure. The changes the government had sought to bring about were based on the recommendations of the Law Commission and had been pending for a long time. The issue had come up in the BMW and other high-profile cases also, when the Commission had recommended changes in the law to contain the dangerous trend of witnesses turning hostile. It suggested that it should be mandatory for the IOs to get the statements of witnesses recorded on oath before a magistrate.

It was proposed to introduce a new legal provision, Section 164(A), in CrPC 1973 under which police officers would be expected to 'forward all persons whose evidence was essential for the just decision in the case, to the nearest Magistrate for recording their statements'. Another provision, Section 311(A) CrPC, was proposed to be added 'allowing any Magistrate, whether he had jurisdiction over the case or not, to record any confession or evidence which should be admissible'. A suggestion made was to insert Section 344(A) that would deal with witnesses turning hostile even after getting their statement recorded under Section 164(A) CrPC and the action might summarily be punishable with imprisonment for a period of three months, extendable to two years.

To oversee the police investigation, it was suggested to amend Section 161 CrPC, making it obligatory for the police to record statements in a Case Diary which should be bound books and not loose sheets, as was being done. Another suggestion was made to substitute Section 162 CrPC with 'statement of witness (required) to be recorded in writing, signed or thumb impression given with date and time and to be forthwith forwarded to the Magistrate'.

These suggestions for legal changes were extremely relevant and had been in demand for a long time. But they could contribute nothing directly to the Jessica Lal case which had to necessarily follow the existing laid-down legal processes. Legal consciousness seemed to prevail upon the concerned and unconcerned officials of Delhi Police, besides the legal fraternity, who were giving their endless opinions on the case.

The trend of the opinions being expressed about the case, official and unofficial, was changing. It now began to be felt in the police department internally that there was no way to add anything substantial to the existing body of evidence on record that had been the basis of the judgement delivered by Trial Judge Justice S.L. Bhayana. It was felt that Justice Bhayana's judgement must be appealed instead of humiliating our own internal team who had actually completed their task adroitly and effectively.

We succeeded in getting the appeal filed and could also get the eminent advocate Additional Solicitor General Gopal Subramanium to argue the case. In order to get the complete picture and more details, he met me separately to take my opinion since in my capacity as DGP Arunachal I was not being officially involved. Some of our other colleagues in Delhi Police who were officially pursuing the matter had kept Gopal Subramanium in complete darkness about some crucial facts of the case, trying to convince him all the time during the briefings that our team had not only bungled, but deliberately created loopholes to damage the case.

Gopal Subramanium had known me for several decades and held me in high esteem. During one of my visits to Delhi from Arunachal later, he took my detailed briefing about this case, following which he decided to rely on me for some more untold facts and not upon some senior officials and their teams who were officially on the job. On several occasions during the High Court appeal proceedings, he took my viewpoint while meeting IO Surender Sharma several times and argued the case meticulously and brilliantly.

13

Resettling the Case: Crime to Criminal

Our real battle began after filing and pursuing the appeal in the High Court. We revisited the entire process once again. Since in any important case where an acquittal has taken place, the detailed, pointed comments of the IO and the opinion of the prosecutor are mandatory, Inspector Surender Sharma and SPP Suresh Saxena utilised this opportunity effectively. We decided to re-examine the investigation from all possible angles by relooking at the evidence on record. Right from the beginning, we found the pace of this meticulous investigation was unusually fast, and the case had been pursued vigorously until the filing of the charge sheet.

The number of PCR vans with Delhi Police had multiplied from just 30 in 1984, when the anti-Sikh riots took place, to nearly 300 in 1999 when the Jessica Lal case occurred. They had generally become the first responders to a large number of crimes. Like in a majority of incidents being reported to the PCR, in the Jessica Lal case too, they received the call and assigned it to the nearest available van. That was PCR van number E-43 led by Head Constable Devi Singh. Head Constable Devi Singh and his team were on *gasht* (patrolling) in the Mehrauli area when at about 2:15 AM a wireless message was received that someone had been shot near the Qutub Minar. While they were proceeding towards the spot, at 2:16 AM another call came that at H-15/6, Mehrauli, a girl had been shot.

Head Constable Devi Singh later stated that at 2:17 AM, when he reached the spot near the main gate of Qutub Colonnade, he found a few vehicles parked there. He went inside the restaurant and found a gunshot hole in the roof and the floor slightly wet. The injured had been taken to Aashlok Hospital. He found no blood on the spot. As a matter of routine, as soon as the local police (police station personnel) arrived, he reported back to the PCR.

SI Sunil Kumar, accompanied by Constable Subhash who had come to the spot, found, like the PCR, that the injured girl had been taken to Aashlok Hospital in Safdarjung Enclave. He proceeded to Aashlok Hospital to further investigate and record the statement of the injured. At Aashlok Hospital, he recorded the statement of the FIR witness Shayan Munshi. Simultaneously, since the information was given to the area police station at Mehrauli as well, SI Sharad Kumar, who was on night emergency duty and had just returned from another call, also joined the investigation when he was handed over the report about the incident.

As recorded by the initial IO, SI Sunil Kumar, he received the information from the Duty Officer of the police station, who had already made a Daily Diary entry (41A) at the police station and handed it over to him at about 2:25 AM. He proceeded to the spot and began his investigation by 2:46 AM on 30 April 1999. When he reached the scene of crime along with Constables Subhash Chand, he found the PCR van already there with Head Constable Devi Singh and others. Two other senior officers, lady ACP Parveen Dutt and Inspector Anand Parkash, who were on routine night patrolling, had also arrived on the spot.

It is interesting to note that all of these police officers went inside and inspected the actual scene of the crime at the restaurant, and they found no blood on the spot but located the bullet hole in the roof that could be seen from the counter. Since the injured Jessica Lal had already been taken to the hospital and there was nothing much to do there except preserving the scene of crime, SI Sunil Kumar, accompanied by Constable Subhash, immediately went to Aashlok Hospital. The scene of the crime was left under the protection of SI Sharad Kumar and Constable Minu Mathew, besides Home Guard Shrawan Kumar (who had arrived on the spot along with SHO Surender Sharma) and was told to maintain a watch on the vehicles outside.

At Aashlok Hospital, where SHO Surender Sharma and ACP O.P. Mishra had also arrived, the SI requested the hospital authorities for permission to record the statement of the injured Jessica Lal. Her condition was reported to be critical and the IO was told that 'the patient was unfit for statement and she was in a coma'. Among the numerous people present at the hospital, including the family members of Jessica Lal, her friends, onlookers and police officers, the co-bartender of Jessica and an eyewitness, Shayan Munshi, was found to be the most suitable person for becoming the formal FIR complainant.

Whatever might have happened to most of the witnesses in the court during the course of the trial, at this point of time Shayan Munshi appeared to be the most natural, truthful and forthcoming eyewitness. In fact, his statement was recorded right there, in the presence of the Ramanis, Jessica's sister Sabrina and others. Shayan Munshi then accompanied SI Sunil Kumar on his scooter as a pillion and returned to Qutub Colonnade. Prior to this, at about 3:40 AM, Bina Ramani and others had shifted Jessica Lal to Apollo Hospital since Aashlok Hospital doctors were unable to treat her.

On coming back to Qutub Colonnade, in the statement recorded by SI Sunil Kumar on 30 April 1999, Shayan again confirmed his previous statement in the FIR. During the examination of the spot along with the SI, he also pointed out the place where Jessica Lal had been shot by a person he described in detail. He further added that during the incident, a tall Sikh, wearing a red turban, about thirty-two years old, was present near the counter along with the person later identified as Manu Sharma and two or three other friends.

Recounting the entire conversation during the site inspection, Shayan Munshi elaborated, 'At this point of time, the boy in the T-shirt demanded drinks and Malini told him again that there was no liquor to serve. The boy (Manu Sharma) told her that while she was herself drinking liquor, why couldn't he get the same. On this, Malini Ramani retorted, "You cannot have even a sip of my drink even if you pay ₹ 1,000." Shayan Munshi recalled and further stated that the boy had said, 'I can pay ₹ 1,000 for a sip of you.' Malini felt offended by this and left the place along with Sanjay Mehtani, her friend and also close to the family.

Shayan Munshi described the incident in minute detail, recounting how the boy in the T-shirt who had shot at Jessica sneaked out of the place along with the Sikh gentleman (later identified as Amardeep alias Tony) in the red turban and two or three other friends. He explained the entire incident, corroborating his statement in the FIR, including the presence of Malini's mother Bina Ramani on the spot, who attempted to stop the person who had shot Jessica Lal.

When Inspector Sharma and ACP Mishra returned to the scene of crime, Home Guard Shrawan Kumar informed them that in the meantime, a black-coloured Tata Safari which had been parked near Qutub Colonnade had been forcibly taken away by a fair complexioned, heavily built boy who had come in a Tata Sierra vehicle which was being driven by a Sikh fellow. When they did not stop the vehicle though he tried to prevent them, he struck the fleeing vehicle with his stick and broke the rear window glass, but they succeeded in escaping.

Meanwhile, as the police investigation relating to the scene of crime was being set into motion, at about 5:30 AM, the security supervisor of Apollo Hospital informed Police Station Mehrauli that Jessica Lal, 34 years old, who had sustained gunshot injury was 'brought dead' from Aashlok Hospital. Later, it was learnt that Jessica Lal had been taken to the Emergency Operation Theatre at Apollo to try to revive her, but that was unsuccessful.

This information was given to SI Sunil Kumar and the 'attempt to murder' case under Section 307 of IPC registered earlier was converted into a murder case under Section 302 IPC. SI Sharad Kumar and other officers were sent to Apollo Hospital while SI Sunil Kumar and the Crime Team of the South Delhi district remained busy at the scene of crime where, among other details, it was pointed out again that there was no blood there.

Simultaneously, the site plans and photographs including that of the dead body were prepared, besides collecting the forensic evidence. The officers in the Delhi Police Crime Team were obviously required to carefully examine the scene of crime in order to collect the evidence without damaging it. But, in the process, inevitably, some disturbance was bound to take place. In the restaurant, the forensic experts found two fired cartridges with 'C' markings on them. They were found near the bar counter, beneath the ice box.

Despite all the efforts made during the night and subsequently when the experts from CFSL inspected the scene of crime, the bullet lead, which had pierced through the tin roof, could not be recovered. The empty cartridges were safely packed and sealed by the IO, to be subsequently sent to CFSL for their ballistic examination and to report and confirm the connection of these items to the case.

By the time it was around 7 AM, Jatinder Raj, the supervisor of the restaurant who had carried the injured Jessica Lal in the car along with others, produced his bloodstained shirt to the investigating officers. Actually, when Bina Ramani was carrying Jessica on the back seat of Sanjay Mehtani's car, Jessica's head was on Jatinder's lap and his shirt got bloodstained. Since Jessica's blood sample was already with the police, the blood on the shirt of Jatinder Raj served the purpose of investigation regarding both of them. Jatinder Raj was among the earliest witnesses. His statement, along with those of others, was recorded suitably to corroborate the initial report and the related developments from the actual crime up to the declared death of Jessica Lal.

Jatinder Raj gave a detailed account of the Thursday Parties being held at Qutub Colonnade where alcohol was routinely served. Jatinder said that this party, on the intervening night of 29–30 April, was almost over by about half-past midnight and he started helping in the cleaning of the place and removal of glasses and bottles.

Surender Chander, who worked in the kitchen of Qutub Colonnade, made a statement on 30 April itself about the cleaning of blood at the site. He said that on the night of 29–30 April, at about 2 AM, while he was cleaning the utensils in the kitchen, he heard two shots being fired. As he went near the counter inside the restaurant, he found Jessica Lal lying on the floor. He added that one of the guests, Rouble Dungley, another family friend, asked for cloth and water with which he cleaned Jessica Lal's face.

Surender Chander cleaned the floor on the direction of someone, whom he subsequently described as a 'male voice' during the PIL that was filed in Delhi High Court, raising issues about the cleaning of the blood from the spot.

Describing the incidents during that night, Jatinder narrated that while some people were generally chatting around, at about 1 AM, his uncle Karan Rajput, who turned out to be a crucial eyewitness but later resiled, came looking for him. Since he was busy, he made Karan Rajput sit inside Tamarind Court. At about 2 AM, the party was almost over, and he was sitting in his office in Qutub Colonnade, when he heard gunshots and rushed to the restaurant.

There was chaos and people were running helter-skelter. Near the counter, Jatinder found Jessica Lal lying on the floor and Rouble Dungley sitting next to her, cleaning blood from her face. At this point, Bina Ramani, with the help of the waiter Madan, put Jessica Lal on a tablecloth to be carried to the car. Jatinder Raj accompanied Jessica to the Aashlok hospital and from there returned to Qutub Colonnade.

SI Sharad Kumar, who had gone to Apollo Hospital in order to conduct the inquest or the statutory enquiry (Section 174 CrPC) into the cause and circumstances of this unnatural death, did not find any clothes on Jessica Lal's dead body. Jessica's sister Sabrina Lal was present throughout, and besides identifying the body, she had also accompanied her for the autopsy (post-mortem examination) that was conducted at All India Institute of Medical Sciences (AIIMS). Following the post-mortem, by about 1 PM on 30 April, Jessica's body was handed over to Sabrina Lal. The police were given the piece of lead recovered from Jessica's skull as well as her blood sample for further investigation.

The information about the actual ownership of Manu Sharma's Tata Safari CH01-W-6535, registered in the name of Venod Sharma's sugar mill Piccadily Agro Industries Ltd, Bhadson, Indri, Karnal, was received from Chandigarh within a couple of hours. Consequently, Inspector Raman Lamba, in-charge, Anti Auto Theft Squad (AATS) of South District Police, was dispatched to Karnal by about 2 PM on 30 April to locate the vehicle and its owner. At Karnal, in the sugar factory, Inspector Lamba met Major R.C. Sood, the chief security officer, who told him that the mills were closed since it was off-season and the general manager and chairman were not available.

When he enquired about the Tata Safari vehicle, Major Sood informed him that it had been taken by the chairman of Piccadily Agro Industries Ltd, Sidharth Vashisht alias Manu Sharma, who was Venod Sharma's son and resident of 229, Sector 29/C Chandigarh. The mill premises were inspected for the crime-related vehicle. Inspector Lamba did not find it there. He then went to search for the car at a guesthouse of the company at Kurukshetra. At the guesthouse, the guard Suraj Bhan informed that Manu Sharma used to come there sometimes along with his friends for rest and overnight stay, but he had not come there in the past fifteen days.

Inspector Lamba also checked the house of one Mr Aggarwal, the general manager of the mills. But there were no clues relevant to the case, and Inspector Lamba returned to Delhi. He brought important details of the vehicle and its user, obviously confirming the possession of Manu Sharma during the crucial time. Meanwhile, another team led by SI Pankaj Malik had already been dispatched to make further enquiries about the vehicle and its owner.

Though I have investigated—either directly or in a supervisory capacity—thousands of cases, including some of the most talked about and sensational cases of murder and other heinous crimes, rarely had I come across a case of this dimension where so many developments took place in less than twenty-four hours of the crime being committed. On 30 April, numerous important statements were being made and recorded simultaneously. Obviously, one such statement happened to be that of the star witness Bina Ramani, married (her second marriage) to Georges Mailhot, a former Canadian International Development Agency (CIDA) official in Delhi. Bina, fifty-six-years-old, was a British national and a well-known Delhi socialite and businesswoman.

Perhaps, in the given situation, Bina had no option but to admit that alcohol was served regularly at the popular Qutub Colonnade during the Thursday Parties. She stated that the party was over on the night of 29–30 April, and the place was being cleaned when the shoot-out took place. The same day, Bina's husband Georges Mailhot, the sixty-year-old Canadian national who claimed to be an artist by profession and lived with Bina's family, corroborated her statement. He said that on the night of 29–30 April, at about 2 AM, after the party was over at Qutub Colonnade and the cleaning work was going on, he was standing in the courtyard when he heard 'two pops' coming from inside the restaurant, and he hurried to the door.

As he was moving towards the spot, Shayan Munshi came running out saying that someone had shot Jessica. Inside, he found Jessica lying near the counter while Bina was following a fair-complexioned stocky man, wearing a white T-shirt. Georges Mailhot further mentioned that he went to the police station at Mehrauli to lodge a report where the Duty Officer told him that the police had already received the information and someone had gone to investigate the matter.

Another twist in the case came in the form of a statement that a white Ambassador car, which supposedly could be the official vehicle of some bureaucrat or police officer, was also seen at Qutub Colonnade. It was already known to the local police that the senior police officer who had come to Qutub Colonnade in a police Ambassador car was Joint Commissioner of Police (New Delhi Range) Y.S. Dadwal. Dadwal had called up in the morning and told me about his visit to the place the previous night. Immediately after the crime, once Dadwal's presence at the party was known to the media, it became an issue in the government as well.

Additional DCP Vivek Gogia was later asked to formally examine Dadwal, which was done in his office at Delhi Police Headquarters. Dadwal stated that on 29 April, at about 11.45 PM, he had gone to Qutub Colonnade along with his friends Mr and Mrs Mohit Jain and Mr and Mrs Raju Singh, 'since it was an open restaurant'. They remained there for around half an hour and left the place at about quarter past midnight as they found the place to be too crowded. Dadwal further clarified that he had known Venod Sharma since he was earlier posted as Inspector General of Police (IGP), Chandigarh, and he had met his son Manu Sharma then. However, he stated that he did not remember having met him (Manu Sharma) at Qutub Colonnade that night.

Although the Crime Team of Delhi Police had already visited the scene of crime early in the morning of 30 April, considering the importance of the case, the CFSL team was also summoned for a thorough inspection. This team examined the preserved place very carefully by applying proper methods, specifically to find bloodstains at the place where Jessica had been shot, but they found none. The team also attempted to locate the fired lead which had pierced through the roof of the restaurant, but it was also not found.

Later, when the Tata Safari vehicle was brought to Police Station Mehrauli, it was thoroughly inspected with sophisticated instruments for any other clues. The driver-side rear glass of the vehicle, which had been broken by Home Guard Shrawan Kumar, was found to have been replaced. This glass was subsequently examined in comparison to the other glasses and the broken glass pieces which had been found in the vehicle at Noida. All put together, the CFSL gave a clear opinion to establish that not only was the glass of the vehicle broken, but another glass had been fixed which was dissimilar to the original one.

During investigation, it transpired that the vehicle was retrieved by Vikas Yadav from the scene of crime along with Amardeep Singh Gill. It was taken away by him and handed over to his loyal driver, Dhanraj, with the responsibility to change the broken glass pane and dispose off the vehicle. Dhanraj got the glass changed and abandoned the Tata Safari in Noida, where it was found by the Noida Police on 2 May.

During this period, from 30 April to 6 May, all-out efforts were made to apprehend the main accused, Manu Sharma. Besides extensive evidence pointing to him, after the arrests of his associates, Amardeep Singh Gill and Alok Khanna, it had been established beyond doubt that Manu Sharma had killed Jessica Lal. Inspector Raman Lamba and his team were continually travelling to different places in Haryana and Chandigarh to locate and arrest him.

Inspector Raman Lamba had already informed us in Delhi that Manu Sharma's mother had told him about Vikas Yadav, son of the well-known politician, former UP Cabinet Minister and Rajya Sabha Member of Parliament Dharam Pal Yadav, and Amardeep Singh Gill alias Tony Gill, being among his best friends who used to move around with him in Delhi. Amardeep Singh Gill was a general manager (GM) in Coca-Cola and resided in Friends Colony in Delhi. The police now had his mobile phone number.

During his investigations, Inspector Lamba conducted repeated raids at Piccadily Restaurant, Piccadily Cinema Halls and other places owned by Venod Sharma and his family. After the initial meeting with Venod Sharma at his house, where also were present Punjab Police Senior Superintendent (SSP) Sumedh Singh Saini, who later rose to become DGP, Punjab, and a noted lawyer, Inspector Lamba could not lay his hands on Venod Sharma. Venod Sharma got himself admitted to Post Graduate Institute (PGI) Hospital, Chandigarh. When Inspector Lamba went to PGI Chandigarh to question Venod Sharma, he was prevented from doing so as Venod had already been shifted to the Cardiac Care Unit (CCU). He thus became inaccessible for any investigation. Instead, Inspector Lamba was confronted by his lawyer Harish Ghai outside the hospital. The Delhi Police officer, with all the support from the Chandigarh Police—then headed by none less than the iconic Kiran Bedi herself—as well as Delhi Police supervisory officer Vivek Gogia's personal contacts, could not make any headway except telling Advocate Harish Ghai to produce Manu Sharma.

After taking their own time, undeterred by a national hunt going on for Jessica's killer, for the reasons that became clear later, Sidharth Vashisht alias Manu Sharma could be arrested by the Delhi Police team led by Inspector Raman Lamba only when he surrendered at Patiala Tourist Bungalow, Chandigarh, at 2:20 PM on 6 May 1999. Manu's advocate Harish Ghai produced only the arms licence, without the suspected crime weapon. The description on the arms licence was of a non-prohibited bore (NPB) pistol with the endorsement of Beretta, made in Italy, with 25 rounds of .22 bore cartridges. The arms licence was seized by ASI Nirbhay Singh under the signature of Sidharth Vashisht. The personal search of this much-wanted accused yielded ₹ 1,900 in cash and small items like a silver *kada* (bangle), a Casio quartz watch and a 'Hanuman Chalisa Gutka' for chanting to dispel fear through prayers.

Manu was taken to his house. He had said that the weapon of offence had been handed over to one Ravinder Sudan alias Teetu, whose address was noted in Manu Sharma's diary. But this diary could not be found. However, the interrogation gave a clue to Teetu's local contact in Delhi—his brother-in-law's telephone number. This was communicated to the senior officers. A manhunt was immediately launched to locate Teetu and recover the weapon.

Manu Sharma was brought to Delhi by about 9 PM. He was immediately questioned by the senior officers of South district and then finally taken to the police station by about 11:30 PM, where he was handed over to the SHO.

Acting further on the clues provided by the team from Chandigarh, another police officer, SI K.P. Malik from South District, was deputed to make inquiries about a Delhi telephone number 2213879, which was reported to be the contact number of Ravinder Sudan. This telephone number was found to be of Sudan's brother-in-law Chander Sain Issar, an employee of Goodyear company, who gave a detailed account of Sudan. He informed that Sudan was an NRI, living in USA for the past 12–13 years. He said that Sudan had come to India on a visit six months ago, from USA.

Sudan had gone to Issar's home on 29 April evening and following a telephone call from some unknown person, the next day morning at about 10 AM, he went away, carrying a handbag. There was no information about Sudan until a telephone call came on 2 May evening that he was going to Bhilai to meet his sisters who lived there. While he was away, on 4 May, another telephone call came from his *bhabhi* (sister-in-law) from the US, inquiring about the flight Sudan was taking to return to the US.

Issar had no information about Sudan after the US phone call, but he gave some important information. Sudan's cousin Inderjeet Bakshi had a flat at Mani Majra near Chandigarh which he had bought two years earlier and had entrusted it to his friend Tony Jain of Panchkula. Inquiries were made from Inderjeet Bakshi at his house in Minto Road Complex in New Delhi, who gave some more details about Sudan's movements. Sudan had visited him in the evening of 3 May and told him about his flight back to the US the same night. Sudan returned to Bakshi's house at about 5 AM the next morning, explaining that his ticket could not be confirmed and he could not take the flight.

The same evening, however, Sudan took his luggage in a three-wheeler scooter saying that he was scheduled to return to USA the same night. Inquiries were made quickly from the Foreigners and Regional Registration Office (FRRO) and the Immigration Authority at the airport, who confirmed the departure of Sudan from India on 4–5 May night by Gulf Air. This was indeed a major setback for the investigators since it was very clear that the crucial evidence of the murder weapon would now be extremely difficult to find in Sudan's absence.

We now understood why Manu Sharma's father Venod Sharma, taking refuge in the leading government hospital PGI, Chandigarh, was evading police investigation. It was clear why he had delayed presenting his protected son to the police. Manu surrendered only after Sudan had left India. They conspired together to ensure the disposal of the murder weapon.

Beginning with the scene of crime investigation on the morning of 30 April, six days later, when Manu Sharma was arrested and taken into custody by Police Station Mehrauli, the first crucial phase of the investigation was over.

14

Socialites and Celebrities: Who's Who of Delhi

In my experience of investigating several major crimes during my different postings, considering the intricacies of the investigations or the mysteries to be untangled, the Jessica Lal murder was a relatively simpler case. In fact, considering the actual circumstances of the Thursday Party at Qutub Colonnade where a large number of people present were known to one another and the organisers, there was nothing much to investigate about their identities. The effort that went in was the legwork and soft skills required to persuade the dramatis personae to come forward to speak the actual facts. For once, the generally publicity-crazy 'Page Three' characters did not want to be named in the case. They had more to conceal than to reveal truthfully and help the investigators.

When we learnt that the crime was committed by the pampered son of a prominent politician, we thought his previous and subsequent conduct could not be kept hidden. We were very hopeful that we would be able to catch the culprit quickly. When compared to some completely blind cases I had handled—like the assassinations of Prime Minister Rajiv Gandhi, Lalit Maken, Arjun Dass and General A.S. Vaidya (when I got associated with the CBI)—all having national and international links and complex ramifications, investigating Jessica's murder appeared to be far easier.

During the investigation, I never expected this case to become such a serious and mammoth affair. The case was not so big or complex; it was made so because a lot of devious characters were involved in it. Obviously, the media hype also led to the High Court suo moto cognisance and the home ministry and other high-ups getting into its details. Even the non-recovery of the offence weapon and the discovery of serious manipulation in the ballistic report coming from CBI's CFSL, which was clarified through a report from the Rajasthan Forensic Science Lab, actually did not seem to damage the case so much in the long run.

We appeared to be well equipped and fortified through an array of direct, indirect and circumstantial evidence. Added to the oral and visual evidence through numerous scenes of crime witnesses who connected the case very accurately, we had fairly strong forensic, documentary and material evidence, all of which put together created several unbroken chains of events that decidedly proved the case. But the story as it unfolded during the prolonged trial, thanks to the celebrities and the socialites involved, turned out to be extremely complicated.

During the investigation, as the details came to light, I marvelled at the creativity and innovative spirit of the Ramanis. The idea of setting up 'Thursday Parties' at Qutub Colonnade on an unexciting mid-week day was a business tactic thought up by the mother–daughter duo. They were quite adept at creating a buzz for any event—they knew the art of attracting celebrities to special parties which served as a magnet for the Page Three crowd. The idea was to get those who really mattered in Delhi to the party where they could develop or firm up their business or social connections. They had a track record of setting up several such sought-after happening places—the Hauz Khas Village, which had become the artistic, ethnic and fashion hub of Delhi, was one of them. The mother and daughter were ably supported by a highly creative Georges Mailhot.

From the first day itself, during investigation, we had some idea of the kind of people who were present at the ninth Thursday Party. The guest list included several well-known celebrities and important persons. Our initial attempt was to identify and apprehend the main accused of the crime, his associates and co-accused, harbourers and conspirators, whose identities were getting revealed.

While we were busy establishing our case methodically, the media was in a frenzy over the guest list. Very quickly, the investigation started getting sucked into the media and celebrity quagmire. Except for Commissioner of Police V.N. Singh, who was primarily interested in a methodical and thorough investigation, all others seemed to be more interested in the dramatis personae than the crime itself.

An elaborate investigation was also required to be done under the orders of the High Court which had taken cognisance of this case through a PIL filed by the NGO, Bhrashtachar Virodhi Morcha. When we decided to examine each and every person who had come to Qutub Colonnade on 29–30 April, invited or uninvited, the investigation became an endless affair.

The owner–organisers of the Thursday Party explained to us that on the night in question, two parties were going on simultaneously in the Qutub Colonnade complex. One was the 'Around the World' farewell party for Georges Mailhot who was going abroad, and the other was the ninth party in the highly successful series of what was called the 'Thursday Party', that was organised by Bina's daughter, Malini Ramani. Mailhot's party was set up mostly on the terrace where, among others, the Hollywood star Steven Seagal and a large number of other guests, who were mostly known to one another, had come through invitations.

We learnt that this brilliant idea of the somewhat informal Thursday Party was conceived by Bina's fashion designer daughter Malini and fully supported by Bina and Mailhot to revive their sagging business at the Qutub Colonnade.

When Georges Mailhot was examined on 30 April, he provided a guest list that was formally seized by the IO as a case document and partly became the basis for the investigation. Subsequently, a detailed roving inquiry had to be conducted from those present or connected to the party in order to prepare a second list to find out who all had attended the Thursday Party.

Later, during the trial, an inappropriate and misleading impression was created about these two lists. The second list of Malini Ramani's guests was produced in my office and later presented in the High Court as just being the result of the investigation in which we had gathered concrete evidence for the case, like it happened with Mailhot's first list.

In order to examine all the persons who were present at the party, another team was constituted under ACP (Public Grievances Cell) Durga Prasad, who examined most of them one by one. Going systematically, he called upon the well-known designer Rohit Bal first, who had called the PCR on the emergency telephone number 100 to give the first information of the crime. When summoned for investigation, Rohit Bal gave a detailed statement about his role and informed that he had come to the party along with the fashion designer Reena Dhaka and her husband Ajay Sharma.

Among the well-known people who attended the party were Anand Seth, Karan Pal, Nakul Nath, Meena Alagh, Parveen, Ramesh, Rouble Dungley, Tarun Tahiliani, Anil Beg, Iyesha Paul, Sanjay Kapoor, Sanjiv Batra, Vishal and Yash. Most of these persons were identified easily since they were celebrities and well-known fashion designers, mostly known to one another. Among others whom Rohit Bal had met in the party were Amarjeet Sethi, Bina Ramani, Malini Ramani, Bindu Wadhera, Vineeta Thukral, Hari Bhartiya, Jessica Lal, Dr Naresh Trehan, Poochi Sikand, Preeti Paul and 15–20 others who were known to be a part of the social group.

At Qutub Colonnade, among those present during the party, apart from the Ramanis with Mailhot and the other crucial witnesses, Rohit Bal was the only one who had something relevant to say. Rohit talked about his nearly ten-year-long association with Bina Ramani and also his acquaintance and friendship with Bina's daughters, Malini and Gita. He gave a description of the Thursday Party. Rohit also knew a number of other visitors to the Qutub Colonnade including Rouble Dungley, whom he met near the unconscious Jessica soon after the shooting.

Rohit said that he had arrived at the party about ten minutes prior to the shooting, following which he heard Malini scream that somebody had fired at Jessica. He had known Jessica for nearly fifteen years, as she had been a model earlier and then worked in events management. As soon as he heard Malini scream, Rohit ran towards Tamarind Court and found Jessica lying in front of the counter. He could see blood flowing from her body and he lifted her hand to check her pulse to see if she was alive.

Rohit immediately dialled 100 from his mobile phone to call the police. He also phoned his personal doctor Alok Chopra, the co-owner of Aashlok Hospital in Safdarjung Enclave. Dr Alok Chopra asked him to bring Jessica to the hospital, while Bina Ramani put her in a car and took her there. Although Rohit Bal had not witnessed the crime or seen the accused person, the next day, at the time of cremation, he overheard people saying that Manu Sharma had killed Jessica Lal.

Among the fashion designers group, Reena Dhaka and her husband Ajay Sharma were examined, and they said that they had been in the party since about 9 PM. They came on the invitation of Malini Ramani who knew them. Reena also knew Jessica Lal. She met her and saw her serving drinks at the bar counter. Most of the people examined had nothing significant to inform about the crime or even about the presence of the accused persons in the party.

Another officer from South District, ACP R.C. Thakur, was also asked to identify other people who had attended the party, prepare a list and carry out further investigations under the supervision of Additional DCP Vivek Gogia. At least twenty-one more persons, the who's who of the fashion world, were examined. Most of them knew the Ramanis or knew several other invitees coming to the Thursday Party, thus forming a chain of known persons, as planned by Malini in this unusual business. The list of known socialites included Manisha Gill, Hanut Singh, Nikhil Khanna, Rohini Trehan, David Chang, Jay Wadia, Jacob Dubey, Bhai Chand Patel, Sukhmati Shah, Dhiren Chauhan, Sonam Lamba, Rajesh Sharma, Veena Sharma and Tarun Tahiliani and his wife Shailja.

Most of these people talked about their acquaintance with the Ramanis and Jessica Lal. But they did not say anything substantial about the crime or the persons connected with it. They also did not say much about the presence of police officers and bureaucrats in the party, a point which was being looked into at the instance of the High Court and the higher levels of the government.

Since serious efforts were made to identify those who had attended the party, several persons came forward to depose voluntarily, in spite of their pronounced ignorance about the case. Among them was Gaurav Karan, the son of the former Commissioner of Police Vijay Karan, who had come to the party along with his sister and two other friends, Aman Chopra and Gautam Monga. They said that there were nearly 300 persons present in the party at about 11:30 PM. They also confirmed the presence of many persons mentioned earlier, besides some other known names in the social circuit like Rohit Gandhi, Shiv Karan, Rahul Khanna, Kismat Kapoor, Arjun Walia, Dharam Sehgal, Shivam and Gaurav.

About the general ambience and the activities in the party, such as coupons, service of liquor and snacks, and the number of people present, they gave a somewhat similar account as Rohit and some of the more expressive guests. All these persons introduced the names of several other persons who attended the party and most of them were identified, contacted and examined.

Surprisingly, in the party there were a large number of people who had come from outside Delhi and even from as far as Mumbai. They had come since they knew the Ramanis. Others had been invited by people in their social network on hearing about the growing popularity of this happening place. During investigation, all these people chose not to disclose anything relevant about the case, even if they appeared to have some knowledge. Despite thorough questioning, they did not go beyond talking about the shortage of liquor and that the place was crowded.

Many of these people found the party interesting because there were plenty of common friends, like Dave Chang met Vivek Sahni, Hanut Singh and Nikhil Khanna. Most of them claimed to have come to know about the incident only the next day. Some of them, like Vivek Sahni, found that the event was purely for making money and was not a private party at all, as the organisers claimed.

Among others in the party, Vikram Aditya Bhatia, a health club owner from Greater Kailash Part II, gave a detailed account of the happenings in the party. Around 60–70 of his friends, including socialites like Sandeep Tahiliani, Miki Kunj, Bindu Wadhera, Rohit Agarwal, Neeraj Khanna and Vikram Walia, also said something similar and corroborated the story. They appeared to have been moving in groups and were generally chatting to socialise and network.

Numerous others who attended the party had plenty to speak about their previous contacts with the Ramanis, about the opportunities for socialising, dance and music in the midst of the big crowd that had collected that night. Poonam Walia from another posh South Delhi colony came through her friend Dhiren. She expressed her ignorance about the illegality of the bar being operated with a young model as a barmaid. Among the well-known people, like many others, Priya Paul and Preeti Paul had come to the place on Malini's invitation, but they found that there was no restriction on the entry of uninvited visitors. They reached the place around 10:30 PM and found 50–60 persons already present, including their friends Vivek Sahni, Tarun Tahiliani, Natasha and Hari Bhartiya.

They knew Jessica, who was serving at the counter, for several years as a model, but they did not know Manu Sharma. Information about the shoot-out came as a shock to them the next day and was a complete dampener on Priya's birthday celebrations, which they did not hold. Many others from high society like Sagari Singh and Sonam Lamba had similar stories to narrate about the night or about the next day when they were told about the incident by someone or they learnt about it through the newspapers. Sagari knew Malini since 1985, as they were schoolmates at the elite Lawrence School in Sanawar in Himachal Pradesh, which was a common connection for many people present that evening.

Most narratives about the events at the party appeared on similar lines, with very little concrete information about the crime and the accused involved. Even the friends of the Ramanis like Rohina Trehan, who was living in the same building as the Ramanis in Saket, did not have much to say. Rohini had come with her brother Rahul and mother Dr Preeta Trehan and remained there for quite some time, leaving the place just before the shoot-out took place.

The Trehans felt that the party was more for fun and for meeting friends. Like others, they purchased a couple of coupons for ₹ 100 each, took a few 'vodkas and beers' besides their dinner at about 1 AM. While leaving the party, as mentioned, they found the place jam-packed, with about 300–400 people, having no inkling of what would soon take place there. They had come to the party uninvited after hearing about it from their friends. Among many others present was Punita Thukral who had attended the party a couple of times earlier and who spent her time greeting people, circulating and socialising. Eminent cardiac surgeon Dr Naresh Trehan was also there for some time.

The party started and proceeded well, but towards the end it degenerated into a kind of a grab and scramble due to the limited supply of alcohol. Among the lucky ones who found themselves comfortable with drinks was a British national, Pura Oxmaira, an early bird and a guest of Vikram Aditya Bhatia. Oxmaira had purchased six or seven coupons when he arrived and that served him well. Soon, the likes of Tarun Tahiliani, Micky Kunj, Bindu Wadhera and Rohit Agarwal were rubbing shoulders with their own clan or others while the gathering already had 300–400 people or maybe more.

It must have been a tough time for the more respectable and status-conscious amongst them. The senior police officer, Joint Police Commissioner Y.S. Dadwal, in the company of Kamaljit Singh alias Raju Singh and Mohit Jain, with their wives coming 'for a change' from Gymkhana Club, found the crowd to be too stuffy and preferred to go to some other place.

By this time, even someone like the celebrity fashion designer Tarun Tahiliani, scion of the well-known Admiral R.H. Tahiliani family, had to go without any drinks or food which finished apparently by 1 AM or so. Tarun Tahiliani asked for a drink but finding the bar closed, unlike Manu Sharma, he retreated gracefully. Friends of Malini, like Rajesh Mukherjee and others, did not stay till the end but some of them witnessed the circumstances which occurred following the shoot-out. Rajesh Mukherjee corroborated the respective roles of Bina Ramani, Sanjay Mehtani, Rohit Bal and some others among the 30–40 people who may have been present at about 2 AM when the crime took place.

In the process of intensive investigation and examination of the people who had come to the party, the specially constituted team led by ACP Durga Prasad examined Andleep Sehgal alias

Andee, and also the crucial witness, Deepak Bhojwani, both of whom had something very important to say. To support Manu's motive and his presence on the scene of crime, Deepak Bhojwani had, perhaps, the most critical statement to make. Talking about his export business of jewellery and his close friendship with Jessica, he mentioned that he had been coming to the Thursday Party at Qutub Colonnade for the past four occasions. On 29–30 night, he had wisely bought four coupons for drinks early and was generally going around meeting friends.

At about 1:30 AM, when Deepak Bhojwani went near the bar, Jessica told him that if he had a few coupons she would quietly give him a couple of drinks since the liquor stock was almost over. Deepak Bhojwani produced two coupons and while he was carrying his two drinks in both hands, Manu Sharma greeted him with a 'hello' and wanted to know how Deepak had two drinks in his hands whereas he was getting none. Deepak told Manu that the bar was closed and that there were no drinks. When they were about to exchange their visiting cards, a Sikh gentleman wearing a red turban walked up to Manu and took him away towards Tamarind Court.

Deepak mentioned that Jessica had told him that after the party was over, all of them would go out for a coffee. At about 2 AM, he heard the gunshots and was told that Jessica had been shot. He found Jessica lying on the floor and some people saying that a person in a white T-shirt who was accompanied by a Sikh in a red turban had shot her. While Deepak Bhojwani was mentally connecting this with the people whom he had met a couple of minutes earlier, Bina and others lifted Jessica and took her to Aashlok Hospital and, subsequently, to Apollo Hospital where, he was told, the doctors declared her dead.

Among the very few persons who could be cited as witnesses to the crime, the well-connected Andleep Sehgal happened to be there along with his wife and had something more to say about Manu's friends and the co-accused. He mentioned Amardeep

Gill and Parikshit Sagar being present, while also confirming the presence of Manu Sharma, Tony Gill, Amit Jhingan, Alok Khanna, Vikas Yadav—he knew all of them as they were from the same social group. Andleep Sehgal had known Manu Sharma since the past three or four months and saw him in a white T-shirt that night near the bar counter. He had met the accused persons before he left the party with his wife at about 1 AM.

Parikshit Sagar had something relevant to say about the presence of Manu Sharma and other accused persons at the party. Parikshit had arrived at about 11 PM at this much-publicised Thursday Party. He had attended such parties three or four times earlier too, since he knew Bina Ramani and Malini Ramani for quite some time. In the party, he met Sidharth Vashisht, Amardeep Singh Gill and Alok Khanna, besides Jessica Lal, whom he knew for nearly three years through meeting her in social gatherings. He knew Tony Gill and Alok Khanna since he used to visit Chandigarh very often when he was studying in school at Sanawar.

It was the common Sanawar group that led to their meeting each other a couple of times. Parikshit mentioned meeting Manu Sharma at about 12:30 AM. Manu asked him 'whether I knew Malini and Jessica and if I could get a drink because the bar is closed'.

Dr Naresh Trehan, perhaps the best-known cardiac surgeon in the country and a celebrated socialite, was also examined in the case. He told us about having heard of this party where a lot of people would get together. On 29 April 1999, he had returned from USA and was invited to this place by some of his friends. At about 11:30 PM, when he came to the party, there were at least 200 people, including Atul Punj and Priya Paul.

Dr Trehan said he found the place too crowded. He stayed there for 5–10 minutes and did not have anything to drink or eat. It was only the next day that he learnt about the crime when Atul rang him up to say that Jessica Lal had been murdered at the restaurant. He was not aware whether it was a private party, legal or illegal, nor did he know Manu Sharma or any bureaucrat or any senior police officer present there.

Sanjay Mehtani, an exporter, who travelled to Hong Kong very frequently and happened to be a close friend of Malini Ramani, was an important witness about the circumstances which preceded the crime. As he was feeling hungry, he had accompanied Malini to Tamarind Cafe at about 2 AM just before the crime. There, as deposed by him, he saw Manu Sharma, a fat, fair-complexioned person, aged about forty, wearing a T-shirt and blue jeans. He also found three or four of his friends with him, including a tall Sikh in a red turban.

As Sanjay Mehtani got his statement recorded, he too was a direct witness about Manu Sharma demanding liquor and the refusal by the waiter. He vividly remembered the presence of Shayan Munshi, Malini Ramani and Jessica Lal at the murder spot and the fact that drinks were over at that time. Sanjay Mehtani, Malini Ramani and Jessica Lal were hanging around with drinks in their hands. By that time the party was over. It seems while Sanjay Mehtani had turned around and was standing a little farther away, as he said, he suddenly heard some loud arguments and Manu Sharma saying something which annoyed Malini. She felt bad and along with Sanjay Mehtani, she left the place.

Minutes later, when Sanjay was still in Tamarind Court, he heard two gunshots and saw Shayan Munshi running out saying that someone had shot Jessica Lal. He went inside and he found Jessica lying on the floor opposite the bar counter, with a gunshot injury on the left forehead. In his statement, he described the entire chain of events exactly as they had happened, which was clearly corroborated by the statements of other eyewitnesses too.

Some of the persons who were examined by the police later, like Arjun Som Dutt from the posh Maharani Bagh area, also came forward with a detailed account of the party. Arjun had known Jessica Lal for nearly five years and, at the party, he was enjoying his drink which he had bought using coupons costing ₹ 100 each. He met Jessica, Malini Ramani and Sanjay Mehtani, besides Nikhil Khanna, Priya Singh, Vivek Sahni, Dave Chang, Rubia Sharma, Reena Dhaka, Harish Aggarwal, Rohit Bal, Natasha Handa, Amarjeet Singh and several others. At about 2 AM, there was a commotion following the shoot-out and he found Jessica Lal lying on the floor inside Tamarind Cafe.

Arminder Gill alias Aman Gill, an exporter by profession, had also come to the party with his wife Jasbir Gill and friend Parikshit Sagar. He met many of his college friends there like Amandeep Singh Gill alias Tony Gill, Alok Khanna, Amit Jhingan along with Vikas Yadav and Manu Sharma. He identified each of them and particularly described Manu Sharma in his white T-shirt and blue jeans. Since he went back with his friend Parikshit at about 1:30 AM before the incident took place, he was not a witness to the actual crime, but he confirmed the presence of Manu and his co-accused friends at the party.

15

Investigation and Manu's Confession

Following the arrest of Manu Sharma and his associates Amardeep Singh Gill and Alok Khanna, intensive searches were carried out for the remaining key conspirators and associates, especially Vikas Yadav and Amit Jhingan. While the very well-known Vikas Yadav continued to remain absconding, creating uproar all over the media, it was not difficult to locate the milder Amit Jhingan in his middle-class Vasant Kunj flat.

On 8 May 1999, when Manu Sharma and Amit Jhingan were brought to Police Station Mehrauli and were present in SHO Surender Sharma's room, it was by sheer chance that Bina Ramani and her daughter Malini too came there in connection with their restaurant's Excise Act case. The investigators took the appropriate legal advantage and brought them face to face to confront and identify one another.

Since Manu and others had already refused to join the Test Identification Parade (TIP), their identification at the police station could be used as evidence in the court. Both Bina and Malini Ramani readily recognised Manu Sharma as the same person who was wearing a white T-shirt and blue jeans and had shot Jessica Lal in the party on 29–30 April night. They also said that about three or four other persons had accompanied Manu Sharma during the shoot-out, one of whom was Amit Jhingan, the person present at the police station in front of them.

Bina Ramani, as per her seasoned ways to communicate, gave a graphic and dramatic account of the incident, explaining how she tried to stop Manu Sharma who went out of the Qutub Colonnade gate along with his friends. Supporting both of them, Bina's husband Georges Mailhot once again endorsed his earlier statement and said that he had seen Manu Sharma wearing a white T-shirt being followed by Bina Ramani after the shoot-out.

Amit Jhingan gave a detailed account of his own conduct besides that of others, including Manu Sharma's. He said Tony Gill called him at about 11 PM on 29 April evening and asked him to come to Qutub Colonnade. In fact, he reached the place even before his other friends, Manu Sharma, Vikas Yadav, Amardeep Singh Gill and Alok Khanna, who arrived a little later. Already, more than 300 people were present. He interacted with some people until about 2 AM, when he heard the gunfire and learned about the shooting. Amit Jhingan sneaked away from the scene and returned home where some time later Tony Gill contacted him on his mobile and asked him to come with his Maruti Gypsy to his residence.

It was at this time, Jhingan admitted, when he returned to Amardeep Singh Gill's house in Friends Colony to assist Manu and others and learnt about Manu Sharma's vehicle being removed. He became a party to the conspiracy that was hatched amongst the five of them to remove the vehicle and to retrieve the weapon of offence. To retrieve the weapon of offence, that is, the .22 Beretta pistol which was used by Manu Sharma and concealed near the Indian Cottage Industries, Amit drove Manu and Vikas to Mehrauli in his Maruti Gypsy.

As per the versions recorded and evidence collected, the three of them came to the small gate of the well-known Indian Cottage Industries near Qutub Minar. There was a tin shed in which Manu Sharma had concealed the weapon while escaping from the scene of crime. In the presence of Amit Jhingan, Manu

Sharma recovered the weapon and they went back to Tony Gill's house in Friends Colony (West). Very truthfully and without any hesitation, following his arrest, Amit Jhingan led the police party to the Indian Cottage Industries and pointed out the place where the weapon had been concealed and was later taken away by Manu Sharma. There was absolutely no discrepancy or variation in the confessional statements made by him and Manu Sharma.

Though these statements were very well understood, believed and accepted by even common people, it was primarily on account of the ways our laws have been framed and structured that both those statements were inadmissible as evidence. Nevertheless, they formed the basis of crucial parts of the investigation concerning the arrested accused persons.

Several police officers from the PCR, the local police and the forensic experts who visited the crucial portion of the crime scene gave identical accounts. As one entered the Tamarind Cafe on the right side, there was a counter and behind the counter, a kitchen. In front of the counter, in the ceiling, there was a hole caused by a gunshot. The bullet which had gone through the roof could never be found. Near the counter, below the ice box, two empty cartridges were recovered with the English letter 'C' inscribed on the bottom. They were sealed and taken into police possession.

When the police, including the SHO Inspector Surender Sharma, had reached the crime spot soon after the crime, they found that among the vehicles on the scene there was one black Tata Safari vehicle number CH01-W-6535 parked near the gate of Qutub Colonnade. Home Guard Shrawan Kumar number 6993/DHG was posted on duty to maintain a watch. By this time, the local police had taken charge of the scene of the crime while the other officers and policemen were on their respective duties and DHG Shrawan Kumar was alone there.

Around 3:30–3:45 AM on 30 April, one white Tata Sierra MP-04V-2634, later found to be belonging to co-accused Alok Khanna, arrived at Qutub Colonnade with the other co-accused, Tony Gill and Vikas Yadav inside. When Vikas Yadav got down from the Tata Sierra and attempted to take away the Tata Safari, Home Guard Shrawan Kumar tried to stop him. When Vikas Yadav was forcibly taking the vehicle away by speeding up, Shrawan Kumar hit the vehicle's driver side rear windowpane with his stick and the glass broke. Despite this, the vehicle was driven away, but its number was noted down by the alert Home Guard Shrawan Kumar. This greatly helped in further investigations, as the owner of the vehicle could be located quickly.

Though Inspector Surender Sharma was transferred from his position as SHO Mehrauli on 18 June 1999, the investigation was handed over to him, and he fully devoted himself to this case. During investigation, through the Chandigarh Police, the Tata Safari bearing registration number CH01-W-6535 was found to be registered with Piccadily Agro Industries Ltd located at Sector-34, Chandigarh. This vehicle was used by Sidharth Vashisht alias Manu Sharma. On 2 May 1999, this Tata Safari was found in Noida with a .22 bore live cartridge, and the Noida Police registered an FIR number 115 under Section 25 of the Arms Act. On 3 May, the vehicle was taken over by the Chief Investigating Officer Surender Sharma from the custody of Noida Police.

During closer examination, it was found that though the rear glass windowpane had been changed and the vehicle had been thoroughly cleaned, a few glass pieces were still present inside the vehicle. This established the fact that the vehicle which had been suspiciously removed from Qutub Colonnade, which had been checked by Shrawan Kumar and which he had tried to stop from being taken away by striking the windowpane with his stick, breaking its glass, was the same as this one. The vehicle, one .22 live cartridge and the broken glass pieces were also taken into formal custody by Delhi Police.

During further investigation, the statements of the witnesses were duly recorded to establish the chain of events. Based on the information provided by Chandigarh Police about the ownership of the Tata Safari and the fact that it was used by Manu Sharma and his companions in Delhi, as well as the statements recorded and evidence collected, on 5 May, Amardeep Singh Gill aka Tony Gill and Alok Khanna were among the first ones to be arrested. They readily admitted to their involvement and disclosed the sequence of events. On 6 May, the main accused Sidharth Vashisht alias Manu Sharma was arrested by the Delhi Police team camping at Chandigarh.

On 8 May, another co-accused who had been present at the spot, Amit Jhingan, was arrested. On 14 May, Shyam Sunder Sharma was arrested. On 15 May, Vikas Gill alias Ruby Gill and Harvinder Chopra were arrested. On the same day, Yograj Singh was arrested. On 30 May, Vikas Yadav was arrested. Thus, nine persons were arrested in the case within a month of the commission of the crime and most of the evidence was collected regarding their respective roles and involvement.

Accused Amardeep Singh Gill alias Tony Gill and Alok Khanna, were both employed as General Managers in the Hindustan Coca-Cola Company. Sidharth Vashisht alias Manu Sharma was a director of Piccadily Agro Industries Ltd, which was a sugar factory. Vikas Yadav was a director of Yadu Overseas Ltd. Amit Jhingan was the owner of MSC Garments Company.

At such moments, my alter ego often became active. It questioned me about all the hard work and scientific methods which we meticulously applied to our investigation work.

My alter ego said, 'You have spent the whole day in recording statements. In the court, these persons will back out from what they have said. You also know that these statements will not have much value as evidence in legal terms.'

I replied, 'My fight is not just with the culprits like these ones. My fight is with the systemic shortcomings in our set-up and the legal processes which provide scope for such culprits to flourish.'

'But what value does this evidence have for you? It will not help you in any way,' my alter ego countered.

I replied, 'Every piece of evidence, admissible or inadmissible, has its value if it is based on truth. If the doors of one legal recourse are closed, that does not mean that truth will succumb. There will be some other paths to get the gates of justice opened. Such evidence will be a source of strength to carry forward the fight for justice.'

My alter ego continued to argue, 'The Indian law, as it stands today, completely rejects any confessional statement made before a police officer except for the part of the disclosure statements which are not in the nature of a confession, and which lead to the discovery of a fact. From a legal point of view, this becomes extremely difficult for the police—it is a very tricky exercise to segregate such disclosure statements which lead to a discovery from the confessional statements. This kind of infructuous fact-finding—present in the statements of Manu Sharma and Amit Jhingan—is found in a majority of the cases where the accused persons are arrested and confess their crime to the police. It can make a person want to give up.'

I answered, 'It is true that such evidence may not be treated as a direct proof in our legal system. But it still has immense value in creating an impression in the court and influencing public opinion. Many people who stand for truth often abandon their fight when they encounter such kinds of roadblocks. Who knows, maybe they are very near victory when they decide to give up. Please do not ever think that I will forsake the truth. And please don't even suggest such things to me.'

Whatever may have been its legal value, Manu Sharma's initial statement on 7 May was comprehensive enough to help us build a framework that would cover and establish an uninterrupted chain of events in the case. Although he remained in police custody for another ten days or so, he added nothing substantial to the statement he had already given.

This confessional statement was audio and video-recorded by us and presented in the court. Remarkably, this evidence was set aside at that moment but eight years later, when the case was reopened following public outcry and scrutiny, it proved to be of tremendous help and was widely publicised by the media.

In such circumstances, my alter ego asked me, 'How do you stay hopeful for success when there are so many holes in the system? You cannot plug all the holes.'

I replied, 'We need to remain positive and look for ways of achieving success within the system. When one door closes, another can open up if we try hard enough. Teetu's escape was definitely a loss, but we never crossed the rule book. After Manu Sharma's arrest, we planned to take him physically to all the spots where he hid and to the people who had helped him. We knew we would get more corroborating facts in that process.'

My team and our prosecutor were taking full advantage of Section 27 of the Indian Evidence Act 1872 which partly compensates for the legal infirmity created by Sections 25 and 26 of the Act. Section 25 says that no confession made to a police officer shall be taken as proof against an accused person; Section 26 says that no confession made by any person while he is in the custody of a police officer, unless it is made in the immediate presence of a magistrate, shall be taken as proof against the person.

Such limitations on the police from taking advantage of confessional statements which are made to them routinely also flows from Section 162 CrPC 1973, which makes all statements made to a police officer, either by a witness or by an accused, inadmissible as evidence under the law. The exception is the confession made under Section 145 of the Indian Evidence Act 1872 wherein any part of such a statement, if duly proved, is used by the accused or for re-examination of the witnesses for the purpose of explaining any matter referred in the cross-examination. Section 27 of the Indian Evidence Act, 1872, however, provides:

> When any fact is deposed as discovered in consequence of information received from a person accused of any offence, in the custody of a police officer, so much of such information, whether it amounts to confession or not, as relates distinctly to the fact thereby discovered, may be proved.

The most logical and appropriate way of collecting evidence for a crime, once it is worked out and the perpetrator is arrested, has to be in its re-constructive and retrospective exercise about the incident. The investigator has to travel to all the places along with the perpetrator, his or her accomplices and associates, the witnesses and others connected to the case, recounting and recording the facts and circumstance of the case.

Under Section 27 of the Indian Evidence Act, during the 'pointing out' exercise of the weapon of offence and its use, and discovery of facts as a consequence of such information given by the accused, the police and non-police witnesses together corroborate the facts. Logically, there appeared to be no scope nor any reason why the transactions could not be established in this case. But when it came to the proceedings in the court and the connected legal gymnastics, dozens of loopholes were pointed out and the case appeared to go to pieces.

16

Charge Sheet in the Trial Court Revisited

The charge sheet in this case was filed by Inspector Jagdish Meena, the SHO of Police Station Mehrauli, through SPP Suresh K. Saxena, on 3 August 1999 in the court of Metropolitan Magistrate V.K. Khanna. From there, the case was committed to the Sessions Court for trial. Along with the charge sheet, seventy-four documents running into hundreds of pages and nine articles including the piece of lead recovered from Jessica's brain; the bloodstained shirt of the manager at Qutub Colonnade; seized documents of Manu Sharma's Tata Safari, Tony Gill's Tata Sierra and Amit Jhingan's Gypsy, besides details of the mobile phones and the cartridges, were submitted.

First, the charge sheet filed pinpointed the names of the two main accused persons—Sidharth Vashisht alias Manu Sharma and Vikas Yadav—who were already in judicial custody. Second, it mentioned seven other persons, namely, Amardeep Singh Gill alias Tony, Alok Khanna, Amit Jhingan, Shyam Sunder Sharma, Harvinder Chopra, Ruby Gill and Yograj Singh, who were all on bail. Third, it mentioned three other persons as accused—Ravinder Sudan alias Teetu, Dhanraj and Raja Chopra; all of them were absconding and were wanted persons. A list of 131 witnesses was also enclosed, the last two witnesses being the Chief Investigation Officer Inspector Surender Sharma and the SHO of Police Station Mehrauli, Inspector Jagdish Meena.

The manner in which a charge sheet has to be filed is provided in Section 173 of the CrPC. The charge sheet has to be filed in the competent court having jurisdiction over the area where the crime has taken place. It has to be a simple affair, with not too many details about the evidence collected by the investigators, most of which is often not admissible under the Indian Evidence Act as it consists of the statements or confessions made before a police officer.

The charge sheet is a bare account of the facts and circumstances and the basic evidence to prima facie establish the offences and charges made out in the FIR or revealed during the investigation. Like the FIR, which remains the basic document for any cognisable crime in several police organisations like the Delhi Police, the charge sheet is drafted with caution and clarity and, if possible, with brevity. The CrPC also lays down a time period within which the charge sheet has to be filed in the court.

The filing of a brief charge sheet is in keeping with the provisions of the CrPC and the Indian Evidence Act. But I often found that such a basic document, with inadequate evidence and material, is highly unsupportive during the trial.

My experience in the CBI was very different. The charge sheets and supporting documents filed by the CBI often ran into hundreds and thousands of pages. These kinds of submissions for trial are now being followed by different police and investigating organisations, including the Delhi Police.

The main charge sheet in the Jessica Lal case was less than thirteen pages, which included nearly two-and-a-half pages of the cover and index page and the FIR. It was subjected to an intense scrutiny, rarely done in most charge sheets. The verbatim reproduction of the FIR in the charge sheet, which was the statement of Shayan Munshi recorded during the night at Aashlok Hospital that disclosed an attempt to murder (under Section 307 IPC) Jessica Lal at Qutub Colonnade, got converted into a murder case (under Section 302 IPC) following her death the next morning.

The charge sheet was filed under different sections of IPC, namely, 302, 201, 212, 120(b)/34 and under Sections 27,54 and 59 of the Arms Act, that is, murder, causing disappearance of evidence and giving false information to screen the offender of a capital offence, harbouring an offender of a capital offence, criminal conspiracy and common intention to commit offence of murder, the use of firearm to commit an offence and so on.

Under the law, nothing is allowed to be changed or improved upon after this document is filed. The exception is when the police decides to conduct further investigations with additional evidence and puts up more charges. Another exception is if the police wants to arrest additional accused persons with adequate evidence that could result in further trial. Section 173(8) CrPC empowers the officer-in-charge (SHO) of the police station to obtain further oral and documentary evidence, beyond what is filed in the charge sheet, and file it before the magistrate under Section 173(2) CrPC, based on which the magistrate takes cognisance. Police officers senior to the SHO in hierarchy are empowered under CrPC and the Police Act(s) and Rules to exercise all powers including the investigation and submission of the final reports to the magistrate, to be forwarded through them under general or special orders of the state government.

In the Jessica Lal case, we had the opportunity to conduct further investigations and file a supplementary charge sheet had we been able to collect more evidence regarding the weapon and the highly suspicious ballistic report prepared by the CBI's CFSL. This report was absolutely contrary to the facts, circumstances and the eyewitness accounts of people connected directly to the scene of the crime.

A supplementary charge sheet could have been filed by the Crime Branch of Delhi Police following an independent investigation by them under the orders of the Commissioner of Police Ajay Raj Sharma since he had been formally apprised through a detailed report of 1999. No further investigation was carried out regarding an obviously incorrect ballistic report, and the charge sheet filed by the police on 3 August 1999 remained the basic document to be contested by the prosecution and defence, besides the entire legal wrangling.

The charge sheet did mention that those who tried to help the main accused Manu Sharma and who in turn became accused, were all influential people backed by their high level of power, position and money. Accused Shyam Sunder Sharma, who was the uncle of the main accused Manu Sharma, was an industrialist and son-in-law of former President of India, Shankar Dayal Sharma; another accused Harvinder Chopra was a chartered accountant in the Piccadily group of industries; the third accused Vikas Gill alias Ruby Gill was the managing director of Punjab Biotech Sugar Ltd, Lalru, Chandigarh; and the fourth accused, Yograj Singh, was an actor in Punjabi films, a former Ranji cricketer and the father of the Indian national cricket team member, Yuvraj Singh.

It was also established that the absconding accused Teetu had met Manu Sharma's uncle Shyam Sunder Sharma and had told him about the possession of the weapon of offence used in the murder. Shyam Sunder Sharma had sent ₹ 70,000 to him and asked him to go to USA. Teetu, an American national, left for USA on 4 May 1999, on a Gulf Air flight.

The suspected murder weapon was a .22 pistol owned by Manu Sharma. It was an Italy-made P-Beretta Number B 56943U and registered in his name vide gun licence number 193/New/DM/CH/98. He had bought it on 31 January 1999, just a few months earlier. The licence also stated that he had bought 25 rounds of .22 bore cartridges from Sonu Gun House, 7 Club Market, Karnal. The evidence we had linking Manu Sharma to Jessica Lal's shooting included the two empties of .22 bore cartridges found at the scene of crime and the live cartridge recovered from Manu Sharma's Tata Safari which were also of .22 bore. All of them had the English letter 'C' inscribed at the bottom. The weapon of offence could not be recovered despite the best efforts but was proved to be owned by Manu Sharma, and circumstantially connected to the NRI Ravinder Sudan alias Teetu, who had absconded and escaped to USA.

During investigation, as per our case, it was established beyond doubt that Sidharth Vashisht alias Manu Sharma, Amardeep Singh Gill alias Tony, Vikas Yadav, Amit Jhingan, Alok Khanna, Shyam Sunder Sharma, Harvinder Chopra, Yograj Singh, Vikas Gill alias Ruby Gill, Raja Chopra, Ravinder Sudan alias Teetu and Dhanraj (the driver who was handed over Manu's Tata Safari vehicle, replaced the broken windowpane, drove the vehicle and finally abandoned it in Noida), had conspired together at Delhi, Manali, Chandigarh and other places in April–May 1999 with the intention of committing the murder of Jessica Lal, destroying evidence in the case, shielding the offenders knowing fully well that they had committed this crime, providing them with shelter and harbouring Manu Sharma. Under this criminal conspiracy, they committed several offences, as acts of commission and omission, we charged.

The investigations of the circumstances, the statements made by witnesses and the presence of Vikas Yadav, Amardeep Singh Gill, Alok Khanna and Amit Jhingan along with Manu Sharma at the time of crime and also soon after that incident, and their deliberate attempt to destroy the evidence related to the case, all established the offences against them. Similarly, Manu Sharma's uncle Shyam Sunder Sharma joined the conspiracy to destroy the evidence, besides actively associating in the escape from India of Ravinder Sudan, who was primarily responsible for the disappearance of the weapon of offence. Similarly, accused Yograj Singh directly helped Manu Sharma in his escape and also harboured him, as did the accused Harvinder Chopra and Vikas Gill. The role of Vikas Yadav's driver Dhanraj who took charge of Manu's Tata Safari from Vikas on 30 April itself, changed the broken windowpane and abandoned the vehicle in

Noida, was very significant. He was made to disappear by the accused persons, being declared an absconder and proclaimed offender while being charge sheeted.

In conclusion, in the charge sheet, Manu Sharma and eleven other accused persons were charged under Section 120B read with 302, 201 and 212 IPC. Manu Sharma was charged under Sections 302, 201 of IPC and 27, 54 and 59 of the Arms Act, being substantive offences. His co-accused Amardeep Singh Gill alias Tony Gill, Alok Khanna, Vikas Yadav and Amit Jhingan were also charged for substantive offences under Section 302 IPC besides Sections 201, 212, 34 IPC. The other accused persons, Shyam Sunder Sharma, Yograj Singh, Vikas Gill, Harvinder Chopra, Ravinder Sudan and Dhanraj were charged for substantive offences under Section 212 IPC. Sidharth Vashisht alias Manu Sharma and Vikas Yadav were produced in the court in judicial custody; the other accused persons were produced on bail, and non-bailable warrants were issued against the three absconding accused persons named in the charge sheet—Ravinder Sudan, Dhanraj and Raja Chopra.

17

Titans in the High Court: Justice Sodhi, Gopal and Ram

The verdict on 21 February 2006 by Judge Sunder Lal Bhayana acquitting all the accused was not acceptable to anybody except the accused persons, the conspirators, abettors and the lawyers who demolished our investigation in the court. At that time, every minute detail and development of the case was in the public domain.

The media, either because of their interest in increasing its popularity with viewers, that is, TRP (television rating points), or because of its role as the fourth estate and an integral wing of democracy, responded with a tirade against the verdict and our investigation became fully embroiled in it. There were candlelight marches, a new trend of lodging such protests, held in different parts of the country, demanding 'Justice for Jessica'.

Star TV did a sting operation in which the hostile witnesses and others assisting them were totally exposed and the stand of the defence counsel, who was the country's leading lawyer—the irrepressible Ram Jethmalani—was completely disproved in the public eye. Barkha Dutt, a leading journalist from NDTV, did incessant reporting and held public meetings. The 'Justice for Jessica' movement grew rapidly. My own story—the factual and authentic version of the police case—however, did not get any attention.

It was a pity that I and my team were facing a self-destructive counter-investigation being carried out by our own colleagues, fanned by a public trial in the media, for our suspectedly 'irresponsible and dubious role' in the investigation of the case. But my convictions held firm and I believed that the High Court would fully vindicate us, establishing that the investigation done by us was foolproof, sincere and efficient.

It was obvious that the evidence getting manipulated or the witnesses becoming hostile were not within our control or even within our legal powers to manage. This was what I had been highlighting throughout—that our criminal justice system provided such loose loopholes to the wrongdoers so that they easily managed to escape justice and completely avoid punishment. This case was even more disturbing. I and my team were not only being blamed for doing substandard work, we were also being charged for letting the accused free themselves from the clutches of the justice system.

My decision to take charge of the case, even though I was far away in Itanagar, was based on all this. Of course, I had to figure out the practical aspects, too. I needed to be either on leave or do this work parallelly while remaining posted at Arunachal Pradesh. But I needed to visit Delhi frequently to fight the trial in the High Court as well as the investigation targeting our team and SPP Saxena.

Amidst the public outcry that followed the Trial Court judgement, my decision proved to be very fruitful. I realised for the first time how our functioning democracy manifested its strength by giving weightage to even informal steps and genuine hard work if it was all done for bringing out the truth.

At Delhi and at Arunachal, I worked relentlessly, mostly unofficially, to support the investigators and the prosecutors, now led by ASG Gopal Subramanium, and clear my own and my team's name.

The support of some of my colleagues in the police department, some important public figures including those in the media, a few top lawyers, and most importantly Gopal Subramanium, who agreed to take up our case in the High Court, started bearing fruit. A number of friends in the media, who had earlier turned a deaf ear and closed their eyes over the sorry state of affairs, started taking interest. Informally, our team led by SPP Suresh Saxena prepared the case which was accepted by the legal team of Delhi Police, appreciating the need for an appeal against Justice Bhayana's judgement. In any case, the entire facts and evidence of the case were all over—from Police Headquarters to Delhi Government which controlled the prosecution department and to the union home ministry. The High Court, having taken suo motu cognisance, went into all the aspects of the case including the efforts made by us, ultimately vindicating our stand and accepting our submissions.

The media reported every step in detail, including the self-goals by the Delhi Police team by finding fault in their own case in an attempt to malign us. In a way, under the close scrutiny of the media which had generated an intense public debate, and the scrutiny of the High Court, our resilient democracy showed its supremacy over all institutions.

Led by the brilliant ASG Gopal Subramanium, it was decided to file an appeal in the High Court against Justice Bhayana's judgement. The appeal would be based entirely upon the evidence already collected by us during the investigation and produced in the Trial Court. This appeal was automatically put on a fast-track mode. It would be worthwhile to partly reproduce the relevant proceedings and the judgement delivered by the High Court Bench led by Justice R.S. Sodhi which summarises the cogent and most effective arguments advanced by ASG Subramanium:

> Challenging the correctness of the judgement under appeal, Shri Gopal Subramanium, learned Additional Solicitor General, argued that the judgement under challenge is

self-destructive, contradictory and omits to appreciate the evidence on record as also a misread evidence.

In support of his contention, learned Additional Solicitor General pointed out that the Court agrees with the Prosecution to the effect that Sidhartha Vashisht @ Manu Sharma was holder of a licensed pistol of .22 bore; that the Tata Safari car No. CH-01-W-6535 was registered in the name of Piccadily Agro Industries Pvt. Ltd., Chandigarh, of which accused Sidharth Vashisht was one of the directors; that Amardeep Singh Gill was allotted the Tata Sierra car bearing registration No. HR- 26-H-4348; that Amardeep Singh Gill was having mobile phone No. 9811100237, Alok Khanna was having mobile phone No. 9811068169 given by Hindustan Coca-Cola Company and that telephone No. 3782072 was installed at the residence of D.P. Yadav, father of Vikas Yadav, and that telephone Nos. 4765152-53 were installed at the Sugar Mill owned by Piccadily Agro Industries Limited of which Sidhartha Vashisht @ Manu Sharma and Harvinder Chopra were directors at the relevant time; that Beena Ramani owned the restaurant 'Once Upon a Time' and she was running a cafe named 'Tamarind Court Café' at Qutub Colonnade at the relevant time and that on 29.4.1999 a private party was going on at the said restaurant which was a regular Thursday party when liquor was served in the restaurant; that the accused Sidhartha Vashisht @ Manu Sharma, along with the co-accused Amardeep Singh Gill, Alok Khanna and Vikas Yadav, was present at the said party at Tamarind Court Cafe on the night of the occurrence when someone fired a shot at Jessica Lal as a result of which she received injuries on the head.

She was removed to Aashlok Hospital from where she was removed to Apollo Hospital and declared 'brought dead'. The body was transferred to the All India Institute of Medical Sciences where postmortem was conducted by Dr. R.K.

> Sharma who opined that the cause of death was head injury caused by fire arm and it was sufficient to cause death in the ordinary course of nature.

Likewise, the judge took cognisance of all the leads in the lodged documents which the prosecution had pursued and the facts which the first investigation team of Delhi Police supervised by me had found out. The judge relied upon the testimony of the witness Deepak Bhojwani, who had stated that Jessica Lal and Shayan Munshi were serving liquor on that night at the bar counter.

The judge said:

> Learned Additional Solicitor General argued that the Prosecution has been able to prove that Sidhartha Vashisht @ Manu Sharma, Amardeep Singh Gill, Alok Khanna and Vikas Yadav were present at the spot of incidence on the night of 29/30.4.1999, their identities having been fixed. . . In other words, the Prosecution has been able to bring home the guilt of the accused beyond shadow of doubt.

The judge also stated:

> Learned Additional Solicitor General submitted that the basis of the judgement of acquittal is clearly erroneous, perverse and deserves to be set aside . . .

The ASG had also stated that this was a case where a host of prosecution witnesses became hostile at the instance and suspected efforts of the defence, which had introduced false evidence into the case from the witnesses who had turned hostile and that the defence had even gone on to tamper with judicial records. The Trial Court should have seen through the game of the defence rather than, with a single stroke, paint the prosecution as the villain of having set up a false case against Manu Sharma.

Rebutting the prosecution's submissions while supporting the Trial Court judgement, the country's leading lawyer Ram Jethmalani along with R.K. Naseem, another leading criminal lawyer of Delhi, as the defence counsels for Manu Sharma, pitched the same facts and evidence already presented by the ASG Gopal Subramanium in the High Court but portrayed them differently. Ram Jethmalani and his supporting lawyers presented the narratives in such a manner that all of us who were so authentically comprehensive in our work, righteous and truthful, appeared to be not only foolishly wrong but also the culprits.

In the light of the detailed arguments so convincingly advanced by ASG Subramanium, it was really interesting to see how Jethmalani twisted them and presented them in a totally different light. Jethmalani's high level of pleading capacity as the country's leading advocate was very good, but unfortunately, it was all used for negative purposes. He was trying to save a group whose names had been on the top in the world of crime. Jethmalani's steps were beautifully recorded by Justice Sodhi in his judgement from which, ultimately, real justice emerged, giving us victory. Here is another quote from Justice Sodhi's judgement about Ram Jethmalani's court manoeuvrings:

> Arguing on behalf of the accused, Sidhartha Vashisht @ Manu Sharma, Shri Ram Jethmalani, learned Senior Advocate, submitted that Manu Sharma was not present at the Qutub Colonnade on 29/30.4.1999. He submitted that there is nothing to prove the presence of Manu Sharma at the spot of occurrence and that the witnesses PW-1, PW-5, PW-6 and PW-19 do not, in any manner, show that they knew the accused and their testimonies cannot be used by the Prosecution to take advantage to fix the presence of

the accused at the spot of occurrence specially when PW-1 already stands stamped as a 'planted witness'.

He submitted that PW-1, Deepak Bhojwani's statement is filled with improvements and contradictions besides the fact that his statement was recorded at a very late stage, the same does not inspire confidence and cannot be relied upon. PW-6, Malini Ramani, has been discussed by the trial court in paragraphs 278 and 292 of the judgement. The findings are justified from the material on record. In addition, he submitted that this witness fainted on hearing that Jessica Lal had been hit and cannot, therefore, be a witness of the occurrence. He also submitted that this witness along with her parents was under extreme Police pressure. She had been interrogated intensely for five days, the photographs were shown to her, the Police had made her to sign statements and put psychological pressure on her, as such was a pliable witness for the Prosecution but not a reliable witness for the Court.

A false excise case was registered to keep the pressure alive during deposition which was subsequently got decided with a paltry fine. Counsel submitted that impermissible leading questions were put to this witness as regards identification which cannot be used as evidence. In any event, this witness was too drunk since she had been drinking from the start up to the finish of the party. She can hardly be expected to remember anything of importance.

From the testimony of PW-2, Shayan Munshi, PW-3, Shiv Dass Yadav and PW-4, Karan Rajput, it is clear that nobody saw Manu Sharma at the place of incidence nor did anybody see Manu Sharma using fire arm to fire two shots let alone to fire the shot that killed Jessica Lal. None of these witnesses were eye witnesses to the occurrence but are witnesses of prior and subsequent events.

PW-2, Shayan Munshi, clearly states that two different people fired from two different weapons. His statement made to the police which is stated to be the FIR was never dictated by him nor read over to him as it was in Hindi, a language not known to him. Counsel submitted that the statement of the witness sought to be used by the Prosecution to establish the guilt of the accused is hit by Section 162 Cr.P.C. since the witnesses were made to sign their statements. The evidentiary value, therefore, has been impaired considerably and cannot be used as pure evidence. Counsel submitted that an atmosphere of prejudicial hate had been created to implicate Manu Sharma while the actual culprits successfully managed to divert the investigation to a wrong direction and escaped.

The theory of two persons having fired two bullets was deliberately abandoned by the Police itself. He submitted that the charge, as framed, is under Section 302 IPC, but when there is a possibility of two bullets being fired by two different persons, there is no certainty that the bullet that killed Jessica Lal was fired by Manu Sharma. He could not, therefore, be convicted under Section 302 IPC. He contended that Beena Ramani was not present in the party. This is evident from the site plan where Beena Ramani has not been shown. Relying upon PW-4, PW-6 and PW-47, counsel submitted that these Prosecution witnesses are not hostile. From their statements it is evident that Beena Ramani did not see the shooting.

Counsel further went on to submit that the Prosecution has failed to prove that the fatal bullet was in possession of the accused, Manu Sharma, at 2.00 a.m. on 29/30.4.1999. The Prosecution has not been able to get rid of the fact that there were two persons who fired two bullets. Even otherwise, there is no proof that Manu Sharma fired the fatal bullet. The FIR based on the statement of Shayan Munshi cannot be treated as an FIR. His statement was got signed by the Police and is hit by Section 162(2) Cr.P.C. He submitted that the Police has manufactured evidence after investigation up to the date of trial. PW-1 had stated that he had told the Police that Manu Sharma was the killer but his statement was recorded on the 14.5.1999, the long delay is fatal. This witness has made 21 improvements. He is known to the deceased and has every reason to make a false statement. In any event, he was too drunk on the date of the occurrence to be a meaningful witness.

There has been a dishonest attempt by the Prosecution to improve the case against Manu Sharma by introduction of PW-1 whose statement lacks independent corroboration. He fully supports the statement of PW-2, Shayan Munshi who, counsel submitted, cannot be relied upon by the Prosecution but the accused has every right to rely upon the same since it was not put to the accused in his statement under Section 313 Cr.P.C. that the motive attributed is inadequate and is of much higher intent and intensity. Shayan Munshi clearly states that two shots were fired by two different persons and there is no reason to disbelieve this witness who finds support from the ballistic evidence, Ex. PW-89/DA. Counsel also went on to submit that the Prosecution has been dishonest and unfair in trying to withhold evidence of the ballistic expert, Roop Singh, which had to be brought on record by the accused who made an application to that effect in the Court. Even the ballistic expert produced by the Prosecution has clearly stated that the two empties examined appear to have been fired from two different fire arms. From the opinion of the expert and the statement of Shayan Munshi, it is not possible for this Court to go against the finding that two persons had fired two shots.

According to the counsel, from the testimony of PW-23, Rouble Dunglay, it is clear that the whole story of non serving liquor being the motive of the crime is a concoction. Jessica Lal died not because she did not give what she did not have, but did not give what she had which had hurt the manhood

> of the assailant. The Prosecution must necessarily succeed as of late and cannot be allowed to create a new one [sic]. Counsel categorically stated that there is nothing on record to show that Manu Sharma fired a shot, there is evidence which discloses that two persons fired shot and one of them had fired a shot in the air. Nobody saw Manu Sharma firing the fatal shot. In any event, Manu Sharma was not there nor did he need a drink. Shayan Munshi is a reliable witness who states that Manu Sharma was not the one who fired a shot in the open.

According to the counsel, Bina Ramani and her husband Mailhot too could not prove that Manu Sharma had fired the fatal shot at the deceased. The evidence was there that Bina Ramani was with the people who took Jessica Lal to the hospital. Counsel Jethmalani also argued that:

> A photograph of Manu Sharma was taken by the Police from the Farmhouse of his father. It was here that his pistol and ammunitions were also taken into possession but no recovery memo was made. This was deliberately done to implicate Manu Sharma in this case.

According to Jethmalani, this clearly showed that the investigation team had deliberately cooked up a false case against Manu Sharma and there remained a question as to whether it was a licensed gun of Manu Sharma used to kill Jessica Lal or some other weapon registered in someone else's name.

The learned lawyer, the late Shri Ram Jethmalani, had a knack of twisting and turning facts and he was the master of the artistry of court proceedings. As a lawyer, he was a winner most of the time. However, the common public understood very well that Jethmalani and his associate lawyers, on the basis of numerous hostile witnesses and concocted defence evidence, had attempted to get the truth killed and establish falsehood. Although in the High Court our case was entirely based upon the evidence collected and presented by our team, the success was attributed to vox-populi, the triumph of democracy—the people were bigger than individuals. The High Court took an early cognisance of the appeal against Justice Bhayana's judgement in view of the widespread public outcry for getting Jessica Lal justice, but it ultimately relied entirely upon the facts and evidence on record.

The loopholes in the criminal justice system of India can be used to manipulate a case and facts can be managed to obtain any result, wrong or right, from the purest platform of virtue and justice. Fortunately, our higher judiciary is one of the biggest saviours for the citizens of the country.

Justice Sodhi's judgement, which came on 18 December 2006, was entirely based on the evidence produced by us during our investigation—in the appeal not even a word could have been added to it—and so meticulously and forcefully presented by ASG Gopal Subramanium. The judgement, which was subsequently fully endorsed by the Supreme Court, completely vindicated our investigation and our bonafides which had been absurdly and mischievously attacked by our own colleagues within Delhi Police.

Justice Sodhi not only saw through the game being played to protect Manu Sharma and the destruction of evidence by his co-accused, but he also clearly brought out the conspiracy to destroy the case itself at every stage by the high-and-mighty. Interestingly, the entire evidence relied upon by the High Court was exactly the same which was distorted and misrepresented, even put to the second self-destructive investigation against me and my team by the reigning top cops of Delhi Police. Throwing all that away, disagreeing with erudite Senior Advocate Jethmalani, even passing serious strictures against Judge Bhayana and the machinations of Delhi Police, while agreeing with ASG Gopal Subramanium, Justice Sodhi and Justice P.K. Bhasin concluded:

> In the totality of circumstances adduced from material on record, the judgement under challenge appears to us to be an immature assessment of material on record which is self-contradictory, based on misreading of material and unsustainable. We find that Beena Ramani has identified Sidhartha Vashisht @ Manu Sharma, Amardeep Singh Gill, Alok Khanna and Vikas Yadav to be the persons present at the Tamarind Cafe at the time of the incidence. She also saw Manu Sharma firing the fatal shot which hit Jessica Lal. Her testimony finds corroboration from the testimony of Malini Ramani and Georges Mailhot. There is evidence on record to show that Manu Sharma had a licensed pistol of .22 bore which he has not produced to establish his innocence and on the contrary has taken false plea that the pistol, its ammunition and license had been removed by the Police on 30.4.1999.
>
> We also find from the material on record that Manu Sharma abandoned his vehicle while making good his escape. We also find that the ammunition used in the causing of the firearm injury to Jessica Lal was of .22 bore which Manu Sharma admittedly possessed and a similar live cartridge was recovered from the abandoned Tata Safari. From this, we have no hesitation in holding that Manu Sharma is guilty of an offence under Section 302 IPC for having committed the murder of Jessica Lal on 29/30.4.1999 at the Tamarind Cafe as also under Section 27 Arms Act.
>
> Coming to the case put up by the Prosecution as regards Vikas Yadav and Amardeep Singh Gill, we have noted above that both these accused were present at the Tamarind Cafe when Manu Sharma caused firearm injuries to Jessica Lal. These two persons subsequently were seen by PW-30 Sharvan Kumar, coming in a white Tata Sierra driven by Amardeep Singh Gill from which Vikas Yadav alighted and

surreptitiously removed the Tata Safari which was being guarded by Sharvan Kumar.

The very fact that Vikas Yadav removed the Tata Safari from Qutub Colonnade is sufficient to bring home his guilt under Section 201 IPC since he and Amardeep Singh Gill, both knowing that an offence has been committed at the Tamarind Cafe by Manu Sharma caused the Tata Safari, which is part of the evidence, to be removed with an intention to screening Manu Sharma. From these circumstances it is evident that the Tata Safari was removed from outside Qutub Colonnade pursuant to a conspiracy between Vikas Yadav, Amardeep Singh Gill and Manu Sharma. Therefore, these three accused are guilty of having conspired to remove the Tata Safari from Qutub Colonnade and are held guilty under Section 201 read with Section 120B IPC.

As regards Shyam Sunder Sharma, he was charged for an offence under Section 212 IPC for harbouring Ravinder Krishan Sudan. We find there is no incriminating evidence to suggest that Shyam Sunder Sharma ever harboured Ravinder Krishan Sudan. Even otherwise, Ravinder Krishan Sudan has been declared a Proclaimed Offender and has not faced trial. This charge against Shyam Sunder Sharma cannot be sustained. Consequently we uphold his acquittal under Section 212 IPC as also 201 IPC and dismiss the appeal qua Shyam Sunder Sharma due to lack of evidence.

The case against Harvinder Chopra is that he arranged for the stay of Sidhartha Vashisht @ Manu Sharma at the house of PW-52, Chander Prakash Chopra, thereby committing an offence under Section 212 IPC. From the material on record, we find there is no evidence to suggest that Harvinder Chopra arranged for stay of Manu Sharma at the house of PW-52, Chander Prakash Chopra. Chander Prakash Chopra himself has not supported the Prosecution's case. We, therefore, find no evidence to convict Harvinder Chopra of the offence under Section 212 IPC. Consequently, we uphold his acquittal under Section 212 IPC and dismiss the appeal qua Harvinder Chopra.

The case against Yograj Singh is that he facilitated Sidhartha Vashisht @ Manu Sharma being taken to Khera, Muktsar in Punjab and harboured Sidhartha Vashisht @ Manu Sharma. To substantiate this case, the Prosecution examined PW-53, PW-64 and PW-65. We find that none of these witnesses have supported the Prosecution's case and there is no other evidence on record which suggests that Yograj Singh is guilty of harbouring Sidhartha Vashisht @ Manu Sharma at Khera in Muktsar (Punjab). Consequently we uphold his acquittal under Section 212 IPC and dismiss the appeal qua Yograj Singh.

The case against Vikas Gill was that he was charged for escorting Sidhartha Vashisht @ Manu Sharma to Panchkula between 30.4.1999 and 1.5.1999 and harboured him with the intention to screening him from legal punishment. We find from the record that there is no evidence to the effect that Vikas Gill took Sidhartha Vashisht @ Manu Sharma to Panchkula from Delhi and/or harboured him at any place. Consequently we uphold his acquittal under Section 212 IPC and dismiss the appeal qua Vikas Gill.

The case against Raja Chopra is that he provided a conveyance to Sidhartha Vashisht @ Manu Sharma within the meaning of Section 52A IPC in order to screen him from legal punishment. From the material on record we find no admissible evidence to substantiate the charge against this accused. Consequently we uphold his acquittal under Section 212 IPC and dismiss the appeal qua Raja Chopra.

As regards the case against Alok Khanna, he was charged under Section 120B read with Section 201 IPC for causing disappearance of Tata Safari from Qutub Colonnade. We find there is no evidence to link Alok Khanna with the conspiracy to remove or destroy evidence. No doubt, his car was used

> by Amardeep Singh Gill and Vikas Yadav to go to Qutub Colonnade to remove the Tata Safari, but this in itself is not sufficient to hold that Alok Khanna consented to or was a part of the conspiracy shared by Amardeep Singh Gill with Vikas Yadav to remove the Tata Safari from the Qutub Colonnade. In that view of the matter, we find that the Prosecution has not been able to bring home its case against Alok Khanna. The appeal qua Alok Khanna is dismissed.
>
> We may also note here that Ravinder Krishan Sudan and Dhanraj were declared Proclaimed Offender by the trial court. Their case is not before us.
>
> In the above analysis, while holding Sidharth Vashisht @ Manu Sharma guilty under Section 302 IPC for the murder of Jessica Lal as also under Section 27 Arms Act and Section 201/120B IPC, we also hold Amardeep Singh Gill and Vikas Yadav guilty for the offence punishable under Section 201 IPC/120B IPC while upholding the acquittal of the remaining respondents of the offences charged against them. Accused Sidharth Vashisht @ Manu Sharma, Vikas Yadav and Amardeep Singh Gill be taken into custody forthwith and lodged in Central Jail, Tihar. The appeal is disposed of in the above terms.

As a consequence of this judgement, Sidharth Vashisht served a life sentence in Tihar jail. Availing himself of various remissions, he was finally released in June 2020. Vikas Yadav and Amardeep Singh Gill each served four years of imprisonment. Jessica's soul must have received solace from the final verdict of the High Court, which was upheld by the Supreme Court, and its execution.

18

Retrospective Justice and Introspection

In retrospect, I feel sad that a large part of our evidence collected through truthful and meticulous investigation against the co-accused, who were party to the destruction of the evidence against Manu Sharma at every stage and who harboured and supported him throughout his escape following the crime when our teams were hot on his chase, couldn't be proved in the High Court. This was entirely on account of the system that permits, and even promotes, lies and falsehood to supress the truth. But with the conviction of Manu Sharma, the main culprit and his co-accused Vikas Yadav and Amardeep Singh Gill, justice triumphed, vindicating our honest and painstaking investigation and giving solace to Jessica's soul.

Although the Supreme Court fully endorsed the High Court judgement, perhaps to uphold the dignity of the higher judiciary, they decided to expunge some of the highly derogatory remarks about Trial Judge S.L. Bhayana, who had been elevated as a judge of the High Court within a few days of his delivery of the judgement on 21 February 2006.

The real issues, however, concerning the blatant abuse of our criminal justice process by offenders and their supporters in this case were partly addressed in the form of a much-delayed common judgement on 22 May 2013 delivered by Justices

Ravindra Bhat and G.P. Mittal and the proceedings initiated by the High Court.

The judges expressed their utter surprise that during the trial thirty-two witnesses including three eyewitnesses of the murder and the CBI ballistic expert turned hostile. They felt, 'That is definitely a sad state of affairs. Witnesses turning hostile appears to be the order of the day. The courts must put an end to this kind of attitude of witnesses turning hostile in order to thwart the course of justice.'

In the interest of justice, the Court directed action under Section 340 of the CrPC which deals with the procedure adopted by the courts for giving false evidence under oath and the penal provision, and also action for the offences committed under Section 195 of the IPC dealing with fabricated and false evidence to procure conviction of offence punishable with imprisonment ranging from seven years to life. The proceedings went on for years against the false-witnesses-turned-accused-persons like Shayan Munshi, Shiv Das Yadav, Karan Rajput, Andleep Sehgal, Ashok Dutt, Prem Sagar Manocha and others, partly vindicating our stand as well.

This case brought a new learning for me. I realised that there was immense power and force even in informal efforts if they were done to support truth and justice. While remaining posted in Arunachal, I visited Delhi innumerable times—on leave, on duty and even when summoned by my own junior and senior colleagues in Delhi Police, conducting a highly disruptive investigation against their own colleagues. Simultaneously, along with my team, I worked incessantly from an informal platform to strengthen the case in the High Court and set it on a path to victory.

When Jessica finally received justice, I also had a big relief for myself and my team, becoming free of all the false charges inflicted upon the investigation team. In my heart, I had the satisfaction of knowing that the hard work and sincere efforts put up by me and my team had not gone waste.

In my way of working and my approach towards my profession, my discomfort with the shortcomings of our criminal justice system continued to trouble me. I wanted to do everything to bring about changes that could plug the holes inherent in the system which give scope to injustice to reign and justice to get suppressed.

19

BMW Caused Bizarre Massacre

My alter ego talked to me constantly and made me restless to search for answers, just like 'Betaal' in the stories of Vikram and Betaal (King Vikramaditya and the Ghost) which we read in our childhood.

One day, my alter ego said, 'You mentioned the BMW hit-and-run case as another typical example of the collapse of the criminal justice system. You feel that the manipulations done by some very senior and reputed law practitioners in this case were even worse than those done by the so-called learned lawyers in the Jessica Lal case. Incidentally, one very senior lawyer defending the accused was common in both the cases. But in terms of the legal jigsaw and wranglings, the BMW case was even murkier because it had a host of senior lawyers defending the accused.'

In the BMW case, it was unprecedented that two so-called legal luminaries defending the accused resorted to such nasty and demeaning practices that the Supreme Court took cognisance and debarred them for a few months from practising law. It was a shame on the entire legal community of India. It became an example to be quoted in perpetuity.

When the phone on my bedside rang at six-thirty on that extremely cold Sunday morning, I knew intuitively that it was not a routine call. The date was 10 January 1999 and, as

I remember, in the quietness of the morning, the shrill ringing of the phone echoed in the whole house—my official residence at Satya Marg, Chanakyapuri, New Delhi. The morning crime and law-and-order briefings used to be given to me by my three district DCPs by about 8 AM every day, though Sundays and holidays were a bit easy. So that early morning call could not possibly be a routine one.

As joint commissioner of the eventful South Delhi Range that covered nearly half of Delhi including South, South-West and West districts of the NCT, every morning I had a lot to report to my meticulous and highly professional senior, Police Commissioner Virendra Narain (VN) Singh, an officer also known for his aristocratic lineage. Out of habit, before making the phone call, I would jot down all the points given by my officers in my Delhi Police Diary that I kept by my bedside.

I don't recall who called me first, the PCR or South Delhi Control or DCP South Pradeep Srivastava. But the information which was urgently intimated was terrible and quite disturbing. My mind started running as to what all had to be done immediately. It appeared to be one of the ghastliest hit-and-run cases by a car in memory. Several persons had been killed. I call the killing a 'massacre' because that is what it was by character—six people, including three policemen, ruthlessly mowed down by a speeding BMW car.

This became the notorious 'BMW Case' after the brand name of the killing machine involved. The initial reports said that early in the morning of 10 January 1999, between 4 and 4:30 AM, a big, black speeding car had broken through a police picket, killing the three policemen who were on duty as well as three other persons whom the policemen were checking, near the Lodhi Road crossing in Delhi. A seventh person was badly injured. Several PCR vans had rushed to the spot within minutes and taken the injured and the dead to the AIIMS hospital.

'Where are you going?' Rekha, my wife, asked sleepily as I got out of bed to get dressed quickly.

'Lodhi Road,' I replied mechanically, debating in my mind whether to call my boss right away or do a spot assessment and then call. I decided to call immediately, given the Commissioner's desire to be told of major events in real time. I sat on the bed again and dialled his residence.

Rekha woke up on hearing me talking on the phone. A gentle, God-fearing person, she was shocked to hear of the incident and helped me get ready quickly.

I reached Police Station Lodhi Colony only a little before the Police Commissioner—my home was closer to the site. So I was there to receive him when he came in. The SHO, Lady Inspector Vimlesh Yadav, who was at the police station at night like most other SHOs, was waiting there along with Assistant Commissioner Mahadev Mehta and DCP Pradeep Srivastava. Pradeep was accompanied by the Additional DCPs attached to him—Vivek Gogia and R.S. Ghumman. Pradeep and Vivek had reached the accident spot while it was still dark and came to the police station after that. SHO Yadav gave a detailed account of the incident.

Inspector Jagdish Pandey from the PCR, who had also rushed to the spot after hearing the news flashed on the police system, informed us about the crucial and concrete lead he had followed. He said, 'Sir, by hitting the barricade hard, the vehicle got damaged. There was an oil leak. I followed the trail of the oil leak. It ended at house number 50, Golf Links.'

Golf Links—those familiar with Delhi will know this place—was one of the poshest residential areas in the capital. The main road on which it was located was called Archbishop Makarios Marg.

'Vivek and I have already visited the house,' said Pradeep at this point. 'We found that a car that looked like having been involved in an accident was parked there. It had been freshly washed, which indicated some untoward event and looked fishy.'

He said that SI Kailash Chand, a rookie cop, was the Night Emergency Officer that day at the police station. He was the first person to investigate the scene of crime. 'Kailash had promptly carried out a thorough investigation of the spot of the crime and had found some vital evidence,' said Pradeep.

Thanks to the methodical, minute and meticulous investigation of the place of the crime carried out by SI Kailash Chand, we soon had crucial, telltale evidence of the incident like broken pieces of the temporary registration number plate and some other details about the car. The findings matched the vehicle found parked at 50, Golf Links.

A boy from Shamli, a small town in Western UP (Uttar Pradesh), SI Kailash Chand had no family pedigree of police service, nor did he have much experience in investigations. But his meticulous work and serious-minded devotion to duty was a critical factor in this case.

When he was woken up from his cosy slumber while in his makeshift bed at Police Station Lodhi Colony at 4:40 AM, he had no idea about the horrifying and macabre scene he would soon confront. Lady Constable Anita from the PCR was the first person who had informed the police station about the accident near the Car Care Centre Petrol Pump on Lodhi Road near Lodhi Hotel.

The FIR and the police station Daily Diary were subsequently registered with offences under Sections 304 (culpable homicide not amounting to murder) and 338 (causing grievous hurt endangering human life), based on a *rukka* (the first report of a crime by the police officer on the spot) sent to the SHO by the officer-complainant from the site. Kailash Chand's *rukka* contained the crucial details which later became the basis of a massive and prolonged defence scrutiny and the material for powerful and attacking arguments in all the esteemed courts by some of the country's most eminent lawyers, including Ram Jethmalani.

When I arrived at the police station, the details of the case as given by Kailash Chand to his seniors were explained to me. The BMW car with the number M-312 LYP was said to be driven at extremely high speed. It was coming from Hazrat Nizamuddin side on Lodhi Road and going towards the Safdarjung monument. It rammed full throttle into a group of seven persons standing there, on the left side of the road near the Car Care Centre. Three persons died on the spot. The other four persons, who had been seriously injured, were rushed to AIIMS by PCR vans. The first PCR van had arrived at the spot even before SI Kailash Chand and his companion, Constable Jaganlal.

Those who died on the spot included the policemen—Home Guard Constable named Ramraj and a Central Reserve Police Force (CRPF) constable named, Rajan Kumar. Both were present there on a night-checking duty. The third dead person was unidentified at that time. He was about thirty-five years of age. The body of Constable Ramraj was found badly crushed. The gory accident scene was so horrendous that the investigators were shocked at its severity.

Ramraj's right leg had been found amputed and lying almost 10–15 feet away. The belly of Constable Rajan Kumar had burst open and blood flowed profusely, spreading all over the area. Investigator Kailash Chand found the broken number plate of the car which became the main clue to identify and locate the culprits. Over the number plate, the words 'Park Lane' and 'BMW' were written. A piece of a black car bumper and a rear-view mirror glass were also found on the spot, all spread in a circle as wide as 100–125 feet.

Even before I had reached the police station, Pradeep and his team had pieced together the trail of the culprit car and located it, while Kailash had found the linking evidence. The case had already been partly worked out. Inspectors Jagdish Pandey and Vimlesh Yadav had reached the house where the BMW car was parked inside and the gate was closed. When they peeped through the gap in the side hinge, they saw three persons, later identified as the houseowner Rajiv Gupta and his two staff Bhola Nath and Shyam Singh, washing the damaged car.

Pradeep and the team explained to me dramatically how, with considerable difficulty, the gate was opened to find the washed car covered with a tarpaulin. It did not have a number plate and was with a broken bumper and lights, all similar to the broken parts already recovered from the spot by SI Kailash Chand. A 'Park Lane' sticker was affixed in the car; it was the same kind as the one found from the accident spot. Despite the hurried washing of the vehicle, blood was still found on the rear left side wheel of the car. Later, some blood was found by forensic experts on the steering wheel of the vehicle as well, providing us with more evidence, which was subsequently developed and presented in the court.

Rajiv Gupta, a rich businessman with high-level contacts and who was later described as a 'man of several hundred crores' by his own lawyers in the court, was questioned by our team immediately after the discovery of the vehicle. He disclosed that the car belonged to Sanjeev Nanda, a friend of his son, Sidharth Gupta. Both of them had gone to the Defence Colony residence of Sanjeev Nanda. A police team was sent to Defence Colony and in no time Sanjeev Nanda along with his friends, Sidharth Gupta and Manik Kapoor, were taken into custody. The whole police team was amazed to learn that Sanjeev Nanda was the grandson of a national celebrity—the former Naval Chief Admiral Sardarilal Mathradas Nanda. Admiral Nanda lived in his house at Golf Links and out of his love for his grandson, tried to protect him. Admiral Nanda himself came forward to produce his grandson to the police.

As per the rule book, it had been already recorded that the accused not only committed a crime and like a coward fled from the scene, but also tried to destroy and erase the evidence by washing the car and hiding it in a house. When we first saw and met Sanjeev Nanda for investigation, his body language itself indicated he had committed a crime. With injuries on his lips and disoriented and sheepish behaviour, Sanjeev Nanda along with his two friends was produced before me. Police Commissioner V.N. Singh had already joined us at Police Station Lodhi Colony when the investigation was in progress. I observed that my calm and composed boss V.N. Singh, whom we always found to be very patient and unruffled, was extremely disturbed looking at the ghastly scene we had inspected.

The investigation progressed very well. It was supervised by the trio from South Delhi Police—Pradeep, Vivek and Ghumman. The work done by the investigating team was later praised by ASJ Vinod Kumar in his exhaustive judgement. As per rules, Sanjeev Nanda and his accomplices and also the only surviving victim of the accident, Manoj Malik, were medically examined at AIIMS. The medico-legal case (MLC) report of Sanjeev with the history of alcohol consumption prepared by Dr T. Milo in the Casualty of AIIMS, stated 'bilaterally dilated pupils, coherent speech and unsteady gait, smell of alcohol, blood clot in left nostril, lacerated wounds in upper and lower lips with swelling and blood clots'.

For reasons unknown, the blood sample of Sanjeev Nanda taken by the doctor was not sent to the Central Forensic Science Laboratory (CFSL), the independent agency that conducts scientific examination of the samples collected by the police, as late as 12 January. This delay later became the subject matter of a legal battle. The blood sample was, in any case, examined by Senior Scientific Officer cum Chemical Examiner Dr Madhulika Sharma. She reported the presence of 0.115 per cent weight/volume ethyl alcohol in Sanjeev's blood which was far beyond the permissible limit of 0.030 per cent as per the Motor Vehicles (MV) Act. Much later, during the trial, another blood sample of Sanjeev Nanda was taken and found to be B-positive. This could not be compared with the earlier putrefied sample which had been sent after a delay to the FSL and became an issue of an argument by the defence lawyers later in the court.

In the chain of scientific and forensic investigations, our team had called the fingerprint expert Nagesh Wadera to the house at Golf Links. He arrived by about 10 AM on 10 January and finding the car wet, he waited for some time and then lifted several fingerprints. The next day, when the vehicle was at the police station, Senior Scientific Officer D.S. Chakotra was called. He re-examined the vehicle minutely and found bloodstains on the steering wheel. All this scientific evidence clearly connected Sanjeev Nanda to the crime.

While I was at the police station along with the Police Commissioner V.N. Singh, the facts of the case were already falling in place under the guidance of the senior supervisory officials. We were finally told about the six dead persons, including Delhi Home Guards Ramraj and Perumal and the CRPF Constable Rajan Kumar, who were checking the passers-by on the road during their night duty. They were said to be standing very close to the footpath adjacent to the Car Care Centre Petrol Pump when the BMW car crashed into them.

The other three dead persons were identified. They were Mehandi Hasan, Nasir and Gulab, all residents of Darbhanga in Bihar. These poor, temporary workers were on their way to Nizamuddin Railway Station to catch a train, but became unfortunate victims of this ghastly tragedy. They were guests of the grievously injured Manoj Kumar, an employee at a dhaba (roadside eatery) belonging to Kailash Chand who lived near CGO Complex. All of them had been taken to AIIMS in the PCR vans which had arrived on the spot within minutes of the accident.

Obviously, SI Kailash Chand and his companion Constable Jagan Lal could not find a witness on the scene of crime. It was natural that in the early hours of a cold January morning, not many people would be on the road. However, we were fortunate to find two crucial witnesses connected to the scene. One was Hari Shankar Yadav, who was present at the Car Care Centre on his night duty. He was the one who rushed to the spot immediately on hearing the loud sound of the crash; but seeing the ghastly sight, he said he got frightened. Hari Shankar went back to the petrol pump and called his manager Brijesh Virmani on phone to inform him about the accident. Brijesh Virmani then called the PCR number 100 and gave the information about the incident.

The other most-important eyewitness was the seriously injured Manoj Malik, the victim who barely survived the accident. Somehow, despite multiple injuries, he remained conscious and talked while being carried in the PCR van to AIIMS. He gave details of the incident to the policemen in the PCR van, describing how, when he and his guests were going on foot to the railway station, they had been stopped by the police party and then all of them were hit by the speeding vehicle.

Whatever might have happened or was talked about in this much-criticised BMW case during the investigation and the prolonged trial which ran for nearly a decade, from the lowest Trial Court to the highest Supreme Court, all appreciated the good and effective investigation work done by Kailash Chand, an inexperienced and unassuming young sub-inspector. He worked sincerely while applying his acumen, and with his very limited resources, he handled a highly challenging case well.

The rough site plan prepared by him was quite good. In the document he mentioned point A to be near the left side footpath close to the Car Care Centre where the first impact of the speeding car occurred, leaving blood marks there. That was followed by point B which was near electric pole number 11 on the central road divider, showing marks of blood. He mentioned the area having blood marks as covered in 38 steps. He described skid marks of the car starting from point A leading to points

B, C and D. He described point C as a spot on the central road divider where there were friction marks of a tyre. In his report, point D was the spot where one dead body was found, with a leg amputated.

According to the description, another dead body was found at point E near electric pole number 12 on the central road divider (like pole 11) and the area around it had many marks of blood and tyre-drag. The third dead body was at point F, 26 steps away from point E, with blood and tyre-drag marks. An amputated leg was lying near electric pole number 13 at point G, which was 5 steps away from point F. He mentioned the evidence seen, found and collected from the spot—the pieces of car registration number, bumper and glass and, most importantly, the oil trail on Lodhi road pointing towards Safdarjung monument. This was all neatly recorded on the site plan and marked clearly.

The performance of the photographer, Constable Ramavtar from the DCP office, was also admirable. He efficiently photographed the scene of occurrence which corroborated and supported Kailash Chand's site plan and the *rukka*. He also videographed the entire process of investigation flawlessly. His video recording remarkably included the oil-leak trail found by the PCR Inspector Jagdish Pandey through which the vehicle causing the accident could be tracked. All processes were available in the form of video. They succeeded in recording perfectly admissible evidence and thus made the case so strong that it could later withstand the powerful assaults by leading criminal lawyers and the judicial scrutiny of the highest court.

Though the case against the accused was strong enough, all these findings with connecting material could become legal evidence only after the Motor Vehicle Expert Devinder Singh carefully inspected the scene of the crime, the items collected and the BMW car involved. He could neatly connect the findings and establish in the court that due to the accident, the steering oil of the BMW car leaked and the reserve in the container emptied out.

The police custody of a person starts from the time when a duly empowered police officer on official duty takes charge or detains a person, but certain laid-down legal formalities and documentation have to be completed to formalise this. Sanjeev Nanda had already been arrested, along with his friends who were present in the car on 10 January morning. He remained in police custody for the next twenty-four hours. On 11 January, he was produced before a metropolitan magistrate, who decided he should be in police remand for two more days for custodial investigations.

While in police remand, Sanjeev Nanda gave all the details of the accident and made several confessions and admissions, most of which were not admissible as evidence under the law. However, his statements helped the police in completing the investigations. His disclosures became the basis of the recovery of his bloodstained woollen sweater and jeans from his residence at D-108 Defence Colony. He was wearing these clothes at the time of the accident and that became the basis of establishing his connection with the crime vehicle and the crime.

A brand-new imported BMW car, with a temporary number M-312 LYP, without a registered number of India, would have been difficult to find, but for the clear, telltale lead from the scene of crime to the place it was found. Once found at the affluent Golf Links house of the rich businessman Rajiv Gupta, our team tracked and linked all the evidence and arrested Sanjeev Nanda, who was alleged to be driving the BMW car at the time of the accident. His friends, Sidharth (son of Rajiv Gupta) and Manik Kapoor were in the car at the time of the accident. The owner of the BMW car was found to be Ms Sonali Nanda,

Sanjeev Nanda's sister. She was the daughter of the super-rich businessman Suresh Nanda and the granddaughter of the celebrated Admiral S.M. Nanda.

Sonali Nanda lived in a posh locality, at 4, Prithviraj Road, from where her brother Sanjeev, as confirmed by the watchman, had taken Sonali's new BMW car the previous evening. The watchman referred to Sanjeev as 'Baba'. Sonali stayed with her wealthy father Suresh Nanda, who retired as a Lt Commander from the Indian Navy. He had taken premature retirement to start his business. He was the owner of a hotel-chain. He had also floated multiple companies, some of them dealing with arms, defence force vehicles, defence weapons and so on. He was later involved in several criminal litigations filed by the CBI.

Sanjeev's mother Renu Nanda, separated from her husband Suresh Nanda, lived in her relatively modest house at B-104 Defence Colony, supported by her father-in-law Admiral Nanda and his wife Sumitra. Sanjeev held a driving licence, acquired in the USA while studying there. He was on a visit to India when he got involved in this case and was arrested. While in India, he generally lived with his mother Renu Nanda, unlike his sister, Sonali, who lived with her father.

As required in the police rules and guidelines, being a heinous crime, the case was classified as a 'Special Report Crime', to be closely supervised by the senior officers of the district. Soon, it came under my purview and direct supervision. However, even before I had a direct role, it looked like the major part of the investigation had been completed and the crime had been solved. It appeared that, with competent investigators and seniors taking interest, after completing due processes, it would be filed in the court, and a judgement, in all likelihood, would be obtained through a final verdict, surely resulting in punishments to the culprits.

But suddenly, to my utter amazement, a peculiar man-made twist was brought about in the case. Though the case in its routine course had soon passed off from me, my attention and curiosity was aroused due to the mysterious entry of an intriguing character—Sunil Kulkarni—into the case. As it was later established, he was deliberately planted by the defence lawyers to deflect the case from its path of linear progression towards justice. A straightforward case being investigated by the local police, which had unfolded fully within hours due to the excellent work in tracking the crime vehicle and the perpetrator, suddenly transformed into a complex case which shook the people and the media for several years.

I was absolutely shocked when I found Manoj Malik, the only survivor of the accident, who had suffered so much and had lost his friends due to the accident, completely backing out in the court from his earlier statements. He was apparently bought over by the defence party. As available in the police records, Manoj had given a complete account to the police during the initial investigation itself since he was fully conscious and coherent immediately after the accident. His statement had been witnessed by all the members of the investigating police team and properly recorded.

It was on record that he had explained about his work at an eatery in the CGO Complex, run by a person named Kailash; he had narrated being stopped near the checkpost opposite the Car Care Centre Petrol Pump by the police party there while he was going to Nizamuddin Railway Station along with his friends Nasir, Mehandi Hasan and Gulab—all his friends had lost their lives in the accident. His statement was recorded under Section 161 CrPC. Deposition to the police was perfectly in order, supporting the prosecution case. The other witness, Hari Shankar Yadav, the worker at the petrol pump, had already turned hostile. The police had recordings of the statements of both the witnesses, but they were not admissible in the court proceedings.

I could sense some questionable oddities or silly oversights in the roles of the checkpost SHO Vimlesh Yadav and SI Ulhas Giri who had taken over the case from SI Kailash Chand.

The unexplainable surprise was the sudden replacement of SI Kailash Chand, who was performing his duties perfectly and so brilliantly. It was questionable why the SHO, Vimlesh Yadav, replaced him by SI Ulhas Giri in the middle of the investigation.

20

Lacklustre Charge Sheet and the Unfolding of the Case

SHO Vimlesh Yadav's charge sheet was something that left a lot to be desired. From the very beginning, her only significant roles were, first, that she was the SHO; and second, that she had gone along with Inspector Jagdish Pandey as a witness to follow the oil trail from the accident site to the Golf Links house where the damaged BMW car was found. As the SHO and hence the officer-in-charge of the Lodhi Colony police station, since she was legally required to do so, she presented the charge sheet in the court. This brief and sparsely drafted challan (that is, final report or charge sheet) was presented in the court on 7 April 1999 through her senior, Assistant Commissioner of Police Mahadev Mehta. Considering the huge media interest the case had already generated and contrary to expectations and the meticulous investigation, the charge sheet was a drab and lacklustre document.

There is always a lot of difference in the content and quality of charge sheets prepared by different agencies. The specialised police agencies like the Crime Branch or Special Units in the State police or the CBI prepare charge sheets with a professional touch in much greater detail as compared to local police stations. This creates a lot of difference in their treatment and appreciation.

The local police and some other police agencies who may have conducted excellent investigations and collected the most valuable admissible evidence, traditionally believe that the charge sheet of the case need not carry all the details. There is a school of police officers that believes that in its narrative, this basic document need not contain the material details except the mention of evidence they intend to rely upon during the trial like the list of witnesses and the material evidence whose actual appreciation has to be done by the prosecution and the Court during the trial.

In retrospect, I find this charge sheet written in Devanagari script and Urdu language in this momentous case to be somewhat casual despite an excellent detection, very fast collection of evidence and a reasonably good investigation. The supervisory officers, as per the prevailing practice, left this document in the hands of the juniors who followed the routine system, stating in the narrative column the concise details of the sections of law being applied, along with the FIR 17/99. The sections applied were 304, 338, 201, 34 IPC and 131, 132, 187 MV Act. There was a brief mention of the circumstances connected with them. The main offence against Sanjeev Nanda under Section 304 IPC along with his co-accused for other offences was 'culpable homicide not amounting to murder, committing the said acts with the intention to cause deaths'.

Sanjeev Nanda, the main accused, was produced before the Sessions Court in judicial custody (that is, while being in jail), whereas his other co-accused—Manik Kapoor, Sidharth Gupta and his father Rajiv Gupta, and their staff who had washed the car at 50, Golf Links, Bhola Nath, Shyam Singh Rana—were all charge sheeted while already released on bail. In all, sixty-six prosecution witnesses were listed for being produced during the trial, which included the police, forensic, technical and medical experts, as well as the crucial eyewitnesses, including Sunil Kulkarni, who was dropped by us later. However, the charge sheet didn't contain the details of the evidence and circumstantial descriptions connecting the crimes to the offenders, their respective and common roles and so on.

Between the filing of the charge sheet on 7 April and the framing of the charges against the individual accused persons on 3 August 1999, the intervening four months passed by in fulfilling the laid-down legal requirements of the court and the prosecutor. The system, as it operates in small and big cases, gives me an impression that the supply of material evidence being relied upon, including the statements and documents within Sections 207 and 208 CrPC, can by itself become a long-winded exercise.

ASJ D.K. Saini heard and considered the arguments and came to the conclusion that there were sufficient grounds for framing specific charges against each person, presuming the accused persons named in the charge sheet had committed the offences. Sanjeev Nanda, Manik Kapoor and Sidharth Gupta, the three persons who were together in the car, were also charged under Sections 201 and 34 IPC for causing disappearance of evidence in the offence committed and for giving false information to screen the offenders with common intention. Charges of the destruction of evidence with common intention under Section 201 and 34 IPC were also framed by the Court against Sidharth Gupta's father, Rajiv Gupta and his two household staff, Shyam Singh Rana and Bhola Nath.

For the main offences directly connected to reckless driving which resulted in the ghastly death of the six persons namely, Home Guards Rajan Kumar, Ram Raj and Constable Perumal besides Mehandi Hasan, Nasir and Gulab and grievous injuries to the seventh person Manoj Kumar, charges were framed by the judge against Sanjeev Nanda, Manik Kapoor and Sidharth Gupta under Sections 304(1), 308, 34 and 35 IPC, that is, committing and attempt, with common intention or knowledge, to commit culpable homicide not amounting to murder.

Amongst the three main accused persons, Sidharth Gupta had been separately charged by the judge under Sections 304(1), 308 and 35 IPC on 3 August; but sometime later, while the prosecution case was still being presented in the Trial Court, the Delhi High Court decided on 20 November 2000 to discharge him. Indeed, Sidharth's discharge came as a blow to the police and prosecution, but it was already realised that collecting evidence and submitting it in the court was just the beginning; a much bigger battle was already being fought in full swing outside the court.

To the investigating and supervisory officers in the district police, the facts of the case appeared to be absolutely clear, seamlessly linked together and well established through direct material, as well as forensic and circumstantial evidence, as reported to us. Starting from the point when on the previous evening, that is on 9 January, Sanjeev Nanda, who didn't have an Indian driving licence, took the unregistered BMW car number M-312 LYP belonging to his sister Sonali Nanda from his father Suresh Nanda's house at 4, Prithviraj Road, to the point he left it at his friend and car-companion Sidharth Gupta's house at 50, Golf Links, every small step seemed to have been traced and connected.

From the facts and evidence on record, it was clear that an inebriated Sanjeev Nanda, who attended a party at a friend's house and got drunk, was recklessly driving back home in the BMW car along with his friends Manik Kapoor and Sidharth Gupta, when at about 4:30 AM on 10 January, he hit the police checkpost, killing six persons and causing grievous injury to a seventh person.

The unfortunate police checkpost that night on Lodhi Road near the Car Care Centre Petrol Pump, not far from the police station, was manned by a CRPF constable and two Home Guards who happened to be there on duty by chance since they were not the staff of that police station. The first person at the accident site and thus the first prosecution witness, Hari Shankar Yadav, was the night attendant on duty at the adjacent Car Care Centre Petrol Pump. Having heard the loud sound, he saw the car crash and provided the information to his manager who, in turn, reported the incident on phone to the police on PCR 100 number.

Witness Hari Shankar, due to his proximity to the site and nature of his duties, was in a position to give a clear eyewitness account of this huge car crash—and initially he did provide that to the police. But, as it happens with many witnesses in our system, Hari Shankar resiled from his previous statement in the court by not telling that he saw a speeding vehicle coming from the Nizamuddin side hit some persons who fell down, injured and died. He was declared a hostile witness since he refused to support the prosecution case, saying that he was so frightened that he came out but then went back to the petrol pump.

Having lost the first witness in the case, though alarmed, we had a lot of hope from the only surviving victim, the badly injured Manoj Malik. He was produced as the second witness. He had been hit by the car when he was proceeding to the Nizamuddin Railway Station along with his three friends, all of whom died in the accident. Up to the point that he and his friends were stopped by the police and their belongings were checked, he narrated the events correctly. But suddenly he changed the location of the picket by saying that he was standing in the middle of the road while it was evident from the site plan and marks on the spot that his position was on the left side of the road.

His next statement that he was hit by a 'truck' and not a car was the height of his dishonest deposition, as against the well-established details of the vehicle which were admitted by Sanjeev Nanda himself. Circumstanstantially and through his conduct, it appeared, this prosecution witness had been clearly influenced and won over while he took cover behind a member of Parliament from Orissa and was most unethically protected by two lawyers.

The depositions of the hostile witnesses Hari Shankar Yadav and Manoj Malik show that their conduct was despicable, to say the least. But, when we look into the arguments of the country's top criminal lawyers like Ram Jethmalani, we start wondering if there was something really wrong with the police handling of this case. Repeatedly, citing numerous rulings, the plea was taken about the unfair trial of the accused on the ground that the prosecution had attempted to surreptitiously conceal the evidence available in the PCR records. In desperate need to strengthen its case, the police was trying to force an eyewitness to depose incorrectly.

Now, as I take out my Delhi Police Diary for the BMW case after so many years, I find the original print on the cover a little faded. On it is written 1999 in black ink. January 9 and 10 were Saturday and Sunday and so were on the same page. With only half the page for me to write on the date-wise diary, I had scribbled on every bit of white space available. All the relevant information was there—the date, time, scene of crime details with recovered items like broken, reassembled and missing number plate M-312 LYP with 'Park Lane' on it and so on.

I find contemporaneous facts in my diary, like the names of the dead and injured, details and respective roles of all arrested accused persons—Sanjeev Nanda, Manik Kapoor, Sidharth Gupta, Rajiv Gupta, Bhola and Shyam Rana. The details include crucial parts of the investigation, about PCR Inspector Jagdish Pandey, oil leak and trail leading to 50 Golf Links house of the co-accused Rajiv and Sidharth Gupta, the offending car taken out by Sanjeev Nanda alias 'Baba' on 9 April from 4, Prithviraj Road, night party at Sainik Farms, accident near Car Care Centre Lodhi Road, the offending vehicle trailed and found being washed at 50, Golf Links.

All this was known to Commissioner of Police V.N. Singh and to me within hours of the crime. The accused persons produced before us admitted their fault through their confessions, though these confessions were legally inadmissible, about this horrifying motor-vehicle massacre. I sincerely thought that it was an extremely bizarre, peculiar case, deserving the highest possible punishment. Commissioner V.N. Singh and I believed, guided and briefed the team led by a seasoned DCP and two Additional DCPs, about the legal provisions ranging between 304-A IPC—causing death by rash and negligent act, and 304(2) IPC—culpable homicide not amounting to murder, but the prolonged litigation established that the latter was not easy to prove.

In retrospect, it appears that despite our clear directions about the application of the appropriate sections of the law, the police presentation of this case wasn't up to the mark, perhaps due to the lack of professionalism and ability to understand the legal nuances at the level of the local police station. Either lack of intellect and legal knowledge or poor language skills or lack of an understanding of the importance of a charge sheet, resulted in submission of a poor and weak document in the court. Such an inadequately drafted charge sheet, though legally acceptable, often affect a proper presentation of the case even in the best-investigated cases, like the BMW case. This makes it difficult to establish the truth and permits plenty of space for legal manipulations as well as falsification of facts.

In such moments, I often became quite disturbed. It was sad to see the plight of our country's judicial system and its misuse. I felt sorry for the Catch-22 situation in which we policemen always found ourselves.

At this juncture, my alter ego started hurling questions at me, asking, 'Why does good work get defeated like this? Why does our system give scope to unscrupulous elements to creep in and vitiate the process?'

I answered, 'When we look into the line of arguments of the country's top criminal lawyers like Ram Jethmalani, we may tend to think there was really something wrong with the police's handling of this case. Our team members, who had done painstaking work which could only be called marvellous, were questioned though they deserved admiration and commendation. This will continue to happen unless we throw away our age-old systems, and substitute them with the new, responding to contemporary requirements.'

In the judicial process, a clear-cut case was completely derailed and the truth completely killed in the court. Repeatedly, citing numerous rulings, the learned lawyers of the accused party fantastically turned the point of the spear towards the investigating team of the police itself.

During the trial, several issues were picked up by the defence counsels from the material on police files, such as the PCR messages flashed during the pick-up and hospitalisation of the only surviving victim—witness Manoj Malik not supporting the prosecution case. Both the Trial and the High Courts, however, rejected the adverse plea trying to establish that the basic story narrated through the FIR and charge sheet was not correct. In spite of the abundant material evidence as well as the forensic and circumstantial evidence supporting the case, at times, the work of the prosecution was on the verge of failing in the court.

Amidst strong evidence placed before the court, an important scientific, though circumstantial, evidence came through the testimony of R.C. Gupta, the director in-charge of Safdarjung Airport Meteorological Office, located close to Lodhi Road, the scene of the crime. He gave a firm scientific opinion that there was a clear visibility of 1,000 metres at the time of the accident. He also said that there was additional brightness caused by the series of street lights switched on at that hour. This helped the case of the prosecution while disproving some crucial contention of the accused.

During the initial period, all the developments taking place at the surface level and also under the carpet were well known to Commissioner of Police V.N. Singh, too, as I was in touch with him professionally and personally. We were getting the inkling of the wrongdoings occurring during the court proceedings, but legally we could do nothing about them.

21

Implanted Kulkarni Planted Deflection

As I browse through the pages of my personal diary of those days, I find a clear note dated 15 January 1999 that a mysterious person named Sunil Kulkarni who claimed to be a resident of Mumbai turned up in my office through DCP Pradeep Srivastava. He had called several times earlier, desperately seeking to meet me to reveal certain facts of the BMW accident which he claimed to have. I had avoided meeting him earlier but finally agreed to meet him.

Unlike the conditions normally seen in Mumbai Police HQ or in several other metropolitan police offices, the Delhi Police HQ was always full of people. The Police Commissioner often met several visitors (40–50 a day on an average)—each having individual pleas—standing or sitting outside the office, with the Staff Officers taking notes for follow-up actions. I was next to the Commissioner in the number of public dealings. The itinerary of my meetings, in those days, used to be prepared by my Staff Officer, Inspector Virender Pundir. My meeting with Kulkarni was also scheduled by Pundir, a meticulous police officer with excellent knowledge of laws, investigation and police procedures.

Sitting outside amongst other visitors, the mercurial Sunil Kulkarni, full of schemes and ideas in his head, must have been quite uncomfortable. Pundir knew about his anxiety to meet me since he had already been briefed by DCP Srivastava, who hadn't met him till then. Slightly built, wheatish towards being dark, with a twinkle in his eyes, smart and pleasant-mannered, Kulkarni entered my room in a hurry to be heard. I called Pundir, who came with some other issues in hand, and sat down to listen to him.

The way Kulkarni dramatically described his presence on the spot in the BMW case, exactly at the time when the incident took place, could be mind-boggling to anyone interested in the case. The media had already got some inkling about this 'socially spirited and crucial eyewitness', which was enough indication for me to be cautious about whatever he said. I asked the DCP to conduct a thorough inquiry about Kulkarni's address and background. He had already been declared a star witness by the media and we had no option but to record his statement at the police station.

For me, an added reason for being suspicious was a past experience, again dealt by DCP Pradeep Srivastava, a couple of years ago when a person from Ranchi in Bihar suddenly declared himself to be the killer of Lalit Maken, member of Parliament, in the sensational terrorist crime in Delhi. My friend from Patna University, Manoranjan Sinha, SSP Ranchi, arrested the man and we sent Srivastava to bring him to Delhi. We interrogated him and found that he was a fake, keen to become famous overnight. He had done most of his homework about the case in minute detail, like Kulkarni—who, it seems, visited the crime scene besides gathering information from the media.

Sunil Kulkarni, from the unverified address of Saki Naka in Mumbai and no other address anywhere, a person with no livelihood or ostensible means of subsistence, followed the official channels to reach me through DCP Srivastava. As he must have planned along with the legal experts, he managed to officially reach the Police Station Lodhi Colony on 15 January 1999, and most cunningly became the guest of SHO

Vimlesh Yadav, who arranged a guesthouse for him to stay for an indefinite period.

Kulkarni's statement was quickly recorded the same day under Section 161 CrPC which empowers the IO to examine any person acquainted with the facts and circumstances of the case orally or in writing and maintain it in a separate record. Under Section 162 CrPC, however, the IO is not empowered to get the witness to sign such a statement, hence making it inadmissible as evidence under the law, except in situations when during inquiry or trial, a part of it is used for contradicting in the court. The IO can use it for making discovery of a new fact under Section 27 of the Indian Evidence Act.

Highly intelligent, well-informed, but for me an obviously unreliable witness, Kulkarni understood the legal nuances; hence, to pin him down, it was decided to produce him before a metropolitan magistrate for recording his statement under Section 164 CrPC. The magistrate, as required, warned him about the use of his statement against him and also made sure that it was made voluntarily and truthfully under oath, which could bring the charge of perjury at some stage, unlike the unsigned statement made to the IO.

The story of Sunil Kulkarni can't be categorised as a detective or investigative one, since it unfolded with his changing tricks from 15 January 1999, when he appeared before me until now, twenty years later. Now Kulkarni is facing a trial in the court of the Chief Metropolitan Magistrate in Delhi's Tis Hazari courts under Section 195 CrPC for contempt of law and offence against public justice on a complaint by the Delhi High Court. I have been summoned in this case by the court as a witness but not yet examined. Meanwhile, as always, Kulkarni is at large, trying to avoid the judicial process.

Since 1999, Kulkarni was found to be mingling with all kinds of people, sometimes inside the court but mostly outside, playing his games with the leading prosecution lawyers. He hobnobbed with defence lawyers, promoting their unethical practices, bluffing the police and misguiding the judicial process. He appeared in the media frequently, misleading all viewers.

Kulkarni's role was quite intriguing to everyone. He appeared in the case quite dramatically. I always believed that he was a worthless witness in the case, and thus rejected him during my first encounter itself, with suitable directions to my juniors—which they followed. However, I also suspected that he could bring a storm through a serious disruptive factor into the case.

According to his initial story, Kulkarni said he was passing through the spot at the time of the accident, on foot, on his way to the Nizamuddin Railway Station to catch a train for Bhopal. He described the accident in considerable detail. He stated that he got completely unnerved seeing the sight of so many people being mowed down by the speeding car. Shocked by the gory scene, he left the place and went to the Nizamuddin Railway Station to catch his train. On reaching the railway station, he tried to call the police emergency number 100 but was unable to get through. He went to Bhopal in a confused state and on coming back to Delhi, being troubled by conscience, he contacted the police to get his statement lodged.

According to the statement recorded by Kulkarni, the accident was caused by a car. He said the car stopped for a while after hitting the men. When it stopped, a man alighted from the driver's seat and examined the front and rear of the car. Then, another person got down from the passenger seat. He called the other by the name 'Sanjeev' and urged that they should go. Kulkarni's statement was recorded under Section 161 CrPC. The following day he was shown Nanda's BMW car at Police Station Lodhi Colony. He identified that it was the same car that had caused the accident.

On 21 January 1999, Kulkarni's statement was recorded by a magistrate under Section 164 CrPC. Before the magistrate, he substantially reiterated the statement made to the police, lacing it up with details about his stay in Delhi from 7 January and his movements in the evening before the accident. In the statement before the magistrate, the manner of identification of Sanjeev Nanda was also the same with the addition that after the accident, when the car moved again, the person on the driving seat was trying to look for the way by craning his head out of the broken glass window and thus Kulkarni was able to see him clearly. He said he could see the driver properly from a distance of no more than three-and-a-half feet when the car passed by his side.

The police wanted to settle the question of the driver's identification. They wanted Kulkarni to identify Sanjeev Nanda in a test identification parade but Sanjeev Nanda refused to take part in anything of that sort. Incidentally, on 31 March 1999 when Sanjeev Nanda was produced in the court, Kulkarni also happened to be there. He immediately identified him as the driver of the car in the accident.

Kulkarni's arrival on the scene as an eyewitness of that terrible accident received wide media coverage and he was generally acclaimed as a champion of public cause. At that time, he appeared to the investigators too as godsent witness, but soon there were reasons to look at him completely differently. Summons issued by the Trial Court and sent to the Mumbai address given by him revealed that the address was fake. The report dated 30 August 1999 on the summons said that he had given a wrong address and his actual address was not known to anyone. It also stated that he was a petty cheat who had defrauded several people in different ways. The report concluded by saying that he seemed to be a person of shady character.

At the same time, Kulkarni was turning and twisting in his fluctuating claims while we proceeded further, establishing the case with appropriate evidence. On 31 August, a habeas corpus petition was filed in the Delhi High Court making the allegation that Kulkarni was being forcibly held by the Delhi Police in wrongful confinement. This twist was shocking for the police. However, on the day following the day of the writ petition (that is, on 1 September), the allegations were denied in court in favour of the police. Kulkarni was personally present in the court then. The court dismissed the writ petition without any directions.

In his next move, Kulkarni filed a new petition through a lawyer before the Trial Court on 13 September. In this petition, he stated that he had told the police that the accident was caused by a 'truck'. But the police was adamant about not changing the version of the FIR that was already registered and on the basis of which five persons had been arrested. He alleged that the police refused to pay heed to what he wanted to say. He also alleged that the police forced him to support its own story aimed against the accused, and that all his earlier statements had been made under police coercion.

On 23 September, suddenly an unforeseen incident occurred which gave a new twist to the whole case. A clash took place between a joint team of Delhi and Mumbai policemen and members of the Bar in the Patiala House Court premises, most strangely, for the 'custody' of Kulkarni. A complaint about the alleged high-handed actions of the police was formally lodged before the Court and a notice was issued to the then joint commissioner of police, who was none other but me, to investigate the peculiar incident and intimate the Court about the truth. In response to the notice, I submitted a long and detailed report to the Court on 27 September 1999.

As I found, Kulkarni had appeared in the court on 23 September when summoned, along with his advocate B.R. Handa. That act was not so simple. He perhaps did so with the intention to hatch a nasty plan in the court. On that day, officers from the Mumbai Police along with a supporting team of Delhi Police were present in the court to arrest Kulkarni in connection with a cheating case lodged against him in Mumbai. When they approached to arrest Kulkarni, Advocate Handa, supported by his other advocate friends present there, strongly opposed the action.

The heated arguments between the Delhi Police and Mumbai Police parties on the one hand and the lawyers supporting Kulkarni and Advocate Handa on the other soon turned into a fight between the two groups. They created a riotous situation in and near the court. That resulted in the registration of a criminal case against Advocate Handa and others. All this led to my intervention on the direction of the judge in the Patiala House Courts. Being the Joint Commissioner of Police, I investigated the mayhem created in the court and outside on the arterial road near India Gate and prepared a report on it, as directed.

In the report, I made a detailed and meticulous explanation about Kulkarni's conduct from the time he became a witness for the prosecution in the BMW case. I strongly defended the actions of the policemen who did hard work and performed an effective investigation. I pointed out the shady background of Kulkarni. I mentioned that he could not give any authentic address or contact details to the police. I also mentioned that his lifestyle had completely changed after getting publicity and mileage through the case. He had begun to live in expensive hotels and move in big cars. All this raised a suspicion that he was getting financed by some hidden sources and he was acting under their influence.

With my report to the Court, I enclosed a copy of the printout of the calls made on Kulkarni's mobile phone, whose number he had given to one of the police officers. It showed that as early as 17 July 1999, he was secretly in close touch with the counsel for the defence, R.K. Anand (representing one of the appellants) and his junior advocate, Jai Bhagwan. The mobile phone records proved that Kulkarni was also secretly in touch with Suresh Nanda, father of Sanjeev Nanda.

I cited several other instances to show the mischievous role and dubious character of Kulkarni. The essence of the report was that Kulkarni had been bought over by the defence and was in clandestine and rather dangerous collusion with it. He was suspected to have received large sums of money from the family of the accused. He was trying to play both the sides to create a deep level of confusion in the case and he was completely unreliable.

On 30 September, the date which was fixed for his examination, Kulkarni was present in the court. He was, however, represented by his own lawyer and not by the prosecuting counsel. He was quite eager to depose. But the prosecution no longer wanted to examine him. I.U. Khan, the special public prosecutor, filed a petition stating that on the instructions of the State he gave up Kulkarni as one of the prosecution witnesses on the ground that he was won over by the accused. He also submitted before the Court my report (Jt Commissioner's report of September 27).

As expected, our allegation that Kulkarni had been won over was denied by both Kulkarni and the accused party. The Court, however, discharged him, leaving the question open as to what inference it would draw as a result of his non-examination by the prosecution. Before Kulkarni's exit from the case, the prosecution had lost the two other key witnesses. After his exit, the prosecution was without an eyewitness.

The trial proceeded in this manner, and over a period of the next four years, the prosecution examined around sixty witnesses on the forensic and other circumstantial aspects of the case. The prosecution finally closed its evidence on 22 August 2003. Thereafter, the accused were examined under Section 313 of CrPC and a list of defence witnesses was presented on their behalf. While the case was fixed for defence evidence, two applications were filed before the Trial Court. One was at the instance of the prosecution seeking a direction by the Court to make the accused Sanjeev Nanda give his blood sample for analysis for comparison with the bloodstains found in the car and on his clothes, and the other was by the defence under Section 311 CrPC for recalling nine prosecution witnesses for their further cross-examination.

Subsequently, during the appeal filed by Sanjeev Nanda and others in the High Court, the defence counsel contended, 'So far the act of prosecution in dropping the said witness was concerned, no fault can be found with the same, but to recall such a witness after a gap of eight years was an astounding fact on earth.' The fact was that the police or the prosecution or the defence never recalled Kulkarni as a prosecution witness; it was the trial judge who decided to summon him as a 'court witness'.

Before Kulkarni appeared in my office the second time on 31 August 1999, there was a whole lot of information about him which was brought to the knowledge of the Court, starting with the allegation of one Gauri Shankar reflecting upon his dubious character. The charges were peculiar but revealed clearly that he was an unreliable character, prone to indulge in acts of fraud. The fact that he had given a mobile phone to Gauri Shankar which was registered in the name of Shivalik Hotel was also not found to be a normal conduct. It raised suspicion that some kind of nasty underhand plan was being cooked. The Trial Court however believed that it was on record that he had stayed at Shivalik Hotel in Delhi until 12:30 PM of 9 January 1999; hence, his presence in Delhi on 10 January couldn't be improbable.

Interestingly, another report from Police suggested that he proceeded to Nahan from there, though he changed his statement to say later that he had gone to Bhopal after witnessing the BMW incident and returned to Delhi on 12 January, but he was not able to explain where he remained for three days before he met me on 15 January. The Court was fully aware that its summons could not be served on Kulkarni and none of his addresses and whereabouts, before and after the crime, could ever be verified.

Going back to Kulkarni's initial appearance before me and his meeting with SHO Inspector Vimlesh Yadav on 15 January, he gave his version in writing, which fully matched the detailed description of the scene of crime prepared by SI Kailash Chand, admittedly inadmissible as evidence under the law, yet given credence by the Trial Court. The Trial Court took serious note of the statement made by Kulkarni before the police and the magistrate, which was in line with the respective positions of the deceased bodies, blood trails, tyre and skid marks and movement of the offending BMW on the scene of occurrence.

Earlier, the same facts had been intimated to the police by witness Manoj Malik, who later turned hostile. Surprisingly, changing his earlier statements to the police and the magistrate, Kulkarni also made a statement that Sidharth Gupta came out of the driver's seat, though it had not been indicated by any other evidence that Gupta was driving the BMW. On the one hand, the Court had released Sidharth Gupta following a Delhi High Court order in an entirely different set of proceedings; on the other, the trial judge found Kulkarni's statements to be very useful for corroborating and authenticating the videography and other evidence of the crime scene.

Restless and ambitious, Kulkarni got trapped into a media sting operation which was partly his own creation. A sting operation carried out by NDTV opened up a Pandora's Box, not only affecting Kulkarni but also a large part of our criminal justice system itself. It was finally dealt by the highest court, something which had never happened earlier. Instead of reproducing his statements and his role as interpreted by different judges making references to me in the case, I find it far more convenient and authentic to reproduce (as I shall do at a later stage of this narrative) the brief narration given by Justice Aftab Alam in the Supreme Court judgement.

It is ironic that a comprehensive report prepared by me as the joint commissioner of police and which was used in the Supreme Court judgement of Justice Aftab Alam of 29 July 2009, never saw the light of the day in the manner it deserved to have. I could lay my hands on my own report while writing this book to revisit the BMW case and to explain to the practitioners of the criminal justice system how necessary it was to plug the holes which the system inherently had.

Concerning the incident at Patiala House Courts between the lawyers and the police, giving a conclusive order based on the account of the New Delhi Bar Association (NDBA), I had been asked to appear before the judge in-charge and explain as to 'what action had been taken against the erring police officials as it amounted to interference in the judicial process'. Briefly, the order stated that at about 3:30 PM the members of NDBA appeared before ASJ Mittal saying that when Senior Advocate B.R. Handa along with other lawyers and Sunil Kulkarni were coming out of ASJ P.K. Bhasin's court at about 1 PM after attending to the matter pertaining to the BMW case, an unsuccessful attempt was made by the police to somehow 'abduct' the witness, Kulkarni. The police officers did not succeed in their 'nefarious designs' due to a large number of lawyers being present, but the policemen followed Senior Advocate Handa and Kulkarni up to Handa's chamber in a bid to interrogate them.

A host of advocates present there wanted to speak to the SHO leading the police team but, it was alleged, they were pushed back and assaulted by the policemen. The president of the Bar Association and executive members also turned up there and the traffic on the main road in and around the court was stopped for quite some time, which caused traffic snarls near India Gate as well. The situation could be controlled only when senior police officers arrived on the spot.

I reported to the judge that the incident occurred simply due to the fact that Sunil Kulkarni was wanted by the Mumbai Police in a cheating case of Sakinaka Police Station but he was being kept in a 'protective custody' by Senior Advocate B.R. Handa. The fracas took place as the Mumbai Police wanted to lawfully arrest him with the help of the Delhi Police. Initially, the policemen had requested and tried to persuade Senior Advocate Handa to hand over Kulkarni, but he plainly refused. It was unlawful. The policemen were not allowed to do their job.

Apart from giving a precise and vivid narrative of the incident in my report, I also mentioned certain related facts such as how Kulkarni, while speaking to the press, could explain quite dramatically that he was so disturbed after witnessing the accident that he couldn't sleep for two nights. He could also show tears while explaining details, as evident in one of his interviews to the *Indian Express*. The national dailies as well as the electronic media covered his statements on 16 January with wide publicity. This was the day just after the day he met me. He was portrayed as a 'public spirited person' who had answered the call of his conscience and decided to tell the police what he saw and subsequently made a voluntary statement before a magistrate under Section 164 CrPC.

Without proof which was admissible in the court, the prosecution had become weak in the judicial proceedings after the crucial witnesses turned hostile. In spite of the high quality of our investigation in terms of the speed and the collection of material, forensic and circumstantial evidence, the police was criticised for doing shoddy work. To our utter sorrow and frustration, the Court severely criticised the police, and said it had misused the ample power and authority provided to it by the system. Interestingly it also, at the same time, rejected the new petition of the defence for recall of witnesses, observing that the power was available only with the Court and not at all with the accused and the defending counsel.

At the end of the order, the Court observed that the only witness in the case whose statement was already recorded under Section 164 of CrPC was Kulkarni. Even though he had been dropped and given up by the prosecution, the Court felt that a proper examination of Kulkarni was important in the given circumstances of the case. That was how Kulkarni, whom we had found to be an imposter and as such did not want him to be there, returned to the scene again, though more dangerously this time for the prosecution. The Court, according to its decision, summoned Kulkarni and he had to appear on 14 May 2007. Kulkarni thus bounced back on the stage with greater vigour than before.

Through our investigation, Kulkarni had been found to be a close friend and associate of the prosecution counsel R.K. Anand and defence counsel I.U. Khan. My detailed report on the case file documented Kulkarni's deep connections with the advocates and the defence party. At one point of time during the trial, Kulkarni was assailed by both these counsels as a cheat and the most unreliable witness in the whole episode. He was apparently planted by the learned lawyers to dupe all parties and bring in twists and complexities in the case.

Kulkarni, in the second round of his testimony, was treated by the trial judge as a 'court witness'. The Court later observed in the order sheet on 10 October 2007 that 'some evidence had come in the deposition of witness Sunil Kulkarni and prior to it there was no evidence against Sanjeev Nanda'. The judge modified his stand later when this was pointed out and emphasised by the defence. The judge then stated, 'I make it clear that it was only a prima facie opinion and the said order sheet should be read that "earlier there was no direct evidence against accused Sanjeev Nanda".'

Based substantially on the 'court witness' Kulkarni's deposition, among other clinching evidence, the final judgement was delivered by ASJ Vinod Kumar on 2 September 2008.

The Delhi High Court disposed the appeal in May 2009 and the Supreme Court in August 2012. Later, the Supreme Court judgement (Criminal Appeal No. 1393 of 2008, R.K. Anand vs Registrar of Delhi High Court), delivered by Justice Aftab Alam on 29 July 2009 became a landmark judgement in the criminal justice system of the country regarding the role of advocates and the media.

The Supreme Court judgement completely denounced the character of Sunil Kulkarni and condemned the complex manipulations done by the media, the lawyers and also the courts. In all the judgements, Sunil Kulkarni occupied a major space. His case was cited as an example of how a maliciously and treacherously planted witness, who actually was nobody in the case, could vitiate the process of justice. Kulkarni's statements, which were made separately before the police, the metropolitan magistrate and in the Trial Court as a 'court witness' (as decided by ASJ Vinod Kumar), is a classic example of how the entire judicial process can be misled to annihilate the truth. A decade later, Justice Aftab Alam, along with his brother judges Justice BN Agarwal and Justice GS Singhvi in their remarkable judgement, partly relying upon my reports, brought out the real story.

22

Khaki and Court Taken for a Ride

Through my personal diaries and my recollections of the contemporary material, when I recall the chain of events concerning the BMW case and Sunil Kulkarni, I am simply left aghast.

Following our initial inquiries determining him to be an unreliable witness, Kulkarni had appeared before the court fully protected by lawyers on 30 August 1999, supposedly under the guidance of his favoured police officers. He had shocked everyone by complaining to the court that he felt terribly insecure even though he was going out of the way to help the prosecution. He was bold enough to keep calling me during that period on the phone, asking me to meet him. He finally met me on 31 August (this was our second meeting), looked desolate and while talking, he started weeping. He said he had qualms of conscience and was being shaken up from inside. He assured me that he had come all the way to speak the truth. He also explained how he had spurned an offer of ₹ 1.5 crore extended to him by the accused party.

While Kulkarni was sitting in my office, I observed that a lawyer, presumably Senior Advocate B.R. Handa, talked to him using an inspector's mobile phone. That was the time when the lawyer had filed a writ petition (habeas corpus) in the High Court with a notice served on us to produce Kulkarni the next day in the court, that is, on 1 September 1999. Moving with police officers, simultaneously, Kulkarni requested for security which was provided to him under court orders. When produced in the High Court, he desired to go with Senior Advocate B.R. Handa, and didn't contact the police thereafter.

It seemed to me he was in touch with the accused party who had managed to get a few policemen in their favour with instructions to provide him with protection. He appeared in the court with Senior Advocate Handa on 13 September. Kulkarni's dubious and double role in the case was something unheard of so far in any other criminal case. It was unprecedented that a prosecution witness had been produced in the court by the opponents, that is, the defence lawyers. For all those years after the accident, we had reported to the court that Kulkarni was an inauthentic person and a double-cross.

During that period, surprisingly, the legal heirs of the deceased persons of the accident filed a petition to transfer the case from the court of ASJ P.K. Bhasin. That was, however, turned down by the Court. The case was then adjourned to 23 September when the shameful brawl between lawyers and police took place in the court premises.

I had very meticulously recorded the facts about the role and the sudden involvement of the Mumbai Police in the case. The Mumbai Police team, led by SI P.A. Repale from Sakinaka Police Station, officially supported by Delhi Police, along with an order from the Andheri Metropolitan Magistrate, Mumbai, addressed to his counterpart in Delhi, had come to arrest Kulkarni in connection with a cheating case filed against him in Mumbai.

The Mumbai police officers had filed an application in the court of Additional Chief Metropolitan Magistrate (Additional CMM) Sangeeta Dhingra Sehgal, making a request to direct Advocate B.R. Handa to hand over the accused to the Mumbai Police team. They gave an undertaking that Kulkarni would be produced on the next date of hearing, that is, 30 September, in the court of ASJ P.K. Bhasin as ordered by Additional CMM Dhingra, but nothing seemed to have happened due to the protests by the lawyers against the police.

In my detailed submission to the judge in charge, I reported about the NDBA complaint against the police in the episode concerning Kulkarni and the lawyers who protected him. It was absolutely clear that all the police officers from Mumbai and Delhi who were present in the Patiala House Courts were performing their respective legal duties. They were legally bound to arrest Kulkarni who was taken into so-called 'protective custody' by the lawyers; but he was not arrested in the court. However, as soon as he went outside, an attempt was made to do so, resulting in the unsavoury clash.

Kulkarni could be seen sitting in the car of the lawyer Handa, who was asked to hand him over, but he refused and went away, while 50–60 advocates gathered, allegedly manhandled the police party and raised slogans. On a separate complaint of the Mumbai police, a case of rioting, obstruction and assault on police officers and facilitating escape of an accused was registered on 23 September 1999. That case, however, remained pending for years and despite everything being on record, finally it was shelved as 'untraced'.

In my written report to the judge at this early stage of the BMW trial, I had tried to bring to light these blatant manipulations, maladies and malpractices. I tried to establish that the policemen in question were not at all at fault. Rather, they remained restrained even in the face of false allegations and humiliations, just to uphold the dignity of the judicial process which was, on the other end, openly being flouted by others. On 27 September, I made a prayer to the Court to direct those holding Sunil Kulkarni to disclose his whereabouts and hand him over to Mumbai police for their investigation. I also requested the Court for his appearance and free-and-fair deposition for trial in the BMW case on 30 September 1999.

I submitted a request to the Court asking, for my own satisfaction, curiosity and clarity, why a prosecution witness had suddenly changed his stand and demanded a counsel for himself. In my two and a half decades of police career until then, I had never seen such a service being provided to a prosecution witness. In my understanding, a witness was an independent person who had to truthfully depose the facts before the court and any attempt to influence him to depose otherwise would amount to tampering with evidence. Whatever was my indignation at that time, my report and submissions remained unattended, gathering dust in the court files for years.

All that happened in the courts, much before the actual trial really progressed through the examination of sixty-one prosecution witnesses by SPP I.U. Khan, a well-known Senior Advocate who had offered to work on the case on a token fee. The police officers and the officials, and the medical, technical and forensic witnesses deposed truthfully and competently. This established the case well, but at the same time, the witnesses who should have been the backbone of that criminal trial lied on oath in the court, and were declared hostile.

Although there were several defence witnesses in the case, in this strange trial, which became the theme of an interesting movie *Jolly LLB* and its sequel, the distinction between prosecution and defence witnesses got completely blurred due to the unusual ways through which the rules were implemented. The case was unique in the sense that all the key eyewitnesses turned hostile and the self-styled, dubious and self-proclaimed witness, Kulkarni, who was strongly rejected by both the defence and prosecution lawyers and also dropped by the police was, out of the way, summoned and examined by the Court itself.

ASJ Vinod Kumar delivered one of the most talked about judgements, particularly regarding the exclusive treatment in the court given to the controversial witness Kulkarni. That had been strongly rebutted in a big way by Senior Advocate Ram Jethmalani. ASJ Vinod Kumar, had discussed in detail the conduct of Kulkarni, prior and subsequent to the crime, and came to the conclusion that he was in Delhi at the time of the crime and was indeed a truthful eyewitness of the incident. He didn't accept the arguments advanced by the defence lawyer Ram Jethmalani asserting that the presence of Kulkarni at the time of crime in Delhi was somewhat impossible and wrongfully claimed. The judge ruled out Jethmalani's arguments about the discrepancies in several of Kulkarni's statements.

Later, challenging the verdict of the Trial Court when this case was being argued in the High Court during appeal, the defence counsel, based on the police investigations itself, mounted a severe attack on this court witness calling the deposition to be 'full of falsehood and self-concoctions'. The defence counsel argued, 'Going into Kulkarni's movements prior to his arrival to the scene of crime at about 4.30 AM on 10th morning, he had come to Delhi on 7th to meet some Minister of State. He stayed first in Ajanta hotel and later in Shiva hotel from where he checked out at 12.30 PM on 9th January '99 getting it noted there that his next destination as per his schedule was Solan. In reality however, he did not go to Solan. Instead, he claimed to have met a friend Sushil Kataria at the New Delhi Railway Station and remained with him from dinner until 3.45 AM. It was near Shiv Mandir, on Maharshi Raman Marg adjoining Lodhi Road, around a bonfire with some three-wheeler drivers that he said he spent some time before he proceeded towards the Nizamuddin Railway Station.'

Without being able to prove all those movements outside the hotel, Kulkarni contradicted himself, saying that he couldn't get a three-wheeler near Lodhi Road. He started walking on foot and witnessed the gory accident by chance. As he said in the court, he tried to wake up persons sleeping at the petrol pump, but nobody woke up, completely contradicting the recorded first information of our witness Hari Shankar Yadav.

Thus, Kulkarni's deposition that he walked a little towards the Nizamuddin Railway Station, hired an auto-rickshaw, attempted to dial 100 from telephones installed at the railway station and boarded a train to Bhopal to again meet another person called Kataria, held no ground. He returned to Delhi two or three days later and made a telephone call to me or perhaps to DCP Srivastava. Most of his depositions remained unverified, as well as his subsequent movements and his addresses, over the years.

Apart from Kulkarni's statements made to the police and the magistrate soon after the crime, when examined as a court witness, the judge found him to be consistent. Additionally, the judge found the descriptions of the scene of crime through Kailash Chand's *rukka*, site plan and videographic presentation, which he personally viewed very minutely, and the statement made by the resiled witness Manoj Malik, to be corroborative. He found a new factor in all these through the solitary eyewitness Kulkarni, who testified that the offending vehicle stopped, and was then driven backwards, trampling and killing those who were stuck under the car.

The police investigations and complete rejection of Kulkarni as a prosecution witness coupled with copious arguments by the defence counsels in line with the police findings did not cut ice with ASJ Vinod Kumar. Ironically, he delivered a very comprehensive judgement, completely accepting our investigations and heavily relying upon Kulkarni—the court witness.

23

What Offence Was Committed? By Whom?

In a sudden change of stand, well-advised by the Senior Advocate Ram Jethmalani and others, during the final arguments, Sanjeev Nanda admitted that he was driving the offending vehicle. Summing up the evidence, submissions and circumstances, the judge concluded that he was in no doubt that Sanjeev Nanda was driving the vehicle at the time of the offence. But the real legal battle started in the Trial Court which was further elaborated in the High Court and the Supreme Court—all three came to different conclusions about the offences committed by Sanjeev Nanda and his co-accused, and thus determined varying quantum of punishment, even handing down discharge and acquittal to some.

To my mind, for the police as the prime movers of the criminal justice system, the most important legal issues, minutely debated and practically settled, were the circumstances and evidence under which such fatal cases of motor vehicle accidents could be decided. Prolonged arguments took place in the Trial Court, to start with, whether this case fell within the ambit and provisions of Section 80 or Section 304-A or Section 304(2) of the IPC. Let us look at these provisions briefly.

Section 80 says:

> Nothing is an offence which is done by an accident or misfortune or without any criminal intention or knowledge

> in doing a lawful act in a lawful manner by lawful means and with proper care and caution.

Section 304-A states:

> Whoever causes the death of any person by doing any rash and negligent act not amounting to culpable homicide, shall be punished with imprisonment of either description for a term which may extend to two years, or with fine or with both.

For us, the BMW case was an exceptional opportunity to learn the practical application of the law on fatal accidents, a situation routinely confronted by the police, prosecution and defence lawyers and the courts. Once the circumstances and evidence in the case appear to be exceeding the realm of Sections 80 and 304-A, getting into 304(2) IPC, we need to understand its altered application—though it becomes extremely difficult to do so, given the imagination and brilliance of Indian lawyers and the endless rulings handed down by the Supreme Court and High Courts. Under Section 299 IPC culpable homicide is defined as:

> Whoever causes death by doing an act with the intention of causing death, or with the intention of causing such bodily injury as is likely to cause death, or with the knowledge that he is likely by such act to cause death, commits the offence of culpable homicide.

The application of Section 304 IPC dealing with the punishment for 'culpable homicide not amounting to murder' in fatal accident cases has to be done with circumspection, and this wise decision was taken by SI Kailash Chand and the seniors officers present on the spot, including Police Commissioner V.N. Singh.

Culpable homicide not amounting to murder is:

> If act by which the death is caused is done with the intention of causing death, or of causing such bodily injury as is likely to cause death. The punishment provided is imprisonment for life, or imprisonment for either description for a term which may to 10 years and shall also be liable to fine.

Part 2 of 304 IPC provides:

> If the act is done with knowledge that it is likely to cause death, but without any intention to cause death, or to cause such bodily injury as is likely to cause death.

The punishment provided is 'imprisonment which may extend to ten years, or with fine, or with both'.

The Trial Court, in the judgement of this case, had gone into great depths to come to a conclusion that the accused Sanjeev Nanda should be covered within Part 2 of Section 304 IPC as 'committing culpable homicide not amounting to murder'. Accordingly, under the law, the other co-accused to be covered within the corresponding provisions of Section 201 IPC for:

> Knowingly or having reason to believe that an offence has been committed, causing disappearance of evidence in the offence committed with the intention of screening the offender from legal punishment, with that intention giving information in respect of the offense which he knows or believes to be false.

The punishment provided for the offence is seven years and a fine if the punishment for the main offence is death; three years if the punishment for the main offence is imprisonment for life; and a quarter of the longest term provided for the offence if that happens to be less than ten years.

In this case, the trial judge began with dispelling the misconception that causing death by a motor vehicle would simply draw criminal liability under Section 304-A, citing a Supreme Court judgement (1976-1SSC 889), wherein death is caused by doing a rash and negligent act not amounting to culpable homicide under Section 299 or a murder under Section 300 IPC:

> If a person wilfully drives a motor vehicle into the midst of a crowd and thereby causes death to some persons it will not be a case of mere rash and negligent driving and the act will amount to culpable homicide. Each case, therefore, will depend upon the particular facts established against the accused.

During the protracted trial and appeal and the continuous bashing by the media, two cases of motor vehicle deaths were prominently reported. The film star Salman Khan allegedly drove his car on the night of 28 September 2002 and rammed it into a laundry and bakery, killing a labourer and leaving four injured. The Sessions Court had held him guilty under Section 304 IPC with a five-year sentence for culpable homicide not amounting to murder, but the Bombay High Court granted him bail the same day and, finding fault with the police and prosecution, set him free completely from all charges in 2015.

In the BMW case, the most prominent case cited in the courts was the State of Maharashtra vs Alister Anthony Pareira (MANU/MH/0655/2007) in which the accused, in somewhat similar fashion to Sanjeev Nanda, drove his car while drunk, about the same time in the morning, and ran over people sleeping on a footpath in Mumbai, causing death of seven persons and injuries to eight others.

The Sessions Court practically let Pareira off with two months' sentence under Section 304-A for causing death by a rash and negligent act, but the Bombay High Court reversed the sentence and convicted the accused with a punishment of three years imprisonment under Section 304(2) IPC. The defence counsel in the BMW case referred to this case and attempted to take the plea that the knowledge of people sleeping on the footpath during night could be attributed but the presence of policemen and private persons in 'the middle of the road (wrongly witnessed) on the chilly morning of 10th January on Lodhi road could never be visualised'.

Considering the overall evidence and circumstances, the Court, in our case, came to a conclusion that reckless driving could be covered both as a murder under Section 300(4)—having the knowledge of an 'act being so imminently dangerous that death would be caused in all probability' or a culpable homicide under Section 299(3rd part) when the offender 'acts with the knowledge that he was likely by such act to cause death'.

In order to cover the case in Part 3 of 299 IPC, the judge cited innumerable cases and personal scrutiny of the evidence even beyond what the IO and experts had to say; and, most importantly, he relied heavily on the court witness Sunil Kulkarni, who was finally cross-examined by the SPP I.U. Khan on 29 and 30 May 2007. These were the days when the sting operation of NDTV created a media storm, making the judge say that both SPP Khan and the defence counsel Senior Advocate R.K. Anand were colluding and that 'the witness Kulkarni was under great mental pressure'.

All accused persons were convicted and ASJ Vinod Kumar went into further details once again, hearing the Public Prosecutor Rajiv Mohan who had replaced SPP I.U. Khan and the defence counsel Ramesh Gupta, both of whom presented their grounds for higher punishment and the mitigating circumstances, respectively. While Mohan mentioned about the seriousness of the crime, almost touching upon murder, Gupta mentioned about the age, jail record including NGO's reports and payments of ₹ 10 lakh each to the family of the deceased and ₹ 5 lakh to the injured and so on.

Drawing a comparison with Mumbai's Pareira case where the High Court had awarded three-year imprisonment with ₹ 5 lakh fine, finding the offence committed by Sanjeev Nanda far graver, he was sentenced to rigorous imprisonment (RI) for five years with benefit of Section 428 CrPC (period of nine-month detention undergone set off). Rajiv Gupta was convicted with a sentence of one year RI and ₹ 10,000 fine while his staff, Shyam Singh and Bhola Nath, were sentenced to six months RI and ₹ 100 fine, each.

Concluding the discussion on the evidence in respect of the co-accused Manik Kapoor, Rajiv Gupta, Bhola Nath and Shyam Singh Rana, the trial judge had a lot to say about the hobnobbing between the defence counsel, prosecution and the IO and for the perfunctory investigation, lamenting, 'This trial was an example how the entire criminal justice had been hijacked by the rich and powerful.' He found the inefficiency in the investigation not incidental but deliberate.

Apart from the judicial file, the judge had thoroughly examined, discussed, even somewhat erroneously shared the police file with the defence and observed that the additional public prosecutor (APP) checked the charge sheet, raising serious objections that led to a *kalandara* (charge) being filed against Sanjeev Nanda's sister Sonali Nanda, to whom the BMW car belonged and who hadn't cooperated during the investigation. The suggestion from the APP led to further statements of the witnesses being recorded about the washing of the car by the co-accused for being charged under Section 201 IPC.

Somewhere, the legal position was lost sight of—that the police file containing the unsigned and inadmissible statements of witnesses recorded under Sections 161 and 162 CrPC and the confidential diaries, that is, the day-by-day proceedings of the investigation setting forth timing, places, and circumstances of the investigation maintained under Section 172 CrPC, had to be outside the reach of anyone except the senior police officers and the concerned court. How all this became available to the defence party in this case should have been taken very seriously. It led to highly disruptive arguments advanced by the Senior Advocate Ram Jethmalani, particularly about the PCR wireless messages of the time when the police was carrying the injured and the dead as well as giving internal reports of their own movements.

All such material as well as the inadmissible Section 161 CrPC statements were freely and inappropriately used during the trial and the police took the blame for inefficiency. However, the messages related to Inspector Jagdish Yadav who tracked and discovered the car from the accident spot to 50, Golf Links through the oil trail and the recovery of the vehicle washed by the co-accused by SHO Vimlesh Yadav could be explained through the PCR messages as well.

Our ample direct and circumstantial evidence, forensic, scientific and expert testimony, as well as documentary and oral evidence given by the police officers, could counter the hostile witnesses. The trial resulted in the conviction of the main accused, Sanjeev Nanda, besides the co-accused Rajiv Gupta, Bhola Nath and Shyam Singh Rana; Manik Kapoor was let off since except for his fingerprints in the car, there was no other evidence against him.

On hindsight, I feel that the concerned police officers should have got all the actions performed and ensured preparation of a proper charge sheet for the court. I also wonder whether all the details of the confidential case diaries should have been made public. These details have to be shared with the defence only when referred to by the police during the trial.

During the trial and appeals before the High Court and Supreme Court, several adverse observations were made by the judges about the manner of presentation of the case, but the basic framework of this investigation was so strong that all through, up to the highest courts, it withstood the onslaughts from the best of lawyers and the worst of manipulations.

The judgement delivered on 5 September 2008 was certainly not the end of the journey we began on 10 January 1999, but it was an important landmark. Thousands of small and big events took place during the investigation and trial of this case. Arguably, it was the best-known case of motor vehicle accident, and one in which all conceivable norms of criminal justice were flouted, surprisingly, presented by none other than the country's top lawyer, the irrepressible Ram Jethmalani, as a case of 'justice delayed is justice denied'.

Submitting that no lapse or delay could be attributed to them during the trial, the prosecution gave a convincing account of the timely submission of charge sheet, charge proceedings for two months on fourteen dates during May to July 1999; the prosecution evidence was completed by August 2003, with nine adjournments taken by the accused and four by the State. Only two adjournments were taken for witnesses being absent; three joint requests were made and seven times the files were in the High Court. Exemptions were sought by Rajiv Gupta ten times and Sanjeev Nanda twelve times; the judge was on leave five times. Defence evidence continued from October 2005 to May 2008, with intervening dates for the court witness Kulkarni, supplementary charge sheets, final arguments with eight prosecution and fifteen defence hearings; and finally, the convictions and sentencing on 2 and 5 September 2008.

When everything appears to be so well explained, then who is responsible for the 'justice distorted and delayed is justice destroyed and denied'? And to whom—the accused or the victim or the society at large represented by the State? Most of the time, like in this case, the specific provisions for expeditious trial under Section 309 CrPC, and those regarding postponement and adjournments, are overlooked. In the High Court later, there were arguments about the Indian Constitution not providing speedy trial as one of the fundamental rights like in USA, though this is covered in the broad sweep of Article 21 which confers the right to every person not to be deprived of life and liberty except through a laid-down procedure which has to be reasonable, fair and just.

24

High Court and Supreme Court: Topsy-Turvy Verdicts

Reading through the High Court judgement in this case, I find my own thoughts of policing, in all aspects, being echoed in the observations of the judge:

> Truth is the cherished principle and is the guiding star of the criminal justice system. For justice to be done, truth must prevail. Truth is the soul of justice. Justice will be said to be done when no innocent person is punished and the guilty person is not allowed to go scot-free.

So far so good, but the problem arises with the observation made further:

> The case opens up in the High Court with the submission, relying upon the inadmissible police document, highlighted and thrown-up by learned lawyer Ram Jethmalani, that the accused Sanjeev Nanda was 'an absolutely honest person since in his very first encounter with the police (on 10th morning at 7 AM), he truthfully and honestly disclosed in his statement under Section 161 CrPC that the said unfortunate accident in which six persons had died and one was injured had occurred when he was driving the said vehicle on the said fateful morning.

Earlier, during the last lap of the trial's final arguments following prolonged litigation, with all possible methods, fair and foul, adopted by many, Jethmalani in his inimitable style of arguments had 'very fairly admitted to the factum of accident and the fact that the accused Sanjeev Nanda was at the driving seat of the BMW car bearing registration number M-312 LYP'. It is only lawyers of abilities at Jethmalani's level who can take liberties with the law even in the highest courts and convert an issue in the police records, which is completely non-admissible in court, into a central point of the arguments.

Jethmalani fiercely attacked the judgement of the Trial Court on all fronts, stating that prosecution totally failed to prove the case and the judge of the Trial Court had failed to appreciate the facts, misapplied the law, indulged in self-research, assumed the role of an expert by viewing the videography, attached undue weightage to the most discredited witness, and displayed prejudice against the rich and mighty, blaming the accused for the ills and misdeeds of greedy lawyers.

Fortunately, the results of our investigation and our track record during the trial could be explained well by our prosecutor against Jethmalani's formidable attack. Remarkably, Jethmalani's attack was mostly against the judge and the prosecutor and not so much against the police. The examination of Sunil Kulkarni as a court witness after a gap of eight years and the personal audience granted to him by the judge in his chamber, were all points of general criticism of the trial judge.

The entry of the self-styled eyewitness Kulkarni on 15 January was perhaps the beginning of complexities in the case, which I had realised very quickly during my first meeting with him itself. Following Kulkarni's volte-face, the points obliquely raised by the defence counsel about this crook and alleged cheat were correct, since he was an out-and-out fake. But, in the light of his methodical preparation to present himself as a witness, and the media, which eulogised him too quickly, initially, we had no option but to examine him. He was appropriately and quickly sent to the police station the same day. He met the officers connected with the case and his statement was recorded by the IO and then by the metropolitan magistrate. Soon, we realised his dubiousness and decided to drop him, thus saving ourselves a lot of trouble.

During the arguments in the High Court, almost all the points raised during the trial were reiterated, but some of the arguments were altogether new. The main issue was about the conviction of Sanjeev Nanda under Section 304 IPC for culpable homicide not amounting to murder and not under Section 304-A—rash and negligent act causing death—for which the defence was fully prepared.

There was a question in my mind regarding the measurement of alcohol in the blood. The AIIMS medical test reported an alcohol content of 0.115 per cent w/v in Sanjeev Nanda's blood—the permissible limit was 30 mg in 100 ml (that is 0.03 per cent w/v)—clearly violating the provisions of the MV Act. Where was the need or opportunity to use a breath analyser as required under Section 185 of the MV Act, 1988? Everyone knows that a breath analyser is used by traffic policeman or the motor vehicle officials on the roadside to check drivers. How could a breath analyser have been used in this case? And after the AIIMS report, what doubt could there be on the accused's state of drunkenness?

The issues relating to the high speed and reckless driving of a large car like the BMW by a drunken young driver, returning in the wee hours with his friends, appeared to be self-evident from the scene of crime and described precisely by the IO through his *rukka* (which became the FIR), the site plan and the videography. These documents proved how the vehicle hit the three policemen and four others towards the left, near the footpath, close to the Car Care Centre Petrol Pump, from where the first informant, Hari Shankar, came, hearing the sound of the accident.

The vehicle hit the seven persons like a blast, turned right and hit the central verge, the driver came out of the vehicle to see what happened, and decided to escape on being prompted by his friend, clearly established the crime, intent and knowledge. No one can deny the fact that the injured were entangled beneath and over the vehicle and were bound to be trampled and killed if the vehicle was driven further—which is exactly what Sanjeev Nanda did, possibly out of panic, as the defence claimed.

That the court witness Kulkarni was a cheat, a conman and liar of an extreme variety, there could be no doubt. His complete unreliability was already crystal clear from his overall conduct from the beginning of the case and his subsequent actions. I submitted a detailed report to the in-charge judge on 27 September 1999, but why this report on the case file was not heeded is a mystery to me.

To hold the police even remotely accountable for whatever Kulkarni did with the case or with the prosecution and defence lawyers or the media and the Trial Court itself, is unjustified since he had faced out-and-out rejection by us. Similarly, the police should not be held responsible for hostile witnesses like Hari Shankar or Manoj Malik, a victim of the horrendous accident, who could have died in the accident itself—both these persons represented unethical collusion.

There was absolutely no doubt in the minds of the judges across the hierarchy—from the ASJ to the High Court and Supreme Court judges—that Sanjeev Nanda was guilty of extremely rash and drunken driving, resulting in a major accident causing six deaths and injury to the seventh person. The High Court examined the Trial Court's reasoning for conviction under Section 304(2), that is, culpable homicide not amounting to murder. It disagreed and decided it was mere rash and negligent driving, causing death.

The Supreme Court disagreed with the interpretation of the High Court and restored the offence of culpable homicide not amounting to murder, but it became somewhat kind to Sanjeev Nanda and spared him further incarceration.

The High Court mentioned about the high value placed by the Trial Court to an article 'Recklessness under Indian Penal Code' published by the Indian Law Institute, an institution situated right next to the Supreme Court, which I visit frequently. The situations envisaged in Part 3 of Section 299 IPC, Section 300(4) IPC and Section 304-A IPC referred in the article were considered by the Trial Court, amongst a large number of judgements. This was objected to by the defence counsel. The Trial Court examined and concluded that in this case, the offender had the knowledge of 'second degree' as provided within Part 3 of Section 299 for 'indulging in the act which he knew was likely to cause death, hence culpable homicide not amounting to murder'.

Briefly discussing the fine distinction between 'rashness' and 'negligence'—the consciousness of mischievous or illegal consequences missing in the latter—the High Court said that keeping in view the totality of the circumstances, that is, two hostile witnesses and a court witness, and also the circumstantial evidence, it was not in agreement with the Trial Court that the offence committed by the appellant was under Section 304 part 3 IPC. The same set of cases were discussed including the remarkably similar one of Alister Anthony Pareira of Mumbai, where seven persons had been killed and six injured on the footpath of the city by a drunken young driver returning from a party, at about the same time as Sanjeev Nanda in the Delhi BMW case. The facts of these two cases—Alister and BMW—were now found to be different.

Another case considered was the Supreme Court case of 1954, Sadhu Singh Harnam Singh vs State of Pepsu, in which the accused had shot dead a revered mahant (priest) who was his guest on that day. He did so just because the mahant was leaving the house without taking meals and he wanted the mahant to spend the night with him. In this case, the Supreme Court had reduced the offence from murder under Section 302 IPC to 304-A, considering it to be just a rash and negligent act, just like our own BMW case.

Having reduced the offence to a rash and negligent act on the part of the main accused Sanjeev Nanda, the High Court drastically reduced the culpability of others as well. Under Section 201 IPC, the two friends of Nanda had already been let off by the Trial Court for whatever they did or didn't do. The Court had a lot to say by way of suggestions for legal changes and by way of critical comments about the role of the prosecution and the investigating authorities, and the need for scientific investigation by the police. Without pin-pointing the actual policemen or their conduct of the lapse or connivance, the Court made a concluding observation, 'We can take corrective measures to ensure that the justice delivery system does not become a laughing stock and is not reduced to mockery by persons like Sunil Kulkarni and police officials of doubtful integrity.'

The BMW incident took place in 1999. The case went on for a good ten years. It was only on 20 July 2009 that the High Court Bench of Justice Kailash Gambhir gave its verdict. The accused was arrested and jailed. However, it took another three years for the proceedings to end and the final judgement to come from the Supreme Court on 3 August 2012. The two judges, Justice Deepak Verma and Justice K.S. Radhakrishnan, who wrote separate judgements, came to the major question straightway—whether Sanjeev Nanda deserved to be held guilty of offence under Section 304(2) IPC or the conviction and sentence awarded to him by the High Court under Section 304-A IPC should be held good and legally tenable.

Accepting and appreciating the investigation carried out by our team and the evidence collected, narrating the facts as briefly as possible, the judges went into the issues and controversial points raised during the trial and appeal. ASG Harin P. Raval assisted by Advocate Siddharth S. Dave for the prosecution and Senior Advocate Ram Jethmalani assisted by Advocate S. Kapur for the defence presented their exhaustive arguments in the Supreme Court trial. Later, in the judgement, the judges summarised the arguments of the senior lawyers. The authorities and citations in both the judgements were mostly the same and included almost the same points as those in other much talked about cases of hit-and-run, namely, SSC 525 State of Maharashtra vs Salman Salim Khan (Bollywood actor) and SCC 648 Alister Anthony Pareira vs State of Maharashtra.

Towards the end of their judgements, however, the two judges differed in their appreciation of the aggravating and mitigating circumstances, as presented by ASG Harin Raval and Senior Advocate Ram Jethmalani and thus gave out different sentences. Justice Deepak Verma set aside the High Court's order and restored the judgement of the Trial Court, and partly agreeing with the appeal, maintained the two-year sentence awarded by the High Court, which Sanjeev Nanda had already undergone.

Justice K.S. Radhakrishnan was not so kind to the accused. Briefly narrating how the six persons died due to the rash and negligent drunken driving by the driver who did not even have a proper driving licence was a clear act of causing death of someone. He noted that the accused escaped without giving a helping hand to the victims dying and crying for help; human lives may have been saved had the accused shown mercy. The accused had the knowledge that the car driven by him had hit human beings, bodies were scattered around and they might die, but he thought only of his safety and left the place. Not reporting the crime to the police even after reaching home and failure to provide medical help even after escape decidedly aggravated the offence.

On the point of sentencing, following the decision that the offence fell within Section 304(2) IPC (culpable homicide not amounting to murder), Justice Radhakrishnan held the view that punishment must be proportionate to the gravity of the crime and the offender should be punished for deterrence to himself and others from committing similar offences. The High Court, according to him, committed a grave error in converting the offence from Section 304(2) IPC to Section 304-A IPC.

In addition to the sentence already awarded by the High Court, the accused was directed to pay an amount of ₹ 50 lakh to the Union of India within six months, to be utilised for providing compensation to the victims of motor vehicles accidents where the vehicle owner and driver are not traced. On default, he would undergo simple imprisonment for one year. The accused Sanjeev Nanda was ordered to perform community service for two years, to be arranged by the Ministry of Social Justice and Empowerment within two months; and on default, he would undergo simple imprisonment for two years.

As a person leading a voluntary organisation which works extensively for the rehabilitation and social reintegration of juveniles and adolescents, I appreciate the positive and substantial value of this reformative judgement of the Supreme Court.

25

Media and Lawyers: Issues Settled in Supreme Court

We have been extremely privileged in the BMW case to have a thoughtful and thorough Supreme Court judge like Justice Aftab Alam who gave a brief and clear account of the complex BMW story. This was particularly so regarding the conman Sunil Kulkarni who took the entire police and legal process for a ride and the NDTV sting operation that revealed the disagreeable roles of two key players—the media and the lawyers. Led by Justice Alam, the Supreme Court settled the issues with this profound judgement on 29 May 2009. The media had been following this case since the day the incident occurred on 10 January 1999.

The most significant chapter in the media story was added to this case on 20 April 2007 when NDTV, a popular news channel, telecasted a half-hour programme on the case. Later, Poonam Agarwal of NDTV received a phone call from Sunil Kulkarni mentioning that he was very impressed with the programme and wished to expose the nexus between the prosecution and defence who, according to him, were hand-in-glove in the case.

A day prior to the telecast, on 19 April, on behalf of Senior Advocate I.U. Khan, the special public prosecutor in the BMW case, his junior, Advocate Vikas Arora had filed a complaint with the NDTV chief editor that Poonam Agarwal had demanded copies of case diaries and statements, failing which she had threatened to expose them. He mentioned that the prosecution and police in the case seemed to have been influenced by the accused. Simultaneously, while Poonam was meeting Kulkarni and planning the sting operations, on 26 April, her channel NDTV gave a reply to Vikas Arora that they were a responsible media and would make all efforts to unravel the truth.

Between 1999 when the BMW case occurred and the investigation was wrapped quickly, and 2007, when the so-called floundering trial was concluding, there must have been endless games and manipulations with which the police officers in the picture were mostly unconnected. I am not aware who among the previous team were being consulted, but for me, whatever appeared in the media from time to time was just shocking news as I was without much idea about what was happening behind the scenes.

I recollect clearly that I.U. Khan, one of the leading criminal lawyers of Delhi, had generously offered to take up this case on a token fee, and DCP Pradeep Srivastava had recommended him very happily. What all happened during these eight years was mostly in the courts, chambers and homes about which Delhi Police officers connected with the case appeared ignorant.

NDTV was a leading channel for investigative journalism at that time, and they contacted me after the sensational Jessica Lal case ended in an acquittal, to our huge discomfiture. Fortunately, the NDTV team working on the BMW case was not involved in police-bashing when Poonam Agarwal and her colleague Deepak Verma were on their mission at Patiala House Courts along with Sunil Kulkarni. On 28 April 2007, when, to unravel the truth, Poonam 'wired' Kulkarni with a concealed button camera connected to a small recorder with a microchip, my detailed report dated 27 September 1999 containing similar truth was lying in the court file for years.

When I read this story again while writing this book, ironically, I was reminded of the preparations for the final act of the Rajiv Gandhi assassination at Sriperumbudur near Madras. Shubha, the associate of the suicide bomber Dhanu, prepared her by fixing the suicide device on her body. But here, unlike Shubha and Dhanu, Kulkarni was on his meandering mission in the BMW game while Poonam was keen to broadcast her planned recording of the ignorant target, the jovial and friendly, Senior Advocate I.U. Khan.

Poonam waited outside Patiala House Courts while the wired Kulkarni, along with Deepak Verma, who had a concealed camera and recording device in his bag, started looking for Advocate Khan, who was found in another crowded chamber. In his usual boisterous and friendly style, Khan stated, 'Meet Kulkarni, he is the prime witness in the BMW case. He is our star witness and he is a very public spirited and devoted man, and he was in Delhi on the day when this unfortunate incident happened. He was going on foot to Nizamuddin Railway Station and incidentally witnessed the incident.' The language used in the recording was Hindi. Here is the gist, with English translation:

KHAN: *Ab* court *ne* (now court . . . he coughs) we dropped you.

KHAN: These were the instructions we received from the (Police) Headquarters and that's why I got the SHO statement recorded that 'on the instruction of the SHO and ACP, such and such witness has been dropped'. Then how can I make a statement? My clients are Delhi Police. Whatever instructions they will give, I will act upon them. I was very keen to examine you.

KULKARNI: Ya, I know that because I still remember, still remember.

KHAN: *Inhone mera hath dabaya, *** bhi dabaya, khoob dabaya, maine kaha main kya karoon, agar* individual client *ho to samjha bhi lo,* department *hai* (They pressured me a lot, but I said what can I do? If it was an individual client, I could convince them, but this is a department).

Kulkarni expressed his anxiety about the statement to be recorded and Khan told him that he could enjoy since he had been dropped as a witness and who was he (Court) to say that it should be recorded? Someone else in the chamber quipped, 'The Court can order investigation but cannot determine the mode of investigation.' Khan agreed to this comment.

Kulkarni suggested that in the evening he would come to Khan's home. Khan welcomed him, saying that in Delhi he was a guest. Khan talked about the personal rapport between the two and asked Kulkarni to have a cold drink. They came out of the chamber and continued talking. Kulkarni spoke about the summons which had gone to Mumbai and were returned.

(Khan cut in) Khan: '*Tum mere ko miloge kab*, *ye bata*o (tell me, when will you meet me)?'

Khan talked about meeting while Kulkarni talked about his conversation with the SHO. Khan wanted to know where he was staying, and Kulkarni said that he was staying outside Delhi.

They discussed the time and day of the meeting at Khan's home and settled for the next evening (Sunday) between 7 to 8 PM. Kulkarni told Khan not to tell anyone about their proposed meeting and Khan assured him that the question did not arise.

KHAN: '*Tumhare liye bahut badhiya* Scotch *rakha hua hai* (I have kept an excellent Scotch for you)!'

KULKARNI: '*Waise meri* K.K. Paul (police commissioner) *se baat hui hai*, *lekin maine abhi tak nahi bola hoon* (I had a talk with K.K. Paul, but I have not spoken till now). I have not received summons at all. *Wo mere ko bata dena* (tell me about it).'

They decided to continue discussions the next day in the evening at Khan's home. We do not know whether Kulkarni met Khan at his home the next day.

The highly sensational sting operation involving I.U. Khan, and his friend, R.K. Anand, a defence lawyer for Sanjeev Nanda at that time, went live on NDTV on 30 May and the whole country saw it. After that the media coverage for the BMW case became tremendously hyped.

The next morning, on 31 May, Khan was interviewed live for 23 minutes on the NDTV channel. He maintained that the clandestine recording of his conversation with Kulkarni was used selectively and out of context to create unwanted twists and controversy. Subsequently, on the issue of Kulkarni's meeting with the so-called 'Bade Saheb (big officer)' alleged to be R.K. Anand, Khan always maintained it was meant to be a senior police officer in the (Police) Headquarters. Anyway, following this shocking exposé and his compromised position as the special public prosecutor, he withdrew from the case on 31 May itself, producing a handwritten letter from Kulkarni stating that he had collected the summons from SHO Lodhi Colony on the advice of I.U. Khan.

Earlier, when Khan's junior, Advocate Vikas Arora, was contacted by the NDTV reporter Poonam on 19 April, they could have got alerted that something was cooking in the media. But neither Khan nor Anand, veterans of the criminal law world, appeared to be prepared for such a sting operation. The incident destroyed their illustrious careers.

Senior Advocate R.K. Anand was one of the best-known criminal lawyers of the country, having defended three prime ministers. He was the president of the Bar Council for many years and the vice-president of the Indian Law Institute, besides being a member of Parliament (MP) and a leading spokesperson of the Congress party. He was a high-profile celebrity in Delhi, highly respected in the society.

On 6 May, without any prior appointment, Kulkarni—wired, directed and fixed by Poonam—arrived at Indira Gandhi International Airport and met R.K. Anand in the domestic VIP lounge. He approached the security at the gate and got an announcement made to call R.K. Anand to the lounge to meet him.

Probably not on full alert or taken by surprise, R.K. Anand responded to the public announcement that someone was requesting him to come to the lounge. He went there after hearing his name announced repeatedly on the airport's public address system and saw Kulkarni waiting for him.

In the VIP lounge, R.K. Anand gave a friendly scolding to Kulkarni, '*Kya badmashi karte rahte ho* (what naughty things do you keep doing)?' Kulkarni said that he had been informing him about all the developments he knew, but Anand did not believe him. Laughing, Anand told him to stop doing wrong things and be a good guy, otherwise he would beat him up. Kulkarni asked Anand what strategy had to be made now. He said he had sent a message through Khan Saab and asked whether Anand had got it. Anand said he had received it.

Anand asked Kulkarni to meet him on his return, after his flight arrived at 9.30 PM the next day.

Kulkarni and Poonam planned a third sting operation for 8 May 2007 outside the Delhi High Court. Kulkarni, duly fitted with a recording device and wired by Poonam, got into the back seat of Anand's car and travelled together with him up to South Extension.

The same evening, the fourth and the last sting operation was carried out by the two in South Extension Part II, where R.K. Anand's office was located. Kulkarni met Anand's junior, Advocate Bhagwan Sharma, and another person called Lovely (Kulbir Singh), reported to be Anand's odd-job man, to negotiate on Anand's behalf. Briefly, the recorded conversations were as follows:

Kulkarni complained why he was not able to meet in the office or at home while everyone was after him; Anand asked why he was meeting him in the office. Kulkarni explained that no one watched them here and asked, '*Achcha abhi kya karna hai batao* (okay, tell what is to be done now)?'

Anand: '*Ab dekho tum***tum***paise***** (now you see***you***you***money****).'

Kulkarni asked how could he talk about all this while they were doing drama?

Anand: '*Baat to tumhare saamne karunga, peechhe to karonga nahi* (I will talk in front of you, not behind your back).'

Again, Anand repeated about talking in his presence, then Kulkarni said, '*Kal kya mere ko nikal rahe ho 311 se* (are you taking me out of 311)?' (Kulkarni was referring to Section 311 of CrPC under which the judge had summoned Kulkarni after nearly eight years of his being dropped as a witness by the police).

Anand: '*Nikal doon* (should I take you out)?'

Kulkarni: '*Nahi . . . nahi, mat nikalna* (no, no, don't take me out).'

Kulkarni pleaded with Anand not to withdraw him from the case when he was prepared to support and do everything for him. He asked Anand why had he filed an application in the High Court—didn't he have trust in him? Yes, he had got angry at times. Anand accepted the plea and Kulkarni said that he would come and depose in the court.

Anand: '*Ab usse kya baat karni hai* (what has to be talked with him)?'

The conversation went on.

Anand: 'I am out of touch.'

Kulkarni: '*Hmm. . .! Paune aath baje* (quarter-to-eight) I'll get back to you.'

Anand gave him a homily about not doing any harm to others, being good to everyone and not implicating anyone like Narsimha Rao (former prime minister) was implicated, whom he had got off; Kulkarni told him that he was prepared to do anything for him and talked about wrong information being fed.

The sting operations were over on 8 May, being the last meeting of Kulkarni with the representatives of R.K. Anand—Bhagwan Singh and Kulbir Singh alias Lovely; this second person was later reported to have died in a freak accident when the Trial and High Courts took cognisance of the telecast on 31 May following the broadcast of the programme on 30 May. In between, Kulkarni was interviewed at the NDTV studio on 13 May. He narrated the sequence of events up to the sting operation and explained how he contacted Poonam Agarwal following a programme about the BMW case.

Kulkarni said that the prosecution and defence were in league and the witnesses were bought over, and he was willing to expose all this through a sting operation with NDTV. Explaining about his sting encounters involving I.U. Khan and R.K. Anand, he said he did all this in the interest of the judiciary and he would ask for NSG (National Security Guard) security from the court. He presented himself as a truthful witness, briefly narrating his statements to the police and the magistrate. True to his character, he did a volte-face within a few days and refused to give his consent for the telecast of the programme to NDTV, who decided to go ahead anyway, on the grounds of serving the larger public interest.

On 30 May 2007, at 8 PM, one of the most sensational programmes ever, 'India 60 Minutes (BMW Special)' was telecast and presented by the most visible NDTV anchors, Sonia Singh and Barkha Dutt. Giving a damning account of the country's criminal justice system, with selective recordings and some of the best-known legal experts freely giving their opinions on this sub-judice day-to-day trial, this was a grand success for the channel.

The channel was able to simultaneously catch R.K. Anand along with the accused Sanjeev Nanda at his residence through a mobile camera unit with a reporter. Anand refused the interview saying he would speak in the court next day, but subsequently he did speak—he was presented awkwardly in the programme. At 9 PM (prime time), the programme continued with Poonam explaining how the entire operation was carried out with Kulkarni.

It is highly intriguing for me, in retrospect, how the developments concerning the sting operations and their telecast on 20, 29, 30 and 31 May, and even subsequently, went on simultaneously, interspersed with the court proceedings.

Sunil Kulkarni had been summoned as a court witness on 19 March and asked to appear on 14 May 2007, that is, after nearly eight years of being dropped as a prosecution witness by the police. And, as in the past, the summons could not be served on any address—he preferred to collect them from the SHO Lodhi Colony, as mentioned by SPP I.U. Khan. This issue, along with further cross-examination of some witnesses, was taken to the High Court and disposed off on 29 May through a detailed order.

The High Court held that witnesses could be recalled and Kulkarni examined as a court witness, but found the Trial Court's criticism of the police unwarranted and expunged it.

Kulkarni kept on playing his games, hoodwinking everyone including the courts. On 14 May, he appeared in the Trial Court but refused to be examined despite persuasion; on 17 May, he appeared and got a police protection order, but he never took the protection; finally, on 19 May, he was cross-examined by SPP I.U. Khan and deviated from the prosecution case significantly. Before I.U. Khan could conclude his cross-examination on the next date, that is, 31 May, on 30 May, the NDTV telecast took place, disrupting the entire legal process. Khan gave up his special public prosecutor's position in the case. R.K. Anand was also in the dock.

All hell broke loose, not only in the media but also in the BMW case. The managing director of NDTV was directed by the Trial Court to produce the entire unedited recording of the sting operation the next day, along with the names of the employees and reporters of NDTV who were a part of the sting operation. Consequently, the cross-examination of Kulkarni scheduled for 31 May was deferred on the request of the SPP Advocate Rajiv Mohan, who replaced I.U. Khan.

The proceedings pertaining to the NDTV sting operation, however, couldn't continue in the Trial Court since, shocked by the outrageous subversion of the criminal justice system by the rich and powerful, the Delhi High Court initiated suo motu proceedings under Writ Petition (Criminal) no. 796 of 2007.

The High Court called for all the material from NDTV and, based on that, issued show cause notices to R.K. Anand, I.U. Khan and Bhagwan Sharma, an associate lawyer of R.K. Anand. Senior Advocate R.K. Anand, a defence counsel for Sanjeev Nanda in the High Court, and Senior Advocate I.U. Khan, the SPP, had been shown to be deeply connected to Sunil Kulkarni in the TV story, supposedly negotiating for a witness to be bought over. Advocate Bhagwan Sharma assisted Anand, along with a person named Kulbir Singh alias Lovely, who had unfortunately died in an accident by the time the High Court initiated the proceedings.

On 31 May, a High Court Bench presided by the Chief Justice directed the Registrar General to collect all available material, that is, CDs, videos and transcripts and submit them within ten days. It further directed NDTV to preserve the original material pertaining to the sting operation. The latter part of the High Court order about leaving the material in the custody of the news channel was challenged in the Supreme Court. The number of microchips and CDs available with NDTV regarding the sting operation also became a subject matter of dispute later. Poonam Agarwal and NDTV were directed to submit detailed affidavits, but they were not given notices for contempt though Senior Advocate Vinay Bhasin argued the same day that the programme amounted to being an interference with the administration of criminal justice.

In the High Court, the matter being connected to senior criminal lawyers with all the legal resources at their command, particularly for someone like R.K. Anand, a series of petitions were filed instead of responding to the show cause notice of contempt. Anand challenged the bonafide of Justice Manmohan Sarin, one of the judges on the bench, asking him to recuse himself from the case on the ground of personal prejudice. The petition was ultimately rejected by Justice Sarin, but the other judges on the bench did not support him. Several interlocutory applications were filed by Anand which were all rejected, while I.U. Khan went ahead, modestly fighting his case claiming misinterpretation of his conversations with Kulkarni.

Almost in the dock on several occasions, the NDTV team went ahead aggressively with their investigative journalism. They further uncovered a very close nexus between Kulkarni and Anand and found details that corroborated my 27 September 1999 report about Kulkarni's deep connections with the defence lawyers and the accused party. The High Court and Sessions Court proceedings were still going on when, on 3 December 2007, NDTV completely exposed the deep relations between Kulkarni and Anand.

In 2000, as per the report, Kulkarni had lived in Anand's villa 'Schilthorn' in Shimla for about an year as his son named Nishikant Anand. He cheated several people there and even acquired a forged driving licence in the false name. He was booked in a police case and remained in jail for forty-five days. My contention before the court in 1999 about Kulkarni's relationships, including the payments of his hotel bills by the Nandas, were all finally accepted in full by the highest court in 2009.

Appearing live on TV on 30 May, when confronted with the reports from the sting operations about his meetings with Kulkarni by the anchor Barkha Dutt, Anand almost admitted his compromised position, from which he unsuccessfully attempted to wriggle out later. The Supreme Court observed that his 'statement made on oath before the High Court thus completely falsifies his denial in the live interview with the anchor of the TV programme about his second meeting with Kulkarni in the car'. He was duty-bound to inform the High Court when the Criminal Revision against the Trial Court order summoning Kulkarni as court witness was heard on several dates, about the same time in May 2007.

Surprisingly, as the Supreme Court later observed, Anand was relying on some of his own sting recordings while calling the NDTV stings fabricated, doctored, morphed and so on in his affidavit which, incidentally, referred to one of my official meetings with Anand when I was DGP Arunachal Pradesh. According to Anand, Kulkarni had attempted to meet him in his office, and as a matter of chance, I was present for some legal discussion. Anand took a plea that 'Kulkarni was rebuffed, rebuked and was asked to leave Respondent's (his) office in the presence of Shri Kanth. Thereafter, Sunil Kulkarni was physically thrown out from the office of the Respondent.' He pleaded that, I (Amod Kanth) 'also rebuked Kulkarni for his conduct in front of Anand'.

I recalled that incident. Sometime in 2005 or 2006, when during a chance meeting with R.K. Anand at Guwahati airport, he gave me some informal opinion in a criminal case. Some more discussion took place when I visited Delhi the next time, and I also visited Anand's office. I was furious when I saw Kulkarni sitting with Anand in his office in South Extension Part II, and got him thrown out, with a rebuke. Completely unconnected with the case at that time, I had no idea about the developments but had extremely unpleasant memories of that dubious and undesirable person, Kulkarni.

Through the recorded conversations with Kulkarni, Anand wanted to establish his admonishment and advice not to take money, and in the Supreme Court reproduced several irrelevant statements, one of which was in relation to me and the police commissioner, '*Uska koi taluk nahi . . . phir bhi ye* Amod Kanth *ke peeche kyon para hai* K.K. Paul (he—Amod Kanth—is not connected in any way, then why is K.K. Paul after him)?'

In a nutshell, the High Court finally convicted Senior Advocates R.K. Anand and I.U. Khan, finding their misconduct within the definition of 'criminal contempt'. The judges expressed their displeasure with Advocate Bhagwan Sharma too, but acquitted him of the charge in their judgement dated 21 August 2008.

By way of punishment, the High Court prohibited R.K. Anand and I.U. Khan from appearing in Delhi High Court and the subordinate courts for a period of four months, but left them free to carry on their professional work like 'consultations, advises, conferences, opinions, etc.' The Court also levied a fine of ₹2,000 on each of them. It also held that as 'senior advocates', R.K. Anand and I.U. Khan had forfeited their right to be designated as such, and recommended to the full court to divest them of the honour which had been bestowed upon them with the trust of the Court and the entire judiciary.

Both R.K. Anand and I.U. Khan filed criminal appeals (Nos 1393 and 1451 of 2008, respectively, R.K. Anand vs Registrar Delhi High Court and I.U. Khan vs Registrar Delhi High Court) under Section 19(1) of the Contempt of Courts Act. The appeals were decided on 29 July 2009 with the delivery of judgements that appeared to be historic in many ways. For all of us—the Delhi Police officers as well as the investigation team which was also subjected to a close scrutiny in this matter—there was a great learning out of it.

Most appropriately, for the police practitioners in the criminal justice system, the Supreme Court went into great detail, taking out this case from the close confines of the culpability of two lawyers under the Contempt of Court Act to 'the very root of the administration of justice in the country and need to be addressed by this Court'. The issues formulated by the Supreme Court included:

> Whether convictions were justified or not? Whether the High Court procedure adopted was fair and reasonable? Whether prohibition of the appellants to appear in High Court and subordinate courts as a punishment was open to them? Whether the given punishments were adequate and commensurate with their misdeeds, considering the facts and circumstances?

While discussing the role of NDTV in the sting operation and the telecast during the period of criminal trial, the Supreme Court threw light on what are called 'media trials'. Adding to our understanding of the issues, the root causes behind the BMW trial becoming directionless, and the declining professional standards among lawyers were also examined threadbare.

To debate on these crucial issues during the High Court proceedings, too, there were some legal minds supporting the contending contemnors, but the Supreme Court obtained assistance from some of the finest lawyers of the country, Senior Advocates Altaf Ahmed appearing for R.K. Anand, P.P. Rao for I.U. Khan and Harish Salve for NDTV. The Court had appointed Senior Advocates Gopal Subramanium and Nageswara Rao as amicus curiae, both of whom were later recommended to be judges in the Supreme Court.

Senior Advocate Harish Salve, though representing NDTV, joined Senior Advocate Gopal Subramanium in a scathing attack of R.K. Anand about his disregard for court proceedings, brazen attempt to browbeat the High Court, even succeeding to the extent of getting a token punishment of not appearing in the courts for four months. The Supreme Court held that trying to suborn the court witness in a criminal trial was reprehensible enough but Anand's absence of any remorse for his misdemeanour and conduct in the High Court was worse.

Agreeing with the legal stalwarts Salve and Subramanium and finding the punishment to be inadequate and incommensurate with the offence, R.K. Anand was found guilty of contempt for influencing the key witness in the BMW case. He was made to tender unconditional apology before the Court and directed to choose between the prescribed six months of imprisonment or donate ₹20 lakh to the Bar Council of India to develop a library or a Computer Centre and also provide free legal aid for one year; Anand chose the second option.

The professional misconduct of I.U. Khan in being familiar with Kulkarni to the extent of inviting him to his home in the evening for high quality whisky was unethical and unprofessional, but the rest of his conversation with him was in the open chamber at Patiala House Courts. For reasons best known to him, I.U. Khan had offered to the police to take up this case on a token fee, and it was a known fact that he was friendly with R.K. Anand and used to call him 'Bade Saheb'. From the circumstances and the sting operation it was clear that he was familiar with Kulkarni and had the knowledge about all his misdoings and the dirtiest possible games he was playing to destroy this case, between 1999 and 2007.

The High Court relied upon the sting operation which uncovered the unholy nexus between the defence and the prosecution and found Khan guilty of contempt of court. Regarding the expression 'Bade Saheb', Kulkarni used it to address the senior officers in Police Headquarters and as understood, he claimed he was in contact with the Police Commissioner Paul as the so-called 'Bade Saheb'.

Khan's culpability, according to the High Court, was that he failed to inform the prosecution that one of its witnesses was in touch with the opponents—he was more than an acquaintance of the defence lawyer. Arguing for Khan, Senior Advocate P.P. Rao strongly pleaded that the High Court denied him the opportunity to defend himself on this point and based the judgement on an assumption. Khan was finally given the benefit of doubt since, according to the Supreme Court, on the basis of the materials on record, the charge of criminal contempt could not be satisfactorily established against him.

Going very deep into the evidence on record which brought into light many of the dark areas of the investigation—which couldn't be done before the Trial Court—the Supreme Court examined and ruled about the procedure adopted by the High Court and the punishment given, transgressing their jurisdiction. The limitations of the courts were also highlighted while discussing the conduct of the respondent lawyers in the context of the Advocates Act and the disciplinary bodies like the Bar Council of India and the State Bar Councils. Most of them were not prepared to play this role, nor were they legally empowered to deal with recalcitrant lawyers.

As expected, when I was somewhat out of the two high profile cases, my alter ego asked me, 'How do you compare these two experiences of Jessica Lal and BMW hit-and-run cases?'

I replied, 'These were simple cases which became much larger than life because of the accused parties, the lawyers and certain high-and-mighty joining hands to subvert the system. Politicians and the media made them big in a bid to save or protect the accused who belonged to the rich and powerful families of the country. Had there been an ordinary person involved as an accused, the police would have successfully closed the cases in a very short time. I recall these episodes, not to remember their occurrence, but to search for answers to the questions which you hurl at me regarding the state of the criminal justice system of our country.

'My answer to your question will remain incomplete if I do not mention some cases of organised and sensational crimes of a very different nature which I handled during my career. For example, I would like to review the case of Romesh Sharma, the politician—don of the land mafia, who had his roots in Delhi and Mumbai but wings spread all over India and beyond—up to the level of large corporates and the international mafia of Dawood Ibrahim. He and his gang indulged in horrifying crimes which ranged from murder and kidnapping to criminal intimidation and terrorist activities, cheating, forgery, treachery and trespassing to drug trafficking, political and sex scandals. A review of his misdeeds will also throw fresh light on our criminal justice system and the serious shortcomings with which it is ridden.'

26

Romesh Sharma and the Mafia Miasma in Delhi

My alter ego once said, 'The stories of the mafia crimes of Mumbai are very popular, particularly in the movies. They have inspired many characters, both in the world of crime and in the world of cops. How about reviewing Romesh Sharma's character and the mafia cases to have a better understanding of the system?'

I replied, 'True! Delhi being the national capital, there are certain aspects here which are not seen in the cases of Mumbai. I happened to experience this myself. My insights are based on the cases which I had handled.'

My alter ego then asked, 'Can you explain the differences and how the demerits of our system become visible in a typical case?'

I replied, 'The police of Delhi, the capital of India, has often been compared with the police of the financial capital, Mumbai, despite both battling very different situations and crimes. NCT Delhi often sees a surfeit of media around every incidence of crime. The witnesses have numerous nefarious designs. Each incidence involves people with multiple levels of political as well as other high-level connections. Remarkably, many mafia crimes that occur not just in NCT but in the National Capital Region (NCR) and even extend to UP, Haryana and Punjab, manifest a common cause—in one form or the other, all kinds of crimes are often related to some land or property.'

The rapid growth of the NCT–NCR and the massive urbanisation plans undertaken from the 1980s onwards by the DDA, HUDA, Noida and Greater Noida Authorities, along with private builders, led to the rise of some deadly land mafias in the sprawling 1,485 sq km area of NCT Delhi. This mafia had connections with politicians, bureaucrats, drug traffickers, arms smugglers and even the Mumbai mafia.

The big property dealers of Delhi often thrive through the support of powerful political networks. They operate throughout Delhi in large numbers, showing their ugly faces everywhere, from villages to the commercial areas mushrooming in and around Delhi. These land mafias invariably have access to different types of people—from the highly powerful politicians and well-placed bureaucrats to the thousands of poor migrant labourers. The land mafias work under the banner of a few registered companies which serve as fronts to cover their misdeeds.

The organised criminal activities of the land mafias of Delhi have their own share of concomitant crimes like cheating in land deals, forgery of land-related documents, circulation of fake documents related to cases of transfer of property, use of violence for land-grabbing, use of musclemen to illegally occupy pieces of land and so on. Despite all this, Delhi Police has always claimed that the crimes by Delhi land mafias have been far less in terms of magnitude and outcomes compared to the Mumbai mafias.

I have my own share of experiences of handling the land mafias of Delhi, but the most memorable one was when, along with my team of Delhi Police, I stumbled upon the notorious Romesh Sharma, whom we arrested on 20 October 1998. That arrest led to perhaps the most elaborate mafia crime investigation in Delhi.

Romesh Sharma's arrest led to the launch of a major joint operation by the Delhi Police, CBI, Income Tax, Excise and Wildlife Authorities. It was also an opportunity for me to work alongside my former comrade-in-arms from the IPS trainee days, Neeraj Kumar, who was the most active officer in the CBI, chasing organised criminals.

It all began in the afternoon of 20 October 1998. We received a tip about H. Suresh Rao, owner of Pushpak Aviation Company, being assaulted by Romesh Sharma and his goons at C-30 Mayfair Gardens, a bungalow belonging to Romesh Sharma in a posh area of South Delhi. The local ACP and SHO who had swung into action finally rescued Suresh Rao from Romesh Sharma's political office at the high-profile government colony on Mahadev Road near Parliament Street, where he had been taken and held illegally in captivity.

The story that emerged was like a Bollywood script. Suresh Rao was only the tip of the mafia iceberg that Romesh Sharma ran. Along with his criminal empire, Romesh Sharma also had political ambitions. He had contested parliamentary elections from Phulpur in UP, a constituency which had once sent Indira Gandhi to the Parliament. He had hired a helicopter from Suresh Rao's company in 1996 for campaigning. Suresh Rao told us of the elaborate paperwork that went into the hiring of the helicopter to evade the Election Commission's electoral expenditure limits.

He explained that although the helicopter had been given on hire, a memorandum of understanding (MoU) for sale was signed to avoid the ceiling of election expenses. The understanding was that the helicopter would be returned after the election and the document would be destroyed. However, following the election, when Rao was transporting the dismantled helicopter by road from Phulpur, near Allahabad, to Mumbai, the truck was forcibly diverted to Delhi and brought to Romesh Sharma's 'Jai Mata Di' farmhouse in Mehrauli.

Romesh Sharma's goons forced Suresh Rao's people to reassemble the helicopter and the documents pertaining to sale and transfer were signed afresh. Apart from the physical muscle, Romesh Sharma also threatened Suresh Rao through telephone calls from Irfan Goga, a Dubai-based henchman of Dawood Ibrahim. From that day until the time the case was registered at Police Station Hauz Khaz in October 1998, the helicopter remained parked with Romesh Sharma while Suresh Rao helplessly went knocking on all possible doors in the police and in the government, without any result.

High-profile and highly placed criminals normally show certain kinds of behaviour and mannerisms when they are arrested and placed in police custody. Romesh Sharma had his own style. He was very keen to narrate his life history. We decided to patiently hear him out and record every bit of what he had to say. There could be no better source to know about Romesh Sharma's crime-ridden adventurous life and the numerous cases he was involved in, than his own confessional statements and explanations, though most of them would be inadmissible as evidence under the law.

We transcribed his verbal statements into written records in our police files. I remember how he bragged to the police about his rags-to-riches story—from his most humble origins in a small village in UP to becoming a powerful politician–mafia lord, operating from Mumbai to as far as NCT Delhi, acquiring the dizzy heights he always aspired. He tried to impress me as well, dropping names of his contacts who could be known to me.

My alter ego asked me, 'Why do you, in police, record in great detail the story of a criminal like Romesh Sharma? How does it benefit the police in its functioning?'

I replied, 'If an accused speaks out, it is very necessary for the police to make sure that it is recorded. In our system, it is a basic requirement that every fact related to the accused must be investigated and put into records. In Romesh Sharma's case, he spoke a lot about himself—even small details of his crimes and criminal and political background in his excessively long confessional statement. So the record of his story contains details which would otherwise have been difficult to come by.'

As Romesh Sharma explained, his massive and fast-expanding mafia operations spread all over Delhi. Some very important people in politics and the corporate world became involved in his affairs. During the same period, the well-known 'N. N. Vohra Report' by the union home secretary about the activities of crime syndicates and mafia organisations having deep involvement of the local as well as the special units of the police, directly patronised by political personalities and government functionaries, was doing the rounds in the power corridors and creating waves in the Parliament.

The Vohra Committee consisted of the home secretary; the secretary, Research and Analysis Wing (RAW); the director, Intelligence Bureau (IB); and the director, CBI. It co-opted the revenue secretary along with a team consisting of the chiefs of the Central Board of Excise and Customs, the Central Board of Direct Taxes, the Central Economic Intelligence Bureau, the Directorate of Enforcement and the Narcotics Control Bureau. The committee came out with some very remarkable and path-breaking findings and recommendations.

The Vohra Committee defined crime syndicates and mafias at the local level as the groups which were engaged in illegal activities like distillation of illicit liquor, gambling, satta, prostitution and forcible occupation of land and buildings in bigger cities, and operated behind the facade of officially registered companies. Over time, the criminal activities graduated to drugs, human trafficking and terrorism, and had international ramifications. The report brought out the roles of various stakeholders in the system.

RAW washed its hands off in the matter, taking the plea of limited strength and the international charter of duties.

The CBI had extensively and also quite intensively handled the Mumbai bomb blast investigations and had come out with a frank and bold report on Romesh Sharma-type cases. This report revealed the extraordinary powers that the crime syndicates had and the influence they exercised in villages, small and big towns and slums as well as metropolitan cities. The shocking point they highlighted was the inability of the local police, partly due to lack of courage and resources, to tackle the syndicates, and mainly because of the patronage provided to them by the law enforcement agencies, bureaucrats and politicians.

The report described how big names in the world of organised crime, like Dawood Ibrahim or Memon brothers or notorious characters like Iqbal Mirchi of Mumbai, blatantly defied the system routinely and indulged in heinous acts. The IB had alerted the senior police officers several times and provided concrete information regarding the linkages between the underworld, the politicians and the bureaucrats, but to no avail.

The N.N. Vohra Committee recommended a strong and urgent need to identify and neutralise the nexus between criminals, mafia and anti-social elements on the one hand, and police, bureaucrats, politicians and their linkages spreading over the electorate as well as the political, economic, law-and-order and administrative apparatus, on the other. An extremely grim picture was presented about how a parallel government was being run by the powerful mafia and how their impact in the political, business as well as the film circles was destroying the socioeconomic fabric and destabilising the economy and democratic polity. Thus our expose of Romesh Sharma's life and work became an appropriate and well-timed case study.

The Vohra Committee recommended establishing a nodal agency exclusively devoted to getting the bigger criminal cases properly addressed. But this report later became the subject of dispute. One dispute was whether the proposed body should be constituted within the IB or the home ministry. It is interesting to know and study how a top secret and detailed report (of which only three copies had been prepared initially—for the union home minister, minister of state for home and the home secretary) could remain a non-starter while mafia bosses like Romesh Sharma flourished right under the nose of the Central Government.

In the backdrop of the extensive mafia operations in the country that were exposed following the investigations into the 1993 Mumbai bomb blasts, the story of the rise and fall of Romesh Sharma made interesting reading. There were many myths about him, often spread and made larger by the media, which we had to first meticulously understand in the course of our investigations.

27

UP Lad Becomes Politician–Mafia Don

Romesh Sharma's own narrative and its police recordings describe how he had risen from complete anonymity to become a mafia don and a leader in business and politics by all kinds of manipulations which can only be described as being purely criminal in nature.

He was born on 12 February 1954 to Kausalya Devi and Satyanarayan Mishra in village Raipur, from where he eventually shifted to village Bibipur near Ugrasenpur in Allahabad (now called Prayagraj) district. As corroborated by the local land and police records, his family jointly owned a dilapidated house and 0.65 hectare of land, all together valued at ₹5 lakh. He was the youngest of five brothers and sisters. He talked about only two of his brothers—Dhanraj, who was an agriculturist and Bhagwan Das who owned two small factories, one of coil wire and another of corrugated boxes.

Among several others, one person, Harish Mishra, a cousin, was a close associate of Romesh in Mumbai. Jagdish Prasad, an agriculturist in the village and an advocate in Varanasi, who was married to his eldest sister, was also a close associate in all matters related to Romesh.

Romesh Sharma, like a typical Mumbai don, spent a nondescript childhood until he was fourteen, when he finally left his parental home, never to return to his village.

He told us that while he was studying in Intermediate College, living in Mugra Badshapur Hostel, in 1969, he suddenly left his studies and soon migrated to Delhi. Initially, he stayed with one of his relatives in Sadar Bazar, a commercial hub in Central Delhi, perhaps to work in a wire factory. He earned the measly wage of ₹4 per week. He then started selling purses, hankies and hangers on the roadside. Getting tired of making ₹5–10 per week, he shifted to Mumbai in 1970 and stayed with a relative named Shukla, who worked at Godrej.

An instinctively ambitious person, Romesh strived to rise in life and acquire money and power. He found a job paying ₹200 per month in a glass factory and went to stay at Santa Cruz with a kind lady, Dr Couten Veera Chrisy, as a paying guest for ₹40–45 per month. Soon, he shifted to Kaiser Woollen Mills. Simultaneously, he also managed to get a diploma in Refrigeration and Air Conditioning from St. John Institute, Matunga. After that, he worked at Blue Bird Refrigeration and Air Conditioning Company as an apprentice. The year was 1973 and his monthly wage was ₹300 now.

In his twentieth year, he met his namesake, Romesh Kapur, an Electronics Engineer fresh from UK, who belonged to the family that owned the famous Copper Chimney chain of restaurants in Mumbai. Besides the restaurant business, the Kapurs also owned a film financing company, Kardar Film Pvt. Ltd. In 1975, Romesh Sharma struck a deal with them and set up a partnership company, Electronics India Ltd, to manufacture deep freezers, refrigerators and coolers. His aim was to sell the products in the local market at low rates.

This shift in occupation changed Romesh Sharma's fortunes and, he claimed, he started earning ₹50,000 a month. Soon, he accumulated some money and turned towards investments in real estate. Unfortunately, in 1976, Romesh Kapur had a fatal car accident and his brother Nonnie Kapur, who took over the company, soon got into a dispute with Romesh Sharma. Just after two months of the accident, the factory closed down.

Meanwhile, destiny and a devious mind had both been at work. By the time the factory closed, Romesh Sharma had turned into a dreaded land-mafia lord. In the world of real estate, he was recognised as a powerful person who had the backing of politicians and rich businessmen. It was difficult to determine how he could manage to acquire sizable properties in a very short period of just two years—1976–78.

He purchased shares in several expensive buildings like Sant Sadan and Union Park of Khar, Pali Hill from Natha Singh, Avtar Singh and Kartar Singh Chawla. This transformed him into a 'big businessman' overnight, he said, as he narrated his story. However, later, when he attempted to transfer the property to one Narendra Bhatia of Raja Constructions, one of the previous owners, Avtar Singh, refused to do that and the property went into litigation.

That litigation taught Romesh Sharma the art and tricks of dabbling in huge property deals and disputed real estate. As per his own admission, he started amassing huge wealth by acquiring disputed properties at low prices. Highly ambitious as he was, he simultaneously started taking interest in politics, often by organising rallies and dharnas (pickets), particularly aiding and facilitating politicians of different types coming from UP and Bihar.

Even before he turned twenty-five, along with his meteoric rise in the field of real estate, in 1978, he took a plunge into politics in the Mumbai region. Romesh Sharma became an office-bearer of the Socialist Party of Maharashtra State through the support of Bhola Prasad Singh, a former home minister of Bihar. He also cultivated Raj Narain, the mercurial politician who made history by defeating Indira Gandhi and became one of the topmost ministers in the Janata Party regime in 1977.

In line with his core character of striving to rise by-hook-or-by-crook, Romesh Sharma had become friendly with Vardrajan Mudaliar (Vardha Bhai), the undisputed lord of the Mumbai underworld. His indoctrination and training took place with Vardha Bhai in terms of both receiving and giving material, manpower and moral support. Romesh revealed that at one of his first rallies with Vardha Bhai at Kala Ghora, he met the dreaded mafia don Dawood Ibrahim, who was introduced to him as a student leader.

Vardha Bhai patronised several followers like Romesh Sharma and Dawood Ibrahim, but the rise of Romesh Sharma was unique and striking. His extensive activities in the political arena gave rise to such a big clout by 1979 itself that he acquired the image of a fast-rising political leader. He claimed to be the treasurer of the Socialist Party of Maharashtra State, the outfit which was able to contest councillors' elections in Mumbai and won at least seven to eight seats at that time.

From 1979 onwards, as he narrated, Romesh Sharma's political fortunes and profile were on ascendance, particularly due to his association with Chaudhary Charan Singh, who was the home minister at that time and later became the prime minister of India for a short period. When Romesh Sharma's political party was merged with Chaudhary Saheb's party, he was made the convener of Janata Party (Socialist) in Maharashtra.

He claimed during interrogation that he often took Charan Singh in his own car to political rallies and other functions and built almost a father–son relationship with him. In 1979, they fought elections together in Maharashtra as the Lok Dal party; the next year, in 1980, he was made an office-bearer of Maharashtra State Lok Dal, and in 1982, he graduated to become a national-level office-bearer of the Lok Dal.

After the death of Charan Singh, Romesh claimed proximity to his son Ajit Singh, who took over the reins of the party, but he could not continue very long with him. Since Ajit Singh lacked his father's stature and went into political wilderness, Romesh looked for other channels for further rise.

All through, he carried on his nefarious activities in real estate by adopting the modus operandi of acquiring disputed properties and then doing manipulations around them. He claimed that along with one B.K. Jajodia, whose brother M.L. Jajodia owned two companies, namely, Victoria and Kamdhenu, he acquired a major share in Connaught Place's majestic Regal Building in New Delhi. During the trial of the CBI case in which Romesh Sharma forcibly took away the helicopter from H. Suresh Rao and kept in his Jai Mata Di Farm, the Reliance Group President V. Balasubramanium and Wing Commander Vinod Manchanda deposed about handing over the crucial documents concerning the helicopter to us. In this case, Romesh Sharma was sentenced to undergo rigorous imprisonment for 10 years with a fine of Rs 17.5 lakh.

By the time Romesh Sharma turned thirty, as he claimed, he had access to dizzy heights in politics and proximity to Rajiv Gandhi, the heir apparent to Indira Gandhi in the Congress party. He claimed to have been considered for a senior position in the party but the equations soon got altered.

It is to be noted that in his confessional statement made to us, Romesh Sharma talked most loudly about his political persona which ran through his entire career, and somewhat underplayed his mafia role. He claimed that in 1985 he became a senior office-bearer of the Quami Ekta Committee and the Kisan Congress, both of them being Congress party outfits. An income tax raid, confirmed by records, was conducted at his house in 1989, resulting in the seizure of ₹3 lakh cash, Toyota and other imported vehicles, and a tax demand of ₹1.15 crore was made on him as an assessee during the years 1987–1988 to 1989–1990. His political rise, the income tax raids notwithstanding, continued during this period.

He made tall claims about contesting an election for the All India Congress Committee and getting a large number of votes, but Narasimha Rao and other top leaders did not approve and the election was declared null and void. In 1994, he took out a Quami Ekta Rath Yatra from Allahabad to Lucknow. During the intervening period, between 1992 and 1996, as he claimed, he became closer to Devi Lal, the future deputy prime minister and his son Om Prakash Chautala, the future chief minister of Haryana, who had also helped in bringing down the V.P. Singh government.

His political ambitions and active association with different political leaders and groups across party lines brought him close to Lalu Prasad Yadav, he claimed. He further claimed that Lalu offered him a Rajya Sabha seat, but it was denied to him at the last moment.

Disenchanted by Lalu's actions and frustrated by his denial of the promised position, Romesh Sharma endeavoured to form his own party called the All India Bhartiya Congress. While he continued to retain several so-called important positions like the ones in the All India Kisan Sangarsh Samaj, the Youth Unity Centre, the Indo-Italian Friendship Society, the Indian Confederation of Labour and so on, what was really important to him were his political ambitions.

In the midst of the joint raid conducted by the Delhi Police, CBI, Income Tax, Excise and Wildlife Authorities, when I visited his place, he welcomed me and exchanged pleasantries as if he had known me for a long time and acted as a good host. The forty-four-year-old mafia-don-turned-politician was living an extremely ostentatious life, full of opulence and comfort, with luxuries of all kinds at his command.

28

Profiling the Mysterious Mafia

His personal dossier, prepared by the investigators, described Romesh Sharma as a person with healthy habits, a non-smoker, who preferred fresh fruits, juice and simple Indian food along with fish and quail. He avoided strong alcohol and preferred red wine for a healthy heart, maintained robust health, though he suffered from gastritis and a bit of hypertension. He was an extremely sharp and shrewd fellow, quick-witted and humorous, and he could anticipate the investigator's next query. But he could also be very short tempered, arrogant and occasionally violent.

Among his weaknesses were a strong desire to acquire more and more disputed property and foreign cars, besides relationships with women. He harboured an incessant ambition to become both the topmost politician of the country and the richest man in the world. To appear politically correct in public, he used to wear a well-tailored and tight-fitting kurta–pyjama, while in private life he preferred flashy clothes, branded shoes, suits and expensive watches. From the raids at his abodes, several expensive ladies watches were recovered, probably meant to be gifted to women friends. An ardent worshiper of Mata Vaishno Devi, he would pray every morning.

Unable to stand even the soft interrogation soon after his arrest, Romesh Sharma, found with his charming girlfriend Kunjum Budhiraja whom he later allegedly got killed while in Tihar Jail, just gave up. With Kunjum by his side for moral support, he kept on telling stories about his life and political and corporate conections, including one senior corporate executive to whose Connaught Place office he led us for some very crucial and sensitive recoveries resulting in a case under the Official Secrets Act. His disclosures led to the investigation of about twenty cases against him, besides the massive enquiries initiated by the income tax authorities and the CBI, whose reports ran into hundreds of pages.

He gave a detailed account of his life, acquisitions and contacts—they were the who's who of the powers that be. He gave information about thirty-one properties—land, flats and independent houses—he owned in Delhi, Mumbai and Haryana. Keys of fifteen vehicles which were found hanging in a concealed keyboard in his house led to the recovery of cars owned or possessed by him like Cielo, Toyota, Audi, BMW, Honda, Pajero, Contessa, Chevrolet, Mercedes and also several smaller cars.

Romesh Sharma had floated several companies which were allegedly being run with the support of a powerful corporate friend.

These companies provided a cover to the huge number of properties that Romesh Sharma acquired through his goons and muscle power. He was in touch with the contacts of Dawood Ibrahim in Mumbai and Dubai. An expert in trapping vulnerable and disputed property owners through women and money, coupled with threats, he made full use of his political and mafia friends. He forced the targeted property owners to sign agreements for rent and sale, besides power-of-attorney documents to transfer the ownerships of the properties.

The documents and details of thirty-one such properties were found during the search of his house. The properties were of all kinds—farmhouses, residential plots, commercial land, industrial land, besides independent houses and flats in Delhi, Haryana, UP and Mumbai. We came across a large number of flats owned by him located in Ghaziabad, Safdarjung Enclave, Palam Vihar, Mehrauli and also in Mumbai. He owned or controlled several flats in Delhi's posh areas like Sarvodaya Enclave, Mayfair Gardens, Connaught Place, besides other expensive properties in Greater Kailash, Lajpat Nagar, Panchsheel, Tughlakabad and Sarvapriya Vihar.

We also learnt that he owned several plots and flats including a penthouse and a huge property at Juhu beach near Sun-n-Sand hotel. It was difficult to track down all the real estate that appeared to be under his control, which included 200 acres of agricultural land in Faridabad. He had some of the better-known chartered accountants and lawyers to look after his property interests.

During the searches, stamps and seals of numerous commercial companies that Romesh Sharma had floated along with his associates, were found. They included companies like Honda Exports, RR Exports, RR Gems and Jewels, Penguin Exports and Indo-American Associates. As an initial estimate, all of us in CBI, Delhi Police, Income Tax and other authorities felt that all these ill-gotten properties could easily be worth over ₹500 crore, a sizable amount in those times.

Among the several property documents that were recovered from his house, there were some unsigned ones too, like the one in favour of Balu pertaining to an expensive plot in Safdarjung Enclave. He wanted to acquire this property from the father-in-law of Janak Raj Gupta, the MP from Jammu, which, fortuitously, could be saved due to timely intervention.

In Mayfair Gardens itself, despite a case being investigated by the Crime Branch with regard to a disputed property, Romesh Sharma was able to secure the rights and a possession letter from Ajay Nayyar, the original seller, who could not to be found. Similarly, the prime property of Regal Building, Connaught Place, was taken from an unknown Sanjay Sabharwal. Romesh Sharma was able to dupe and even coerce a powerful politician,

M.K. Subba, an MP from Assam. Subba had a property in the Mehrauli area held in the name of his tribal wife, Karma Kamu.

Despite a case being registered by Subba regarding an adjacent property in Mehrauli, Delhi Police Crime Branch and the Special Task Force could not proceed further until our team arrested Romesh Sharma and the investigation was carried out in greater depth. A twist took place in our investigations when the Delhi land matters got connected with some land matters of Mumbai and through this surfaced the connection of Romesh Sharma with the most-wanted international crook, Dawood Ibrahim. In Mumbai, a property located on Royal Turner Road and, most importantly, the allegedly disputed prime property at Juhu beach, had become a sort of a bone of contention between Romesh Sharma and Dawood Ibrahim.

In Delhi Police, we had a new insight into the Romesh Sharma case when we came to learn, with the help of the Mumbai Police, that Dawood was keen to acquire the Sun-n-Sand hotel in Juhu in Mumbai, at that time under the forced occupation of Romesh Sharma. Dawood probably planned to carry out his illicit business of smuggling, camouflaged under the operations of the famous hotel. When Romesh Sharma refused to part with this property, the D-Company (as the Dawood gang was called) acted with vengeance. Some Mumbai-based gangsters, on the directions of D-Company, organised a lethal attack on the property, ransacked everything and put it on fire. Everything there got burnt, we were told.

Romesh Sharma said that he did not give up, nor did he succumb to D-Company's pressure. With the support of his political connections in Delhi, he remained in occupation of the property, he claimed. Using his own goons and with the help of his self-developed political clout and his committed cousin brother, Harish Mishra, he continued to maintain an office at that very site and monitor his Mumbai operations.

As he had started a fight with the D-Company, the matter was not going to die down easily. The Mumbai incident of the fire in the Sun-n-Sand hotel initiated an interaction between Dawood and Romesh Sharma. It could not be said that they compromised with each other nor that they internally harboured a dislike for each other. It was a kind of a status quo. Around the same time, H. Suresh Rao's helicopter-related dispute erupted and the matter flared up, suggesting a connection with Dawood.

Suresh Rao complained to us that he started getting telephone calls from Irfan Goga of Dubai, Dawood's henchman, threatening to kill him if he did not comply with Romesh Sharma's wishes. He could be rescued and saved from the continuous threats and torture only with our 20 October raids and the registration of cases.

Our investigations revealed that in several property-related cases, Romesh Sharma took the support of the Dawood gang. To grab the posh Mayfair Gardens property, Romesh Sharma impersonated the Mumbai-based property dealer Rajendra Kumar Sharma and utilised his D-Company underworld connections to the hilt.

In another case registered with the police, he terrorised one Lakshman Jiwanani, a Mumbai businessman. Along with Jiwanani he cheated and terrorised a Mumbai-based lady, Mandakani Hule. In December 1992, Romesh Sharma threatened them to force them to release a property.

Romesh admitted that he had threatened Jiwanani while he (Romesh) was in Dubai, under the care of the D-Company. He had gone to Dubai to participate in Dawood Ibrahim's birthday celebrations which used to be organised on a large scale, he claimed. As per police records, Romesh Sharma had threatened Jiwanani that he and his family would be eliminated in case he did not forget about the said property.

Around October 1998, when our joint team exposed and brought to light Romesh Sharma's mafia activities, the Delhi

Police had already registered several cases against him. Interestingly, the charges included the deal in which Romesh Sharma was in close contact with the MP, M.K. Subba, in an illicit property transaction in Chhatarpur, Delhi.

Another important case pending investigation with Delhi Police was that of retired Wing Commander Romesh Malik's property which his tenant Ashok Malik, the managing director of Modi Rubber Ltd, was allegedly attempting to take over. In his typical style, Romesh Sharma got involved in that case. He involved the dreaded criminal Abu Salem, Dawood Ibrahim's close associate in India, in the transaction. Abu Salem made threatening calls to Romesh Malik, asking him to forget about his property. Romesh Malik later gave the telephone number of Abu Salem to the police, which was subsequently verified and found to be correct.

All these and many other similar activities opened up numerous cases of the Romesh Sharma–Dawood Ibrahim association and several deals between them of a criminal nature. Interestingly, all these criminal relationships had crystallised from 1978 onwards through the common patronage of the big gangster Vardha Bhai (Vardrajan Mudaliar). From that original gang, among others, emanated two major mafia streams flowing as two separate entities, Dawood's so-called D-Company and Romesh Sharma's land mafia coupled with strong political aspirations.

Romesh Sharma claimed that by 1985 he had become so powerful that he was considered to be a frontrunner in the world of international gangsters. Once, in a dispute over a property at Juhu beach where the Chandragupta Hotel was built, he got into direct confrontation with Vardha Bhai's sons and, he claimed, he had an upper hand in the dispute. He also claimed that once he got his own mentor Vardha Bhai arrested with the help of DCP Pawar of Mumbai Police. Vardha Bhai got so disturbed by that arrest that he soon shifted to Chennai and ultimately died there.

The conflicts between Dawood and Sharma took place only during the initial years—until 1992, when they had a grand reunion at a dinner organised by Dawood Ibrahim at his White House in Dubai, he claimed.

The partnership and camaraderie between Dawood and Sharma flourished and became stronger with the passage of time. Despite the clear involvement of Dawood and his gang members in terrorism cases and being the most-wanted criminals, Romesh Sharma remained in continuous touch with Dawood's brothers and associates like Anees and Shakeel. In July 1993, following the Mumbai bomb blasts, Dawood wanted to get his mother Aminabi Ibrahim Kaskar, whose passport had expired, out of India. Romesh Sharma claimed to have organised the entire operation for her exit from India.

As disclosed by Sharma, Aminabi met him through Nizami Nurul Hasan of Hazrat Nizamuddin Dargah. With the help of his trusted aides, Arvind alias Bali and V.K. Luthra alias Billoo Sharma, he managed to get her passport extended by giving false information to the under secretary, ministry of external affairs, that her son-in-law was injured in an accident in Dubai and was on his deathbed.

Amina's passport was extended through Sharma's connections in the external affairs ministry and she left for Dubai by flight EL701 on 20 July 1998. While Sharma's henchmen Bali and Billoo were initially arrested in this passport case since they were the supposedly respectable referees, the external affairs ministry's file having been 'lost', the CBI could never prove the case, even after Sharma was arrested.

The investigation of Romesh Sharma's case was an altogether different experience and it gave us a new learning of the criminal justice system of our country. My talks with my alter ego continued as I tried to resolve the queries arising in my mind. Throughout, I felt that our system provided the leeway for the rise of such dangerous gangsters who posed an immense threat to national security, while harming our sociopolitical life.

My alter ego asked, 'If the police were aware of all this, why was Romesh Sharma not arrested earlier or why was he allowed to rise so much?'

I replied, 'The Indian police is affected by two phenomena—first, its sincere work gets defeated in the judicial process because the court system requires cogent and admissible evidence. Second, the police structure itself is not foolproof and it is prone to influence by power and money.'

My alter ego asked further, 'How do you feel when a high profile mafia–gangster with a network all over supporting his criminal activities—like Romesh Sharma—gets arrested and thoroughly investigated, and then held guilty by the court, resulting in a punishment? And once inside, he can't escape from the jail, no matter what his connections or resources are. Despite the gaping holes and endless weaknesses in the system, it is the strength of our country's justice system that such characters remain incarcerated for years.'

I replied, 'The manner in which the information was developed about the criminal-cum-mafia activities of Romesh Sharma with the help of my CBI colleague Neeraj Kumar, which led to a massive multi-agency investigation resulting in his prolonged incarceration, was a matter of great satisfaction to all of us. We could do all this by successfully negotiating the pitfalls of our criminal justice system.

India's prison system is not at all foolproof, but Tihar Jail does keep for long the types of Romesh Sharma within its confines. It's debatable whether the prisons are too lenient, too stringent or just 'manageable' by the inmates. Often, a lot depends on who the prisoner is and the level or category he or she occupies. As an example, let us review the long incarceration and the historic escape from jail by the notorious Charles Sobhraj, the international criminal who played at will with India's legal system and the largest jail for decades.'

29

Charles and I: Early Acquaintances

It was a routine that started after my marriage—carrying home-made lunch to work. Since 1974, whenever together, Rekha, my wife, chooses to be a 'domestic engineer' as she calls herself, and takes up this job quite passionately and diligently. Cooking delicious recipes suitable for the particular person being her forte, she always ensures that I have something tasty and healthy to eat for lunch. That day in 1986 was no different.

I was sitting in my makeshift investigation centre in the basement of the newly constructed Ashok Vihar Police Station. This basement housed the lock-up which witnessed the custodial investigations of some famous and fascinating, though extremely unsavoury, criminals. Along with my team, I was interrogating two of them at that time—the prime accused of the internationally talked about Tihar Jail escape case, Charles Gurumukh Sobhraj, and his companion, David Richard Hall, who were in the lock-up on police remand.

As I opened my lunch box to find home-made parathas with a spicy masala aloo sabzi, of course a Rekha recipe, an idea came to me about David, who was practically on hunger strike at that time. I called the constable on duty.

'David *ko le kar aao* (bring David),' I instructed him.

Soon David walked in.

'So, David, I believe you don't like the food we have been giving you here,' I said without preamble.

David Richard Hall, a Briton who had been earlier arrested from Delhi airport with charas (cannabis) in his possession and released prior to Charles's escape from Tihar jail, was a photographer by profession—a sensitive person by all accounts. He was in our custody, having been again arrested with his more famous, or rather infamous, companion, Charles. I was interrogating both of them to find out the details of Charles's escape from Tihar jail along with his dreaded co-accused, in which David had played a very crucial role, and their criminal history.

Unlike his notorious companion, David was finding life in the lock-up quite difficult. Temperamentally, he was always like that—being a creative artist who was caught in a situation of becoming a hard-core conspirator-accused under the influence of Charles Sobhraj.

David mumbled something in response to my comment on food as I gestured to him to sit.

'Have some lunch,' I offered, pointing to my lunch.

'David *ke liye* plate *lao* (bring a plate for David),' I asked the astonished constable, who was watching me closely.

'My wife has made this food. I am sure you will like it,' I told David.

The mention of my wife and my kind tone were enough to make David start blubbering. Soon, this man, who had been a key actor in one of the most daring jailbreaks in Indian history, who had so far maintained a stubborn silence during interrogation, was weeping like a child.

My wife's cooking brought out his own concern for his wife. He appeared to be an emotional wreck, worried terribly about her safety—he feared his dreaded co-criminal would cause her harm—and desperate to get out of the mess he was in.

Rekha's parathas could help to achieve what several hours of interrogation by experienced professionals could not. David

Hall sang like a canary and revealed the diabolical plan that had led to the escape from Tihar Jail of the notorious Bikini Killer, Charles Sobhraj. The story is a part of our police investigation records, which led to a thorough investigation and then a trial of Charles, along with numerous others, resulting in a ten-year incarceration of Charles. David was released after some time, and he soon joined his nurse-wife Maria Hall at Leamington Spa in the UK.

To continue the story of Charles and his association with me—on 28 October 2015, the *Times of India* published a story 'Charles Confesses to Randeep Hooda in Jail Why He Couldn't Stop *Main aur Charles*' along with a poster signed by Charles Sobhraj when he met Randeep in Kathmandu Jail. Several filmmakers had unsuccessfully attempted a film on Sobhraj, one of the most notorious international criminals also known as the 'Bikini Killer'. He had earned this sobriquet for drugging and cold-bloodedly murdering many unsuspecting young women in bikinis whom he had befriended.

He was also called 'Serpent' for his extremely deceptive and cunning modus operandi. His sensational killings had earned him a dubious celebrity status and, contrary to my experience with this dirty character, many—particularly some women who fell for him—described him as 'handsome, charming and knowledgeable'.

When Randeep Hooda and the director Prawaal Raman called me from Mumbai and said that they were trying to meet Charles in Nepal where he was jailed, I was terribly put off and tried to dissuade them. Charles, with his sharp, scheming brain, had learnt how he could subvert the system. He realised he could use his notoriety to make a killing by invoking the copyright clause on his life story whenever anyone approached him for an interview or sought to make a movie on him. But Randeep and Prawaal were wiser than me. Prawaal succeeded in making *Main aur Charles*, the first ever full-scale film on Charles, without paying a single penny to him. In fact, they also managed to secure his full support along with a signed poster as endorsement.

Charles told Randeep in Kathmandu Jail, 'I have not given anyone the rights to make a film on me. I consulted my lawyer in France and tried to stop you. But because you had taken the rights from Amod Kanth, I knew I could not do anything. That was a good move on your part.'

Once again, I had managed to out-think the Serpent whom I had arrested after his audacious jailbreak from Tihar. Since the movie *Main aur Charles* was made from my perspective and was my story, he could not invoke the copyright laws on the film. All he could do was watch the movie!

Randeep told the media, 'Charles asked us to convey his salaam to Amod Kanth.' Charles also asked Randeep and Prawaal to meet him in the court on the next hearing. 'I have many more stories, meet me, we will negotiate,' he said. He did not want to let go an opportunity to try and make some money from them.

For me and for the entire *Main Aur Charles* team including Randeep Hooda who played Charles, Adil Hussain who played Amod Kanth and Raman Prawaal, the director who made the movie, it was all a cathartic experience. I have been connected to Prawaal in a very personal and completely non-commercial way, and I permitted him to make the film purely due to his love for me and his deep attachment for my charity 'Prayas' which figures in the culmination of the movie.

I had understood the true character of Charles well—the most cunning and perhaps the most obnoxious criminal I came across during my entire police career. I can never forget the foul stench emanating from him. It was an olfactory assault when

I spent endless hours with him in the newly built Ashok Vihar Police station lock-up. Following his sensational Tihar Jail escape, thanks to DGP Maharashtra Suryakant Jog who was earlier my Police Commissioner in Delhi, Charles was arrested by Mumbai Police Inspector Madhukar Zende in Goa, from where he was taken to Mumbai by the Mumbai Police team and, most unhappily, I had to bring him back to Delhi in a chartered Border Security Force (BSF) aircraft.

Prawaal was a critically acclaimed director of psychological thrillers like *Darna Mana Hai* and *404*. I knew him since his childhood and was his local guardian in Delhi. He was aware that I had investigated Charles after he escaped from Tihar Jail in 1986. In 2010, he met me and I formally shared my experience of how we pieced together the details of his escape, tracked him down to Goa and investigated this marathon case.

Prawaal partly took the story from the public domain and fictionalised my character along with Charles Sobhraj's. *Main aur Charles* earned critical success due to his direction and also the brilliant acting by the internationally acclaimed actors Adil Hussain and Randeep Hooda. Adil played me and Randeep played Charles, both having the uncanny ability to get inside the skin of the characters they portrayed.

The making of the film was as exciting for me as the actual investigation. Earlier, it was being jointly produced by Mahesh and Pooja Bhatt, and Prawaal. The working title of this project, which was given up by the Bhatt–Prawaal team due to some issues between them, was 'Bad'. In 2013, when the film was in its early stages of production, I was in Mumbai to visit the Umarkhari Juvenile Home as a part of my work with delinquent children. I still remember the meeting I had with the entire film crew at the hotel. Instead of discussing the Charles story, Mahesh Bhatt got into an involved discussion with me on Buddha's death. So Randeep and Prawaal had to travel with me to the airport in torrential rain, to try and get all the information from me about the Charles story!

I have taken out my Delhi Police Diary of 1986 with its pages all yellow and brittle and turned to the relevant pages. The date reads 16 March, a Sunday. It was an old habit of mine—I kept a detailed journal of all the big crimes and events in my police work. I locate the entry 'Case FIR no. 139 dated 16/3/86 u/s (under sections) 222, 223, 224, 228, 161, 328 r/w (read with) 120B and 34 IPC, Police Station Janakpuri, West Delhi District'.

This sensational case occupies an unusually large and disproportionate space in my diary—more than 10 pages of minute scribblings that explain a major part of this most complex and devious jail escape. As against this, about the same period, there is a brief half-page reference to (Harjinder Singh) Jinda's escape from judicial custody in Ahmedabad while being taken to the court.

Terrorist Jinda and his gang had earlier committed numerous sensational terrorist killings in Delhi and outside. He came in the limelight for the assassinations of the brilliant parliamentarian Lalit Maken, a close Gandhi family associate and Councillor Arjun Dass. After escaping from custody, he killed the former army chief during Operation Blue Star, General Arun Shridhar Vaidya.

Coming back to Charles Sobhraj, my encounter with him is etched unforgettably in my mind. Much before he gained notoriety as an international criminal and his most ingeniously planned and executed Tihar Jail escape on 16 March 1986, our Crime Branch and the Crime Record Office (CRO) had started keeping his track.

In the dossier, he was Charles Gurumukh Sobhraj, son of Hotchand Sobhraj, born in Saigon (now called Ho Chi Minh City) in Vietnam on 6 April 1944. His mother was Therese Phung, a French national with an address in Marseilles. He lived with her in Paris and claimed to have graduated in Science from La Sorbonne University in 1966. By then he was already an offender, being a juvenile delinquent for some time. He had started indulging in small crimes and could manage to travel abroad extensively.

Charles came to India for the first time in 1961–1962, but he did not come to the notice of any law enforcement authority and returned to France. Soon after completing college, in 1967, he had a 'love marriage' with Chantal Compagnon, a French national said to be 'coming from a conservative Parisian family'. Charles had a daughter with Chantal named Usha Sobhraj in 1970 while they were in Mumbai. This marriage did not last long and Usha stayed with her mother after the separation. Charles returned to India the same year Usha was born.

By this time, Charles's father Hotchand had got married again. His new wife was Kamla Sobhraj and they settled in Pune. From this marriage of Hotchand, Charles Sobhraj had several half-siblings. Among them, Jaidev and Suresh lived in Pune and Gobind went to the US. Hotchand died in 1973, leaving behind this large family in India and a vagabond half-French son Charles, who was obviously hugely enamoured with India. But Hotchand had been alive when Charles began his criminal career and had established his signature modus operandi.

The first record by Delhi Police of Charles's criminal career was on 1 November 1971. He was found without any passport and was arrested near the diplomatic area of Chanakyapuri in New Delhi. Exactly forty-five days later, on 16 December, he played his trademark trick of feigning illness, and while being taken to Wellington Hospital (now called Ram Manohar Lohia Hospital), he escaped from custody.

For these two crimes—having no documents and running away from custody—when he was apprehended in 1978–1979, he was sentenced to two years simple imprisonments for each crime by Metropolitan Magistrate A.K. Srivastava and my old friend, Magistrate S.K. Tandon. S.K. Tandon narrated the stories about Charles to me and gave some insights about him as he had, by then, acquired a reputation of sorts.

During this period, his activities didn't come to the notice of the Indian police prominently. But he was caught by the immigration authorities at the Palam Airport while posing as Dr Gillian Claire, holding a British passport on which he had affixed his own photograph. In the same series of court verdicts in 1978, Charles was convicted on three counts for a total rigorous imprisonment of five years, with fines.

I had joined the Indian Police Service (IPS) in 1974 and following the initial 'foundational course' at Mussoorie at the Lal Bahadur Shastri National Academy of Administration along with IAS and other services, we went to Mount Abu in Rajasthan to the Sardar Vallabhbhai Patel National Police Academy, which was soon shifted to Hyderabad—along with us. Concluding my hardcore police training at Hyderabad and three months rigorous attachment at the Punjab Police Training Academy, Phillaur, I joined Delhi Police, having been allotted the Union Territories (UT) cadre of the IPS.

I was posted for one year of field training to India's smallest but most sensitive district—New Delhi. It was a stimulating team to learn and work with, attached to the Chanakyapuri sub-division with the wiry, smart and elusive Sub Divisional Police Officer (SDPO) Ram Pal Singh (or 'RP' as he was called), whose wife Bina bhabhi liked me and my wife Rekha a lot. This period was thought-provoking and the training provided me with an opportunity to learn from brilliant police officers of the cadre—Maxwell Pereira and my co-trainee, Qamar Ahmad.

I was deep into learning about criminal investigations, along with the SHOs and IOs of New Delhi district. My training required me to study different types of cases. My district training location was at the Superintendent of Police's (SP's) office in the Parliament Street Police Station complex and at Police Station Chanakyapuri.

This was an interesting time as I lived in a small, two-room apartment within the police station complex—on duty 24x7—along with my small family of five members as my parents and my sister Rupa were with Rekha and me for several months during this period. With the highly supportive trainer RP, I had the opportunity to study different kinds of policing functions—important crimes were only a few in the district, but law-and-order problems like protests, rallies and dharnas were in abundance.

Very close to the New Delhi District Headquarters at Parliament Street—the hub of national-level political activities—on Jai Singh Road was located the Young Men's Christian Association (YMCA) hostel. This was a popular and relatively safe, decent and cheap place to stay for foreigners. Conveniently located amidst foreigners, Charles Sobhraj stayed there with a false passport and the assumed name, Cornaire David. It was with this name that on 6 June 1976 he committed one of the more serious crimes during my training. He booked room 307 and stayed with his girlfriend Mary Ellen Ether, close to a group of tourists from his own country. His French victims had booked room 454, one floor above his room.

Who knows, our paths may have unknowingly crossed at this time—I on my way to work and he on the lookout for potential victims.

30

International Crook

In his typical style, which he had already adopted and kept practising all through his criminal career, Charles and his girlfriend became very friendly with the unsuspecting group of foreigners at the YMCA hostel and administered them tranquillisers. Together, Charles and Ellen robbed all of them. Since by now Charles Sobhraj was notorious for such crimes which targeted innocent and gullible foreigners and drugged them after befriending them, his handiwork was recognised and he was soon apprehended.

Much later, on 22 October 1981, while being in judicial custody (that is, in jail) in Delhi, along with other cases he was tried and convicted to undergo five years and three months rigorous imprisonment (RI) by ASJ T.S. Oberoi. Ellen Esther, in an unusual conduct for the women co-accused with Charles Sobhraj, somehow came out of his spell and decided to depose against him. She became an approver in the case and was released after being given a pardon.

Charles had earlier managed to return to Europe following his involvements and arrests in the crimes in Delhi and elsewhere in India during 1970–1972. Back home in France, he spent time with his wife and getting to know his daughter until 1974, when he divorced Chantal. The incorrigible liar and deceiver that he was, the real hallmark of this notorious cheat was that he spared no one—not even the most intimate persons, including his wife Chantal, were spared his criminal perfidy. Perpetually restless, a traveller with cold-blooded designs, at times appearing to be psychopathic—though I prefer not to assign him the benefit of being a psychological case—he was compelled by an inexplicable urge to commit the most heinous crimes.

In my understanding of him, Charles, who was always completely in control of the situation and himself, was wilfully treading the path of crime out of greed as much as owing to a cruel streak. In early 1976, he came back to India from Europe and committed several crimes, including the drugging–robbery at YMCA for which he was arrested by Delhi Police in July 1976. He was in jail, this time for ten years, from 1976 to 1986—there was no going back or release or escape. He stayed in the jail until 16 March 1986, when he made his audacious escape from Tihar.

When Charles escaped from Tihar, along with the investigations we carried out in minute detail, we looked for his record in the Delhi Police dossier on him. There was only sparse information available about his life and crimes there. Far more material about him could be found in the stories which he himself generated in the media about his exploits and in the so-called non-fiction books like *Serpentine* (published in 1979) written by Thomas Thomson, *Life and Crimes of Charles Sobhraj* (1980) written by Richard Neville and Julie Clarke and the article in *Reader's Digest* 'The Bikini Murders' (1982) written by Noel Barber, which gave him the notorious title of 'Bikini Killer' and, of course, he was included among the 'Great Cases of the Interpol'.

From the reports in India and abroad and from the stories floating around about him, we could build a reasonable record of his criminal antecedents and an authentic life-profile. Separation of his parents and desertion by his father made him dependent as a teenager on his mother's boyfriend, a French army lieutenant who took them to Indo-China. In his younger days, he kept moving between France, Indochina and India, as he narrated. He also became friendly with his half-brother Andrien with whom, subsequently, he committed some serious crimes outside France before abandoning him in a jail, like he abandoned many others.

Going back to his criminal records, he started off as a 'juvenile delinquent' but the first reported crime committed by him as a 'young offender' was in 1963. It was a burglary for which he served a jail sentence in Poissy Prison near Paris. In jail he learnt some tricks for gaining confidence of the jail officials and the other prison inmates. He became very friendly with Felix d'Escogne, said to be a wealthy and kind jail volunteer, with whom he remained friendly even when released from prison. On parole from jail, he displayed his typical dual personality—moving between high society and crimes like burglary and cheating, making a good income out of both.

Charles was smart, but not smart enough to stay out of the reach of police as was evident from his second arrest for driving a stolen car right on the day he had proposed to Chantal. Chantal, like most of his besotted girlfriends, was not deterred and waited for eight months to marry him while he served a sentence for auto theft.

His irrepressible criminal instincts soon grew stronger and also engulfed his pregnant, enamoured, loving wife Chantal, who escaped with Charles from France to Eastern Europe, entered Asia on fake travel documents and arrived in Mumbai, where their daughter Usha was born. By then Charles was deep into cheating, thefts and gambling, and graduating to serious crimes. He was arrested in a failed robbery attempt in Delhi's famous Ashoka Hotel's jewellery shop. In 1973, getting himself bailed out with money from his father Hotchand, he escaped to Kabul, where he developed his new modus operandi of targeting hippies who were always on the move all over Asia including Afghanistan, looking for kicks and drugs.

In Kabul, Charles was again caught while robbing tourists, but escaped custody by feigning illness and drugging the hospital guards. Chantal couldn't bear it any more and went back to Paris with Usha, swearing she would never meet him again.

Charles now had the freedom to commit crimes along with his half-brother Andrien, who had joined him. Using multiple fake passports which they acquired from their foreigner victims, both of them kept country-hopping, committing crimes in Eastern Europe and the Middle East until they were arrested in Athens and handed over by the Greeks to the Turkish police. From here, Charles escaped, deserting his half-brother, who was convicted and served jail sentences for eighteen years.

Already wanted by the French, Indian, Afghan, Greek and Turkish police, Charles expanded his criminal playground to the global tourist destination, Thailand. He was joined by Marie-Andree Leclerc, a Canadian tourist craving for adventure. In Thailand, Charles honed his skills further, becoming a fake-jewellery and drug dealer, targeting tourists.

Confidence trickster and a hardened crook that he was, he would drug his newly acquired tourist friends and steal their passports. Sometimes he would administer drugs and cause dysentery in his victims and then offer to help cure them and recover their documents. Along with Leclerc, in these and many other crimes, he was joined by an Indian, Ajay Chowdhury, with whom he committed several murders in Thailand and Nepal—the popular hippie and backpacker destinations where they found their prey in plenty.

This was the period when places like Thailand and Nepal, and locations like Varanasi and Goa in India, were overflowing with hippies in small and large groups, exploring their new-found spirituality in drugs and distorted forms of Hinduism, Buddhism and so on. Charles, adept in all kinds of con jobs including fake spirituality, drugs and glib talks, pretended to be a saviour and a Good Samaritan and presented Leclerc and Ajay Chowdhury as 'family' to build confidence.

Together, the three of them regularly targeted the 'family members' among the foreign tourists whom they brought in the group drugged, robbed and killed. Teresa Knowlton, a young

American tourist from Seattle, was a victim who was found drowned in the tidal pool of Thailand Gulf in a flowered bikini. Another victim was Charmayne Carrou, a French girl whose body was found on the beach in a similar kind of a flowered bikini.

Carrou's nomadic Turkish boyfriend, Vitali Hakim's burnt body was found near a Pattaya resort where Charles and 'family' lived together. Charles had invited his Hong Kong acquaintances, Henker Bintanja and his fiancee Cornelia Hemker, to the 'Thailand family' to live together. He initially drugged and later nursed them back to health to gain their confidence. At that time, when the victims had disappeared, Charles was suspected. Though their bodies were found on 18 December 1975, before they could be identified by the Thailand police, Sobhraj and Leclerc escaped and crossed over to Nepal on forged passports by affixing their own photographs.

Charles, now in 2022, is serving a life sentence in Nepal, where he had been tried for the murder of two tourists, the Canadian national Lauret Ormond Carriere, 26, and the American national from California, Connie Bronzich, 29, whose burnt bodies were found on 22 December 1975. Sobhraj and Lelerc used the passports of Carriere and Bronzich to go to Thailand before the Nepal Police could identify the bodies. The French 'family members' meanwhile became suspicious of Charles and his partner, and they went back to Paris, tipping off the local authorities.

At that time Charles was questioned by the Thailand police but they let him off. A Dutch diplomat, Herman Knippenberg and his wife Angela Kane, it appears, got deeply interested in the murder of Bintanja and Hemker, and they collected evidence against Charles to build a case which helped both the Thailand and Nepal Police, who ultimately caught him.

In between, within a short period, Charles kept travelling and went to Kolkata where he allegedly murdered an Israeli scholar Avoni Jacob to take his passport for use. It appears he went to

Singapore, Malaysia and Thailand, where he was questioned by the police for the 'bikini murders' without any evidence in hand. In Malaysia, Charles, Leclerc and Ajay Chowdhury actively dealt in precious gems, planning to go to Switzerland for business. While Charles and Leclerc continued their travels, Chowdhury mysteriously disappeared, never to be found. It is suspected that he too may have been killed by Charles.

Charles and Leclerc came to India and here they created a 'family' again, with two French tourists, Barbara Sheryl Smith and Mary Ellen Eather, whom they met in Mumbai. Sobhraj came to Delhi and befriended another French tourist, Jean-Luc Soloman. In Delhi, Sobhraj, Leclerc, Smith and Eather joined hands to pretend to be guides for a group of French tourists whom they served drugs to cause dysentery, as they had done so many times earlier, intending to win their confidence by helping them recover. The drug acted faster than planned and those who had consumed it started falling ill. Raising alarm, they called the police. Jean-Luc Soloman died, Charles was arrested along with his three women accomplices and landed in Tihar Jail.

All of them were tried and Charles was sentenced to life imprisonment. Leclerc turned an approver against Charles, being privy to the entire chain of events. Finally, she was pardoned by the court and allowed to go back to Canada. Smith and Eather couldn't adjust to the jail conditions and even before the trial, they attempted to commit suicide.

This was the brief story of Charles's life and crimes before he was arrested by us in July 1976. He was incarcerated for the next ten years in Tihar Jail which gave him the notoriety that he encashed all his life after that, until he was arrested and sentenced in Nepal in 2004. In his longest incarceration, now serving a life sentence in Kathmandu Jail for the past eighteen years, he has been playing all his tricks including a so-called marriage with a young girl.

31

Charles in Tihar: The Master Escape

The told and untold stories of Charles in Tihar Jail, Asia's largest prison, are legion. The stories actually began in 1976. This was the time when a gang of jail inmates had become very prominent in Tihar on account of their cleverly crafted litigations against the jail authorities 'to protect their human rights' in the prison. Charles joined hands with the notorious jail inmates Sunil Batra, Vipin Jaggi, Ravinder Kapur and Shahnawaj Khan, who were all being tried, convicted or serving sentences in Delhi's first big, armed, bank-van robbery, which had taken place on 28 September 1970.

Sunil Batra, the spoiled brat of a rich family, led the sensational Union Bank van robbery in which the driver and gunman were shot dead and the others in the van were forced to hand over two cash boxes containing ₹ 6 lakh, which the robbers carried away in their stolen car. Batra was sentenced to death by the Trial Court and the others were given life imprisonment, which were subsequently altered by the High Court and the Supreme Court.

Batra got into a prolonged litigation not only about his own death sentence but also about the prison conditions through writs which went up to the Supreme Court, attracting arguments supporting him by leading lawyers like Ram Jethmalani and S.P. Minocha. The judgement was delivered by legendary human rights supporting Supreme Court judge, Justice V.R. Krishna Iyer.

Subsequently, in the case—Sunil Batra vs Delhi Administration (1980 SC 488)—regarding a prisoner tortured by inserting a baton in the anus for refusing to pay a bribe, Justice Krishna Iyer observed about Tihar Jail, 'Bribery at the point of barbarity is a flourishing trade within the house of punishment itself.'

Charles Sobhraj seized the opportunity to get into this gang led by Sunil Batra, who had become a celebrity in the jail as the defender of the rights of prisoners through his cases, which became famous for their rulings. Sobhraj banded with Batra and group and, together, they kept the prison officials in dread, threatening them by filing petitions in the higher courts on small issues.

Sobhraj quickly learned the ropes of how to control the prison system in Tihar while intimidating the prisoners and also encouraging them to file petitions. In due course of time, he became the real 'lord' of the jail, becoming friendly with the prison officials, bribing them and using all types of inducements to ultimately control them. Within a decade of his stay at Tihar Jail, in 1986, all this culminated in perhaps the most talked about jail escape case.

At about 2:50 PM on 16 March 1986, the superintendent of Tihar Jail, Rajesh Somaal, was enjoying his siesta when his deputy superintendent from Jail No. 3, V.D. Pushkarna, informed him that some escape had taken place from the *deorhi* (main gate) of his jail. The siren was sounded and Somaal, along with Pushkarna and other jail officials, rushed from the inside route, while some others, along with V.K. Munniswami, the assistant commandant of Tamil Nadu Armed Police—the force guarding the jail, on deputation from the state of Tamil Nadu—reached the spot from the outside.

Somaal and Munniswami found Constables Suleman and Selvam, who were assigned frisking and searching duty, lying against the table in a semi-conscious state. Jhuman Singh, the warder on gatekeeping duty, was lying unconscious with a tape hanging around his neck. The warder Ram Chander, on sentry (guard) duty from 12 noon to 3 PM, was also lying unconscious with his rifle lying next to him. The unconscious or semi-conscious Assistant Superintendent S.R. Yadav, warders Jhuman Singh, Anand Prakash and Ram Chander, were all taken to Deen Dayal Upadhyay Hospital for medical treatment.

The undertrial prisoner Mohammed Atiq, an eyewitness to the incident, who had gone to the Jail Hospital and, at the time of the occurrence, was waiting at the *deorhi* of Jail No. 3 for his escort to take him to his Camp Jail, gave a detailed account of the incident. He saw Charles Sobhraj escape along with the notorious undertrial prisoners Laxmi Narain, Ajay Singh, Brij Mohan and Bajrang, besides the convicted criminals Bhola and Dinesh Kumar. He had seen four friends of Charles Sobhraj serving burfi (milk fudge), custard, grapes, puris and so on to all the staff on duty. When the jail officials became unconscious, Charles and his friends escaped from the main gate and got into a car waiting outside. Atiq said that when he peeped out through the gate to see what was happening, Charles Sobhraj pointed a pistol towards him, and out of fear, he retreated inside.

A case was registered on the complaint of Rajesh Somaal at Police Station Janakpuri and then the investigation was transferred to the Crime Branch of Delhi Police, of which I was the DCP. It all happened without any loss of time since the Police Commissioner Ved Marwah himself called and directed me to swing into action without the routine formalities.

Thus began our full-time commitment to one particular case for over a month, at a time when I had many more cases, perhaps far more important, in my hands. It was partly because of the dramatic and sensational nature of the escape of these notorious criminals involved in very serious crimes, and mostly for the reason that the nefarious operation was led by the notorious international criminal, Charles Gurumukh Sobhraj.

For me, Tihar Jail wasn't an unknown place—not because I was ever an inmate or resident of the place, but because a couple of years earlier, when I was DCP West Delhi, this sprawling area was a part of my jurisdiction. I had several occasions to go inside the jail and protect the jail officials on some highly sensitive occasions like the one when Sant Bhindrawale had come there with his heavily armed storm-troopers whom I had to confront personally to establish the jail manual protocol. Little did I know at that time that six years later I would end up spending a lot of my time in this jail as DCP Crime, investigating a jail escape.

I was horrified to discover that the jail officials had violated all the protocols and systems laid down in the jail manuals. Over the years, Tihar Jail had changed considerably. It expanded in capacity and perhaps improved in its facilities, but it had completely broken down as an institution with all rules and regulations thrown to the winds—it majorly worked under the influence of Charles and his ilk, who operated in connivance with the highly corrupt jail officials. Much more than the investigation of the escape, it turned out to be a thorough probe into the detailed reasons and circumstances under which Charles controlled the part of jail (No. 3) he lived in. How he executed his escape became fodder for the media for a long time.

When we examined Anand Prakash, one of the semi-conscious jail warders who had apparently given the first information about the escape, his statements were found to be inconsistent. In any case, Anand Prakash was soon arrested along with three other jail warders, Ram Chander, Prem Bahadur and Jhuman Singh, along with two Tamil Nadu Special Police constables, Suleman and Selvam, and the deputy jail superintendent of Jail No. 3, V.D. Pushkarna. All of them were remanded to police custody up to 24 March for investigations. They were charged with negligence of duty under Section 223 IPC for allowing the jailbreak to take place. They were the directly responsible public servants and hence charged.

Stories, activities and intentions of Charles Sobhraj were no secret in the jail. We started our work by trying to find more information about Charles, his co-escapees, and visitors and friends, both within and outside the jail. Among some of the persons who came to meet Charles were David Richard Hall, a recently released British co-prisoner; and a young lady advocate Sneh Sengar, working with Advocate N.M. Ghatate, who had visited Charles about thirty-one times on record (and many more times otherwise) and was said to be a close associate of Charles. David was reported to have helped Charles in this meticulously planned escape. Among journalists, the names that figured were of the well-known Kumkum Chadha and Dibang, who had become close confidants of Charles.

Most of the information about the planning, background and circumstances of this sensational jail escape, clearly orchestrated in great detail by Charles, became known to us from the thorough custodial interrogations of the jail officials. The mandatory jail registers did not record many of the visits by the conspirators and facilitators, yet we were able to get most of the crucial leads. Surveillance of the suspects also added to some leads. Interestingly, while the successful biographers of Charles came handy, the prospective ones like Dibang became suspects.

Our manhunt continued, and we carried out numerous lookouts and house searches. Simultaneously, we began interrogating the jail staff and other undertrials who had been in contact with Charles. At every stage of our questioning, glaring, system-related and long-standing irregularities committed in total violation of the prison manual came to light. The fact that was highlighted was that the jail officials had been heavily bribed at every step. As a matter of training and professional habit, I became deeply involved in the investigations concerning Charles's entire file, particularly his transfer from Jail No. 1 to Jail No. 3, medical and hospital reports of David Hall and all others, duty rosters of the staff dealing with the escapees and so on.

Patterns began to emerge and a lot of incriminating material came to light. Since the escape was extremely sensational and widely publicised nationally and internationally, our investigations evoked keen interest everywhere and we received support from all quarters in India and abroad—IB, CBI, Interpol and other police forces—when our police parties fanned out in search of the wanted criminals.

Many clues were found from Ashoka Palace Guest House at Anand Niketan in South Delhi, which turned out to be the den where the conspiracy was hatched. This was where several foreign and Indian associates of Charles, his close friends and others connected with co-prisoners like the relatives of the well-known international business tycoon Rajinder Sethia, met regularly over a period of two months before the actual jailbreak.

Besides Rajinder Sethia, another major suspect was the country's most notorious kidnapper, Raju Bhatnagar. He came under suspicion because not only did he have several meetings with Charles and David, but his own associates Bhola and Dinesh, who had been in jail with Charles, were also among the escapees. We received concrete information about the movements of Charles, David, Ajay Singh and Brij Mohan going towards Rajasthan to reach Mumbai.

Luckily, our recently transferred Delhi Police Commissioner Suryakant Jog, a thorough professional who was keen to help his successor, Commissioner Ved Marwah, had taken over as the director general (DGP) of Maharashtra Police. From associates and sources, we received precise information about the hotel near Mumbai Central where Charles was staying. His other co-accused spread out in different hotels and guest houses to avoid identification.

By the time the Mumbai Police party reached the hotel, Charles had already left. But his associate Ajay Singh, a local Delhi boy from the walled city who was yet to learn the tricks of the criminal world, made the silly mistake of travelling with a grenade and was apprehended by a smart railway policeman during routine frisking at the Victoria Terminus (VT) Railway Station (now called Chhatrapati Shivaji Terminus) while attempting to board a train.

At this time, DGP Suryakant Jog had called the well-known Charles tracker of Mumbai, Inspector Madhukar Zende, who had earlier arrested and investigated him, and asked him to follow up the leads regarding Charles's sighting in Goa. In Delhi Police in those times, unlike Mumbai or Maharashtra Police, the senior officers preferred to go by hierarchy, and we depended on the DCPs to brief or take work from their juniors.

It was now clear to us that Charles and David had proceeded from Mumbai to Goa. Goa was the ideal place for Charles. As a global tourist destination with thousands of foreigners, Charles and David could hang around unnoticed in the hundreds of small and big hotels, guest houses, shacks and eating places. They could easily mingle with the crowd and not attract attention to themselves. On my request, Ved Marwah agreed to send our colleague, IPS officer Shamsher Deol, who had just come back from Goa after having served as a popular SP there. He had developed a deep knowledge of the place and also had a good network of contacts and informers.

So now we had two more teams tracking Charles and David—Shamsher Deol and his Goa Police team and Inspector Madhukar Zende with his men from Mumbai Police. They arrived at the popular restaurant in Porvorin called O'Coqueiro, where Charles and David were likely to come. On 6 April 1986, in the evening, Shamsher spent some time at the restaurant and left. But Madhukar, the smart investigator that he was, stayed on, completely merged with the crowd and the typical ambience of the place and waited patiently.

DGP Jog was correct. Madhukar Zende was the right choice to track down Charles. In a smart and quick action, taking the help of the restaurant staff, Zende was not only able to catch the armed Charles Sobhraj and David Hall, but also bundle them into his vehicle. He headed straightway to Mumbai instead of informing or taking the support of Goa Police.

The news of the arrest made international headlines. It also gave Charles a chance to boast that police officers gained as much as he did from media coverage.

Soon after the formal arrest of Charles and David, I arrived in Mumbai onboard a specially requisitioned BSF aircraft. I was received at the airport near the runway by the officers of Mumbai Police. We drove directly to the Police Headquarters to meet the senior officers and take the custody of Charles and David.

The atmosphere was rather tense given the circumstances of the arrest. We were miffed that Inspector Zende had stolen our catch from right under our nose and, to add insult to injury, had whisked him off to Mumbai rather than handing him to us in Goa itself. It was not easy for me to negotiate with Mumbai Police during the course of the day to carry out the requisite legal formalities and also gather all the crucial evidence found on the escapees.

We flew back under high security cover. Escaping the media at the Delhi airport, evading their vehicles, we soon managed to reach the safety of the remotely located, newly built Ashok Vihar Police Station. We finally had Charles and David back in our custody, firmly locked up after getting a remand from the magistrate.

At Ashok Vihar Police Station, the lock-up was located in the basement. Soon, this became my office for all practical purposes and an extension of the Crime Branch for nearly a month following the arrest. Incidentally, this was also the same lock-up where we had kept some of the far more sensitive prisoners in police custody, who were wanted in the country's most sensational terrorist crimes.

In my police career, I handled several sensitive cases like the assassinations of Rajiv Gandhi, Lalit Maken, Arjun Dass, and assisting the CBI in the General A.S. Vaidya case. I also handled highly sophisticated economic and corruption-related crimes like the hawala and the bank scam–share market cases along with their prisoners like Harshad Mehta and V. Krishnamurthy. In all these cases, there appeared some common features that helped us get the complete facts and evidence out of the arrested persons.

I never believed that third degree or custodial torture were the appropriate tools for arriving at the truth, which indisputably is the objective of a successful investigations. Charles Sobhraj and David Hall were no exceptions for me. My tactic of questioning Charles was to play on his psyche. Given his monstrous ego, I figured that I needed to establish right away who the boss was. So my calculated plan to demoralise him was to never offer him a chair to sit while he was being interrogated.

Charles was made to sit on the floor of the lock-up and we sat on chairs during the long hours of questioning. For him, this was unthinkable since he fancied himself as an international celebrity. This was a big blow to his ego, especially because he was used to being greatly pampered. Charles found it all extremely upsetting—being denied the importance that had been bestowed on him by the media, jail officials and fellow prisoners.

One more reason I preferred he was made to sit a little away was the stink emanating from his mouth. Perhaps due to his unhygienic oral habits or some medical issue, his halitosis made it unbearable for me to have him within smelling distance. It still beats me as to how this smelly, obnoxious man was able to charm most people he met, especially the women.

32

Why and How Did He Escape?

During those twenty days, between 16 March and 6 April 1986, when Charles was at large—a free man after nearly ten years in captivity in Tihar Jail—we were able to piece together a detailed character study of this criminal from the jail records and from the statements of his extensive network of co-prisoners, jail functionaries and associates. This enabled us to form a clear picture of how and why he escaped, and how we could bring him back to prison. As I went through his file, it was clear that the prime motive for the escape and its timing was the extradition proceeding going on against him.

Corroborating his criminal antecedents which we had thoroughly investigated, we discovered that most of his crimes and court cases in India had been disposed and he had undergone all the sentences given to him with his prolonged incarceration. What was clearly hanging over his head was a death sentence likely to be given to him in Thailand. The extradition request from the Government of Thailand to the Government of India gave him sleepless nights. The five murders in Thailand, which had earned him notoriety as the 'Bikini Killer', now demanded retribution.

Delhi's Chief Metropolitan Magistrate Subhash Wasan, hearing the extradition case, had decided against Charles and recommended his extradition to Thailand. The appeal against the order was filed by his advocate N.M. Ghatate in the Delhi High Court, but the case was decided against him on 12 December

1985. It was during these legal interactions that the young trainee–advocate working with Ghatate, Sneh Sengar, became enamoured with Charles. Charles asked N.M. Ghatate to file an appeal in the Supreme Court, but he was not hopeful of any favourable decision. So he decided that he had to commit an offence that was serious and sensational enough to continue staying in Tihar Jail, which in any case had been much more than a home to him for most of his life. Interpol's Red Corner Notice pending against him from the courts of Thailand was valid for twenty years. The statute of limitations would have run its course by the time he finished the sentence for jailbreak. Thus he could escape the death sentence.

Charles had obviously used his time in prison well—he had mastered the functioning of India's labyrinthine legal and prison system. When he was captured after the jailbreak, Charles did not have any cases pending trial to continue being in jail, but he was now a 'state prisoner' under the Bengal and Bombay Prisoners Regulations of 1817 and 1819 vintage, reproduced as an Act of 1858. In retrospect, it is clear that Charles completely succeeded in achieving his designs. Here was a textbook case of how criminal minds can use the legal system to their advantage.

There have been numerous jail escapes which have been the plots of popular stories and movies. Most of the escapes were daring ones. But none of them could match the highly intricate and extremely devious but meticulously planned escape from Tihar Jail as done by Charles. His plan went into the minutest details. To that extent, for me, it was a very interesting piece of investigation that unfolded within the jail premises itself while Charles was at large, and the findings were later confirmed by Charles, David and the other associates.

Earlier, in November 1985, his friends in the jail, Brij Mohan and Laxmi Narain, facing trials in nineteen and twenty-one cases of murders, kidnappings, robberies and dacoities (robbery committed by five or more persons) respectively, had offered Charles an escape plan. But Charles, hopeful of a favourable judgement in his extradition case, delayed it till the 12 December adverse High Court order. After the disappointing verdict, he started a clandestine escape plan and preparations started on a war-footing. Others to join him were Ajay Singh and Bajrang, both facing trials in murder and house-robbery cases.

It was difficult for us to believe how a foreigner, a prisoner in a high-security jail that lodged some of the most important political prisoners and other criminals involved in highly sensitive cases, could control the security system to the extent that Charles did at Tihar. He was able to manipulate the entire system to suit his plans. He was able to get his transfer from the high security Jail No. 1 to Jail No. 3. Here he was able to get cell number 8 in ward 2 allotted to himself so that he was in close proximity of his notorious co-conspirators, Brij Mohan, Laxmi Narain, Ajay Singh and Bajrang, who were in the adjacent cell number 7. Our investigations later revealed that he had almost converted Jail No. 3 into his fiefdom.

For the escape, Charles came up with the plan to drug all the jail officials and security staff on duty near the *deorhi*, and the others agreed to it.

As the layers of the case started opening up, we learnt that among the close associates of Charles in prison was a rich businessman, Rajinder Sethia. Sethia was a London-based international trader who had been arrested by CBI in a much-publicised bank fraud case and kept in Jail No. 1 since March 1985. Charles had also been kept in the same jail after being transferred from Karwar Jail in Karnataka on 28 April 1985.

Charles bribed, charmed, cajoled and coerced the officials in Jail No. 1 and exercised a huge influence on them. He acted as a Good Samaritan to several inmates including Rajinder Sethia. Charles facilitated meetings of Sethia with his family members and relatives coming from London. Sethia became very obliged and he trusted Charles blindly. He provided the biggest support to him from inside the jail while Charles's UK-based friend and later co-accused, David Richard Hall, fully implemented his plans from outside the jail.

David Hall was a British national arrested at Palam Airport on 23 December 1985 for being in possession of 1.5 kg of charas. We found that Charles befriended and supported him when he was a helpless prisoner. Planning to use David to the hilt, Charles helped him secure bail on false medical grounds with the help of the young advocate Sneh Sengar. Charles managed to get David admitted in a hospital and prepared his application himself, stating grounds for bail that his kidney was damaged and he was passing blood in his urine.

Charles arranged a false medical report from the jail doctor, Dr Tarlok Jhumat, on consideration and submitted it in the court of the ASJ through Sneh Sengar. She appeared and secured the bail for David for a surety of ₹ 12,000. Surprisingly, Sneh was able to secure the release of David on 10 February 1986 without any surety, just on the basis of a cash security which was paid by Charles. David was totally under obligation to Charles and fully paid back through his support. While these facts were yet to be revealed, Dr Jhumat, who had taken leave on 17 March, the day after the jail escape, pretended that he had to go to the UK to see his ailing brother-in-law and left India without leave or permission from the chief medical officer.

We arrested Sneh Sengar, the young apprentice–advocate, on 28 March after finding conclusive evidence against her. She was the most active conspirator in the escape plan. We also found damning documentary evidence for which she had no answer—a forged passport made in her name that was recovered from her home at Lalitpur in Madhya Pradesh. This passport was organised for her by Charles through his friend, ex-COFEPOSA (Conservation of Foreign Exchange and

Prevention of Smuggling Activities Act) detenu at Tihar, Rajesh Mongia of Systems International. The passport itself was made in a hurry for Sneh Sengar since she was expected to go abroad along with Charles once he was out. She admitted that she was enamoured with Charles when she heard him arguing his own case in the High Court.

Sneh Sengar started visiting Charles (and Rajinder Sethia) in the jail almost daily. The visits were totally unconnected with her profession. The jail records showed thirty-one visits and our investigation suggested that she probably met him on an equal number of occasions, unrecorded. From her conduct, including her photograph taken inside the jail by Gordon Greenall, another conspirator in the case, it was evident that she was more like a girlfriend of Charles, willingly supporting his illegal activities.

We had ample evidence to show that she mediated and passed money between Charles and Sethia and became a confidant of David Hall, besides being close to several other co-accused and connected persons. She regularly met Sethia's nephew Daljit Singh Bhalla who came from London to facilitate the escape, just like David's wife Maria Ann Hall, her friend Patricia Baldwin, Donald Sutcliff and others, all connected with the escape related events. Besides assisting others, she collected 6,700 Swiss Francs which had been deposited as the amount found during the personal search of T. Hartman, an NDPS (Narcotic Drugs and Psychotropic Substances) Act-accused friend of Charles Sobhraj, and admitted to passing it on to Charles. There were numerous such transactions made by Sengar which kept getting discovered during our investigations.

Rajinder Sethia's role appeared to be peripheral to us in the beginning. It was difficult to nail down his involvement, but he could not explain the conduct of his nephew (sister's son) Daljit Singh Bhalla alias Happy, a UK national. Happy came to India at his uncle's behest and continued to be in Delhi, getting involved deeper and deeper into the planning and preparations of the jail escape. He was also in close contact with David's wife in UK itself and, while in Delhi in December 1985, he opened a non-resident–external (NRE) account bearing number 34045 in Grindlays Bank, Connaught Place. Laxmi Sethia, Rajinder Sethia's wife, remitted 99,000 dollars in this account on 4 March 1986, from which Daljit withdrew ₹ 3 lakh on 7 March and ₹ 5.5 lakh on 15 March and spent the entire amount on behalf of his uncle, as corroborated separately from investigations and David's statement on the escape of Charles and other connected acts.

Like several journalists who were looking for juicy and sensational stories from Charles, one of the regulars in the Police Headquarters was the freelancer Dibang. Not only did he become friendly with Charles, he also became a part of the conspiracy. He met several of the co-accused of Charles through him and visited the jail many times with Gordon Greenall, Sneh Sengar and David Hall, giving his residential address as Ashoka Palace—the seat of conspiracy, besides the jail premises. Dibang visited Yashpal Kathuria, the money-changer, along with David Hall, collected from Charles Sobhraj ₹ 2 lakh in Indian currency and converted ₹ 195,000 out of it into 13,000 dollars.

33

David Richard Hall Opens His Heart

Before and after their arrest and our custodial interrogations of Charles and David, plenty of information was coming to us, but there was something significant which the reticent and extremely glum creative director and art photographer David Richard Hall did not disclose to us until the fifth or the sixth day of his questioning. I used to talk to Charles and David in turns. That day, at lunchtime, I called David and shared the food sent by my wife Rekha with him. The result was some cathartic disclosures of David.

Unlike what I did to Charles, I used to provide a chair to David during his interrogation. I found him generally a decent and sensitive person. I had been told that he had not been eating for days, except taking some coffee and bread. My gesture made him emotional, especially at the mention of the lunch prepared by my wife, and he expressed his apprehensions about his wife Maria being at risk. When I offered to arrange for him to speak to her at Leamington Spa, UK, and assured him that nothing untoward would happen to her, he burst into tears, became lucid and started 'singing', as we call it in police lingo. David, who was all quiet and refusing to tell anything until then, kept speaking for several hours, completely opening up about the undisclosed parts of the conspiracy, plans, preparations and execution of the prison break—leaving nothing out.

But look at the irony of our legal system. Whatever David Richard Hall disclosed to us during custodial interrogation could not be used by us as evidence in the court, except the portions that resulted in the discovery of some facts.

I was acutely conscious of the limitations placed by the law while speaking to David or anyone else in our custody. The misuse of the limited window provided in the law to extract confessional statement by the police investigators adopting short-cut routes through torture and other unlawful methods are a major bane of our justice system.

This was also the period when the Terrorist and Disruptive Activities Prevention (TADA) Act 1985 was enacted. This Act remained in force till 1995, after being extended a few times. It had extraordinary provisions including detention up to one year, confessions made to senior police officers (superintendent of police and above) admissible and burden of proof being cast on the accused to prove innocence.

These controversial provisions and popular opinion against giving such powers to the police officers led to this Act being allowed to lapse. In some form or the other, such laws have found a place in the statute books and have remained a subject matter of criticism, the police being at the receiving end, distrusted and denied such authority.

As mentioned, the highly emotional and charged David started a rambling monologue—almost oblivious of my presence and our respective positions. I called the IO to take his statement, which was duly recorded in about seventeen pages by the meticulous Crime Branch Inspector Pratap Singh. To start with, David stated:

> I am a British national. I was arrested on 23.12.85 at Palam Airport for carrying 1.5 kg of hashish. I was sent to Jail No. 1. in Tihar Jail. The moment I stepped in, one person met me at the main gate and introduced himself as Charles Sobhraj.

> He assured me of all possible help. The next day I was transferred to the Foreigners Ward and I met him again. I also joined the Christmas party arranged by him in the jail on 25.12.85. The other participants were Hartman, Peter, Rajinder Sethia, Capt. Rathore and some others. It was that day that Charles Sobhraj introduced me to Rajinder Sethia, who was in jail in a bank fraud case. Sethia also (be)friended me and told me that one of his relatives Daljit Bhalla alias Happy had come to India and had been trying to arrange for his bail and that he would be of help to me and Charles Sobhraj.

We recorded David's statement in chronological order of the events taking place, making everything crystal clear, corroborating much of the investigation and evidence already collected. All the pieces started falling into place and it became easy to collect and collate the facts according to the logical flow of the story.

David continued his story:

> A few days later Charles Sobhraj told me that his appeal relating to his extradition to Thailand had been dismissed in Delhi High Court on 12.12.85 and he was worried because in case he was sent to Thailand, he would have to face the death sentence. He, however, told me that he was trying to move the Supreme Court of India in that matter.

Charles, David and Rajinder met frequently and meticulously planned David's bail, which was the first step in the bigger jailbreak conspiracy.

On one occasion David said:

> Rajinder Sethia broke down and stated that on account of an important witness (Swami Satsangi) in his bank fraud case he was apprehensive of conviction—and was prepared to spend any amount if that witness was liquidated.

It was decided that Sethia would pay 50,000 dollars for the killing of Satsangi through Charles's hitman in England. David would also help Charles in the escape after getting bail, and all expenses were to be borne by Rajinder Sethia.

David told us about the bank account opened by Rajinder's nephew Daljit Singh alias Happy to meet all the expenses and also about Rajinder writing and signing a slip of paper in his presence which read, '20,000 dollars to be paid to the bearer. With many Thanks, Raj'. The amount was to be collected from Mr Bathuria, a director of ESAL Commodities Limited in London. Charles gave this paper to David, who subsequently photographed it in an open briefcase full of currency—the evidence came handy during Rajinder's prosecution.

David gave us plenty of material to understand how Charles had manipulated and controlled the jail officials through expensive gifts and cash bribes, making sure that anyone could visit him and his friends like David and Rajinder, any number of times, freely. Among the visitors was David's friend Gordon Greenall, who had come to India on 5 January 1986 to arrange for his bail. He stayed at Ashoka Palace, Anand Niketan, where David's other friend, Donald Sutcliff, also joined him.

Greenall visited David thrice and Charles another four or five times. Charles introduced him to his friend Sneh Sengar. They planned David's release on bail on medical grounds, which was done using false medical papers. On 18 January 1986, Charles managed to get transferred from Jail No. 1 to Jail No. 3, where he occupied cell number 7, next to his co-conspirators, with whom he escaped.

David gave a detailed account of the planning done in Jail No. 3. Charles arranged to get David admitted in the hospital located in Jail No. 3, to which all of them—Charles, Brij Mohan, Ajay Singh, Bajrang and Laxmi Narain—had free access, thanks to the jail staff and the hospital doctor. In the hospital, they worked out the details of the escape planned in the first week of February. David told us:

> All these persons had come to see me and all of us planned that they would escape from the jail after drugging the jail staff on duty and when released on bail I shall supply the necessary drugs and make arrangements as would be directed by Charles Sobhraj.

David led our teams to several places, including the famous chemist Kemp & Co. at Connaught Place for corroborative documents to be collected as evidence.

As meticulously planned by Charles, Sneh Sengar got David bailed out on 10 February simply on a cash security of ₹ 12,000, paid by Charles, without any surety. David's wife Maria Hall and her friend Patricia reached Delhi on 11 February and all of them, including Gordon Greenall and Donald Sutcliff, stayed together at Ashoka Palace. For all of them, Tihar Jail was like home where, as described in detail by David, they met Charles freely on numerous occasions, often without permissions or entries being made. Daljit Bhalla, who was there full-time to serve his uncle Sethia and provide financial assistance to Charles and others, would also be with them.

As instructed by Charles, Gordon Greenall was provided air tickets through Jaggi of Moon Travels, a contact man of Rajinder Sethia who had also provided tickets to Maria Hall and Patricia. Gordon Greenall travelled across half the globe to various locations to study the security loopholes which might enable Charles to escape in case he had to go out of the country. Charles wanted to transfer 250,000 US dollars from a bank in the Bahamas to Geneva, and he entrusted this task to Greenall.

Initially, Charles wanted his Australian girlfriend Carol Kashaw to do this work, but considering Greenall's track record, he preferred Greenall. Greenall opened a joint bank account in

Geneva in which Charles got 40,000 dollars transferred. Greenall withdrew 32,000 dollars and returned to India. Such an amazing plan, and many other far more complex manoeuvres, planned and executed from inside the jail, were revealed by David.

David continued the narrative:

> Sneh Sengar had been visiting jail frequently; no entries were being made in the jail records. Charles and Ms Sengar used to meet, locked-up in the assistant jail superintendent's office and nobody was there to interfere with them. Sengar also carried messages to Rajinder Sethia in Jail No. 1 and vice-versa. She had developed personal relations with Charles Sobhraj who had managed to procure a passport for her which was a forged one. She had accompanied myself, Daljit Bhalla, Maria Hall—my wife, Ms Patricia Baldwin, Donald Sutcliff and others who used to meet Charles during that period, to jail and other places in Delhi. She had also carried money from Sethia to Charles Sobhraj on 4-5 occasions.
>
> On three occasions I accompanied Sneh Sengar to the house of Daljit Bhalla in Rajinder Nagar but he was available only once. He said that he and Rajinder Sethia were financing the escape and he had withdrawn large sums of money from the bank. This he told on 14.3.86. I used to go by taxi to PG Women's hostel to pick up Sneh Sengar to be taken to Tihar Jail to meet Charles Sobhraj.

While giving us a detailed account of the financial transactions between Charles, Sethia, Bhalla and others regarding the escape and other illegal activities, David admitted to converting foreign exchange through Yashpal and also gave the photographic evidence of the slip of paper with Sethia's signature and a briefcase containing 20,000 dollars. He explained how Sethia gave the slip of paper which read '20,000 dollars to be paid to the bearer' to Charles:

> Charles Sobhraj gave this chit to Gordon Greenall in my presence and directed him to execute the plan with the help of one Keith William in Australia and obtain 20,000 dollars after producing this letter to Mr Bathuria in London. Charles Sobhraj had also given me some names and addresses including that of Swami Satsangi for safe custody which had been entered in my diary.

During the investigation conducted by the CBI Joint Director P.C. Sharma (later director), then camping in London, the diary was seized with the help of Interpol from David Hall's house through his wife Maria at Leamington Spa in UK.

Revealing details of how he procured the huge quantity of Larpose tablets which were used to stupefy the numerous jail and police officials, David disclosed:

> Charles had also directed me and Gordon Greenall to purchase Larpose tablets in large quantities as the same were to be mixed-up in the eatables to be served to the jail staff present at the *deorhi* while escaping. Sobhraj also told me that the food would be prepared by Ajay Singh, Laxmi Narain, Bajrang Lal and Brij Mohan.
>
> I had purchased more than a thousand such tablets from a chemist shop (Kemp & Co., from where we made a recovery of the requisite documents under Section 27 of the Indian Evidence Act) in Connaught Place using different names. Similarly, Gordon Greenall had also purchased 200 tablets of Larpose and all the quantity so purchased had been handed over to Charles Sobhraj in the jail and lastly on 14.3.86.

David gave us the details of the preparations for the escape, including the milk and sweets supplied by Pandit Bhojraj, a routine supplier of Charles, which was required for the most important part of the escape plan—the burfi, which contained over 500 tablets of powdered Larpose for drugging the jail staff. He also spoke about the getaway vehicles, weapons and a grenade—all of which we recovered and connected to the case.

David said that Raju Bhatnagar (a notorious criminal and very smart kidnapper) had also been lodged in jail but he was released in December 1985. Even after his release he was in constant communication with Charles Sobhraj in jail through his carrier, Dev Kumar Tyagi.

Earlier, according to David, the plan to escape was to be executed on 9 March. But when Charles was informed that the arrangements for transport could not be made, the plan was abandoned and a fresh date was to be decided by him.

David told us:

> Charles told me to purchase a motorcycle and a car to be used in the escape. I purchased a motorcycle with registration number DIZ 4515 from Karol Bagh. I also purchased a Fiat car with licence number DHA 9961 from Lajpat Nagar on 14 March 1986 for ₹ 35,000. I had assumed the name Nathial Lehrep son of Richard John for this purpose.

The documents prepared by David and Dev Kumar Tyagi for both the vehicles including delivery receipts and so on were recovered later, thus making our evidence perfect.

David continued talking:

> In the meantime, I had shifted to Ashok Yatri Niwas (a tourist hotel in the central part of New Delhi) and had been residing in the name of Greenall who had already left by then. Raju Bhatnagar had given his personal Llama pistol with two live cartridges . . . delivered to Charles Sobhraj on 14.3.86 at about 4 PM. S.R. Yadav, assistant superintendent was on duty. He had forbidden his staff on duty to search the bag containing the pistol. I had taken two photographs of this pistol in room

number 1819 of Ashok Yatri Niwas before it was delivered to Charles Sobhraj.

All these photographs were recovered at his instance, making this part of the statement made to us admissible under the law. David told us about another weapon purchased through Raju Bhatnagar for ₹ 15,000, and also about a hand grenade wrapped in polythene which was removed by the room service boy from the waste paper basket where he had kept it. The boy was paid 100 dollars to keep this a secret.

Faithfully complying with the minute directions of Charles Sobhraj, David Richard Hall completed all the arrangements by 15 March, that is, a day prior to the jail escape.

I spent a lot of time with David, more than I did with Charles, while questioning them. David struck me as a meticulous and sensitive professional besides being an emotional person attached to his wife Maria—about whose safety he was deeply concerned. He explained the actions in great detail and got facts faithfully and truthfully recorded.

I had not expected so much cooperation from David. It could partly be because of his confidence that we would protect his wife as he had a deadly fear of Charles and partly for the reason that he had understood Charles better than most people. Even though he was as much in awe and enamoured with him as others, he did not want him to be let off, free to continue his criminal activities.

34

Deviously Planned and Perfectly Executed Jail Escape

From the material and evidence we had collected about the jail escape, it was clear that Charles made sure that everything was in place as planned. Nothing was left to chance. The sensational jailbreak, which left everyone in the jail administration and the government totally shocked, went as planned. Charles and his friends literally walked out of jail.

The repercussions were felt till long after the event. The escape revealed the endless irregularities, a completely compromised administration and a thoroughly exposed security system in Asia's largest, high-security prison.

Charles personally supervised the most important part of the escape—the preparations of the burfi, custard and grapes, mixed with powdered Larpose in adequate quantity—five tablets for each person. He made sure that the items were stored properly during the night and remained fresh for serving the next morning.

In the morning of 16 March, Charles came to the *deorhi* at about 9:30 along with Laxmi Narain, who was deputed to get the other three—Ajay Singh, Brij Mohan and Bajrang—to serve the foodstuff. As scheduled, David Hall came to the main gate at 11:30 AM and apprised Charles about all the arrangements including the locations of the getaway vehicles.

Charles was supremely confident for he had been keeping all the jail officials in good humour all the time. He directed David to remove the backup escape car DEA 8887 from Centaur Hotel near the airport, bring it near the jail, hand it over to Raju Bhatnagar and keep it in readiness near Mayapuri Jail Road crossing. He did so to guard against any hindrance in the escape through the outer gate—if that happened, he could run across the jail farm and reach this vehicle.

David Hall came back to Jail No. 3 at 1:40 PM and parked the car number DHA 9961 outside the main gate, with Dev Kumar Tyagi at the wheel. On David's arrival, with all the arrangements in place, Charles had the foodstuff brought in and served to the jail officials. An attempt was made to make sure that the drug-laced food was served to everyone near the main gate. At about 2:30 PM, when the staff, including all those in jail security and the policemen on duty, became unconscious, Charles, followed by Ajay Singh, Brij Mohan, Laxmi Narain and Bajrang, coolly walked out of the jail.

David Hall, as per his habit, took photographs of the entire escape episode—which reminds me of the Rajiv Gandhi assassination at Sriperumbudur in which LTTE had contracted the local Chennai resident Haribabu to take photographs of the event, which became our clinching evidence in that case.

During our questioning, David disclosed:

> I drove the car number DHA 9961 from Jail No. 3 to Kirby Place.... Charles Sobhraj also said that he had used the pistol to scare away an inmate of the jail.... At Kirby Place, Charles told me that he would ride the motorcycle; we both rode the motorcycle ahead of the car up to Sohna, where the motorcycle went out of order and was left there. We travelled in the same car to Alwar where we abandoned the car and took the train to Jaipur. I also took photographs of Charles Sobhraj on the railway platform and in the train. All the escapees went

> together by train to Baroda from where we took two taxis and reached Bombay on the morning of 18.3.86. Brij Mohan, Laxmi Narain and Bajrang got separated from us. I, Charles Sobhraj, Dev Kumar Tyagi (Raju Bhatnagar's carrier who had driven one of the getaway cars) and Ajay Singh stayed in different hotels in Bombay.

True to his character, covering his tracks, Charles wanted to get rid of Dev Kumar Tyagi and Ajay Singh, and he gave them the slip in Mumbai. The first arrest thus made by Mumbai Railway Police was of Ajay Singh who was found with the grenade.

David continued:

> I and Sobhraj went to Goa. On 6.3.86 we were arrested by the police. All the negatives of the photographs which I had taken either in jail or on the way to Bombay had been taken by Charles Sobhraj, which were recovered by the police when we were arrested. At the time of arrest, the pistol which I had given to Charles Sobhraj, and which he had used on 16.3.86 to threaten an inmate of the jail, was recovered from Charles Sobhraj, besides charas, ganja, ₹28,000 and 6,200 dollars.

Thus, the most significant leads for a cast-iron case were provided by David Hall. Every detail given by him was fully corroborated through documentary, oral and material evidence. Clearly, Charles had planned his escape in order to evade a likely death sentence in Thailand for the murders he had committed there. David Hall, Rajinder Sethia and several others were nothing but pawns in his game.

The elaborate criminal conspiracy Charles hatched included his main co-escapees Brij Mohan, Laxmi Narain, Bajrang and Ajay Singh—the last one was arrested in Mumbai while the other three absconded. Sufficient evidence was found against the jail and police officials, namely, V.D. Pushkarna, S.R. Yadav,

Dr Tarlok Jhumat, Anand Prakash, Ram Chander, Prem Bahadur, constables Suleman and Selvam—all public servants, duty-bound to keep Charles and others in confinement. They were prosecuted under several sections of the law connected to escape from lawful custody and conspiracy under Sections 224, 225, 327, 328, 120B IPC, additional Sections 221 and 222 IPC being applied on the public servants' intentional omissions to apprehend the persons.

Along with Charles and four other conspiring co-accused escapees, taking advantage of the situation, two convicted prisoners, Dinesh and Bhola, also escaped from lawful custody and were charged accordingly. Along with Charles and David Hall, Dev Kumar Tyagi, Rajinder Sethia, Ms Sneh Sengar, Daljit Singh Bhalla, (journalist) Dibang and Yashpal Kathuria, were also charged for conspiring and actively helping the escape of the prisoners.

Unlike all other co-escapees who were either convicts or undertrials, Charles Sobhraj had no criminal case against him. He was a 'state prisoner' awaiting extradition or deportation out of India. His worst fear was the threat of deportation to Thailand—that warrant would lapse in twenty years after it was issued in 1975. Nine years after the jail escape, in 1995, the Tihar Jail escape case was the only criminal case pending trial against him in India, thanks to the protection provided to this most devious character by India's long-winded criminal justice system.

The Thai warrant expired on 2 March 1995, as Charles Sobhraj expected. Incidentally, he had been granted bail on a surety of ₹50,000 by the Delhi High Court six years earlier, on 6 March 1989. He refused to furnish sureties and preferred to stay within the protective umbrella of Tihar Jail which continued to grant him safety, comfort and privileges.

Everyone except the media and some of us directly connected with the case seems to have forgotten the terrible misdeeds of Charles Sobhraj. His co-escapees of 1986 were released on bail a long time ago. Charles remained in jail, playing all his tricks. Friends in the media and even senior criminologists found him so suave and intelligent—an 'ideal criminal'—that some of them started exchanging addresses with him within five minutes of meeting him in jail.

Thoroughly impressed with his conduct in jail, even the seniormost officers felt he was really an intellectual, busy reading and writing. Charles boasted in the media about the celebrated DG Prisons Kiran Bedi, 'I think Kiran is an ideal Indian woman, so why not write about her?' He claimed he was writing a book on one of India's best-known cops.

I was in the CBI when the journalist Vitusha Oberoi quoted me, expressing my honest feelings, 'Sobhraj is not a psychopath, just an out-and-out crook—wants money at any cost.' I always held this opinion about him, based entirely on my interactions with him during the investigation in 1986.

He was not like other criminals, I felt, 'Not because Sobhraj is an extraordinary character who ought to find a place in the history of crime, but because of his utter lack of feelings.... In criminals, too, there is something genuine. But Sobhraj has a habit of harming the person who trusts him most.... Sobhraj is at best an average character who has read a little law while in custody. He has also taken advantage of the English he knows, bad English, and his mixed parentage and foreign connections.'

35

Khaki on Broken Wings

A series of thoughts crowded my mind when I recently saw the *Indian Express* headline '21-Year Old Commits Suicide Hours after Being Questioned by Cops'. I felt terribly disturbed. Was this only about the police as the most visible face of the criminal justice system, or did the other wings of the system contribute equally or less or more towards this ignominy?

Son of a poor, casual labourer living in a jhuggi (slum-habitat with a tin or thatched roof), a young second-year undergraduate student of Delhi University, Suraj Thakur, who also worked as a helper in a garment shop to support his poor family, gave up his life after a routine act of the police. Before hanging himself in his makeshift dwelling, crying bitterly, he video-recorded a somewhat longish statement ('Dying Declaration', I presume) which can be translated thus:

> They (police) made me sit on a bike and took me to the station. *Meri koi galti nahi thi* (I did nothing wrong). They asked me to call my friends. They assured me that if I tell them about Ankit's whereabouts, they will leave me. I called Ankit and he came.... They asked me if I am involved in such phone snatching and said that I take smack... they would send me home. I didn't do anything wrong. I am innocent. My parents' reputation is at stake. I am depressed... I am

committing suicide and I am responsible for this. I won't blame anyone.

I have nothing much to say here about this sad incident and the flaws in the system that need to be corrected, but this example and its instant impact on my feelings takes me back to my memories of thousands of interactions, small and big, as a policeman. They include the landmark cases which raised many questions on the efficacy of the criminal justice system of our country. I have been searching for answers to those questions. I alone cannot suggest solutions to the massive problems and issues which envelop our system. But I can at least attempt to pave a little ground for the initiation of thoughts, discussions and debates on such issues.

In this book I have attempted to explain the predicaments of the police while functioning within India's extremely complex criminal justice system (CJS). This book is about some nationally known offenders and criminal cases which tested and very clearly exposed the fragility, infirmity and hollowness of the four wings of the CJS, the Indian police being the over-arching first wing.

The omnipresent 'Khaki' or the police has numerous duties to perform in each wing of the CJS—law-and-order, enforcements and crime investigations; the prosecution and defence lawyers and the related processes; the judicial, quasi-judicial services and the courts; and the correctional agencies, jails and the diverse prison and legal detention systems of India. Each wing has millions of extremely disturbing stories to tell. Together or separately, they deal with highly sensitive incidents and human transactions concerning different levels of criminal and non-criminal acts and propensity to commit them, real or perceived—one small example was Suraj Thakur's case of suicide.

The police, being the country's main and most visible law enforcement body, the 'prime movers' of the justice machinery and its ubiquitous wing, has to be accountable at all levels. From the smallest and apparently insignificant situations to national level security issues, the police, in its myriad forms and roles, is embedded in the sociopolitical–administrative–legal structure of our country. Obviously, the mosaic of the Indian police in all its forms presents the most variegated picture of governance—from the Centre including the NCT Delhi to the states and union territories, from the remotest villages in the Himalayas and Gangetic plains to the shores of the South, to Arunachal and Andamans, many of which I had opportunities to closely observe, interact and serve through criminal justice, even juvenile justice, systems.

I lived my two parallel lives simultaneously for almost twenty years with equal intensity—deeply involved in police work as well as community service through voluntary organisations. I consider myself very fortunate to have had the real, practical experience of the two seemingly incompatible systems, within the government and also outside. Managing the police and community service affairs concurrently was quite a challenge and a great learning for me. Chairing Delhi's Child Rights Commission for three years soon after my retirement provided me another opportunity to look beyond the stereotypes. My life and work, which have obviously shaped my perceptions, are naturally multidimensional, giving me many opportunities to be a dispassionate insider–outsider.

The much talked about Jessica Lal murder case, which I had the opportunity to investigate, promoted popular protests in the country, led by the media. The country witnessed, for the first time, several candlelight marches at India Gate in New Delhi as well as in many other cities. This also created a major demand for changes in the archaic criminal laws. On a very different footing, the notorious BMW case exposed the obnoxious ways in which the investigations and trials, lawyers and judges, were all taken for a ride. The proceedings and historic verdicts delivered by the judges, from the Trial Court to the Apex Court, created benchmarks and a base for future changes. The stories of the two notorious mavericks, Romesh Sharma and Charles Sobhraj, presented unique insights about two entirely different types of criminal minds. The first highlighted the nexus between the mafia–politics–corporate world and the second demonstrated how the prison and the criminal justice system can be played with in a manner no one could ever imagine, providing many lessons for those who cared.

I was deeply connected with all these historic cases and investigated these high-profile criminals. I had the rare opportunity to gain first-hand experience of the manner in which the rich-and-the-powerful, the high-and-mighty interacted with the mafia and hardcore gangsters. Beginning with my mid-career experiments in the serious enforcement of the social legislation—I was somewhat disenchanted with the decay in the system as it operated—I pursued my chosen path of closely aligning with the deprived and vulnerable groups of the society who came in close contact with the police. The extremely pathetic and atrocious treatment given to the poor and have-nots by India's criminal justice system (CJS), with the police being the most visible and active wing, always remained a challenge for me.

In the midst of all these experiences, it has been a subject of deep contemplation for me as to how the Indian police, which is a major part of the CJS and the JJS (juvenile justice system—one of my chosen fields), can perform within the boundaries and limitations of our country's democratic systems and processes. How we measure up in fulfilling the basic tenets of the Constitution is increasingly acquiring greater significance with the changing times and assaults from both the state as well as the non-state forces. Many promises made by the visionary architects of the Constitution actually fall at the doorsteps of the police stations—less fulfilled, more frustrated.

Flowing from the top to the bottom, changes are required at both macro as well as micro levels. At the macro level, the basic concept and role of the Indian police must change alongside India's criminal justice system; the civil laws and the related justice processes are far more appalling though a little less painful. The Indian police, I believe, should not remain just the enforcer of criminal laws and the protector of the country's law-and-order, and continue to be involved mostly in doing what suits the administrators and politicians. The Indian police has to play a role much beyond that, as agents of change.

It is not difficult to understand, in the light of the rising aspirations of the people at large, why the prime function and structure of the police should not be of a controller but that of a benefactor or a friend of the people. The methods used by the police are outmoded in most respects and unsuitable for a modern, democratic society. The demand to have better defined roles and involvement for the police in serving the needy and the have-nots of the society can't be postponed indefinitely. The police should first protect the poor, the weak, the destitute, the elderly, the children and the women, rather than spend most of its scarce time and resources to serve the rich and the powerful.

The image and position of the Indian police, as determined by the Indian Police Act and Rules, operating within the seemingly infallible age-old troika—CrPC, IPC and Indian Evidence Act—is supposed to be that of the enforcer of the laws and the preserver of public order. There is no doubt that its vastness and all-encompassing position in our CJS is most important, yet untenable. When the Indian Constitution was being drafted, dismantling of this people-unfriendly system was not contemplated, perhaps, as it would have resulted in bringing about a number of unforeseen disruptions which would have rocked our entire system during those tumultuous times. At the same time, it is also true that the overwhelming position of the police in the whole administrative set-up is so deeply entrenched that merely a few bits of reforms will not bring about any appreciable change in the system.

It is my effort to ignite the thought that immediate action must be undertaken to redefine the role of the Indian police and its place in the socio–legal–political system. The police has to operate in our highly surcharged democracy with our society's complex realities. Our nation's gross domestic product (GDP) and the size of our militia including the security forces places us as the fifth and the third-largest global power, along with our 131st position in the Human Development Index (HDI) amongst 193 member countries of the UN. This presents a picture of huge contradictions, socioeconomic injustice and inequity, which is bound to create endless conflicts at all levels. And as the main law enforcer, the police often becomes at least the arbiter, if not dispenser of justice.

I am also aware of the view of many of my erudite colleagues and learned friends that the framework which has been developed over so many years, enriched by the contributions of so many thoughtful police leaders, can't possibly be so useless. But I believe that we have to begin the process of making the police of India a distinct entity within the ongoing dynamic changes, giving it the role and image of a friend and protector of the common people and not a force to create fear—mostly in the powerless. This will necessitate insulating the police from the inappropriate influence of the politicians and the others wielding power; at the same time, the system should prevent the police from misusing the powers entrusted to it by the law.

That is all at the macro level. At the micro level, a comprehensive exercise should be undertaken to identify every area of operation where essential changes are required and actions should be taken to ensure the requisite transformation.

One of these areas is to change the system of filing complaints, including registration and handling of FIRs, making the process easier and more convenient for the common person. An FIR should be like any other complaint, made in the language and manner suitable for the complainant or the informant, irrespective of the geographic jurisdiction. An FIR need not be the only signed statement in a criminal case admissible in the court as evidence; all other statements made to the police should carry some value, subject to judicial scrutiny and independent corroboration.

To justify our position, we have to make serious efforts for police reforms, far beyond what is envisaged in the reports of various commissions and court judgements so far. The functioning of the police should be designed and structured largely for the purpose of playing a supportive and beneficial role towards those who are the really needy and helpless members of our society.

The present police system was set up long ago to serve and sustain British colonial imperialism; it is definitely not the right form in which it should continue to exist. The changes made so far through a periodic, somewhat one-sided or reluctant or even reactive reforms, mostly under judicial compulsions, have not brought about the desired changes in the fundamental structure of the police system. As a result, its form and content largely continue to be the same as in colonial times, with the British being substituted by those who inherited the systems.

Even the reforms of 2006 initiated by the Supreme Court, formulated through the well-known Prakash Singh case, which were based on some institutional level recommendations aimed at functional and infrastructural changes in the existing police system, will not bring about any basic changes in the Indian police. The basic character of the police system will remain intact and nothing much will happen except some tinkering with the system. The creation of public grievance committees, security commissions and police establishment boards with quasi-judicial powers, political–bureaucratic and token civil society participations; separating investigation work from the law-and-order activities and empowering investigative bodies with resources, equipment, skilled manpower, training and so on; and providing fixed minimum tenures for crucial functionaries like DGPs are not likely to go beyond the level of just superficial changes.

No doubt, these are meaningful suggestions but they serve, in essence, a limited purpose of just improving the day-to-day functioning of the police, which is connected to the well-entrenched system in which it operates. But these suggestions will not bring about any radical or fundamental changes in the system, since the police will continue to function within the boundaries of the traditional police–judicial–administrative mechanism, just as it has remained within our archaic and mostly outdated justice delivery system.

These reforms will not alter the police–community relationships, or deliver the much-needed services expected of the Indian police as the main law enforcement machinery and the crucial security service delivery agency. The daunting tasks before the Indian police may not be comparable with any other police force or service across the globe, as its tasks range from tackling the ever-springing millions of lawless situations across the country to dealing with hardcore national security and sophisticated crimes.

Over time, there have been a few structural changes to serve the socioeconomically disadvantaged and legally deprived poor and marginalised people in our society. The present police structure and its functioning within our federal system of polity and governance seems to be wavering between the archaic criminal justice system and some highly progressive social legislation. In the Indian police set-up, the exuberant new seems to be somehow superimposed over the feeble old and archaic. This inherent contradiction presents a peculiar situation before those who look or try for newer police reforms. Obviously, at times it appears that the police is neither new nor old but perhaps both and if that is so, then how can the system grow?

As per the laid-down procedure, the empowered policeman at the scene of crime or any incident under investigation or inquiry, collects the evidence and records them as the most truthful accounts. But as per our archaic system, the oral and visual evidence recorded by him are not conclusive proof in the eyes of the law. Is it not a major lacuna or shortcoming in the system that in most of the cases, such recording done by the police has no value as judicial evidence? This means that there is an inbuilt assumption that in any situation of crime, a policeman is unreliable and, sadly, can get influenced and drawn into corruption. Thus begins an unending series of lies and distorted investigations, unfortunately sometimes at the hand of the police itself, undermining the very root of our basic objective of being with truth and justice.

Through an examination of the systems and maladies affecting a few much talked about cases, I have tried to analyse and understand the issues and problems of the role of the Indian police in our CJS concerning a broad spectrum of matters, ranging from crime investigations to different legal interventions, including larger or smaller judicial proceedings, from the magisterial courts to the apex Supreme Court.

From this analysis, supplemented by authentic and detailed narratives, several questions are likely to arise. Should we look for incremental changes and attempt to push them from within the system? Or, should the old system be largely dismantled to pave the way for an entirely new form of policing in India? Should we completely transform the so-called police mindset created by the existing system? Or, should we make a constructive use of the existing time-tested systems, and only change their direction so that they evolve alongside the aspirational changes taking place? Such questions keep agitating the minds of a sizable number of policemen as well, from the ranks of constables to police chiefs, who understand the limitations of this system which seems to have tied their hands and dampened their spirit for change.

A much talked about thought comes to my mind. Can a remedy be found in the constitutionally mandated Indian tradition of village panchayats, where each member of the local community, including the village watchman, may act as a policeman, and operate within the system of checks and balances? But will an attempt to revive an old system of policing be non-progressive in nature? Or, will it be more useful to borrow some relevant parts from the old system in order to draw a new format, suitable for the present requirements? Like in many advanced countries, police being a municipal function, can the routine urban policing be carried out, supervised and accountable to the local self-governments? The successful experiments, like the Japanese and London metropolitan police combining the highly advanced and sophisticated gadgets and methods with community-based policing, could be the models to emulate.

In the ever-growing complexity of India's policing and law-enforcement systems within the framework of the present CJS, JJS and political–bureaucratic systems, there are probably myriad experiments which are already being carried out in bits and pieces at several places. The federal system prevailing in India, operating at the levels of the Central as well as the states and the union territories police organisations, has been carrying out highly contradictory and, in a way, confusing police functions for several decades.

Innumerable good efforts by righteous and innovative policemen are often ineffective and eventually forgotten. The examples of bad police work keep on multiplying and are somewhat commonplace. Simultaneously, there are examples of absolutely modern measures undertaken within the given police structure, especially in the areas of sophisticated forensic applications or investigations to curb child abuse or digital and cyber-security-related crimes.

In terms of working for the society, several police organisations and police leaders have done remarkable and novel work in the social sector, for example, providing services in terms of mitigating tribulations of life in urban slums or rescuing people from human trafficking or community-based policing or rendering effective services in times of riots or communal clashes.

Khaki, in its present form and functions, astride the broken wings of our chaotic criminal justice system, does not seem to be serving or not able to serve, the envisioned goals in the true sense. Its efficacy has not been realised according to our cherished vision of India@75. As agents of law within the constitutional framework to bring real justice to the needy, the police will be required to play the role of change agents for the much-needed socioeconomic transformation within a hugely unequal, unfair and fragmented society.

Operating under the watchful eyes of the higher judiciary, India's justice delivery system is bursting at the seams with over 470 lakh pending court cases and more than 66 lakh cases added annually; there are nearly 4.5 lakh persons in jails with over 76 per cent being undertrial prisoners. In a recent, highest-level meeting, both the Prime Minister and the Chief Justice of India lamented this massive violation of human rights entailing the jurisprudential 'presumption of innocence', while shifting the responsibility to act on each other. Men and women in khaki, being the most visible arm of the CJS, become the obvious targets of the people's wrath. Reforms, either not implemented or implemented, in small incremental chunks, do not change the face or image of the Indian police.

To me, it appears that in the fast-changing, extremely volatile sociopolitical scenario which heavily influences the police and governance alongside the criminal justice and the related systems in the country, the only guiding principles can be the Preamble and the Articles of our Constitution. The value and relevance of this dream document have turned out to be more meaningful and profound with the passage of time.

We have to do soul-searching and deliberate upon how we should position the police in India's functional democracy, being the most visible provider and protector of our people, considering the hierarchy of the people's actual needs. Our role lies in enabling them to be the citizens and beneficiaries of the sovereign, socialist, secular, democratic republic; securing justice—social, economic and political; liberty of thought, expression, belief, faith and worship; ensuring equality of status and opportunity; promoting fraternity, with dignity of the individual and securing the unity and integrity of the nation.

INDEX